THE
DECEIVER'S
HEART

JENNIFER A. NIELSEN

THE DECEIVER'S HEART

· BOOK TWO ·

SCHOLASTIC PRESS · NEW YORK

All rights reserved. Published by Scholastic Press, an imprint of Scholastic Inc.,
Publishers since 1920. SCHOLASTIC, SCHOLASTIC PRESS, and associated logos are
trademarks and/or registered trademarks of Scholastic Inc.

Library of Congress Cataloging-in-Publication Data available

ISBN 978-1-338-04541-3

10 9 8 7 6 5 4 3 2 1   19 20 21 22 23

Printed in the U.S.A. 23
First edition, March 2019

Book design by Christopher Stengel

To Joan, for an amazing ten years.
To Lisa, for the privilege of ten books.
And my hope for many, many more
yet to come.

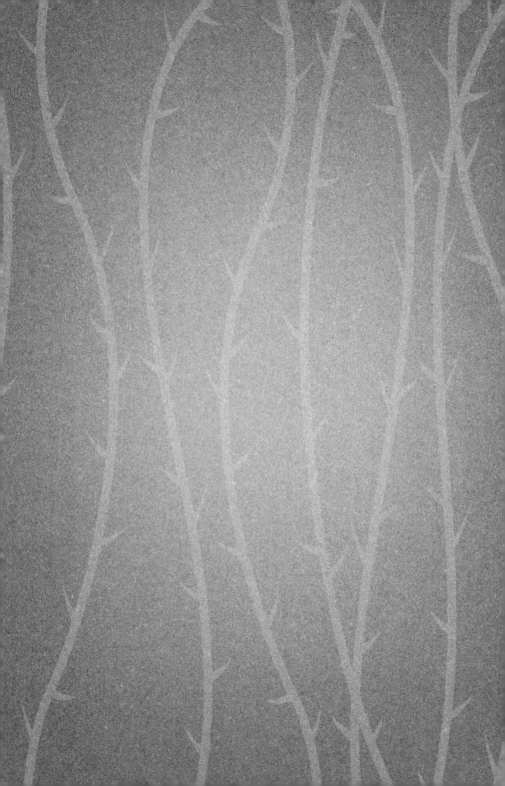

The deceiver's heart is fickle.

A captive of its desires.

A prisoner to its fate.

It pulses for revenge,

Or a quest,

Or love,

Or an enemy to slay.

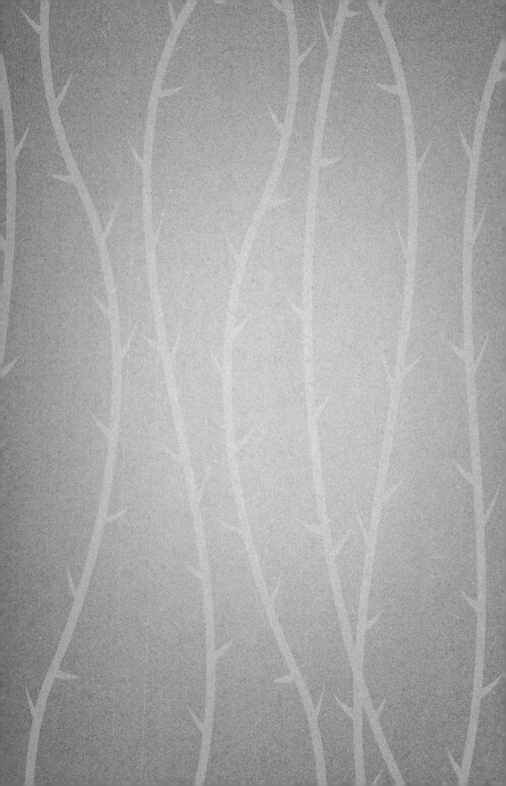

⋆ O N E ⋆

KESTRA

Barely daring to breathe, I crept forward, hoping Lord Endrick wouldn't be aware of my presence until I was closer. He had summoned me here, so there was no chance of surprising him, but I didn't need him watching my every move as I trekked across the great hall toward the Scarlet Throne.

The throne itself was a grand display of rubies and garnets, occupied for the past thousand years by whichever Antoran family was currently in power. But never by an outsider. Never by anyone as evil as Lord Endrick.

Lord Endrick was a head taller than the average Antoran and thick in his build. Today he wore the black uniform of Dominion officers, highly decorated with medals he had never earned, and with green accents signifying his rank as king, a position he had seized from the Dallisor family. In public, he wore a mask to disguise his true nature, but he rarely wore it in his palace. I hated having to look upon him. Every murder he had committed against his own people had grayed his flesh and deepened the lines of his skin until he now resembled a monster more than a person.

Such thoughts made it easier to do what I had to do, but I continued walking forward. My heart ached just to think of what was about to happen.

Endrick sat in close conference with Sir Henry, his chief enforcer, confidant, and the man who had pretended to be my father for all of my sixteen years. Even now, he didn't know that I knew the truth, nor could I tell him until this was over.

If I was lucky, that would be within the next few minutes.

The Olden Blade was in its usual spot, tucked in a garter around my right thigh. But I'd deliberately worn a skirt with only a single sash around the waist today, so it wouldn't be hard to get to the weapon when I needed it. My pulse was racing and my body was much too tense. I needed to slow down, to breathe. I needed to keep thinking.

"Kestra, my daughter, you are late." Sir Henry never missed an opportunity to scold me, though I figured most of his disapproval would come after I killed Lord Endrick. *If* I could do it. I had to do it.

I gave the appropriate bow to the throne, subtly checking with my hand that the Olden Blade's handle was where I expected, and it was. Good.

"Forgive my delay." My tone was deliberately obstinate. Foolishly inciteful. "I'd rather not have come at all."

"Kestra!"

Lord Endrick held up his hand for silence, then gestured for me to rise, which I did.

"You've shown an unusual streak of defiance since returning from the Lava Fields," he said.

I tilted my head. "You must know that defiance is not unusual for me. Wasn't that the reason I was sent to the Lava Fields in the first place?"

"In hopes it would tame you, not encourage you," Sir Henry said. "We—"

He stopped mid-sentence and immediately dipped his head, feeling the burn from Endrick's scathing glare, a reminder that the king did not appreciate being interrupted. I rather enjoyed that. Never in my life had I seen Sir Henry shrink to anyone.

Then Lord Endrick continued, "Some defiance can be tolerated in the young. It's natural to push against one's elders. But it ends here, Miss Dallisor. Before your disappearance several days ago, a wedding was planned for you. Sir Basil has expressed his willingness to continue with the wedding. I only need your promise that when you stand before the people, you will accept him."

I straightened my spine, hoping it would give me courage. "I will not."

Lord Endrick thrust out his hand, and with it came a force that hit me squarely in the chest, knocking the breath from my lungs and sending me sprawling backward. That had hurt far more than I'd expected, but it had to happen. I needed to draw Lord Endrick nearer to me, away from Sir Henry. And I needed to be in a position to quietly reach beneath my skirts.

"Get up, girl!" Sir Henry called to me. I wasn't sure if his order was meant to demand I show Endrick more respect, or to warn of what Endrick would do next if I didn't get up.

Either way, I couldn't obey him, not yet. "If I get up, he'll do that again!"

Endrick's tone darkened. "And if you don't, things will get worse until you agree to the marriage."

"As far as I can tell, marriage itself is far worse than anything you can do to me." Which may have sounded flippant, except in this case it was true. Endrick had already forced Basil to agree to kill me on our wedding night, something Basil himself had confirmed in our private conversations over the past few days.

But Lord Endrick didn't take kindly to my words. He stood, threw his cloak off his shoulders, and marched down the stairs from the Scarlet Throne. "On your knees, girl."

By then, I'd already worked the Olden Blade free of the garter. It was now in my hand, with part of my skirt wrapped around the blade to hide it. I rolled to my knees.

This was it, the moment I would kill him. The timing had to be perfect. He could not see it, could not suspect, until the blade was piercing his gut.

Lord Endrick held out his right hand, and a servant ran forward with a grip glove, fastening it to the king's palm. The grip glove would intensify anything that Endrick's magic could already do. I'd experienced a lesser version of his punishments before, and it was awful.

Sir Henry had remained in his seat, which he rarely did. He was ordinarily the punisher, and if not, he usually relished the pleasure of being up close when Endrick did the job instead. But maybe somewhere, deep in his miserable, shriveled heart, he had tender feelings for me.

Either that, or he didn't want to bother himself with walking down the steps, only to climb them a minute or two later. That was probably it.

I lowered my head and redoubled my grip on the Olden Blade. Endrick's footsteps were behind me and coming closer. It felt like he was deliberately walking slowly, drawing out the torture. Maybe he was.

Finally, I sensed his presence behind me, like a corporeal shadow, like he was death itself. He raised his hand to part my hair, seeking a solid grip on my neck, but as he did, I leapt to my feet, swinging around with the blade and leaving a deep cut in his side.

"No!" Now Sir Henry was rushing down the steps, his sword already out.

I swung back in the opposite direction, this time with a much better aim. I started to bring the blade down on Endrick's chest, but he grabbed my arm, using the grip glove to send a wave of pain through me. Had he not been injured, that pulse of magic probably would have stopped my heart.

I fell to the ground, gasping with breath. Endrick stood over me, clutching his wound and shouting, "A Dallisor child is the Infidante? Where did you find that blade?"

I couldn't speak, couldn't form words, but I stumbled to my feet, trying to put any distance between us. Sir Henry tried to dart forward, but Endrick raised a hand, motioning him back.

"It doesn't matter where I found it," I said. "It's mine, and I will kill you with it."

"You won't," Endrick said. "But if you give it to me now, I may let you live."

Only a fool would believe such lies. I raised the blade again, ready to thrust it at him if he took another step closer to me. Hoping he would, and that I would do better this time.

"Come and get it," I said.

This time, when Lord Endrick shot magic at me, I instinctively put the blade forward and blocked it, something I hadn't known was possible. It reflected back, knocking him off his feet, the mighty Lord of the Dominion reduced to sprawling backward across the marble floor. He was mortal after all, I understood that now. I started toward him, but he immediately sat up and hit me with a force so powerful it hurled me to the windows at the far end of the throne room. As black dots swarmed in my vision, I used the blade to smash the glass, and then I rolled backward over the edge.

It was a long fall into a frost-covered morning, and the hardened tree limbs below would have killed me, except this was the escape I'd already planned to use if anything went wrong. I landed on a web of rope in the upper branches, planted there last night by Basil and me.

While the fall didn't kill me, Lord Endrick nearly had, and I was struggling to remain conscious. I didn't have long. Above me, orders were being shouted to the Ironhearts to bring me in alive.

I rolled down the webbing to the ground, unable to get a grip on the rungs. Basil breathed out my name and darted from a hiding place to break my fall. Certain that we'd be celebrating at this point, I'd told him not to come. How relieved I was to see him now.

Dizzy, and with the world at a distinct angle, I wrapped the Olden Blade in the sash at my waist and pushed it into his hands.

"Take this."

He did, but said, "Let me help you first!"

"I can't get away in time, but you can protect the blade. If I don't survive, it must go to the Coracks. Now go and hide it somewhere no one will suspect, not even me." Especially not me.

I wasn't awake long enough to know if he successfully escaped. All I knew was that I didn't. Ironhearts were shouting my name, surrounding me.

My eyes closed and, I feared, might never open again. I had failed.

· TWO ·

―――――

KESTRA

Kestra!"

My eyes fluttered open to the sound of someone calling my name. I recognized the voice but couldn't understand it.

"Where am I?"

"You're with your father."

"Darrow?"

Immediately, I knew that was the wrong thing to say. I opened my eyes to see Sir Henry seated in front of me, his mouth pressed into a tight line.

"Your former servant, Darrow, received a death worthy of his crimes against the Dominion." Henry's flat, apathetic tone could only come from a man who had ceased to feel for any of the hundreds of people he'd sent to their deaths. "It will be an eternal punishment."

"Eternal punishment?" That was the fate of those who had been killed in All Spirits Forest during the war. To wander forever in a half-life without rest. I shook my head. "Darrow was killed inside a building during a Dominion attack. I saw it happen."

Henry smiled, and my stomach turned. "We captured him before that explosion and brought him to this very room, where he unwisely refused to discuss your training in the Lava Fields. He gave Lord Endrick no choice but to send him to All Spirits Forest to join the other . . . prisoners there."

Tears filled my eyes, but Henry rested his hand on my arm. "You miss your true father, how touching. Once we're finished, I'm sure you'll have the privilege of joining him."

I suspected that would happen soon. My arms and legs were attached with binding cords to the chair in which I was seated. Other than our two chairs, the only furniture in this small dark room was a table, bare except for a single clearstone, our sole source of light.

I began trembling. This room had pulled confessions from the lips of innocent men and women, and had melted the wills of the strongest among them. Whatever might happen to me in here would be awful, but the true punishment would come afterward. The eternal punishment.

The door behind me opened and an icy shudder tore through me. I knew who had come. "Is the girl ready?" Endrick asked. Without a second look at me, Henry immediately vacated his seat for his king, though the gesture was ignored.

Instead, Endrick's deeply lined face came into my field of vision. I recoiled from it, terrified of whatever might happen to me next, and I nearly became sick when he clutched my jaw, turning my face from one side to the other.

"You had a terrible accident," Lord Endrick said. "You fell through a castle window."

That wasn't an accident. That was my escape after I'd failed to kill him, and we both knew it. My eyes flicked to where I had cut him with the Olden Blade, and I was disappointed not to see bandages.

Then he had the power to heal himself too. The next Infidante ought to know that. I wished I had known that.

He pushed back the hair on my forehead tenderly, as if he had any feelings for me warmer than loathing. I noticed a grip glove on that hand, and my panic deepened. I tried to pull away, but the cords had no mercy.

"How were you able to handle the Olden Blade?" he asked. "A Dallisor should not have been able to touch it."

I pressed my lips together, determined to say nothing because if I did, I might tell him everything, simply out of fear. When it was obvious I wouldn't respond, Sir Henry said, "She is adopted, my Lord. Perhaps there is Halderian blood in her."

I was half Halderian, to be exact. And half Endrean. With the same blood as Lord Endrick, though I had no magic of my own.

"Where is the Olden Blade?" His tone remained so calm that it unnerved me. My legs were already beginning to shake.

All I could do was mumble, "I don't know."

Endrick looked at Sir Henry, who said, "If she were lying, I'd know."

Endrick's expression toward me became one almost of admiration. "You've hidden it even from yourself, very wise. Tell me, child, who has the secret?"

A tear escaped me, and though I had every possible lie in my head, when the words came out, they were the perfect truth. "It will go to the Coracks."

"How appropriate, since you helped that Corack boy get into Woodcourt to find it. What is his name?"

I faced forward again, determined not to reveal Simon's name, nor Trina's, the other Corack who'd come with me into Woodcourt. They didn't appear to know about her.

"We know the Coracks forced you to betray us," Endrick continued. "Now we're returning the favor."

I shook my head. "You'll have to kill me first."

Endrick smiled, hearing the quiver in my voice. "I'd rather not. You're such an insignificant threat to me as Infidante, I'd rather keep you alive."

"If I'm insignificant, then I have no power to stop the Coracks."

"You may not, but I do. Understand, my dear, that from this moment forward, there will be no choice, no path in which you have any chance to win." The grip glove slid downward, leaving an icy trail down my neck, and stopped directly over my heart. "You're afraid. But you shouldn't be, for the worst of your fate has already happened."

My heart seemed to tighten inside my chest, constricting, restricting my breaths. "What do you mean?"

"What do you know about the Ironhearts?"

My breaths came sharper. "You didn't."

"Some of my servants cannot be trusted, so I must have ways of ensuring their obedience." He pressed in on my chest and the constriction tightened, making it nearly impossible to breathe. "I take a piece of their heart for myself. It allows me to sense disloyalty and, if necessary, I will then crush the traitor's heart."

He was doing it now, putting a squeeze on my heart that was making the details of this room fade around me. Pain shot through my limbs, making the darkness spin. Through harsh breaths, I asked, "Why not kill me here?"

"You're returning to the Coracks, my dear. This time in my service."

Finally, he released my heart, and tears streamed down my cheeks as I struggled to stay conscious. "I don't know how to find them."

"But they will find you. To make it easy, I've even rescheduled your wedding for two days from now and allowed that fool Basil to sneak a messenger out of Highwyn to them. They'll bring you into their fold like a lamb, but you'll be my wolf."

"I won't."

"You will." He showed me a stone embedded into his grip glove, one that looked like a pearl, only as gray and as lined as his face. "This will be my wedding gift to you, my dear. It will register everything you see and hear while you are with the Coracks. Once I get it back, I will have the means to find the Olden Blade. Then I will destroy them."

At first, I wasn't sure why he was telling me all this so freely. Then his grip glove returned to my forehead, and with a tremor of fear surging through me, I understood. "You're taking my memory of this conversation?"

He laughed. "No, my dear. I'm taking much more than that." His fingertips widened, then pressed down on the sides and top of my head. "I'll take everything I want from you. Darrow, those three years in the Lava Fields, your training with a sword. I'll take it all and rebuild your memories with ideas more suited to a loyal daughter of the Dominion."

I squirmed, attempting to stop him, but I already felt his magic exploring my past, infecting my thoughts, ready to erase. The harder I fought it, the tighter he squeezed on my heart. "Please don't do this!"

"I already am." With his fingers pressing down on my brow, Endrick nodded toward a man in the corner of the room. "That is your father, Sir Henry, who loves you, and you love him. Every memory of a father is of him, is it not?"

More relaxed now, I smiled over at my father. "Of course it is."

When my eyes roamed back to Endrick, he said, "You will forget every event that led to you finding the Olden Blade and becoming the Infidante, and everything that connected you to the Corack rebellion."

I'd heard of the Corack rebellion. They were thugs and thieves and liars, and wholly unconnected to me, thankfully.

Endrick continued, "I am your king, and you will bow to me, obey my every command, and seek to serve me."

"What is your command, my Lord?" That seemed to please him.

Lord Endrick repositioned his fingers and I drew in a gasp, feeling something—magic, perhaps?—shift away from my mind. "I have only one command, my dear, and I am burying it deep within your heart. You will not even remember my words until the time comes to act, but when you hear them, you will know that you must obey."

"What must I do?"

He smiled, and I felt a pinch inside my chest. "There is a rumor of great concern to me. Find the Corack boy who brought you into Woodcourt and kill him. You have seven days in which to succeed. Fail to do this, and you will die."

"Yes, my Lord." I nodded at him, eager to obey, even as my father looked on with concern. I briefly wondered why.

Lord Endrick began brushing his hand across my forehead, and with each stroke I became increasingly tired. "Sleep now. When you wake up, you are Kestra Dallisor. You mean nothing to Antora save for one purpose, and that is to carry out my orders. You are mine, child. You are a weapon of the Dominion."

My eyes were already growing heavy. His words floated through my head like tufts of clouds I might reach for but could never catch.

"What if she fails?" my father asked.

"I have another spy in place to ensure my success."

His words seemed important, like they should have mattered to me somehow, but they didn't. Nothing mattered.

Yet one last spark flared within me as my heart reached out to try to clutch a single thought before it was taken from me too.

Save Simon.

The words lit through me for a brief instant, then were gone.

I didn't know who Simon was or why he needed saving.

And then the name itself vanished.

"How do you know she will obey?" my father asked, believing me already to be asleep.

"Because Antorans have simple minds. When she awakes, she will only remember what I have allowed her to keep or what I have inserted in place of what I have stolen. She will be on our side."

I would be on his side. That was my final thought before falling asleep. When I awoke, I'd be his uncaged wolf, at his service.

If I refused, he would kill me.

For I was an Ironheart now.

· THREE ·

SIMON

I first saw her in the market square.

It was the last place I'd expected her to be, but the greater surprise was how casually she wandered from stall to stall, carefree, even aimless, while she openly laughed and joked with those around her, as if the most serious concern on her mind was whether to wear red or blue at supper tonight. It was so unlike the Kestra Dallisor I had known that I moved in closer, wanting to be certain it was her.

This *was* her. Same dark hair, same smile. Same compelling eyes. Same, but not the same.

Her long hair was elaborately braided with ribbons, probably by one of the four girls surrounding her, competing with one another to fulfill Kestra's every wish before she thought to express it. I hadn't seen that gray longcoat before, nor the green dress beneath it, and I wondered if the Olden Blade was hidden beneath it, against her thigh. She always kept a weapon there, and since she had claimed the Olden Blade, it had not left her possession.

It was the sole weapon that could kill Lord Endrick, and she alone could wield it.

Against my wishes, she had returned here, to the capital of Highwyn, less than a fortnight after renouncing her place within a family that loyally served Endrick. She was here to kill the king.

If that was still her plan, then why was she in this marketplace, holding up dresses to herself and dancing behind them? Whispering to her ladies-in-waiting, and causing them to burst with laughter?

The plan had changed, obviously. But I had rushed here from the southern tip of Antora as soon as I was able to ride. I'd barely slept, eaten only what I could forage along the way, and had been desperately worried for her safety. It was good to see her safe. It was good to see her at all, but something still felt wrong.

I moved toward her, careful to avoid drawing the attention of her guards, two burly men who were watching her with uncommon focus. I didn't recognize either of them, but I had no doubt Sir Henry would have described me to every Loyalist in the city and promised a significant reward for my capture.

My arrest—and execution—would be swift, painful, and public, not only for Kestra's kidnapping, but also because I was a Corack, part of the rebellion.

Or rather, I *used to be* a Corack. Now I was on my own. Still committed to helping Kestra complete her quest. Still committed to Kestra. She and I needed to talk somewhere in private. Not here.

By now, I was one stall away from her. Through the crowd of traders, buyers, and a few ragged children hoping to steal a bite to eat, I only saw Kestra. Seeing her again was like my first sip of water in weeks, my first spark of daylight in a darkened world.

The intensity of my stare must have caught her attention. Our eyes met, and at first I thought she knew me, but then she blinked and almost immediately looked away, clearly uncomfortable, then loudly told her attendants it was time to move on.

I followed, curious about her strange reaction. Obviously, she'd be as surprised to see me here as I'd been to see her, but what I saw wasn't surprise, nor excitement or relief or concern.

It simply wasn't anything. She'd looked past me like I was an open window.

Kestra was nearly to the edge of the market now, standing beside the road and probably waiting for her carriage. If she and I were going to talk, it needed to be now. I needed to separate her from her attendants. I needed a big distraction.

I moved closer, hoping to figure out something by the time I reached her. Except someone linked one arm with mine, pulling me back, and a voice hissed in my other ear, "Simon, no."

I turned to see Trina, a Corack who had been part of our original mission to force Kestra to find the Olden Blade. Trina had hated Kestra from the beginning. She was the last person I wanted to see now.

The person who had grabbed my arm was Gabe, another Corack and a longtime friend. Or maybe he wasn't a friend anymore. Not if he was here with Trina. Not if he had chosen sides against me.

I freed my arm and scowled at them both. "What are you doing here?"

"What are *you* doing?" Trina countered. "Before leaving the Hiplands, Tenger told you to let us handle this!"

"And you think I trust him anymore? That I trust you?" Any vow I'd made to the Coracks seemed irrelevant after Captain Tenger tried to kill me, and then Kestra.

"You trust me," Gabe said with a half-smile.

"I don't trust the Coracks. I don't trust whatever orders Tenger gave you." My glare shifted to Trina. "You thought you were the Infidante, but it's not—"

"I don't need that reminder," she snapped. "But for now, all we care about is making sure Kestra still has the Olden Blade, and that she's still prepared to use it against Lord Endrick. Neither of those questions are certain."

By then, Kestra was climbing into her carriage. She waved at a few Loyalists, promising to see them again later that night, then giggled again with her ladies. Since when did Kestra giggle? And what was happening tonight?

"We're fools to let her leave here," I said.

"We have another plan in place already," Trina said. "That's what we're trying to tell you; everything is arranged."

"And it can't involve you," Gabe said. "Sorry, Simon, but you left the Coracks, and this is our mission. I understand why you want to be involved, you have feelings for Kestra—"

"This isn't about that," I said. "I'm as concerned about the Blade as both of you."

"You came here for Kestra," Trina said flatly. "You're not objective, which means you're not safe. But we will get her out of Highwyn tonight, I promise."

I started to ask, to insist I be made part of the plot, when a cheer rose in the market behind us. I followed the applause to the sound of horses clopping up the cobblestone street, and there was Sir Basil, waving at the people and soaking in their affection like the thirsty rag he was.

Gabe pushed me off the street with him to make way for the horses. Basil never noticed us.

Why was he here, and so triumphantly? Kestra's plan had been to reject marriage to Sir Basil, which would force a meeting with Lord Endrick. Basil should have been back in Reddengrad now, wringing his hands while his father arranged a wedding with some other pawn from a powerful family.

But he was here. Which meant Kestra's plan had failed in some way.

Which meant there would still be a wedding. That was happening *tonight*.

Through gritted teeth, I asked, "Exactly when were you planning to get Kestra out of Highwyn? Before or after they're married?"

Trina sighed. "Simon—"

"She'll be with her attendants for the rest of the day," Gabe said. "Our only choice is to wait until she's alone . . . or mostly alone."

My hand instinctively found my sword. That meant after the wedding, which was entirely unacceptable.

Trina started toward me until I raised the sword. "Do not interfere!"

Interfere? Of course I would interfere.

Gabe raised his hands, trying to calm me. "Look at yourself now, Simon. This is why you have to stay away tonight, for our safety and Kestra's."

"I'm coming with you."

"How? Every guard in Highwyn is watching for you. If you're caught, our plan falls apart and Kestra ends up dead."

I took a deep breath. "Tell me the plan, then."

Trina shook her head. "All you need to know is that we're going to keep Kestra alive and make sure the Olden Blade is safe."

"Are you stopping the wedding?"

Trina and Gabe exchanged a glance. *That* was all I needed to know. I marched away, ignoring their calls for me to stop.

I'd come up with a plan of my own.

· F O U R ·

KESTRA

B y the end of this evening, I'd be married, a thought that had sent flutters through my belly at least a hundred times in the last hour. Could anything be more absurd?

I didn't feel old enough to become someone's wife, and especially not to take on the role of future queen of Reddengrad, Sir Basil's country to the south of Antora. It was difficult to imagine committing my life to someone I barely knew.

"My lady, you are late. I warned you not to go to the market." Although she was new to my service, my handmaiden, Imri Stout, seemed to be tired of me already. That was little surprise. Imri was originally from our neighboring country of Brill. Brillians considered themselves superior to all other people in the western realm, so I was sure it was incomprehensible to her to find herself subject to the Dominion.

I sat up straight while Imri prepared my hair, setting it in curls and ribbons and with tiny flowers to dot the dark tresses as they fell down my back. Then I stood with my arms held out as my ladies dressed me in a silver wedding gown. It was slightly off the shoulder with long sleeves that hung low, tight in the bodice, and it shimmered when I twirled in circles.

"It's about time you showed your excitement, my lady," Imri scolded. Even as a compliment, she still seemed displeased with me.

I smiled back at her. "Who wouldn't be excited for tonight?"

I wouldn't be. At best, the idea of marriage terrified me. My father had assured me that Basil would be the finest of husbands, but I knew I'd be a disappointing wife. I was here because those were the orders of my king, and nothing more.

"You will have to become more serious, now that you will be the princess of Reddengrad," Imri said. "A princess cannot laugh away the affairs of the country."

"Perhaps not." I smiled up at her. "But if I do not laugh, how else will I stay awake as the affairs are discussed?"

It wasn't that at all. My laughter was a disguise, a distraction from injuries I'd sustained during a fall from a castle window a few days ago. If Lord Endrick had not intervened, I'd have lost my life. But the fall had still left me with gaps in my memories, some of them more significant than I'd ever admit aloud. If anyone knew that a daughter of the Dominion was damaged, they might wonder if the Dominion itself was flawed.

"Is there nothing in life that you take seriously?" Imri asked with a sigh.

I tossed back my head and giggled. "What is life but a series of jokes? We either laugh with them or become the object of them."

We were interrupted by a messenger at the door who informed us that Lord Endrick had come to bid his congratulations and everyone else was to leave.

Imri's eyes flashed with something that briefly resembled alarm, which was ridiculous considering that the king honored us with his presence. My room emptied out in a panicked flurry, but I sank to my knees in humility.

"Remain as you are," Endrick said as he entered. An unexpected flash of fear rushed through me, and I privately scolded myself for such disloyalty. Lord Endrick had always been uncommonly kind to me. He wore the mask he often donned in public appearances, though I wished he wouldn't have found that necessary. Perhaps the burden of ruling Antora had lined and grayed his face, but if the people saw him as he really was, they would know how much he'd sacrificed on our behalf.

"You intend to marry tonight?" he asked.

"Yes, my Lord. As my father arranged and as you command."

"That pleases me."

I felt his hands on my neck and realized he was fastening a necklace there. When he finished, I lifted my head and saw a silver pendant with a stone that looked like a gray pearl, with deep lines etched into it. The pendant was heavier than it appeared and sent a strange tremor through me, though it quickly passed.

"This is my wedding gift to you," Endrick said. "As your king, I ask you to never take this off."

Never was a long time, but I dipped my head in respect. "Will you be at the wedding, my Lord?"

"I'm afraid not. I need to rest and recover my strength in the Blue Caves. It's been a difficult week."

"I'm sorry to hear that. I hope the person who caused your difficulties was properly reprimanded."

A beat passed before he said, "They were, I assure you."

He kissed the top of my head, then departed, and within minutes, my ladies returned to escort me to a pre-wedding celebration here at Woodcourt. Every Dallisor within Antora was required to attend, and any Loyalist hoping to gain more power in the Dominion would squeeze in at the back of the room and be grateful for it. My stomach was already in knots.

I waited outside the ballroom door until I heard the herald announce, "Loyalists of the Dominion, Sir Henry Dallisor wishes to thank each of you for attending this celebration of his beloved daughter's wedding."

Unexpectedly, my hands began to tremble, but I tucked them into the folds of my dress, hoping no one would notice. Surely this was excitement, the anticipation of seeing my beloved what's-his-name . . . Basil. Did all brides feel this way? Terror-stricken?

Yes, that must be how they all felt.

Regardless, I was not ready to be anyone's bride.

I did not want this.

Imri touched my arm. "Don't be nervous, my lady. You'll do fine."

I smiled over at her and tossed back my head. "Of course."

I wasn't sure what it meant to "do fine" in regard to one's marriage, but that seemed like an attainable goal. I would marry Basil and "do fine." Years and years and years at his side, doing fine.

The herald continued, "Please join Sir Henry in welcoming his daughter, Lady Kestra Dallisor. By the end of the evening, she will be the bride of Sir Basil the Fifth, son of King Albert and heir to the throne of Reddengrad."

Enthusiastic applause rose from the crowd, and my ladies practically pushed me into the ballroom. Basil walked onto the dais, gave me a respectful bow, then wrapped his arms around my waist and surprised me with a kiss.

It wasn't our first kiss, of course, but this one was more passionate than before, as if he'd been caught up in the excitement of the crowd, or perhaps he wanted them to see the love between us. The love that was supposed to be between us. My father assured me those feelings would come over time, as it had for him and my mother. Memories of my mother were some of the most painful losses from my fall, and I missed her all the more today because of that. When we parted, Basil kept one arm around my waist and waved to the audience, drawing another cheer.

Only then did I really get my first look at the people who had come. They whispered to one another while smiling at me and nodding in approval. Everyone appeared just as they ought to at a pre-wedding party.

Except for one guard at the back of the room. The visor of his helmet was pushed low and his head was down, so I couldn't see his face, but that wasn't necessary. Both hands were balled into fists and one was pounding against his thigh. He was angry. As soon as I had the chance, I'd speak to my father about removing him.

With Basil a sudden fixture at my side, we began circling the room, greeting the guests and receiving their good wishes. I smiled at each of them, said the things it felt like I ought to say, and snuggled against Basil whenever he gave my side a squeeze.

But I couldn't get my mind off the guard in the back of the room. From different positions, I caught different parts of his face. The angle of his jaw, set forward. His lips pressed together in a tight frown. I even saw the corner of his eye, only for a brief second, but long enough to know he was glaring at me.

At me? Why should he be focused on me? The weight of his half-hidden eyes upon me was tangible, and becoming heavier each minute, but I didn't want to disrupt the party by having him hauled out. We only had a few minutes until the wedding began anyway.

Indeed, as soon as we finished greeting the last of the guests, the herald said, "Loyalists of the Dominion, a wedding tent has been set up in the ward, on the north end of the property. Our betrothed couple will take their places."

"Come with me, my love." Basil took my hand and led me from the ballroom into the gardens. "Are you cold?"

A chill breeze was in the air, sweeping through the layers of my dress. My father had taught me that strength made one resistant to temperature. I didn't see how that could possibly be true, but it compelled me to shake my head now.

This area of the gardens had few lights tonight, most of the clearstones of Woodcourt being used to light the path the guests were taking toward the wedding arch. I suspected the dark evening worked in Basil's favor. A mischievous, romantic look gleamed in his eyes.

We stopped in a corner of the gardens, tall hedges behind us and thick bushes in front of us. For a moment, I thought I saw a shadow there, but then a sharper gust of wind caused the bushes to flutter in the wind. It was nothing, only my nerves.

Basil pulled me to him, holding me close around my waist. He studied my face a moment before asking, "Kestra, do you want to marry me?"

"Of course." What else was I supposed to say, given that our wedding was minutes away? I could hardly tell him that my heart was pounding in my throat and that I'd already considered three escape routes from these gardens.

"If this night goes differently than you expect, will you trust that it's for your own good?"

What an odd question. I grinned. "Is this a surprise, or a problem?"

"Not a problem, just . . . a change of plans."

He continued staring at me, his hands sliding to my shoulders. I lifted my face and accepted his kiss. He clearly had strong feelings for me, and I wondered how it was that I had no strong feelings about anything at all, and certainly not for him.

Something was definitely wrong with me. But if I couldn't explain that to myself, how could I ever make him understand?

So I kissed him back, with more passion than I felt. I doubted I could pretend my way through an entire marriage, but I could at least manage the next hour until we were wed.

Basil returned for a second kiss, but we were interrupted by a cough, and then the words "Sir Basil, a message has come for you from Reddengrad. The rider is out front."

It was the guard who had been angry in the ballroom, and though his visor was still low, his emotions were obviously no calmer now. Basil barely looked at him to say, "The rider will have to wait."

But the guard stepped forward. "He says it is urgent, from your father. It involves a promise you made regarding this wedding."

Basil's eyes widened and he released my hand like it stung him. "Forgive me, Kestra, but I must meet him."

"I'll go with you," I offered.

"No!" His tone had changed. A sort of panic was inside Basil now, though I couldn't understand why. What promise had he made regarding our wedding?

Basil gestured to the guard. "Will you wait here with the lady until I return? It won't be more than a few minutes, I'm sure."

"No—" Before I could finish protesting, Basil had hurried away.

Leaving me with this guard. He immediately removed his helmet, and now I had a full view of his face. He was handsome enough, with hair as dark as mine but close-cropped and untidy, and an expression in his brown eyes so intense I could barely look away. New emotions seemed to rise above his anger as he studied me. What was it? Expectation? Hope?

Hope for what?

If he thought I should say something, he'd be disappointed. I turned away, with more interest in the nearby geraniums than in him.

After a few seconds of silence, his head tilted. "Do you know me, Kes?"

"Should I?"

He blinked hard, then tried again. "Do you know me?"

I put ice in my stare back at him, unwilling to repeat myself.

He mumbled something under his breath, then said, "I'm the change of plans your beloved Basil mentioned."

"He's not my beloved." The guard arched an eyebrow, and I quickly added, "He's my *most* beloved. Obviously." Then, "What's the change of plans?"

"You're to come with me." When I hesitated, he added, "It's all right, your . . . most beloved knows."

I waved him away. "Leave, or I'll report you."

But he stepped closer. "My lady, I'm here as your protector. Please trust me."

I shook my head. "I saw you in the ballroom before. Why were you angry?" Not that it mattered, but I was stalling now, hoping Basil would hurry back.

He offered me his hand, clearly eager to hurry us both away from the gardens. "My anger is only for those who would harm you."

But I wouldn't take his hand. I wouldn't go anywhere with this boy.

"Kestra?" That was Basil's voice.

I started to call out, but the guard grabbed my arm and pulled me against him. Basil rounded the corner and froze as soon as he saw the guard, mumbling, "Simon?" He knew this boy? Basil raised his hands, showing he was no threat. "You're early. The wedding is only a few minutes away."

Simon hesitated, only for a moment, but I noticed. "She must leave *now*."

My jaw clenched. "He's telling me the truth?"

Basil reached out for me, as if a pat on the arm would make everything better. "Go with him, my love. I'll find you again soon."

"You won't," Simon countered.

Now Basil hesitated. "Simon, are you working with the Coracks or not?"

"The *Coracks*?" I couldn't believe what I was hearing. Basil had made plans with the group rebelling against my family? I tried to tug my arm away, but Simon tightened his grip and with his other hand pulled out a knife.

Basil shook his head at Simon as we left. "You're in over your head."

This rebel had a knife, and he had me. So I was fairly sure that of the three of us, I was the one most in over my head. But as Simon began leading me from the gardens, Basil called, "I'll see you soon, my love!"

Simon scowled and pushed me to walk faster, taking us on a route that an outsider to Woodcourt should not have known. There must be an explanation for that.

Just outside a small gate was a sturdy horse with an old leather satchel tied to the saddle. My heart lurched into my throat.

"I need a carriage. I don't ride on the backs of animals"—I caught Simon's eye—"or with animals."

He peeled off his guard's uniform, revealing civilian clothes with tears in the fabric and frayed seams. If he had two coins to his name, I'd be shocked.

He faced me once more. "Kes, we're alone now. Do you know who I am?"

"I know that you're a fool to have done this."

"I'm sure you're right," he said, his voice as cold as the night air. "Now get on the horse or I'll drag you behind it."

"You're no protector." I reached for the horse's reins. "Not if you speak to me as an enemy."

He clicked his tongue, irritated. "My lady, right now, I am the only friend you've got." With that, he swung into the saddle behind me, wrapped his filthy arms on either side of me, and rode us into the dark night.

Rode me away from the only home I'd ever known, into an outside world I barely knew. Whatever this boy's intentions, wherever we were going, I'd never been so terrified in my life.

· FIVE ·

SIMON

Fifteen minutes had passed since we left Woodcourt, and my mind was still trying to sort out what had happened.

Basil had referenced that I was early for the plan. Was that the same plan Trina and Gabe had tried to tell me about? Were they working together now? How was such a thing possible?

More concerning still was that Kestra did not seem to know me. This was obviously the work of Lord Endrick, though I didn't yet know the extent of the damage he'd caused within her mind, her memories. I only knew that he'd separated me from anything she did remember and taken with it emotions that I thought had run as deeply within her as they did me.

Erasing them.

Erasing me.

The way she'd kissed Basil back there, or allowed him to kiss her, had ripped me up. And I wasn't sure how long I was supposed to pretend that I was only her indifferent protector, a nameless part of some Corack plan. I didn't even know *how* to pretend such a thing, not when every instinct within me was to close my arms around her and tell her how I truly felt. Whatever Endrick had done to her mind, he had done far worse to my heart.

"Can you loosen your arm around my waist?" Kestra asked. "I'd like to breathe."

"If you can speak, you can breathe."

She scoffed, then asked, "Your name is Simon?"

"Simon Hatch. We've met before."

We'd met before. We'd fought before. We'd embraced each other, shared moments together where there was no one in the world but us. I remembered every detail of every kiss, every brush of her hand over mine, the softness of her cheek against my palm.

And yet she looked at me as if I were a stranger. Or worse, as if I were an enemy.

Slowing the horse to a canter, I said, "I need you to raise the skirt on your right thigh."

She twisted around, eyes blazing. "I will not!"

"Do it, or I'll search you. I know exactly how you'd feel about that, so I suggest you do as I ask."

She huffed, then raised the skirt, very briefly, but enough for me to verify there was no garter, no weapon. Then, without me having to ask, she did the same for her left thigh, with the same results. I wished I had found a knife on her. It would have been some glimmer of the Kestra I'd known, the one always ready for a fight. But it also brought up another question of far greater significance.

Where was the Olden Blade?

"If it's a ransom you want, my father will pay what you ask," she said, cutting into my thoughts.

"I don't want a ransom." Yet I did note that these words were almost the very opposite of what she had told me the last time we were in this situation.

"Then you must think you're saving me from something," she continued. "What is it?" When I didn't answer, she added, "Maybe from the luxuries of being a Dallisor? Or the protection that comes from serving Lord Endrick? Maybe a lifetime of happiness with Basil? Is that what you're saving me from, Simon?"

I bit my tongue to keep from saying the truth. She couldn't possibly believe the things she was saying, unless . . . unless she did. Unless Endrick had done more than erase certain memories from her. What if he had replaced them with a belief that her happiness began and ended with obedience to him?

And if she truly believed that, how was I ever to convince her otherwise? To tell her that she had no Dallisor blood, but instead was half Endrean, just like Lord Endrick, and half Halderian, the enemy clan to the Dallisors. I'd never convince her that Lord Endrick had planned this marriage upon Basil's promise to kill her on their wedding night. The lifetime of happiness she anticipated wasn't even supposed to last until midnight.

Kestra spent the next half hour of our ride warning me that Lord Endrick's armies would already be on our trail, that his oro-pods would eat me alive, and that if I happened to survive, I would be hung where the crows could make mincemeat of my body. Eventually, I stopped listening.

Despite her threats, I breathed easier once we passed the Sentries, the two enormous statues outside Highwyn, one that greeted visitors to the capital and the other that offered a farewell. From there, I planned to turn us east and stick to the coastline as much as possible. This route would offer us plenty of caves in which to hide until I figured out a way to restore her memories.

If there was a way. I might sooner darken the sun than break through Lord Endrick's magic.

We were still within easy sight of the Sentries when I spotted our first sign of trouble, though it wasn't what I'd expected.

Captain Tenger was seated on horseback beside a girl I didn't recognize. Her naturally red lips, skin a shade darker than mine, and nearly translucent white hair immediately gave away her origins. She was from Brill, the neighboring country to the east. Brillians generally kept to themselves and rarely left their own borders. The exception to that rule was directly in front of me with a disk bow ready to fire and a lever blade at her side. Beside her, Tenger looked furious.

Good, because I was more than angry with him.

I halted my horse, then tightened my arms around Kestra. Her breaths had become shallow, as if she was trying to figure out whether Tenger was rescuing her or whether he was the real threat.

I knew the answer. He was a very real threat, absolutely, to both of us.

"How'd you know I'd be on this road?" I asked.

"We've got people stationed on every road out of Highwyn." Tenger's voice was usually stern, but that barely described the chill in his tone now. "You were told not to interfere tonight."

"Yes, but I don't take orders from you anymore," I countered.

Kestra leaned forward. "Please, sir, if you are a man of honor, you will return me to my father."

Tenger smiled and slid off his horse. He walked over to Kestra and took her hand. "My sweet young lady, I am Captain Grey Tenger, commander of the Corack rebellion. I offer my deepest apologies for all you must have suffered tonight. If you'll come with me, we'll make everything right."

She started to leave, but my hand tightened again around her waist. "He's no friend to you," I warned.

"And you are?" She punctuated her question with an elbow to my gut. "You threatened to drag me behind your horse!"

Tenger chuckled, and this time it was genuine. "That's the Simon I remember! Come back to the Coracks, give me your oath. I need you."

I shook my head, refusing to look directly at him. Instead, I kept my focus on the Brillian girl's disk bow still aimed at my chest.

"If you won't join us, then we have a problem," Tenger continued. "Obviously I can't allow you to leave with Lady Dallisor. If you refuse to give her up, then I'll have to kill you here." His eyes darkened. "And I will, Simon. You know that I will."

I did know that. Nor could I start any fight with Tenger right now. Even if I dodged a disk, which was doubtful, I wouldn't risk Kestra getting hit.

Through gritted teeth, I said, "If you truly believe I've abandoned the mission, then you'll never accept my oath."

"I'll never trust you again as I did before, that's true." Tenger brushed his hand over his close-cut beard. "You'll pay an extra price for leaving us the first time." His eyes dropped to my sword.

"No." My sword was not negotiable.

"Very well." Tenger raised two fingers, ready to signal to the girl beside him. "This is Wynnow, a recent volunteer. As she is a Brillian, you can be sure that her aim is excellent. But will she have to hit Kestra to get you?"

I kept my arm tight around Kestra. Not to make her a target, but because I knew how much more danger she'd be in with Tenger.

Tenger had already tried to kill Kestra once, before she was declared the Infidante. Now that she was, he had promised to support her, but I knew he'd still rather see Trina in that role. I suspected the only reason he hadn't yet ordered Wynnow to shoot us was because no one knew what had happened to the Olden Blade. Possibly even Kestra didn't know.

"Make your choice," Tenger said. "Enough stalling!" Wynnow raised her bow. All she needed was the order to fire.

"Take my sword, and accept my oath." I hated speaking the words, but there was no other choice. "I'll return to the Coracks and follow your orders, like before. But Kestra stays with me."

Tenger held out his hand for my sword, and I gave it to him. I still had my knife, but the sword had a far greater significance. I wondered if Tenger knew that.

"If you are following my orders, then this is your first test," Tenger said. "Let Kestra go. She'll ride with someone else, someone she won't try to escape from."

My spine stiffened. "You? Because if she—"

"Not me." The sound of approaching horses caught my attention, and seconds later, Gabe and Trina rounded the bend in the road. Most unexpectedly, Basil was with them.

Behind me, Kestra let out a gasp of relief. I wanted to hurl my knife in Basil's direction and hope the sharp end hit him first. Tenger would probably consider that a violation of my oath. I really didn't care.

"Kestra will ride with her betrothed," Tenger said.

Basil smiled and held out a winter cloak for her, which she gratefully accepted. Deflated and suddenly queasy, I let Kestra go. My heart felt as if that knife might've hit me instead.

Or maybe I simply wished it had.

I was a Corack again, with an oath to serve a captain I no longer trusted, who would never again trust me.

I'd given him my sword, a weapon I had once promised to protect with my life.

And the affection shining in Kestra's eyes that used to be reserved for me was now for Basil. When she looked at me, it was with fear and loathing, and a hope never to have to speak to me again.

But I had no intention of giving up now. She and I would definitely be speaking again.

· SIX ·

KESTRA

Basil took my hand and lifted me onto the horse with him. "Are you well? He didn't hurt you, I hope."

Rather than answer, I cast him a glare. "Are we their captives, or guests?"

He shrugged. "Honestly, Kestra, I'm not sure. Maybe we're both."

"And you planned this?"

"Please, just trust me." That was all he could say. Which was hardly enough for my comfort.

The two Coracks with Basil were both as young as Simon, a girl dressed in riding crops with her hair in a single braid down her back, and a rather handsome boy who rode forward, addressing the man I now knew as Captain Tenger.

The boy said, "Ironhearts might have seen us leaving."

Tenger started toward his horse. "Then let's go."

We followed him for an hour before he announced it was too dark to safely continue and led us to some caves on the northern coastline. Basil and I were ushered deepest inside, which I didn't like at all, and the others filled in to guard the entrance. Bedrolls were passed back to us, though I wasn't tired. But everyone else settled in for the night, so I did too.

"This cave is loaded with terrador plants," the handsome Corack called out. "For anyone who's feeling hungry, listen carefully. Eat one, and you'll be uncomfortable all night. Eat two and you'll wish you were dead. Eat three, and you will be."

Near me was a patch of small leafy plants with tiny white flowers near the stems. Terrador. His advice was met with groans, but he only responded with, "Don't say I never warned you."

From behind me, Basil touched my arm and tried to explain what was happening, but I rolled away from him. Not only was I angry, but the Coracks were talking and I wanted to listen in on their conversation.

Their voices were low, so I couldn't hear everything, but Simon and the two Coracks who had come with Basil were clearly in an argument.

". . . told you not to interfere." The girl said that.

". . . this complicates everything." That was the other Corack.

"You don't care about Kestra." Simon's words came through with perfect clarity. "Only her mission."

"And you've forgotten her mission." The girl said something more after that, but it was drowned out by a horse's snort.

Basil must have suspected I was still awake, because he leaned over and whispered, "The next few days may be confusing. But—"

"What mission are they talking about?" I asked, loud enough for everyone to hear.

The Coracks went silent, waiting for Basil's response. And all he came up with was, "My love, your mission is to survive until you can go home."

In the darkness, someone snorted with irritation, probably Simon. I merely rolled over and pretended to fall asleep, free of guilt for the deception after Basil had offered me such a half-hearted answer. I'd ask someone else later, if I met anyone here I could trust with the truth.

As the trio of Coracks continued arguing, I figured out their names. Trina was the girl, and most of the bickering was between her and Simon. The other boy was named Gabe. He struck me as a kind of peacemaker, an odd trait for a Corack whose every waking minute was dedicated to making war against us. Clearly he had been friends with Simon, and yet something had gone wrong between them. Simon and Trina seemed to have been friends once too. But no more.

Eventually, Tenger ordered all of them to hush and told Simon to take first watch. The cave went quiet, except for Simon's occasional footsteps as he paced back and forth. When he finally stopped walking, I took a chance and peeked up to see where he was. He stood at the cave entrance, almost perfectly still, and although it was dark I was certain that he was watching me.

I ducked my head again and stayed that way until I fell asleep.

⸻

Dawn had barely broken when Wynnow awoke everyone with a shout that oropods were headed our way. "Hurry! I'll stay behind and shoot down any riders I can."

I'd never in my life seen anyone move as fast as the Coracks did, gathering up last night's supplies and practically flying onto their horses. Basil lifted me onto his horse and raced us out of the cave at a full gallop directly behind Tenger.

By the time we made it to the road, I glanced back and saw the dirt being kicked up by the powerful oropod legs. At the speed they were traveling, I doubted we'd get very far.

"Head toward the river!" Tenger shouted.

It was a smart decision. For as fast as they were on land, oropods could not swim, especially nothing as formidable as the Longfinger River ahead. It was wide and deep, and a person would have to be insane to consider crossing it. Yet once we reached its shores, Tenger immediately jumped in with his horse, holding tight to the reins as the current carried him downriver and the horse swam forward.

"Don't follow them in," I told Basil. "I can't swim."

"Yes, you can," he replied. "And we have to go in."

Seconds later, we were in the water too. I gasped with its chill, but Basil assured me we'd be safe. We were, until the water rose as high as my chest. Before I could help myself, the current took hold of my long skirts, pulling me out from beneath Basil's arms.

He called for help and others of our group began shouting my name, but my head was bobbing in and out of the water as it carried me away. I rounded a bend, struggling for each breath but mostly swallowing water and feeling increasingly weighted down by my heavy skirts.

Within minutes, Basil and the Coracks were out of sight, as was any hope of rescue. I turned long enough to see that I was drifting toward the dead black trees of All Spirits Forest, and my heart froze. What had been fear before became a terrifying certainty that I was about to die. This was haunted territory, and no one loyal to Lord Endrick survived these woods. Ever.

At the border of the forest, my body slammed against a rock jutting from the water, hitting my right leg the hardest. I twisted around, desperate to get a hand on it. The rock was slippery, and spray blasted against my face, but I found a narrow grip and dug my fingers into it. The water was frigid, though I didn't know if that was the cause of my shivering, or the sure knowledge that my life was as tenuous as my hold on this rock.

I had to hold on and go no farther. The dead were watching me. I knew that, as certain as I felt my heart pounding. A daughter of the Dominion was within their clutches. Claiming me would be a satisfactory revenge against Lord Endrick.

Above the noise of the river and the cries in my head to tighten my grip, I thought I heard a horse approaching, maybe someone calling my name. I tried to look, but the rock blocked my view.

It didn't matter anyway, because invisible hands beneath the water seemed intent on grabbing my long skirts, tugging me off the rock, pulling me under. Keeping me under. These were the spirits of the dead, and no matter how I struggled upward, they were winning.

The clammy hands of half-life spirits clutched at me on all sides, as if competing for who could drag me to the river bottom the fastest. Their wispy faces crowded around me, angry and wild-eyed, drowning me. My last breath burst from my lungs and I inhaled water instead. I tried again to break free, but by then, I was so battered by the current that I couldn't tell which way was up. Even if I knew, it wouldn't matter. They'd only pull me down again.

This was death.

This was worse than death.

Then, as quickly as they'd come, the spirits vanished, as if repelled. With one exception, a presence that seemed strangely familiar. I heard no voice, saw nothing in the blurry water, but I knew I was being pushed out of the deep river.

From out of nowhere, an arm reached around my waist from above and the pull became more tangible. I fought it at first, confused and disoriented. A few seconds later, my head surfaced, but I still couldn't breathe.

"Stop fighting, let me help you!" That was Simon's voice. He was holding on to me with one hand and to his horse with the other.

I wasn't fighting him. I needed air, needed to escape the spirits who were still surrounding me, gripping at my throat. I thrashed around, suffocating even in this open air.

Simon directed his horse to swim to shore, and as the water became shallower, he pulled me into the saddle ahead of him. He immediately kicked the horse into a run, muttering something about me holding on.

As soon as we cleared the borders of the forest, sunlight hit my face and I drew my first real breath since going under the water. I choked on what I'd swallowed, then continued pulling in as much air as I could get. When I was more settled, I looked back toward the dead forest, hoping to see any sign of what had happened.

"It's all right," Simon said, misunderstanding my interest in the forest. "We're far enough away now." He stopped the horse at the side of the road and helped me out of the saddle, where I collapsed beside a large rock to continue catching my breath.

"Why did they attack you?" he asked.

"They attack everyone loyal to Lord Endrick," I replied, wondering how he could miss the most obvious detail. "They pulled me under."

"Yes, at first. But then something pushed you out, or I'd never have reached you. What was that?"

One of the spirits in that forest wanted me to live, which was something I couldn't begin to explain. Nor would I explain anything to *him*.

He said, "You've been there before, Kes. They let you enter before."

If I'd had the strength for it, I would've laughed in his face. "Impossible! I am a Dallisor!"

He stared at me and something in his expression changed. "That's right. You are a Dallisor," he said, as if this was somehow new information.

"And you're that boy who was watching me in the market earlier today," I said, finally recognizing him. "I don't know why you're so focused on me, but let me be clear. I desire neither your attention nor your friendship."

He clicked his tongue, so I knew I'd successfully irritated him. "If you're ready, we'll return to the others. Let's hope your beloved Basil doesn't almost get you killed again."

"It was an accident."

"This time," he mumbled. Or at least, I thought that's what he'd said. He pulled out his knife and marched toward me so fast that I stood, frightened of what he'd do next, until I realized his target was the extra fabric of my dress. He gathered the ends into his hands and cut away the excess with his knife, then tossed it back into the river.

I shuddered to watch it drift away, slowing sinking beneath the surface. If not for Simon, that would've been me.

"It's all right," he said when he noticed my distress. "You're safe now."

"We both know I'm not."

He stared at me without responding for what felt like a very long time, then lifted me onto his horse to return to the group.

Basil let out an audible sigh of relief when he saw me and eagerly rode forward. "My love, I'm so relieved."

"You returned her?" Tenger was clearly surprised to see us.

Simon cocked his head. "Wasn't that your order?"

Tenger leaned into his saddle. "Wasn't that your order . . . ?" He waited.

"Sir." Simon finished the sentence with a bite to his voice. "Wasn't that your order, *sir*?"

I watched him walk over to Gabe, where they spoke in low voices. Simon was clearly angry, but his eyes continually flitted back to me, and despite what I had told him earlier, I found myself watching him. I hated him for stealing me away from all that was familiar, but something about him felt familiar too. As impossible as that was, I wanted to understand him better.

No, if I was going to survive this, then I *needed* to understand him, this boy who treated me like a prisoner, spoke to me like an enemy, but who looked at me with such hunger, as if I held a place in his heart.

· SEVEN ·

SIMON

I was finally ready to accept at least one fact about Kestra: My feelings for her would never be indifferent, nor even mild. Either she'd keep me on the edge of my temper, or so passionate that I'd go over a cliff just to see her again. It was awful to be apart from her, but torture to be close to her when I couldn't get closer still. My heart stopped whenever I caught a glimpse of her smile and split apart every time she looked at me like I was the mud beneath her boot. She claimed to be my prisoner, but in fact, I was hers. She was a far greater threat to me than I ever could be to her.

After we returned to the others, I released her to Basil only because I needed to breathe again without having to inhale her scent, her essence, and the tragedy that something had fundamentally changed about her. The Kestra I had known was gone, possibly forever. What happened in All Spirits Forest had proved that. She was truly a Dallisor now.

After assuring us the oropods were no longer on our trail, Tenger led us southward, I suspected toward the Drybelt. The Coracks had a secret camp there known as Lonetree, which was a fairly accurate description of its appearance above ground. Below, however, was a vast system of underground caves that from the surface only appeared as a small crevice in the earth. It was our oldest camp, our largest, and the best prepared for defense, if that ever became necessary. So far, the Dominion had never found it.

I rode up beside Tenger. "Don't you think we got away from those oropods rather easily? The Dominion never just gives up."

"Agreed. They could have a trap laid out ahead for us." Tenger sighed. "You have a good mind for leadership, Simon. What a pity to have lost you."

"You have my oath again. I gave you my sword, and I returned Kestra, as ordered. Tell me the plan now."

Tenger clicked his tongue. "You can't believe it'll be that simple."

I arched a brow but tried not to let my irritation show. "Pulling her out of that river wasn't simple."

"You didn't do that because I ordered you to. You didn't even do it to protect the Olden Blade."

"But I did do it. Do we know where the Olden Blade is . . . sir?"

Tenger looked sideways at me. "As I already said, Hatch, it won't be that easy for you to come back. You would've been my next in line, my hope for the rebellion to continue if I ever fell in battle. But now . . . you are the water boy. The person who brings my meals and scrubs my dishes, and you'll do it with a smile on your face until I'm convinced you mean it, if you want to continue having access to her."

"I want to know—"

Tenger cocked his head. "What was that?"

My grip tightened on my reins. "Yes, sir."

"Then ride at the back. You have no right to be up here."

I slowed my horse, steering to the side of the trail. "Yes, sir, Captain Tenger."

Yes, sir, because I would smile and carry out his orders and do whatever I had to do for now. But only until I got my sword back, and Kestra as she was before, if either were possible.

I waited there for Trina and Gabe to pass. He offered me an apologetic smile, and Trina grunted my name. Basil and Kestra came next. Basil thanked me again for saving Kestra. She didn't even blink in my direction.

And I fell in line at the end, trying to watch anything but her. Doing a miserable job of ignoring the way she observed the scenery as we passed, the gentle pat of her hand on her horse. The brush of her fingers along her right thigh where she once had been accustomed to feeling a weapon.

Sending me to a place so near her, and so far apart, was a punishment beyond anything Tenger could have imagined. Every mile forward tore deeper into me. I was sure he knew it too.

We rode into Lonetree Camp early that evening, all of us road-weary and hungry. The Drybelt was the arid center of Antora, with flat plains in the north and deep crevices in the land farther south. In the early days of the rebellion, the Coracks had fled here to hide and had come upon an underground river and natural vents in the cave ceiling to provide fresh air. Thus, Lonetree Camp was barely detectable from most places above ground. As many as four hundred people could live underground here, for extended periods of time, if necessary. Although the surrounding land was hostile, it also provided us the advantage of sparse population and few Dominion soldiers ever passing this way.

I didn't know most of the Coracks who came out to greet Tenger, but when a young boy offered to attend to my horse, his eyes widened. "You're Simon Hatch! We've heard about you out here."

My smile was wary. "About me?"

"The mission, to find the Olden Blade. My mother was surprised the captain put so much trust in someone your age. Someone . . . so near her age."

Oh. "I wasn't the captain's first choice."

"Maybe not. But you found the Blade."

Only for it to be lost now. Or lost to me. Surely Tenger knew more than he was saying about what Kestra had done with it.

"What happens now?" Basil asked Tenger.

"Everyone needs to sleep, then we'll talk in the morning." With that, Tenger nodded at the gathered Coracks, who immediately pulled out disk bows and surrounded me, Kestra, and Basil. They already had their orders.

"I'm sorry," Gabe told me. "Tenger also wants your knife." I pulled my knife from its sheath and, holding it by the blade, offered it to Gabe. He frowned at me before tucking it inside his belt. "You understand why it has to be this way."

"Just take me there." I sighed. "Anywhere I can get some sleep."

Inside one of the caves were cells meant to hold captured Ironhearts until whoever commanded this base passed sentence on them. On occasion, it was used to discipline Coracks who had overstepped their bounds.

Me, I supposed.

There were two cells side by side, with embedded rock and earth at the back and bars on the front and between the cells. I entered the first cell without objection, followed by Basil, who objected very much.

"I must speak to your captain in private," he said. "About our agreement."

"The captain will gladly speak with you . . . in the morning," Gabe said, pushing him into the same cell as me.

Kestra was given the neighboring cell, and wool blankets were tossed in after each of us, as well as a single clearstone for us to share for light. I grabbed my blanket and wrapped it around my shoulders, then leaned against the cave wall. I hoped they wouldn't warm the clearstone. I didn't need to see any more of them.

But Kestra immediately warmed it, lighting the cells enough for me to see Basil rush to the bars, pleading again for her forgiveness. "My love, please believe me. This wasn't part of our agreement. They said nothing about locking us up."

She leaned against the opposite bars, far out of his reach. "And you said nothing at all to me."

Basil tossed a needy glance my way. I arched a brow, as if to say he was on his own for this one, and I hoped it all blew up in his face.

"You promised to trust me if yesterday evening didn't go as planned," he said.

"I thought you were worried about forgetting your vows or tripping on my gown. Not that you'd work with this filthy Corack to kidnap me!" She waved her hands angrily in my direction.

"We're not working together," Basil and I said at almost the same time.

"So you separately planned to kidnap me last night." She sighed. "I've been kidnapped twice."

I leaned forward. "Technically, princess, last night marks your third and fourth kidnappings, which has got to be some sort of record. Though the second was really more of a temporary detention, not a kidnapping."

She paused, her eyes set in deep thought. She was trying to remember. But as soon as she caught me looking, she turned away.

"Please don't upset her," Basil said.

"Upset me?" Her cheeks reddened. "Do you really think anything he says could upset me more than your agreement already has?"

"Which agreement?" I asked Basil. "The one with the Coracks, or your agreement with Lord Endrick?"

Before he squirmed through that answer, I pulled my blanket higher, alone with my self-satisfaction to have stung Basil. Small compensation for the hurt he'd caused me, and not enough to overcome my exhaustion. I welcomed a decent night of sleep, even in a cell. At least here I wouldn't have to worry about Kestra's safety.

When I awoke, Basil and Kestra were both leaning against their shared bars, his hand over hers as they slept. It seemed they had made up again. A perfect start to my day.

Basil must have heard me stirring, because he looked up. He warmed the clearstone before standing, and despite my glare, he sat down at my side. My back was against the wall, with my knees up and hands resting upon them. It would have been easy to reach over and punch him; I'd gladly do it if the opportunity arose. But he quietly said, "I know how you feel about her, Simon, so I know how you feel about me too, but I'm not the villain here. I made this arrangement to protect Kestra—"

"This wasn't for her. You bargained with Tenger to protect your country."

"Yes, I have to protect my country! I won't apologize for that. But I also had to get Kestra out of Highwyn."

"In what way is she any safer with you?"

"She's still alive because of me! Kestra tried to kill Endrick, but failed, and he took her captive. He did something to her afterward, twisting her memories or removing them entirely—I don't know. For some reason, Endrick wants to keep her alive."

I clicked my tongue. If that was true, then it was because he knew who she was. If he could not take the Infidante out of the girl, he would take the girl out of the Infidante.

Basil continued, "There are times when I think I see a flicker of recognition in her eyes, but it quickly disappears, and then a minute later, she's professing loyalty to the Dominion and laughing with her attendants. It's her, but it's obvious this is not the same person she was several days ago. And she's certainly no longer capable of killing Lord Endrick."

That was my sense too. I asked, "How much of her memory did he take?"

"I can't be sure. Whenever the conversation shifts to her past, she closes up. The Kestra we used to know is gone."

"She's not gone. We just have to restore the memories."

"I tried, Simon, but nothing worked. That's when I decided to contact Tenger."

"Why him?" I asked. "Of all people, why would you go to the Coracks?"

Basil lowered his eyes. "Because we each have something the other wants."

I was about to ask him to explain when Gabe reentered the room. He had changed clothes and brought some bread and cider for us, so I gathered it was morning.

"Sir Basil," he said, "Captain Tenger is ready to see you. He'll share breakfast with you in his office."

Gabe's entrance awoke Kestra, whose expression soured as it traveled from Basil to me. Gabe unlocked the door, giving me another sympathetic smile. With a farewell to Kestra, Basil disappeared, leaving the two of us alone.

She sat on the floor and began eating her bread. I'd already forgotten mine.

Instead, I said, "I think I know what happened to—"

"You don't know anything."

"And you do? Why did Basil bring you here? What do the Coracks want with you?"

Her eyes flashed back at me. "What do *you* want?"

I held her gaze until she finally looked away. Even if the truth was locked deep within her, surely she must know that she had become my only reason to do anything.

· EIGHT ·

—————

KESTRA

An hour after Basil was taken away, Trina came to bring me to Captain Tenger.

"Where's Basil?" He hadn't come back from his meeting with Tenger. Would I?

"Let's go," Trina said, ignoring my question.

I glanced back at Simon as I left the cell. He was watching me, as always, but this time gave a slight nod as if to suggest that everything was fine, as if he knew my thoughts. I wished I knew any of his.

As she led me through the corridor, Trina's frown became increasingly pronounced. "We've only just met," I said. "What could I possibly have done in such a short time to deserve your anger?"

For a moment, I believed her glare might actually collapse the narrow tunnel where we were walking. "I hate you *more* since last night, that's true. But I've been working on these feelings for some time now."

My laugh was sharp, but it served the same purpose it had back at Woodcourt, to cover up my fears. "My father says it's better to be hated as a Dallisor than loved as one of the pathetic masses." I winked at her. "That's you, one of the pathetic masses."

"You'll feel differently when the Coracks take the Scarlet Throne and occupy the royal palace."

I shrugged her off. "A skunk may live among the flowers, but that doesn't make it smell any better."

Trina stopped, closed her eyes, and I noticed her fists were clenched, but she gradually let them relax and, without a word, opened the nearby door to a room where Wynnow was waiting inside. In contrast to Trina's near-constant scathing glares, Wynnow smiled at me. "My lady, I've been eager to meet you."

I appreciated Wynnow's politeness but questioned the false humility. Like Imri Stout, my handmaiden back at Woodcourt, and like all Brillians, Wynnow probably was as superior as she believed herself to be. Brillians were highly intelligent, and their hearing and eyesight exceeded that of most Antorans, and their other senses probably did as well. They were also exceptionally long lived, so although Wynnow appeared to be a year or two younger than me, she might have been two or three times as old as I was.

Beyond that, it was well known that the Brillians greatly desired magic. Since Brillians could not obtain it, the Dominion believed that their scientists were attempting to imitate Endrick's magic—his technologies, his weapons. Lord Endrick would not tolerate that for long. Maybe that was why Wynnow was fighting with the Coracks, hoping to defeat the Dominion before he turned an eye to Brill.

When Trina saw my cool greeting, she added, "Wynnow isn't just any Corack. She's heir to the throne of Brill."

Wynnow said, "My mother, the queen, entrusted me to find a way to protect my country from any future invasion by the Dominion. That's why I'm here."

If they hoped to impress me, they'd be disappointed. I could hardly cheer for Wynnow's dedication to a cause that threatened my family, my king. I said, "If you hope to kill Lord Endrick, you'd more easily catch sunlight in a jar. It's impossible."

Trina pushed between us. "For you, it obviously was."

Before I could ask what she meant, Wynnow shot Trina a disapproving glare, then motioned for me to follow her deeper into what appeared to be a weapons supply room. Lever blades, swords, and disk bows filled various crates along the wall, in addition to a few other scattered Dominion weapons that must have been collected in post-battle scavenges.

Hanging from a hook embedded into the wall was a woman's tunic with riding breeches, similar to what Trina wore. "It's mine," Trina explained. "We're about the same size, and if we need to do any more riding, this will mean you don't have to go sidesaddle."

I shook my head. "I've never ridden a horse on my own. Riding breeches won't do me any good."

"But they're better here than skirts." Wynnow pointed to a small wooden room that looked hastily built in one corner. "You can change in there."

"You're joking." And to prove it, I laughed extra loud. "It's dark and there's barely enough room for a single person."

"Does that bother you?" Flecks of suspicion were in Trina's voice. "To be in such a small space?"

I groaned. "It doesn't bother me. It's just inconvenient."

Trina snorted, but Wynnow added in a gentler tone, "Do you know how to change your own clothes, my lady?"

I shook my head to her question, and she undid the buttons down my back before assuring me I could figure out the rest of it. I entered the room, which was almost too small for me to turn around. A little light filtered in from above, which helped, but it was taking a long time to change and Trina was making it clear through her numerous huffs that she was growing impatient.

Then she said, "I would've offered to help, if you didn't treat everyone around you like they're servants."

"Most people around me are servants," I said. "Why should I treat them otherwise?"

Trina muttered something that might've been an insult, had I heard it. Instead, for reasons I couldn't explain, I was hit with a sudden rush of fear. That the walls would cave in on me, that I wouldn't get enough air, that I'd be trapped in this tiny space forever. What was this?

I closed my eyes, attempting to stay calm, which only worsened the feeling that I was not safe if I remained in here. I knew it was only my imagination, but that didn't matter. I was terrified. I tried to dress blind, but then it was taking even longer to finish and every time I opened my eyes, this tiny room felt smaller than before. Surely the air was thinner.

Even before I had finished changing, I darted from the room, out of breath and with my heart threatening to pound out of my chest.

"My lady?" Wynnow's brows were pressed together in concern. That was the expression I expected. Not Trina's gaze of suspicion, which I couldn't at all explain.

Trina leaned in to me. "You were nervous in there."

"Nervous? No." That simple word failed to describe the wave of horror that had shot through me. But how could I explain that, with no logical reason to justify what I'd felt?

"I saw it on your face as you exited, heard it in your voice. I've seen you panic in small spaces before, and I recognized it now."

I was feeling calmer now, and I needed to take back control. "We've never met, Trina."

Her eyes narrowed as she continued staring at me, as if I were the one who was lying or making up stories. She was worse than unkind and possibly insane, as Coracks often were, according to my father.

Wynnow broke the rising tension by saying, "You'll need help with your hair, I think."

I sat in a nearby chair facing away from Trina, and as Wynnow began working at what had become a mop overnight, I repeated Simon's question from this morning. "What do the Coracks want with me?"

Trina said, "Captain Tenger will explain that."

I was sure he would and that it probably would all be a lie. Because all Coracks lied.

I asked, "Is Simon a Corack?"

Trina answered, "He was, until recently. Now . . . we'll have to see."

"Why did he leave?"

She sighed. "The truth is that Simon has become . . . . a problem."

"How?"

Trina walked around until she was facing me. "Honestly, Kestra, the problem is you. If you haven't already noticed, Simon has a rather intense interest in you."

I frowned. "Yes, I might have noticed that."

Wynnow added, "Now that we're in camp, the captain should be able to put an end to that." She finished my braid. "There!"

Trina opened the door for us. "Let's take her to Tenger."

We returned to the cave corridor, where we almost immediately bumped into Basil, being escorted by the boy who had tended to

Simon's horse last night. After meeting with Tenger, Basil seemed no worse than before, a great relief, but his eyes widened as he looked me over. "Trousers?"

"Riding breeches," Trina said. "Far more practical out here."

"I agree." Basil forced a smile to his face, as if his approval was even remotely on my mind. "I've taken care of everything, my love. Very soon, I can explain all of this."

I gave him a polite nod. I had only made up with Basil last night to keep Simon at a distance. As with nearly everything else in my life, what I said and what I felt had little in common.

While Wynnow left with Basil, Trina led me onward to the far end of the corridor, opening the door to the same room from which Basil had just come.

The room's layout was far more established than I'd expected, given the primitive cells and rough carved walls of this cave system. A large table stood between us, with a map of Antora and the surrounding countries, carved into the wood. The rough-hewn walls were lined with dried skins painted with estimates of military strengths in various areas, weapon designs, and lists of names. I deliberately ignored them. The less I knew, the safer I was.

Except Captain Tenger surely wanted information from me. He'd be disappointed though. I knew little of the affairs of my kingdom and probably held fewer secrets than the lowliest servant at Woodcourt.

But if I had nothing of value to offer him, would he conclude that I was of no worth as a prisoner? Maybe he already had, which was why he felt secure about bringing me into this room.

My heart began pounding. I glanced over at Trina. "I won't go in there."

"We're friends here." I hardly believed that, but Trina ducked her head in and said to Tenger, "She didn't like the closet. Everything else seems sincere."

I turned back to her, sensing that she had somehow revealed something of great importance. I took note of that and swore I would never let those feelings of panic be observed by anyone here again.

Tenger smiled and rose to his feet to greet me. "Before we begin, let me introduce you to our physician, Loelle." An aging woman approached me from the corner. Over a simple calf-length skirt, she wore a longcoat lined with pockets and a coif over her hair. The gentle lines on her face seemed kind, even compassionate, but I hardly considered that a reason to trust her.

Loelle set down a mug of steaming tea, placing it near another full mug that smelled enticing. Then she stepped forward. "Lady Dallisor, I heard you were recently in an accident."

"I fell from a window. If Lord Endrick had not been there to heal me, I wouldn't have survived."

"How very . . . *lucky* for you." She'd chosen her words as carefully as I'd chosen mine, but in fact, I had been exceptionally lucky. It must have been draining for Lord Endrick to heal me. Perhaps that was why he needed to rest at the Blue Caves.

Loelle picked up the second mug of tea and held it out to me. "The cells where they held you last night are drafty. This will help warm you."

I took the mug but stared into its dark liquid. "What's in it?"

She picked up her tea again. "If there were anything harmful, I wouldn't be drinking it too."

She sipped from hers and I smelled mine, as if that would give me any clue to its ingredients. But I was terribly cold and thirsty, and so I took a small taste, as a test. It was sweeter than I'd expected, but delicious. I survived the sip, so I took more. And then more again.

Loelle continued, "After you were healed, did you lose any memories?"

How would she know that? I tried to smile that away, as if it was a minor thing. "My father has assured me there's nothing forgotten of any consequence."

"Your mind is not like the ordinary Antoran's. There is a chance for you to recover some of these memories, especially now." Her gaze fell to my mug.

It was almost empty. My eyes narrowed. "What was in that tea?"

"A combination of herbs that absorb some effects of magic. I hope they will help to restore your memories, though there are no guarantees. I promise it will cause you no harm." Loelle stepped closer to me, but I backed away. She added, "I'm also told that something unusual happened to you in All Spirits Forest."

My back stiffened. "I don't know what you mean."

"Something pulled you under the water. Then something . . . or someone . . . pushed you up. Can you tell me more?"

"Only that it never happened." That was a lie, but telling her the truth would have required an explanation I couldn't provide.

When I didn't answer further, she reached out to touch the gray pearl necklace I still wore. "What is this?"

"A gift." I tried to push her hand down, but she kept hold of it.

"From Lord Endrick?" Loelle moved the necklace aside, then pressed her palm over my heart. After several beats, she gave Tenger a distinct frown, wordlessly communicating a concern I did not understand.

He cursed, then walked over to examine the necklace closer. "What do you know about this so-called gift?"

I shrugged, feeling a strange pinch in my chest, like a warning to be careful with my words. "It's a wedding gift, nothing more."

Eyeing Loelle, Tenger said, "We can't take the risk. She must go to the caves."

"What caves?" I asked.

When he saw my curious, widened eyes, Tenger patted my hand, then released it. "Don't let that concern you now." With his nod, Loelle dismissed herself, and Tenger added, "You must have questions for me."

I had a thousand questions, though none of them mattered more than my first. "Whatever I ask, will you promise to answer honestly?"

"As honestly as I can. Please, my lady, sit down." Tenger gestured to a chair in front of him and offered me a tray of sliced bread and apples. "Are you hungry?"

I reached for a slice of bread. Maybe it would dull the effects of the tea, for Loelle had to have tricked me. What was the point of absorbing the effects of magic if no magic had been used on me?

While I ate, Tenger gestured at the table showing the countries surrounding Antora. He pointed to Reddengrad, which lined the entire southern border of Antora.

"Sir Basil's country is under threat of war," he said.

He hadn't mentioned anything about war to me. "From whom?"

He frowned. "From your king, my lady."

My eyes widened. "Lord Endrick intends to attack Reddengrad?"

"Yes. Basil asked us to help him protect his home, and we've agreed."

"Then you've agreed to die. Lord Endrick is immortal and has exceptionally powerful magic. Any fight against him will ultimately fail."

"We're working on that problem." Tenger briefly studied me. "I hoped you might know of a way to stop him."

I shook my head. "There is no way. And even if I did know, I wouldn't tell you. I remain loyal to the Dominion." My chest tightened again. "Why am I here?"

His fingers clasped. "For now, you are here only because Basil is your betrothed. He had to leave Highwyn to seek us out and didn't want you left behind."

I smiled, though my irritation with Basil was rapidly growing. "How very thoughtful of him." A beat passed, then I added, "Is Simon on your side, or is he a Loyalist?"

"He's no Loyalist, that's certain." A corner of Tenger's mouth lifted. "Simon and I are on the same side, but I'm no longer sure what his true goals are."

"Your goal is to kill Lord Endrick." I stood, hoping to relieve the increasing pressure in my chest. "And as such, you may as well hang yourself tonight and save my father the trouble. You've taken me captive, and for that, he will come for you with a particular vengeance."

"A thoughtful suggestion, thank you." Tenger dipped his head, mocking me, but I had been sincerely trying to warn him. "All I ask is that you stay here for now, as our guest. No harm will come to you as long as you promise to obey our rules."

"Locked in that cell, do I have any other choice?"

"You are a guest, my lady. I am not returning you to the cells." Tenger opened the door for me, and Basil was waiting on the other side with Trina. His smile was tentative, but it faded when he saw my cool expression.

If Trina noticed, she didn't care. "I'll take you both to your rooms," she offered.

I accepted Basil's hand as he led me into the corridor. "Did Tenger explain?" he asked.

He explained in carefully worded sentences meant to tell me nothing more than they had to. I'd gotten little from them and worried they'd gotten far more from me.

"They explained." The less I said, the better.

Basil breathed a noticeable sigh of relief. He reached for me, but we were forced apart when Simon entered, roughly pushing between us with an elbow thrown out particularly wide for Basil. Gabe followed him, chuckling loudly until Tenger hushed him.

Inside the room, Simon stood with his arms folded and legs spread apart, facing Tenger like he was ready to defend himself from an attack. "You summoned me, *sir*?"

Tenger nodded at Basil. "Take your betrothed to her room."

"Yes, Captain," Basil said, wrapping his arm tight around me.

And Simon definitely noticed. Before the door shut, he had turned around and was staring at me again.

· NINE ·

SIMON

For the first time since seeing Kestra again, she wasn't at the forefront of my thoughts. I saw Basil's hold on her, the expression of victory in his eyes when he knew I'd seen it, but I'd also seen Kestra squirm. She knew she was being used as a tool to bolster his bargaining power. Or I hoped she did.

But no matter how I wanted to see Kestra continue to resist him, for now, Tenger was standing in front of me, relishing this moment.

Did he think I'd beg? That I'd do anything he asked to get back into his good graces? I was here only because I had to be, and he'd be a fool not to know that.

Tenger *tsked*. "I had to hit you that night, Simon. It wasn't personal."

"Yes, sir." If I said what I really thought, he'd make me regret my words, probably with that grip glove on his right hand. He had taken that from Kestra the night we captured her carriage. I wondered if she had recognized it, or even known what it was.

Tenger continued, "I admit it, I thought Trina would be the Infidante. Indeed, I still believe she would have been chosen had Kestra not claimed the dagger first. And yes, if Trina had been chosen, she would have named me king over the Halderians, and future king of Antora, once Endrick was defeated."

"Yes, sir." I noticed a small knife on the floor at the corner of his desk, three steps ahead of me. It must have fallen without him noticing.

Tenger nodded toward Gabe, who'd been standing watch at the back of the room. "Wait in the corridor." When he'd left, Tenger sighed like the disappointed parent he believed himself to be. "We were friends, Simon. I had your respect, your loyalty."

"You crashed a rock down on my head . . . sir."

"I did what had to be done, based on what I knew at the time. We needed a king among the Coracks, some way of controlling the future of Antora."

I remained silent while Tenger leaned down behind his desk. I used the distraction to walk forward until I could place my foot over the knife. Tenger sat up with my sword in his hands, which he laid out across the desk. He said, "Little did I know then that the Halderians already have a king."

My muscles tensed, but I kept my head down, unwilling to risk any betrayal of my thoughts.

"Did you think I'd miss the look exchanged between you and Kestra when she was asked to name the next king? I'm embarrassed that she figured you out before I did."

"It's not what—"

"I knew you carried a Halderian sword. But it never occurred to me that you have *the* sword. Then Trina informed me she saw King Gareth's ring in your satchel. Did he name you his successor?"

"I'm not Halderian."

Tenger grinned. "That wasn't my question." When I remained silent, he added, "Never mind the answer—with these two items, you have enough claim on the crown. So I suppose my real question is: *Why* haven't you claimed it?"

"I already gave you an answer."

"Because you're not Halderian? Thrones have been claimed over thinner justifications than that. Nor do I believe that's your true reason."

I shifted my stance. "You didn't summon me here to understand the way I think. What do you want from me . . . sir?"

"Obviously, I want you to claim the Halderian crown."

That hadn't been obvious at all. I'd expected to receive some sort of punishment, or to be assigned to a district as far from Kestra as possible, or to be forced into begging for his mercy. This possibility had never occurred to me.

"Claim the crown? Why?"

Tenger gestured to the area of the table where Reddengrad's border with Antora had been carved into the wood. Tucked in a little pocket immediately to the west of both countries was an unclaimed and largely unwanted area known as the Hiplands, the refuge where most Halderians had gathered.

Tenger tapped a knuckle on the Hiplands. "If Endrick takes Reddengrad, the Halderians will be trapped. One day, Endrick will figure out how numerous they've become, and how prosperous. The Halderians must defend Reddengrad if they also expect to survive."

The fact that the Halderians had survived the last several years was a miracle in itself. The Dominion referred to them as the Banished and believed that only small colonies of that clan remained, struggling for survival. But they were wrong. The Halderians had far greater numbers than the Dominion knew, and had built a thriving city in the Hiplands due to their trade with Reddengrad. Once Endrick discovered them, he'd slaughter every last Halderian before they had any hope of mounting a defense.

And suddenly the pieces fit together in my mind. Basil wanted the Coracks to help defend Reddengrad. And Tenger wanted my help in getting the Halderians to join that fight.

"No," I said.

Tenger arched a brow. "No?"

"No, *sir*, I will not claim the throne. And if I did, my first order would not be to send Halderian armies into a hopeless battle. Because as long as Endrick reigns, the battle is hopeless, and you know it!"

"Everyone knows it," Tenger snapped. "But I had to make an agreement with Basil, and those were his terms."

"Because otherwise, he won't say where the Olden Blade is."

"Even if Kestra's memory came back, he claims that she doesn't know where it is. She instructed him to hide it so that if things went badly with Endrick in that final meeting—which they clearly did—he wouldn't get the information from her. But Basil won't reveal where it is until we're fully committed to Reddengrad's defense. That's why I need you, Simon. To get the Halderians involved until Basil reveals to us the Olden Blade."

"Which does us no good while Kestra's memories are gone. As she is now, I doubt she even knows which end of the dagger to aim at Endrick."

"Loelle gave her a medicinal tea that may help to recover some memories. And she's got an Endrean mind, which we hope will heal quickly against Endrick's magic. But that's only part of the problem."

He drew in a deep breath. "What do you know about that necklace Kestra is wearing?"

I'd seen it, but it looked like nothing more than Dominion jewelry. The way Tenger asked the question concerned me though, and probably for good reason.

"Endrick gave it to her?"

"The stone set into the pendant isn't natural. He must have created it. Endrick doesn't give gifts—it's there for a reason."

I agreed, but with Endrick, anything was possible. Did the necklace affect her memories, or control her behavior? Could it read her thoughts or did it have some other malicious intent? I said, "We've got to get rid of it."

"Unless that harms her," Tenger said. "We can't touch the necklace until we understand it."

"And we won't understand if we can't touch it," I mused, batting a fist against my thigh.

Tenger continued, "Loelle confirmed something else to me: Kestra is an Ironheart now."

My gut twisted, and I took a slow breath to absorb that before mumbling, "He's controlling her?"

"Not exactly. But he has some awareness of her and can kill her if he senses any disloyalty in her words or actions. But he hasn't yet, so he still has a use for her."

I knew what the Ironhearts were, but when we fought them, it was always them or us to fall in battle. We'd never tried reclaiming an Ironheart. I didn't even know if it was possible.

Tenger must have sensed my thoughts. "An Ironheart is created through magic. You cannot heal her with anything less."

The tension in my muscles worsened, as if I'd been kicking against a brick wall for weeks, and in some ways, I obviously had. "What are we supposed to do? Endrick will never give up control of her, and we have no means to force him."

"No, we don't. Nor can we fully restore her memories. Endrick has corrupted them too much for Loelle to rebuild everything." Tenger clasped his hands together and lowered his voice. "But we have a plan."

My eyes narrowed, sensing the cure was worse than the cause. "No, Tenger."

"We think the only way to fully heal her is to give her magic. We've got to take her to the Blue Caves."

The anger that had been festering beneath the surface now exploded. "Are you insane?"

Tenger arched a brow. "What was that?"

I straightened my posture and took a deep breath to calm myself. "Are you insane . . . sir? You'll risk her whole future simply because you *think* it will help?"

"We *know* that nothing else will, and maybe magic will be good for her." Tenger's voice remained calmer than I could pretend to be. "Loelle has magic. That's how she's healed hundreds of Coracks over the years."

This wasn't a surprise, but I also knew that over time, any Endrean with magic would turn bad. Loelle was no different. The instant she began to show signs of corruption, her fate was already decided.

"What about your orders to kill any living Endreans?" I asked.

"Obviously Kestra must be an exception." Tenger hesitated again, longer than he should have. "At least until she completes her quest."

I did a double take, certain I could not have heard him correctly. "And after Endrick is dead? Then what?"

Tenger sank back into his chair. If he wanted to appear a reasonable leader who acted solely for the good of the country, he wouldn't get far with me. He couldn't justify such thoughts in his mind without being every bit the villain that Endrick was.

Tenger clasped his hands together and said, "I know you have feelings for Kestra, and perhaps she used to like you too, before Endrick got to her. But she is part of his army now, an Infidante who is fully loyal to him. Magic is the only way to restore her."

My hands balled into fists. "It will corrupt her!"

"Yes, over time it will. She'll eventually become a girl as foreign to you as she is now. But there's no other way for her to complete her quest, and despite your feelings, that is the purpose of her life now. Nothing else."

"She is more than the Infidante!"

Tenger stood, barking out, "No, Simon, she is only the Infidante! Nothing else matters but that. And when she completes her quest, she will be a highly powerful Endrean with magic. We will have to put her down before she becomes as dangerous as Endrick!"

"No!" Angrily, I swiped my arm, knocking papers from his desk, then muttered an apology under my breath. As if I knew I'd gone too far, when in reality, I was only beginning to overstep my bounds with him. I leaned down to pick up the knife, now hidden in my hand when I returned Tenger's papers.

By then, his temper had calmed. In a quieter voice, he said, "Once you see how the magic affects her, you'll agree with me."

I shook my head. "No, *sir*, I will not."

"Do you think I want this to happen to her? I don't! I'd much rather find a way to let her live."

"If that's true, then give me time to——"

"Time will only entrench her false memories and set her true memories farther from her reach. Every passing hour, she will get worse, not better." He took a breath and lowered his voice. "I know you think I'm cruel, but I'm simply speaking the truth. Although she may recover some memories on her own without magic, she'll never get them all back, and only magic can save her heart from Endrick's grip. Nothing you can do will change this."

I couldn't let myself believe that, I wouldn't believe it. But even if Tenger was wrong, I had no idea how to find the right solution.

Tenger tapped my sword again. "My decision about Kestra has been made. Now give me your answer."

Still angry for a number of reasons, I shook my head. "I won't claim the throne."

Tenger sighed, then rang a bell on the table and Gabe opened the door. "Take him back to his cell. He doesn't eat until he's ready to obey me."

I kept my focus on Tenger. "If I am the person you believe me to be, then you have no right to order me to do anything."

Like he'd shoo a fly, Tenger waved me away. "If you will not be that person, then you have no rights at all."

Without another word, I twisted the knife to hide it in my hand and followed Gabe out the door.

· TEN ·

SIMON

I waited until we had rounded a corner of the cave tunnels before I grabbed Gabe's arm and pressed the knife against his side.

He looked down at it, unimpressed, then rolled his eyes at me. "Really, Hatch?"

"Where is she?"

"You won't hurt me."

"I won't kill you, but I will hurt you if I have to." And I meant it.

"How long have we been friends?"

"Long enough that you should know why I have to do this." I released his arm and turned to face him. "Please, Gabe."

"It isn't me you have to get through. There's over a hundred Coracks here in camp and they'll all obey Tenger."

"Not if they don't see us."

"Then have you considered why she's here? Simon, from the moment she became the Infidante, she ceased to have any future with you." His words hit me hard, and he must have sensed that because in a gentler voice, he added, "She can never be yours."

"That's not what this is about."

"That's exactly what this is about." Gabe's tone softened further. "Even if you have other reasons."

More determined than ever, I pressed the blade tighter against Gabe's side. "Where is she?"

He opened his mouth to respond, when an explosion from above ground shook the earth, sending whole chunks of dirt down on our heads. We ducked and eyed each other with a mutual understanding. Lonetree was under attack.

My voice became more earnest. "Gabe?"

This time, he relented, pointing down the tunnel. "Last door on the right."

I tapped his shoulder in appreciation then ran down the corridor while he went the other way. More Coracks were emptying from every part of the cave, calling out orders and distributing weapons from the cache rooms. There were no other explosions, so maybe that had been a mere warning, but it was one we had to take seriously.

Loelle appeared at the far end of the corridors. "Everyone return to your quarters, where it's safe! Let the captain work this out."

But if anyone heard her, they didn't listen. Instead, someone called out, "Dominion?"

From the surface, another person answered, "No. Brown and blue. Halderian colors."

The very fact that they were openly wearing their colors was significant, given that just being identified as Halderian made a person a target of the Dominion. They hadn't launched an organized attack since losing the war, and they shouldn't have any complaint against us. Our alliance wasn't official, but it had been reliable since the Coracks' earliest years. What had changed?

Kestra. They knew she was here.

The Halderians were far from enthusiastic about Kestra as the Infidante, but I'd thought they had accepted her. Certainly Thorne, the current Halderian leader, supported Kestra. Why wasn't he stopping this? And how did the Halderians know she was here anyway?

"Captain!" Breaking the silence, Trina lowered herself down a ladder and burst through the corridor right past me. "They've sent a messenger through. We have ten minutes to respond."

Tenger darted from his office and must have heard her, because he said, "What's the message?"

Trina handed him a paper, which he held up to an embedded clearstone to read, then his face tightened into a grimace. "Unacceptable."

Behind him, Loelle seemed to have guessed at what the paper said. "We must move Kestra to safety, Captain."

"Agreed." He looked around until he found me. "Hatch, you're coming with me to speak to them. Someone find Basil, he's coming too!"

"I'll get Kestra," Loelle offered.

But Tenger shook his head. "You need to prepare for our wounded, though I hope it won't come to that."

"Let me go," I offered. "I'll protect her better than anyone in this camp, you know that!"

Tenger snorted. "You're with me, and you'd better remember your orders. Trina, wherever Kestra is, Basil will be there too. Send him to me, and then you stay with her."

"Yes, sir." Trina eyed me as if she'd just achieved some sort of victory. Maybe she had.

Tenger sent me up the ladder ahead of him, then once we were on top, he cursed and said, "I should have brought your sword . . . Your Highness."

He raised a hand to signal someone to go down for it, but I grabbed his arm and shook my head. "I meant what I said before. I won't claim any title from these people, certainly not now while they're attacking us!"

"They only wanted our attention."

"No, they want Kestra, and that explosion was their way of saying they intend to leave with her, one way or the other. Isn't that what the message said?"

Tenger nodded. "They demand that she return with them to the Hiplands. I've got to offer them a compromise, for all our sakes."

"What compromise?"

By then, Basil poked his head above the surface. "Halderians?" he asked. "I thought they were on our side."

"I thought so too." Tenger pressed his lips together and began walking forward. I followed on his right and Basil was on his left. The thought occurred to me that if we were forced to negotiate, I might offer Basil in exchange for Kestra. Or better yet, exchange him for nothing at all. Either way, she was not leaving with them, not under any circumstances.

We approached a line of blue-and-brown flags carried by a half dozen men in similar colors. In front of them were another ten Halderians with thick leather tunics and fur cloaks, each wearing a brown sash with three thin blue stripes over one shoulder. I immediately noticed Gerald, the man who'd been a spy in Woodcourt when

I was there. Because of his bluish skin, he was easy to spot, but he was watching me too, with a stern expression that struck me as a warning. Beside him was a girl near my age who had latched on to me with her eyes, though I couldn't tell if it was friendly or not. In the center of them all, a man dismounted, obviously in command. It wasn't Thorne, but I had seen this man before, in the audience when Kestra claimed the Olden Blade. He was large, had closely shaved hair, and was the only one with armor over his chest. The Halderians definitely wanted their presence known.

"We expected to see Thorne," Captain Tenger called out. "Isn't he here?"

"Thorne lost a challenge for his leadership," the man facing us responded. "He was too enamored with the idea of Kestra Dallisor as the Infidante. My name is Commander Mindall."

"Kestra might bear the Dallisor name, but you must have been there the night she became the Infidante," Tenger said. "She has no Dallisor blood."

"She has Endrean blood, which is worse," Mindall said. "Endrick's blood."

"She is half Halderian," I said. "Her father—"

"Yes, I was there, I know!" Mindall set his eyes on Basil. "Who are you?"

"He is Sir Basil, heir to the throne of Reddengrad and soon to be husband to Kestra Dallisor," Tenger said.

Speaking with more authority than I'd have expected, Basil added, "Our trade agreements have saved the Halderians, supported you through your darkest years. Continue to attack this camp, and all of the privileges you have enjoyed from us will end."

Mindall laughed. "Some would say that Reddengrad has benefitted more from the labor of Halderians. We don't need your trade agreements. We intend to reclaim the Scarlet Throne of Antora."

"Without a king?" Tenger eyed me.

When Mindall failed to respond, from behind him, Gerald said, "That's a detail yet to be resolved." He was still looking at me, but this time, I pretended not to notice.

"Anything the Halderians want, you need Kestra alive to get it," Tenger said.

"No, Captain, the opposite is true. We need a new Infidante, one we trust to wield the Blade for the good of Halderians."

The only way they'd get a new Infidante was with Kestra's death. If we told them she had no memory of her quest, they'd feel more certain they were doing the right thing. If we told them the Olden Blade was missing again, and that only Basil knew where it was, they'd wring the information from him in an instant.

"And what if we don't give Kestra up?" Tenger asked. "I've grown fond of the girl. If you killed her, I'd feel very put out."

"If you don't hand her over to us within the next five minutes, your entire camp will feel 'put out.'" Mindall waved his arm forward, and a man to his right lifted a square metal box with hammered wires leading toward camp, obviously suggesting that more explosives were already in place.

"Why would we agree to this?" Basil asked. "To send her to her death?"

Mindall didn't so much as blink. "With apologies, as she is your future bride, what about our agreement that anyone with Endrean blood must die? Surely you can see the risk of putting the Olden

Blade into the hands of any Endrean. If she succeeds, we'll replace one tyrant with another."

"Perhaps you're right." Tenger looked at me with a slight shift in his eyes, a silent order I well understood. Aloud, he said, "Simon, go get Kestra."

"Sir! They intend to—"

"They intend to destroy this camp. The Coracks and Halderians are allies, and until they have a legitimate king to say otherwise, we will do as they ask." I started to protest again, but Tenger added, "Basil, go with him. Make sure he does exactly as I ordered."

"My daughter, Harlyn, will come as well," Mindall said, and the girl who had been watching me earlier slid from her horse. She was tall and lean with wide brows, curly black hair cut short, and she seemed comfortable with the blade at her side.

I twisted my face into a grimace, but nodded curtly at her and Basil to follow me. I wasn't particularly comforted by being in either one's company.

As we walked, my mind raced for what to do. Under no circumstances would I hand Kestra over to the Halderians, yet Harlyn was clearly here to ensure otherwise. Unless she struck first, it wasn't in me to harm this girl, and if we attempted to take her hostage, we risked the explosives collapsing the Lonetree caves.

Basil looked over at me, his mouth pressed tight and his eyes full of questions I couldn't answer. But he was my best solution, *if* he had enough brains to decode the conversation we were about to have.

"Basil will take you to Kestra," I said, "although she's still in our prison cells at the far end of the camp. I'll get a horse ready for her to ride out with you."

Harlyn chuckled. "What I'm hearing is that Basil will distract me for a few minutes, possibly even try to lock me in the cells, while you help Kestra escape."

I cursed under my breath while Basil made his best attempt to negotiate. "If your people do anything to harm Kestra, you will incur the wrath of Reddengrad—"

"The wrath of Reddengrad—what is that?" She poked my arm with her elbow as if we were sharing a joke. "We use pole weapons like yours to practice for our real weapons." Before either of us could argue that, she locked one arm in mine and the other in Basil's and said, "Listen carefully, because you're both laughably transparent. The Halderians are split over what to do about the Infidante. Half want to give her a chance. Half want her dead. My father is with that second half . . . but I am not, so here's what you're going to do. When we're out of sight, I'll give Simon my sword to temporarily hold me hostage while Basil gets his betrothed as far from this camp as possible. Then release me and I'll go crying back to my father about how she disappeared on her own when she saw us coming. I'll claim to have fought and injured Basil here at camp . . . despite his fearsome pole weapon. Simon, you'll return with me and give the same story. Agreed?"

I stared at her a moment, taken aback by her candor. But when she opened her mouth to speak again, I quickly said, "Agreed, except Basil and I are switching positions," and felt surprised that Basil didn't object.

Instead, he asked, "How do we know we can trust you?"

"Well, you don't, obviously." Harlyn sighed, withdrew her sword and handed it over to him, then turned to me with an oddly timed smile. "Games of suspicion are tiresome. Don't you agree?"

While Basil waited with Harlyn, I descended back into the tunnels. My first stop was in Tenger's office, where I retrieved my sword. From there, I went to the room where Trina was supposed to be guarding Kestra.

I opened the door. "Kes—"

But neither she nor Trina was there. Back in the corridor, I grabbed Gabe's arm as he rushed past me. "Where's Kestra?"

Gabe pointed to the right. "Trina was taking her to the launch room."

The launch room was adjacent to our underground stables and was the place from which we rode to the surface. Trina had no reason to be there with Kestra. Then realization crashed into me. How stupid I'd been!

"Trina wants to be the Infidante," I told Gabe, though it was more than that. Trina believed she deserved to be the Infidante and that Kestra had stolen her place. Maybe Trina thought she still could fill that role if there was no more Kestra. And if that was true, then Trina could be the reason the Halderians knew to come here. And now she would deliver Kestra to them. What if this had been her plan all along?

"I'll find Kestra," I said, already hurrying toward the launch room, "but you must make sure the Halderians are stopped here!"

· ELEVEN ·

KESTRA

My conversation with Basil hadn't gone as well as I'd hoped, and the deflated expression on his face was punctuated by the sudden explosion above ground. Someone out in the corridors shouted that it was the Halderians. My heart began to race with a fear I'd never known before. Nothing in my past could prepare me for something like this.

Nothing in the past I remembered. Their physician, Loelle, seemed to think something was wrong with my memories. Yes, perhaps I was missing a few moments here and there, but surely nothing that would tell me what to do now.

Basil wiped at his eyes, the last time he would likely think about me. "The Halderians are supposed to be allies with the Coracks. Why would they attack?"

"It's me." My jaw clenched. "It's because I'm a Dallisor."

Basil's shoulders fell. "No, Kestra, you're—"

The door burst open and Trina rushed through it. "Basil, you're wanted at the surface. Tenger needs your help now."

Basil nodded, reached for my hand, and gave it a kiss, saying, "I'll make things right between us, I promise." Then he hurried from the room without another word.

Trina's eyes were wide with alarm. "They're here for you."

Again. They were here for me *again*. As soon as Trina spoke, that was the word that had followed in my mind. I couldn't explain why.

Trina tilted her head. "Do you remember it, Kestra?"

I drew back, realizing I'd covered my mouth with my hand. "Remember what?"

Now she simply pointed to a satchel hanging from a hook embedded in the cave wall. "Pack a bag. It's going to be a cold day."

"What should I take?"

"I already packed most of what we'll need, but take this." Trina tossed me a winter cloak that I quickly buttoned around my neck, then grabbed a blanket off a nearby bunk, a fire starter, and a cup, which she tossed to me to fill the satchel. She looked around the room but there wasn't much else here. "This will have to do. Let's go."

I followed her out of the room and was half-trampled by Corack fighters who were scrambling in every direction while Trina merely breezed around them. "How do you do it?" I asked. "I can't imagine being someone who's always thinking of fighting."

"Can't you?" She smiled back at me as if we were sharing a joke. I only frowned in response. I'd meant what I'd said.

By then, we'd reached the underground stables, where a horse was already laden with riding bags. She dumped the items she had collected into one bag, then attached my rolled blanket to the saddle.

On the outside of one saddlebag was a binding cord, an invention of Lord Endrick's. One end of the cord could be snapped onto the wrist of a prisoner and would not release without its master's order. I didn't know why she had one and didn't like that she was bringing it along.

"I'll wait here." I stepped back, overwhelmed with alarm. "Tenger wanted me to stay in camp."

"Stay in camp and the Halderians will find you. Can you get into a saddle on your own?"

"I've never tried."

She groaned and steadied the horse for me to climb up. She began to follow, when Simon yelled, "Stop!"

He had his sword again, and it was outstretched toward Trina. The expression on his face was deadly serious, but so was hers.

She raised her hands. "I'm moving her to safety."

"Back away."

Trina snorted. "I'll come with you. You need my help."

"No, I don't." Simon advanced, separating us with a gesture of his sword. "Don't try to follow us."

"Simon, this isn't a good idea. It'll mean trouble for you."

His chuckle was harsh. "No doubt, but only if Tenger finds us. And he won't."

I'd begun to slide off the horse, but when he saw me move, he pushed Trina aside, then nearly leapt into the saddle behind me, shaking the reins to race us up the ramp out of the underground camp.

I squirmed within his arms. "Where are you taking me?"

If he heard me, his only response was to pull me in closer. I felt the tension in his muscles, saw the stiff grip of his hands. He was furious, or frightened. I was both.

We rode fast until the camp was long out of sight, and still Simon pushed us forward, ignoring my questions, my threats, and anything else I could think of to slow him down. The first few minutes of escape from the camp lengthened into what might have put us an hour away from the others. We were deeper into the Drybelt—the dusty landscape confirmed that. There wouldn't be many people out this way, and if they were here, they probably weren't Loyalists. I'd have to free myself. Somehow.

Finally, he brought us to a walking speed. I thrust an elbow behind me. "Do you have to sit so close?"

"Yes."

I rolled my eyes, unamused. "Please," I said, pointing up ahead at a thin stream. "I need a rest, and a drink."

This was true enough. In this arid part of the land, it might be some time before we encountered another water supply.

After a few seconds in which I'd thought he was ignoring me, Simon slowed his horse to a stop. He dismounted first, then helped me off. "Stay where I can see you," he said, then led the horse farther downstream for a drink.

I knelt beside the stream and looked around until I found a piece of rock, maybe sharp enough to be a weapon. He wouldn't believe that I could use it, and perhaps he'd be right. We'd find out together.

With the rock clasped in my hand, I took a quick survey of my surroundings. The stream flowed from a pass between two sparse hills ahead of me. I didn't see anywhere to hide, but if I got a good start, I might be able to outrun him.

I glanced back to see Simon looking the horse over, inspecting its legs and hooves. This was my chance. I took a deep breath, then set off at a full run. However, I wasn't a stone's throw away before Simon grabbed my waist and yanked me down with him onto the sandy hillside.

I fought against his grip, and even got in a decent cut on his arm before he wrenched the rock out of my hand. Then he knelt over me and pulled the binding cord from where it had been hung across his shoulders. He snapped one end against his wrist, which instantly curled and sealed in a full circle.

"Don't you dare!" I cried.

But he lifted my arm and snapped the other end against my wrist, where it did the very same thing. Only then did he release me and get back to his feet.

I pulled at the cord, and when it failed to release, I tried to roll my wrist through the opening, but it wouldn't budge. He gave the cord a tug of his own, though I noticed on his end, it widened when he pulled at it. The cord had recognized Simon as its master.

"Release me," I said as firmly as possible. "You have no right—"

"No, but I have every responsibility." The sharpness of his tone softened, though the urgency remained. "I'm your protector, Kestra, and in my judgment, the best protection is to get you away from the Coracks, away from the Halderians, and safe from Lord Endrick."

"I can protect myself."

"With a rock?" Simon withdrew his knife from its sheath and offered it to me. "Use this instead . . . if you can."

Sensing a trick, I was slow to reach for it, and as I did, my eyes caught on the faint scar on my palm, a square cross. I clenched my hand into a fist and pulled my arm back.

With his eyes on my fist, Simon replaced the knife. He walked forward, taking my hand in his and opening it. Brushing his thumb over the scar, he said, "I can tell you about this."

I already knew. "As a girl, I once tried practicing with my father's dagger, but I misused it and cut my hand."

Simon shook his head. "That never happened, Kes. It's a false memory."

"It did happen! It frightened me so much, I've never picked up a weapon since."

"Kes—"

"I remember it, Simon! Enough with your lies!"

He stared at me, looking genuinely disappointed. It was probably nothing to the expression he'd wear after I escaped. Because more than ever before, that had to be my goal. First opportunity I had, I was leaving.

· TWELVE ·

SIMON

We rode for hours, with only the occasional tug of her arm against mine and my repeated pleas for her to talk to me, to help me understand what she did and didn't remember, but she ignored every request as if I weren't even there. It was a cold day, with slowly gathering storm clouds, a perfect parallel for Kestra's mood. Rain was coming, and if that was another sign for Kestra and me, then I dreaded knowing what it was. I hoped at least that we'd get to a decent shelter before the storm came.

Our route that late afternoon was largely determined by occasional gashes in the earth known as the slots, steep-walled crevices that created a maze through the land. If we were being followed, our pursuers would have to stay on our same route, unless they traveled through the base of the slots.

And I knew in my heart that they were somewhere behind us. If we were caught this time, Tenger would probably kill me outright. This violation of my oath would be considered inexcusable. There was no going back for either of us.

After yet another failed request to get Kestra to talk to me, I decided on a new tactic: a story of my own.

"I once protected a girl very much like you. Equally stubborn, but I eventually learned that the more she cared about something, the more stubborn she became. I think you might be similar."

"I'm not," she insisted, unwittingly proving how stubborn she was.

"Obviously." I chuckled at that and briefly felt her sharp glare, but when our eyes met, she blinked a few times, then looked forward again.

"She was curious and had a fierce intensity about her. She felt everything with such passion that it was impossible to be around her and not get caught up in it too." Slowly, I exhaled, like breathing was an afterthought. "It was impossible to be around her and not feel passionate about her."

I stopped there, realizing that I wasn't only saying those words for her, I was feeling them more intensely than I wished. Kestra was right in front of me, so close that she was in every direction I looked, part of every breath I drew in. But if I couldn't find a way to undo Endrick's magic, I would lose her for good.

After a moment, Kestra asked, "What happened to this girl?"

A brief pause. I wanted to be careful here. "She fell into Lord Endrick's clutches. He took her from me."

She turned enough that I saw a hint of moisture in her eyes, but her voice was steady when she said, "If she was part of the rebellion, then he had to stop her, to protect the Dominion."

Likely without realizing it, she had relaxed in the saddle to lean against me, turning my struggles in having her so close to sheer torture. I said, "It was his second attack on her. The first time, he sent so much pain through her body that she barely survived it, leaving behind a tracking ball at the base of her neck. We got it out, but it left a scar that would still be fresh."

"You mean, it'd be fresh if Lord Endrick hadn't killed her in the second attack."

My eyes settled on her. "I never said he killed her. Only that he took her."

Kestra sat up straight again. "Simon, stop—"

"Took her memories and made her believe in a history that isn't true."

"I'm not—"

"She has servants to bathe her and do her hair. It's possible that in the week since she's been awake, she's never felt the back of her own neck."

"I don't have a scar there."

I took her hand. She tried to pull it free, but I kept hold of it and lifted it to her neck, leaving my hand in place until she stopped fighting and felt the scar. Her breaths came in short, harsh bursts, a single tear falling to her cheek.

"What caused that?"

"You were shaking for almost an hour afterward, and he could have done worse. Trina dug the tracker out of your neck, but it left a deep scar that we sealed with wax."

She turned around enough to face me directly, and this time her eyes betrayed a flicker of recognition. If I had reached some part of the real her, then I had to make this moment matter.

"Lord Endrick is an enemy to you, Kes."

I knew immediately that I'd gone too far and wished for a way to take back my words. She blinked hard, and then she was gone again, or trying to make me think so. "He is your enemy. He is my king and I have to serve him." She returned for one long look. "No, I *want* to serve him."

"With or without your memories, tell me how you can kneel to such an evil man?"

"Please stop." The intensity of her tone forced my obedience, yet I saw the questions in her eyes, her frustration with not even knowing what to ask to get the answers she needed. And I saw fear.

A fear deep enough to pierce my heart. I didn't think she was afraid of me, though that was possible. Rather, I thought of how confused her world must be right now. If she did remember anything, who would she trust with that secret? Not me, for reasons I completely understood. Maybe we needed a rest.

After another few minutes, we came to a ridge that was tall enough to hide our horse, should anyone happen by on the trail behind us. Safely behind it, we dismounted, then while I began digging through the various bags attached to the saddle, she sat down, fingering the necklace from Lord Endrick. I wondered again what it really was.

"Are you hungry?" I asked, hoping to distract her. "Did you pack any food in here?"

"Trina packed the bags, and no, I'm not hungry."

"Good, because we'll need to stretch our supplies." I pulled out a pad of pressed papers, which was flipped open to the top page. Something in its angle against the sunlight caught my eye.

"Why does Trina dislike me?"

"The question isn't why, it's how much." I held the blank page up to the sun, getting the angle just right. I angled it again, then pinched the bridge of my nose, sighing loudly as I did. "Are you sure that Trina packed these bags?"

"That's what she told me."

"Then this must be her notepad. I can read the impression of the last note she wrote."

Kestra leaned forward. "What does it say?"

I wished I didn't have to answer the way I did. "It was addressed to Commander Mindall, of the Halderians. Instructions for how to find you."

For a moment, she couldn't speak. And when she did, she mumbled, "Why?"

I waited until Kestra looked at me again, then said, "That must have been her plan this morning. While the Halderians distracted us, Trina intended to ride you out of Lonetree Camp and turn you over to them herself." I shook my head in disbelief. "I never thought she'd be capable of that."

The clopping sound of approaching horses caught my attention and then hers. I took the horse's reins with one hand, then withdrew my knife before grabbing Kestra with the other, pulling us against the ridge.

"I thought you wouldn't hurt me."

"If we're discovered, I'll hurt them, and I really don't want to." It wasn't likely to be travelers or traders this deep into the Drybelt. Chances were much higher that it was Coracks tracking us, and possibly friends of mine. Silently, I prayed it wasn't that.

We waited in that position for less than a minute before the horses started past us on the road. I immediately recognized Wynnow's voice in conversation.

". . . this wasn't the only way they could have come," she was saying. "Let's split up. It does little good for the three of us to be in a single place."

"I know where Simon will go, and this is their route." Trina was the second person. "He'd better hope we don't find him. Tenger is furious."

"Simon knows the risks," Gabe said, the third member of their party. "But all he cares about is her."

Kestra met my eyes and I held her gaze. But she immediately lowered her eyes when Trina said, "I knew his loyalties were already shifting on the first night of our mission. I should've forced him out then. This is my fault."

Their conversation continued, but by then they were out of range. Kestra was clearly upset about something they had said, but I didn't know why.

In a commanding voice, she asked, "Do you know what that conversation was about?"

"Yes."

"When Trina said your loyalties shifted, what does that mean?"

"You know what it means."

She shook her head. "You think there's some connection between us, and that this connection gives you the right to keep me here. But there's nothing between us, Simon. Accident or not, I'd never forget—"

"That was no accident, Kestra." My temper felt brittle and I was out of patience. "You either jumped from that window or were pushed from it because you are now enemy number one to the Dominion. And you haven't just forgotten certain details from your life. They were taken from you by Lord Endrick and that evil man you call Father! He isn't—"

She cut me off with a slap to my face. "Never speak about my father that way! He loves me, he'd never let such a thing—"

"He doesn't love you. If he's pretended to care for you, then it's only because those are his orders from Lord Endrick."

She shook her head again, so furious that she spat out each word. "Lord Endrick saved my life! And I won't hear this treasonous talk from you any longer! I demand you release me at once!"

"I can't do that."

"If you're my protector, then you're my servant. You must obey me."

"Right now, I'm protecting you from yourself."

She faced forward again, but not before tossing back a glare that made me nervous. She wasn't simply angry anymore. She was calculating.

Kestra was beginning to plan. If any of the old Kestra was still active inside her, I knew I should be worried.

· THIRTEEN ·

KESTRA

I spent most of the remaining afternoon trying to sort out all that Simon had said to me. There had been a cruelty to his words, but was that because he was cruel enough to lie to me? Or because the truth itself was cruel?

He had remained quiet too, and I wondered what he was thinking. Creating more lies, no doubt. He must be lying, because Endrick had no reason to deceive me. Nothing else made sense.

Simon finally pointed ahead. "A trail leads to the bottom of that slot. If we take it, we could reach Rutherhouse late tonight."

"Rutherhouse?"

"It's a little inn run by a woman I know and trust."

I pointed at the skies, with clouds notably darker than they'd been earlier. "What if it rains?"

He looked up, obviously disappointed. "You're right. We'll camp here tonight."

I dreaded the idea of sleeping outside in this treacherous area during what would likely be a major storm. Even more, I dreaded traveling through it.

Just off the trail was a mound barely large enough to qualify as a hill. Facing the slots was a narrow cave with a small rock overhang.

I pointed it out to Simon, but he only shook his head, saying, "It's too visible."

"The cave will shelter us if it rains, and the hill will keep out any night winds." I glanced up at the darkening skies. "No one will be out looking for us once the storm begins."

Simon clicked his tongue as if he disagreed, but turned us off the trail anyway. While I cleared out loose debris inside the cave, Simon began unpacking the blankets from the saddle, tossing in one for each of us.

"I packed a fire starter," I pointed out.

"We won't have a fire." He pulled out a water skin and took a sip, then returned it to the satchels. "I haven't brought you all this way just to send a signal of our whereabouts up into the sky. Are you cold?"

"If I am, protector of mine, can you protect me from it?"

Simon smirked back at me. "I can, though I doubt you want me that close."

I didn't. While Simon saw to the horse, I sat on a blanket, curling my legs beneath me and reminding myself to breathe. It was going to be a long night.

Near my foot was a flowering plant that I recognized from the caves where I had slept with the Coracks on the night they took me from Woodcourt. Gabe had called it terrador and warned that it was poisonous.

Immediately a plan began to form in my mind. Three leaves consumed directly were lethal, but if I diluted only two of them in Simon's water skin, he'd get sick enough that I could easily make an escape.

I didn't know where I'd go afterward or how I'd get there. But at last, I had a plan, and any guilt for what I was about to do was muted when I remembered that it was his fault I was here in the first place.

I picked the leaves and stuffed them into my boot just as Simon sat down across from me. His eyes fixed on mine, solemn and intense, and I felt a tightening in my belly, heat rushing through me. I could no longer deny that I was drawn to him in ways I couldn't explain and certainly couldn't understand, but the pull was as real to me as the binding cord on my wrist. It frightened me, and yet I was still staring back at him.

After a moment, he said, "I owe you an apology for what I said earlier. You didn't deserve that."

I said nothing and became the first to look away.

He added, "If it feels like a lot of different groups have been fighting over you, then there's a reason for it."

"What does it matter?" I let out a sarcastic, humorless laugh. "Whatever their reasons, they are mistaken. There is nothing special about me, nothing noteworthy. There is nothing to me at all, and I don't know how to make you see that."

When I looked up, his gaze back at me had softened. "Do you really believe that of yourself?"

I wasn't about to surrender to the tender expression in his eyes or the gentleness in his voice. Arching my neck, I said, "Whatever I believe, you or someone else will be there to tell me I'm wrong."

"You *are* wrong, Kes. If you describe yourself in such small terms, then you are wrong."

I needed to escape this conversation. Escape him. Something about his presence kept my pulse uneven, and I couldn't allow it to continue. But as soon as I began walking, he stood and pulled on the binding cord, stopping me.

"I'm trying to help you, but I need your help." Simon closed the distance between us. "Can you trust me, maybe a little? I am your friend, Kes."

I laughed again, keeping my defenses up. "A Corack and a Dallisor, friends? If you wanted to lie, you could have done better than that."

"We *were* friends. Even something more."

"I love Basil." Why had I said that? I didn't love Basil, and he'd never made my heart race the way it now was.

Simon didn't even blink at my words. "You don't love him. You were only following orders to marry him."

He stepped closer to me, and I countered with a step back. "If we were friends, I would remember it. I'd remember how I feel . . . when you're close."

He took another step toward me, and this time I refused to step back, refused to acknowledge that strange emotions were flaring up within me, filling my chest until it seemed I couldn't breathe. I fought them, tried to push them down or to ignore them, but the harder I tried, the stronger they became.

As he drew even closer, he asked softly, "How do I make you feel?"

"Nauseous."

That wasn't true. There was a fierceness in his eyes that kept me as captive in his gaze as I was with this binding cord. When his fingers brushed against mine, a shiver raced up my spine, though I couldn't explain why. I only knew that when his glance shifted down to my lips, my heart stopped altogether.

Then his hand went to my cheek, cupping it in his palm. He was so close to me, his face nearly against mine. His body even closer. I couldn't catch my breath.

That single thought triggered something in me, something deeper than emotion or reason. It was familiarity, a memory just beyond my reach.

It set my heart racing in an entirely different way than it ever had before. What was happening to me?

"We've been here before, Kes, in a different place, but in this very position. Do you remember it?"

I barely heard him. Panic was exploding within me. I wanted to hide or fight, or to escape from some terrible danger I couldn't see, but which I certainly felt. Invisible walls seemed to press in around me, blocking out my air. Why couldn't I breathe?

I pushed Simon back, drawing a harsh breath as I did. Struggling for my next breath.

Simon looked at me, eyes widened with concern. "It's all right, Kes. Everything is fine."

How could he say that? Nothing was fine! Why had he come so close? Why had he looked at me that way, made me feel that way? And why had it stirred up such feelings of panic?

With a sympathetic sigh, Simon said, "You felt closed in, trapped."

How could he have known that?

As my breathing calmed, I touched my face, almost where his hand had been. This moment had happened before. Deep inside, I knew that it had. But when?

"You're remembering something."

"I'm not. You just frightened me. If I feel anything when I'm around you, it's a passionate, burning need to delouse myself. Never come that close to me again."

Simon flinched at my words and gave me a long time to recover. Eventually, he pulled an apple from one of the satchels. "Can I come close enough to give you this, or shall I roll it over there?"

"You can give me water." I had a plan and I had to stick to it, free of guilt, free of the emotions he stirred up in me. I just needed to escape and then everything would be fine again.

He smiled and handed me his water skin. I drank a few sips, then said, "Is there anything to eat other than apples?"

I was far too nervous to eat, but I needed him distracted while I dropped one terrador leaf into the water skin, then a second one. By the time he turned again with some bread for me, I had tucked the last leaf back inside my boot in case I needed it later.

While I nibbled on the bread, I offered the water skin to Simon. "You must be thirsty too."

He stared at it a moment, then looked at me. "Are you feeling better?"

"I will feel better soon . . . I hope." I followed that with a smile, so forced and false that I was sure he'd suspect the truth.

Instead, he smiled back and reached for the water, taking a long drink before recapping it and returning it to the pile.

Simon was about to have a terrible night, no doubt. I'd ask him to release the binding cord, promising to find some herbs to help him feel better. I'd get them, and by morning he'd be on his way to full recovery, and I'd be gone.

Now all I had to do was wait.

When Simon finally sat on his blanket, he asked me, "What if I'm right? Do you deny that Lord Endrick is powerful enough that he could have affected your memories?"

I shrugged. "I don't deny his power, only his willingness to cause me harm. I've never been disloyal to him, not a day in my life."

"What if you were?"

I groaned. "He saved my life, Simon. I remember very clearly waking up in Lord Endrick's palace, feeling groggy and weak. He personally attended to me, asking me question after question to determine how much damage the fall caused."

"Asking you questions to determine which memories to take and how to replace them with pure fiction. Who knows how much you told him while you were under his influence?"

My expression darkened. "How much I told him about what?"

He went quiet, almost as if he were biting his tongue to keep himself from saying anything more. That was good. He needed to save his strength.

By the time the first drops of rain started to fall, he'd begun to clutch at his side and his voice seemed weaker as he said, "You'll get wet if you try to sleep out there. Come back by me, beneath this ledge."

"I will, after you release the binding cord."

"I can't do that."

"You claim we were friends. Then treat me as a friend!"

He shook his head. "As you are now, Kes, we are not friends. I am your protector and nothing more."

"No," I countered. "You are a kidnapper, nothing more."

He started to argue, then drew in a sharp breath and lay back on his blanket. "As you wish."

I wrapped my blanket over my head to keep out the rain, but my eyes remained open, as I listened to his shallow breaths and occasional grunts of pain. The poison was working.

"Does your mouth taste like metal?" he asked. "I think maybe we—"

"Good night, Simon." Silently, I added the words I didn't dare say aloud: *I'm so very sorry, but it had to be done.*

· FOURTEEN ·

SIMON

Sometime over the next few hours, the rain worsened and was accompanied by fierce lightning and thunder. I sat up and saw her crouched in a tight ball, obviously afraid.

I motioned her over to me, beneath the ledge, but she shook her head. Why did she have to make this a fight, especially on a night when I was becoming increasingly sick? The ache in my bones had worsened and spread through my limbs, and I was sure I had a fever. I started to crawl out from my blanket, but she held up a hand to stop me, then scooted over beside me. With the next flash of lightning, I realized she was watching me, but I didn't want her to know I was sick. She'd use that as an opportunity to try escaping.

I faked a smile, then wrapped my dry blanket around her shoulders and pulled her close to offer her some warmth. Her hand brushed against my chest, then my thigh, as if she wasn't sure where to rest it, so I clasped her hand in mine and was surprised she didn't pull away. She was shivering, I realized, or maybe I was. With her head against my shoulder, she said, "You're not well. Let me go find some herbs to help you."

I'd have to release the binding cord to do that, and within an hour, she'd be as far from this camp as she could go. In this storm, and with a long list of enemies hunting for her, she might not see morning.

Unless this fever broke, I might not see it either.

"Help!"

I sat up straighter, wondering if I'd just heard a voice. Kestra had sat up too and she looked at me with concern.

Then I heard, "Simon!" It was Trina's voice, but it wasn't the voice that had called out first.

I heard it again, louder. "Help!" This was Gabe.

From the direction it had come, I knew what the problem was. They must have spotted our camp and were trying to cross the slot from the other side. They hadn't anticipated how much rain there would be, and all of it was pouring into the slot. It was flooding, and now Gabe was trapped.

I held out a hand to Kestra. "I need your help to save him."

I'd expected a fight, but she immediately stood and walked with me. "What can I do?"

I wasn't sure, until another call for help gave me a sense of direction, and a flash of lightning showed me the area. I pointed across the ravine to where Trina was jumping up and down to get my attention. When I motioned back to her, she gestured down into the slot, as I had feared. She shouted something over at me, but her words were lost against a crack of thunder.

I peered down to see Gabe halfway up the slot wall, but he was holding on to an exposed tree root as a torrent of water rushed over him. It wasn't too much different from when I had seen Kestra in the river, half-drowned.

Yesterday, I'd felt strong enough to pull Kestra out. I couldn't do that now for Gabe. My vision was blurring and I was burning up with fever, despite this cold night's rain.

I pointed to a thick bush near the edge of the ravine and said to Kestra, "Get behind that and hold on. I need you as a brace."

"A brace for what?"

I detached the binding cord from my wrist and began coiling it. "I'll try to manage his weight, but if I can't, don't let go of that bush or you'll go over the edge."

Her brows furrowed. "Simon, I have to tell you—"

"I'll be all right."

"You won't. I—"

"Get to your position and hold on. Hurry!" As soon as she signaled that she was ready, I called to Gabe to grab the rope, then tossed it to him. My first throw missed, but I gathered the rope again and he caught it the second time.

"Attach it to your wrist!" I shouted.

He nodded and smacked it against his wrist. I immediately began pulling, though once he let go of the tree root, he was thrown directly into the current. With my illness, I wasn't able to pull as hard as I wanted. Across the ravine, Trina was shouting again but I couldn't pay attention to her. All I could think about was giving another tug upward.

Then I felt the load lighten. At first, I thought Gabe had somehow fallen off, but I turned and saw Kestra at my side, helping to pull the rope. She nodded over at me, and together we began to make progress. My head swam with dizziness, and Trina's shouts blurred along with everything else. This was worse than mere illness. I was dying.

I was dying.

It was that water Kestra had given me earlier tonight. I'd thought then that it had a funny taste, but skins sometimes picked up strange odors. I'd never tasted anything like this before though.

Kestra had poisoned me.

I looked over at her and she frowned back. She knew what was happening to me, and she wasn't stopping it.

Gabe's head poked over the top of the ravine. "We knew where you were camped," he said as he rolled his body over the edge. "We planned to sneak up on you in the night and get everything sorted. I guess this serves us right for trying to trick you."

I started to answer him, but I didn't have the chance before my vision darkened entirely and my body crumpled to the ground.

· FIFTEEN ·

KESTRA

From across the ridge, Trina screamed when Simon collapsed, the echo filling my ears, chilling my soul. Gabe clambered over to Simon, even as he continued choking on the water he had swallowed down in the ravine.

"What happened to him?" Gabe asked.

I knew how bad this looked, how awful it sounded, but Simon was far worse than I'd expected. I needed to tell Gabe the truth. "I only gave him two leaves, and I diluted it in water. You said two would make a person sick."

Gabe's sudden glare caused me to step back in fear. "Two leaves . . . of what?" He grabbed my arm and yanked me to the ground beside Simon. "Are you talking about those terrador plants I saw in the cave? Those were young plants. The ones out here could've been growing for years!"

I still had the last leaf in my boot and I pulled it out to show him. He held it up against a flash of lightning, his expression turning murderous. "Water intensifies the poison, Kestra. What have you done?"

"I didn't mean to . . . I never wanted—"

"Simon would never hurt you, but I will. I don't care who you are or what you're supposed to do for Antora. If he doesn't walk away from this, neither will you."

Suddenly terrified, I asked, "What can I do?"

Gabe began scouring the area. "Look for a purple flower with a blue center. They call it arquin and it grows near large rocks. Find it!"

I did as he said, though I couldn't see much between flashes of lightning. While I looked, I asked, "How do you know this flower will heal him?"

"It won't, but it will slow the effects, *if* we're not too late." He paused to glare at me. "Lord Endrick would be proud of you tonight. What a fine Dallisor you've turned out to be."

I should have felt pleased by his words, but I wasn't. I didn't want to be a Dallisor like *this*. If he died, would I be responsible?

Of course I would, and I felt terrible. I searched harder for the arquin, hoping to fix what I'd done.

"I found some!" Gabe said with the next flash of lightning. I noticed at the same time that Trina was no longer beside the ravine. And where was Wynnow? I'd nearly forgotten that she was with them earlier. When I asked Gabe about it, he simply said, "We split up."

Gabe picked a handful of leaves and then I held Simon's mouth open while he stuffed them inside.

In my whole life, I'd never felt so helpless, and my heart ached for it. "I'm sorry," I mumbled.

"Yeah, an apology should fix this mess." Gabe rolled his eyes. "Help me carry him back to camp. We saw your shelter."

I lifted Simon's legs while Gabe carried his arms, the walk feeling much farther now than I'd remembered. Once in camp, we laid him on the blanket and pushed him in as deep beneath the ledge as possible for protection from the rain.

"He's still not responding." Gabe leaned over him, checking for a pulse. "How could you do this?"

"I had to do something!" I pointed to the binding cord in a heap on the ground. "He captured me."

"He saved you from the Halderians! He's trying to protect you. The fact is, there are a lot of people out there who want to kill you, and not many people who care if you survive. Simon is fighting for you harder than anyone, and the only way you'll live is if you start to listen to what he's telling you."

I lowered my eyes. "If I knew how to do anything more for him, I would."

Gabe pulled Simon's satchel off his shoulder and tossed it to me. "Look in there. He might have some medicines from Loelle."

I shuffled through the contents, feeling around blindly between the occasional flashes of lightning. There was a roll of rags that could act as bandages, another knife, a binding of paper with a lead pencil, and at the bottom was a thick and heavy ring.

"No medicines," I said to Gabe, who cursed, making sure I heard my name attached to it.

I sat in the open rain, clutching the satchel to my chest as if it could offer me any comfort. Gabe continued to tend to Simon, though nothing he was doing now would matter. Either Simon would live, or he wouldn't, and I couldn't think of the blame I bore for that without shuddering in horror.

Gabe barely glanced at me to say, "Leave."

"Please, I'd rather—"

"I don't know where Wynnow is, but Trina is on the other side of that slot with our horses. She'll be here by morning. Simon didn't trust her with you, and if he's right, then you'd better leave while you can. I'll tell her you escaped."

"I can still help!"

"You never help, Kestra, you only make things worse. If you're still here in the morning, I won't protect you from Trina, understand? Now get out of this camp."

"I don't know where to go."

"And I don't care. Just leave."

Woodenly, I nodded and stood, feeling as if I were in a trance. Wishing this was simply another nightmare that would end if I only opened my eyes. I left with no particular direction in mind, as long as it was away from the slots. I was soaked through and shivering with cold, but I was barely aware of that.

Mostly my heart hurt. It shouldn't have. I'd done what was necessary to escape, and I had succeeded. I should have been celebrating now, not only because I'd proven that I was stronger than anyone believed, but also because I had rid the world of another Corack.

As a Dallisor, that's how I should have felt. But all I really wanted was to know if Simon had somehow survived what I'd done, and if he understood why I'd done it.

I didn't understand, not really. Not anymore. I was thoroughly disgusted with myself.

Eventually, the lightning passed and the rain calmed. By morning, I'd have to find a secure place to hide if Trina came searching for me, which she surely would. Until then, I needed to rest. I found a little juniper tree and leaned against it, indifferent to the thick drops of water that rolled off the needles. I closed my eyes, fighting back tears of exhaustion and fear and a consuming guilt. And fell asleep sobbing.

I dreamed that night of Lord Endrick. In the dream, I was a child again, maybe six or seven years old, and I'd followed a ladybird beetle through Woodcourt's gardens until I accidentally crawled right onto Lord Endrick's boot, hitting his leg. I wanted to run away, but crouched there instead, frozen with fear.

In the dream, he knelt beside me and looked at the ladybird. "Why are you letting this insect lead you where it wants to go? Command it to follow you instead."

That struck me as funny, though when I laughed, his expression tightened with irritation, frightening me. Summoning my courage to state the obvious to a king, I said, "An insect won't follow my commands."

"Then I want you to crush it."

"No!"

"Look at me, my dear child." I did, though it took all the courage in my young heart to do it. "We are the Dominion, and I am its king. All others are insects to us. They must obey or be crushed." His voice was cold, cruel, dismissive of life. Small as I was, I knew my existence mattered as little to him as this beetle's.

He continued, "When I was young, my people were outcasts, mistrusted and feared by all other Antorans. We kept to the mountains and caves, despite our unquestionable superiority. I begged my superiors to let me leave, especially since I hadn't found my powers and was considered a defect, but they never allowed it. Then, one day, Halderian soldiers invaded our territories and tried to banish us from Antora. I fought back, the only Endrean to resist expulsion, and in doing so, discovered my powers. The Halderians are the Banished now, and I am in control." His eyes narrowed. "You are part of the Dominion, child. Learn to control your world. Crush that insect."

I shook my head, but something larger than me, something unseen, forced my hand to cover the ladybird, ready to smash it flat. Endrick's magic.

"Once you've tasted control, nothing less will satisfy you," he said. "Now do as I've commanded."

Gritting my teeth, I folded my fingers around the ladybird. He smiled, anticipating my obedience, but instead, I picked it up and flung it deeper within the gardens where I hoped it would land safely away from him.

Lord Endrick stretched out his arm and a fire immediately burst across the entire garden. I reared back from the flames, but he grabbed my wrist. "How dare you?" he snarled.

"Lady Kestra!" A young servant boy of Woodcourt darted out from behind the garden wall. "Your mother is calling for you. She begs you to come right away."

Lord Endrick glared down at me, then released my wrist, leaving it red and sore. "Go to your mother, child. We will continue this lesson another day. I will remember you . . ."

With that, I'd startled myself awake, dripping with sweat as if I'd actually been next to that fire and not out here on a cold night. My heart pounded, and for several awful minutes I was sure I was about to be sick. Because deep inside, I knew that hadn't just been a dream. It had happened.

I didn't close my eyes again that night. I didn't dare.

· SIXTEEN ·

KESTRA

The dark morning gradually turned to dawn, and despite my every wish to remain curled up beneath this tree, I knew I'd have to face the day. I stood and only then realized that Simon's satchel was on the ground beside me.

I scowled under my breath, cursing my own stupidity. It wasn't enough to kill him; I had to steal his most prized possessions too? The ring at least was heavy, so I suspected it could fetch a fair price at market. I pulled it out of his satchel and studied it.

The gold band was plain on the outside, but it had an inscription inside. I held it up to catch the angle of the rising sun and read, "Behold with reverence the Scarlet Throne."

This was no ordinary ring. But if it was connected to the throne, then why did Simon have it?

I dropped it back into his satchel, but it slipped between the weathered pages of his notebook. Not wanting it to get lost, I pulled out the notebook and it fell open as the ring tumbled to the bottom of the bag.

There I saw a sketch Simon must have drawn, done so well that I recognized myself instantly. Except he'd gotten a few details wrong.

My eyes never had the fire in them that he portrayed, nor had I ever worn the mischievous grin he'd drawn.

I turned the page and saw more drawings of me, some of them only my eyes or a partially finished sketch. There were other drawings too, of places he must have visited in his travels or images that had captured his imagination. But again and again, his work returned to me. He couldn't have done all of these since the other night when he took me from Woodcourt, nor even in the four days since I'd met him . . . if it had only been four days.

I scanned the pages again, comparing myself to the girl he'd drawn. And I couldn't help but think of the way he had described the girl last night who he later claimed was me. He admitted that he'd had feelings for her.

For me.

These drawings were my proof of that. No one could have drawn these the way he had, with such detail and care, if he was indifferent to the girl in the picture.

And what if that girl had looked back at him through those mischievous, fiery eyes, and had feelings for him too?

I felt worse than empty inside. Brushing back tears, I replaced the notebook and folded over the satchel flap, then hung it across my shoulder, the way Simon wore it. I had to return it to him, or if . . . if that was impossible now, then I'd give it to Gabe. Maybe Simon had family here in Antora, or someone who cared for him. They had the right to his things.

The walk back to Simon's camp seemed to take me ten times longer than it had to escape it. The closer I came, the heavier my steps felt, mostly because my thoughts were growing heavier than before.

One question weighed on me more than the others: What if Simon was right—what if Lord Endrick had taken my memories? Because the more I pondered last night's dream, the more real it became.

When I approached the camp, Gabe was leaning against the side of the hill, clearly asleep. I tiptoed past him for one final look at Simon, who appeared far worse in the morning light than he had seemed during the night. The flesh of his cheeks had sunken in, his hair was damp with sweat, and his lashes were fluttering unevenly.

I knelt at Simon's side and touched a hand to his chest. It was rising and falling, though not as deeply as I would've liked. I stared at him, studying every detail of his face. How much younger he looked now, how innocent. I pulled a few broken pieces of late-autumn leaves from his hair. My hand lingered on his cheek.

Had I known this boy once, maybe even had feelings for him? Did Endrick know that, rejoicing as he erased those memories? And if he had, then what else had Endrick taken from me? Last night when Gabe was angry, he had referenced something I was supposed to do for Antora. What could that possibly be? And was Simon trying to save me from this responsibility or trying to preserve me for it?

Whatever it was, I needed to find the answers, but I'd hardly get help from Gabe. Simon was alive, and I'd returned his satchel. That had to be enough.

At his side was a knife, still in its sheath. He'd offered it to me yesterday. If I was going to be on my own, I needed it now. As quietly as possible, I undid the latch holding the knife in place, then slipped it free. When I did, Simon's hand moved to mine.

I caught my breath in my throat. His breaths seemed lighter, but his eyes didn't open. Did he know I was there?

I put my other hand back on his cheek, and with that his face relaxed again and he released my hand with the knife. I rolled onto the balls of my feet, preparing to leave, when Simon began coughing.

Gabe woke up to the sound and immediately noticed me, crouched in front of Simon with the knife over his chest.

"No," I said. "I wasn't—"

Gabe leapt toward me and yanked the knife from my hand, then shoved me away from Simon, keeping one hand gripped like a vise on my arm. In the commotion, Simon's eyes fluttered again and this time they opened.

"What . . ." he mumbled, then he saw Gabe with his knife and me nearly on my back. "Gabe, what are you doing?"

"She was about to stab you," Gabe said. "This, after poisoning you last night."

I shook my head. "I wasn't . . . I mean, I did poison you last night, but I wasn't trying to hurt you just now."

"Then why are you here?" Gabe asked.

I nodded toward Simon's satchel, which I had left by his side. "I accidentally brought that with me last night. I couldn't keep it, not after . . ."

My voice trailed off when I saw Simon staring at me. I didn't want him to know that I had seen the inscription on the ring or especially that I had seen his drawings . . . what the drawings revealed about his feelings for me. I didn't want him to know what Gabe had said last night or that I had begun to have doubts about my memories. I couldn't possibly apologize for almost killing him. I doubted a person *could* apologize for something like that.

"Let her go," Simon mumbled. "Gabe, please."

Gabe released me, and I immediately scrambled away from that knife.

Simon closed his eyes a moment before opening them long enough to say, "Get me to Rutherhouse. That's my only chance now."

"Rutherhouse?"

"Bring Kes."

Gabe shook his head. "Absolutely not. Not after what she did."

He waited for a response, but Simon had fallen back into unconsciousness.

"Will he survive?" I asked.

Gabe's glare could've melted iron. "Well, I don't know, but how kind you are to ask. I'll put Simon on my horse, and I'm going to ride fast. If you can't follow, I'll leave you behind and never look to see if you're there. I'm only offering this much because Simon wants it."

I'd freed myself, but Simon was still far from safe, and I couldn't rest until I knew he'd recover.

He had to recover from this. He had to. Because if he didn't . . .

Tears filled my eyes and I quickly packed up our supplies and tied them to the same horse that Simon and I had shared last night.

If he didn't recover, I'd become what Lord Endrick had wanted me to be in that dream. And for the first time I could remember in my life, I wanted to be as far from the Dominion as possible.

· SEVENTEEN ·

KESTRA

With my help, Gabe lifted Simon onto his horse, though anyone who saw them would think Gabe was carrying an already dead body. Simon was laid over the saddle facedown with his arms flopped over his head.

"Don't look at him like that," Gabe said, scowling at me.

"Like what?"

"Like you had nothing to do with the reason he's unconscious. Get on your horse."

I climbed up on the horse Simon had been riding, gave it a pat on one side, then shook the reins the way Simon had done. Nothing happened at first, but when Gabe's mount trotted out, my horse followed of its own accord. Gabe glanced back at me then picked up his pace. Fortunately, by now, I'd developed a feel for riding. It came as naturally to me as if . . .

As if I'd done this many times before.

I mulled that while keeping within easy sight of Gabe. I knew he'd have questions for me, and whatever I said, he'd twist my words faster than I could defend myself.

Though if Simon died, I'd have no defense. I wouldn't even try.

The problem was that I had questions for Gabe too. I caught up with him and asked, "What happens when Trina gets to that camp?"

"She'll probably regroup with Wynnow and the other Coracks searching for you. That'll buy us some time."

"Does Trina know about Rutherhouse? Will she lead the Coracks there?"

"I don't know. I should take Simon to the Coracks. Loelle could save him, but again, everything has to revolve around you, doesn't it?"

"He asked you to take him to Rutherhouse. I didn't."

"Because it's safer there for you, not for him!" Gabe rode faster, then shook his head and slowed again enough to ask, "Do you remember Celia?"

Celia? There was nobody in my life with that name . . . that I remembered.

"She was your handmaiden for a while, until you drove her so insane that she joined the Coracks. She told me once that being difficult was woven into every fiber of your existence. That you never chose to be a problem for everyone around you, but you didn't have the choice to be any other way. She told me there was no difference between being Kestra and being a problem."

I didn't know how to respond to that, or if I was supposed to respond to that. So I modified my original question. "Last night, you said that you didn't care what I was supposed to do for Antora. What am I supposed to do, Gabe?"

"As you are, there's nothing you can do for us. I hate to say it, but maybe we should've let the Halderians take you yesterday."

I pulled back on the horse and Gabe rode ahead without looking back. If he'd intended to hurt me, he'd succeeded, not because he was unkind, but because he was right. His words soaked through me, draining me of any remaining shreds of pride.

What was I supposed to do? If Gabe liked the idea of turning me over to the Halderians, then as soon as I knew Simon was safe, I needed to escape. But where? The idea of returning home, to a place that would celebrate me for what I'd done to Simon, turned my stomach.

We were leaving the Drybelt now. Although a few slots still lay ahead of us, they were shallower, and patches of farmland gradually appeared ahead along with trees and small streams. Which meant we should see homes soon too. Perhaps I'd find someone to take me in until I sorted out my thoughts.

Absentmindedly, I fingered the necklace from Endrick. I'd never seen a gray pearl like this one, so it had to be worth a great amount of money. I might not find many Loyalists out here, but I'd surely find plenty of Antorans who'd temporarily shift their politics for a bribe.

Except that Lord Endrick had instructed me to always wear it, and I'd never go against the orders of my king.

But . . . what if I did?

When I looked up again, Gabe had ridden on far ahead of me. I shook the reins until the horse picked up its pace. The last thing I wanted was too much time to think, because every question led to a hundred more questions, and those I could answer left me feeling emptier and more hopeless than before.

As promised, Gabe rode fast, keeping us in a southeastern direction for most of the day. He only stopped once, to let his horse drink from a water hole left by last night's rain. By the time I caught up, he was already headed away.

"Is Simon still alive?" I called. Gabe gave no answer, but he continued riding, so I hoped for the best.

He slowed again in the late afternoon as we entered a valley of good farmland, largely hidden by a few remaining slots, their walls as steep as the others but not nearly as tall. In the distance, a small farmhouse was nestled within a pocket of thick trees. A friendly looking dog with brown spots ran out to greet us, sending chickens scurrying in all directions. I assumed this must be Rutherhouse, though the name seemed far too grand for this humble place.

As he was still riding up, Gabe called out and a woman ran from inside the home. She immediately rushed to Simon, asking questions faster than Gabe could answer them. He slid off his horse and pulled Simon down, then carried him inside the home.

I had no idea what to do next. Simon had told Gabe to bring me here, which technically, Gabe had done. I didn't dare invite myself inside. How would that go, if I knocked on the door and announced that I was the one who had nearly killed Simon, and could I come in for some tea and scones? Nor did I dare leave. I had nowhere to go.

I tied my horse to the fence post, then stood beside it for what seemed like hours. The woman's dog stared at me for most of that time, and I began to wonder if it sensed the kind of person I truly was and considered itself on guard duty. Around me, the sun was dipping low and the early evening felt chill. It was going to be a cold night. And I might be left out in it.

Gabe had used the blankets from our camp to pad Simon's ride here. I had the fire starter, but if it was true that I was inherently troublesome, then I'd likely start a small fire, which would spread to the house and not only finish off Simon but also Gabe and the woman who was inside tending to him. I left the fire starter inside the saddlebag and wrapped my arms around myself for warmth.

Several minutes later, the door opened and Gabe stood in the entry, looking anywhere but at me. "You might as well come in."

"How is Simon?" I'd been desperate to ask the question, though I was terrified of the answer, and when it came, it offered little comfort.

"I don't know. Tillie says we'll have to watch him all night."

"I can help."

"You've already helped him more than enough. Come inside, you're letting the heat out."

Finally, I took a step forward, though I wouldn't look at him either. "Tillie. Is that the woman who tends this inn?"

"You're Kestra?" The same woman I'd seen before rounded the corner now, brushing her hands on her simple apron before holding out her arms for an embrace. Her hair was capped and her cheeks were rosy, and her eyes were full of kindness and sympathy. "If I'd known you were out there, I would've sent for you sooner." She hugged me tight, though my arms were caught in her grip, so I stood there stiffly until she released me. "Goodness, child, I can feel the cold in your bones. I have a room where you can bathe and get warm again."

"Simon—"

Her eyes darted to a room at the back of the small home. "I've done all I can for him. He needs to rest."

"Can I see him?"

"No," Gabe said firmly. Then with a kinder tone, he said to Tillie, "I'll stay with Simon."

Tillie nodded, then led me to a room with a small basin tub in one corner. "It's not as fancy as what you're used to, and there'll be no one to tend to you, but I do have a clean dress from my daughter that should fit you. There's some water over my fire. I think it's hot enough to start a bath."

I shook my head. "Let me help with Simon. I don't need a bath."

She smiled. "Yes, you do, child. All of you do. It's a wonder the Coracks aren't taken out with disease, the way some of them care for themselves."

"I'm not a Corack. I'm a Dallisor, and I promise that once I'm home, my father will reward you for—"

"You're not a Dallisor either, from what I'm told. And the best reward you can give me is to ensure that the Dominion never knows I'm out here. Now, let's see to your bath."

Tillie bustled around, filling my bath and setting out soaps for my hair and body. I merely stared at them, motionless, until she said, "You'll enjoy it more if you finish before the water turns to ice." Then she shut the door and left me alone.

The first thing I did was to unclasp Lord Endrick's necklace—I didn't want the soaps to ruin it. But the instant I pulled it off, I was struck with a pain that sent me to my knees. I dropped the necklace and felt almost frozen in place, a suffocating clench on my heart.

From somewhere deep inside me, a voice seemed to say, *You are mine, child. You are a weapon of the Dominion.* It wasn't a true voice, but rather an echo of my past. I'd heard the words before.

I fumbled for the necklace and pressed it back to my chest. The pain remained, but it was better, and with some effort, I was able to latch the clasp again. Then I curled my legs into a ball and held them until my tremors passed.

Simon was right—this was no ordinary necklace. It had power and purpose, and I was its slave. But the necklace itself didn't terrify me half as much as the consequences for removing it. Lord Endrick had ordered me to keep the necklace on at all times. In disobeying him, I had felt as if his very fist were wrapped around my heart, squeezing it until I could no longer breathe.

There could be only one explanation for that. The heart-shaped pendant was a symbol for what Lord Endrick had really done to me. It all made sense now.

I was an Ironheart.

Anger burned inside me. For my entire life, I'd been loyal to Endrick, obeyed his every wish, and he'd repaid that with control over each beat of my heart. Why me?

Simon probably knew the answer, and for all his help to me, I'd done nearly the same thing to Simon's heart as Endrick had done to mine.

I was no better than my king. Could I call him a villain and deny the same of myself?

Eventually, I made it into the bathwater, which washed away the sweat and dirt and dust, but did nothing for the hurt I felt inside. I spent most of the bath in tears, for what I'd done to Simon, for what Lord Endrick had done to me and would yet do if I failed to obey him. And I cried because there was obviously something I was expected to do for Antora. Something that would force me to disobey Endrick.

And then he would do to me what always happened to Ironhearts who disobeyed him. He never showed mercy to traitors.

When I began to dress myself, I decided there was only one thing for me to do. I had to get away from the Coracks. Because if I stayed, I would either become Endrick's weapon or his next victim.

· EIGHTEEN ·

SIMON

I awoke sometime in the night inside a dim room I vaguely recognized. In the corner, a person stirred.

"Simon?" That was Gabe's voice.

Someone placed a damp rag over my forehead and told me to stay quiet. I knew that voice too: Tillie. Which meant Gabe had done as I'd asked. I was at Rutherhouse.

A cup of water was offered to me and I took a few sips.

"No poison in this one." If Gabe thought that was funny, he was wrong. The water made me feel a little better, though the awful taste of metal in my mouth remained.

"We almost lost you." Tillie was speaking, though my vision was blurry, and I had trouble seeing her. "If Kestra had given you that third leaf, or if you weren't as strong . . . but I think you're past the worst of it now."

"Where's—" I cleared my dry throat and accepted another drink of water before trying again. "Where is she?"

"In the back room," Gabe said. "Closed the door to take a bath and we haven't seen her since."

"Go find her."

"She'll be asleep."

"Go find her, Gabe."

He grunted but left the room.

Tillie turned over the rag on my forehead and leaned in. "That is our Infidante? The girl who will save Antora?" When I didn't respond, she added, "Gabe told me what you believe happened to her. Can you bring her memories back?"

I shook my head, feeling the weight of having failed her. "Our physician believes her mind has a better chance to heal than if she were only Antoran. She also gave her a tea that was supposed to help." I rapped a fist against the bed. "But I haven't noticed any difference."

"Maybe she needs more time."

"Maybe. But her memories are only one complication." I closed my eyes to rest, then said, "I can't get her back, Tillie. Not as she was before."

"You barely got her back as she is now." Gabe pushed Kestra through the door, the binding cord around one of her hands. "I found her outside, saddling a horse."

I caught Kestra's eye, but she quickly looked away. Gabe was obviously angry with Kestra, but I smiled a little. Trying to run away was something the old Kestra might have done.

I motioned to a nearby chair and asked her, "Will you stay?"

Gabe snorted. "Are you serious?"

"I won't do anything more to him," Kestra said.

"What more *can* you do?" Gabe turned to me. "If she stays, I'll stay too."

"Then I'll leave," Tillie said, already walking away. "No sense in me crowding up the room." After a moment, Kestra sat in the corner, though she still refused to look at me.

"Remove the binding cord," I said to Gabe.

He sighed but did as I asked, then retreated to the opposite corner of the room. I noticed he withdrew his knife and held it in his hands. I was sure he wanted Kestra to notice too.

"Where were you going?" I asked. "When Gabe found you just now."

"I don't know."

"Kes—"

"I need to find the truth."

"Simon's told you the truth," Gabe said to her. "I've told you the truth, but you refuse to believe it."

She pointed out the nearby window. "What if I were to tell you that it's daylight out there?"

Gabe shrugged. "It's obviously night."

"What if I insist that you're wrong, that you must be seeing things, because the sun is shining as bright as it ever has?"

"I see your point," Gabe said. "That's what we're all saying to you. But we're *all* saying it. If I were the only person to see nighttime in a crowd of people who see the sun, I would ask myself if maybe I'm wrong."

"And if I am wrong, then isn't it better that I discover the truth safely, away from you?"

"You want the truth?" Gabe leaned forward, his voice rising in pitch. "Kestra, the truth is that terrible things happen to people who are around you. Just over two weeks ago, you were in a room with Captain Tenger, bargaining for the life of one of our captives, a man named Darrow."

She shrugged. "I've never heard the name."

"Oh, you've heard it. He cared for you for most of the past three years, at a time when you were exiled from your family's home."

She shook her head. "That's a lie! I have memories of being at home, with my father."

"Endrick put that in your head. You were with your real father those three years. You were with Darrow."

From my perspective on the bed, I saw her fingers begin to tremble. "Don't say anything more," she whispered.

Gabe nodded at me. "Tell her, Simon."

I drew in a breath, and when she turned my way, I said, "Darrow spent those three years in your service, training you with weapons and horses and to fight. He was preparing you for the life he knew was coming. At the time, you thought he was a loyal servant. Less than two weeks ago, you learned he was your father."

Her voice wavered. *"Was?"*

The next part was harder to say. "He was killed during a Dominion attack."

She looked from me over to Gabe, who nodded his agreement. But she closed her eyes, then said, "I remember being in a lava field and cutting my leg on some rock. My father—Sir Henry—found me and helped me back into a house."

"That was Darrow."

"No!" she shouted. "No, I see the memory in my mind, as if it happened only yesterday! Don't tell me that the things I see, the things I feel and remember and know as well as my own name, are not true!"

Silence fell heavy in the room until Gabe smiled sardonically. "You already tried to kill Simon. Must you yell at him too?"

She drew in a couple of harsh breaths, then folded her arms and sat down again.

I decided to try a different tactic. "After you and Gabe brought me back to our camp, I wasn't always unconscious, even if I couldn't respond. You went through my saddlebag."

"Yes."

"She *stole* your saddlebag," Gabe said.

"I didn't!" she protested. "Gabe sent me away from the camp, and I was so upset, I didn't realize I had it with me. But I returned it the next morning."

I smiled, glad to see the fire in her. Then asked, "Why did you return it?"

She hesitated and pressed her mouth shut. She had her reasons but didn't want to share them. Maybe not with Gabe here. Maybe not with me.

"He's getting tired again," Gabe said. "We should let him sleep."

I hadn't realized that my eyes were closed, but Gabe was right. I was exhausted.

"Let me stay with him," Kestra said. "If he needs anything, I'll take care of it."

"I don't trust you," Gabe said.

"But I do," I mumbled. "Leave us alone, Gabe."

He stood, and I had no doubt that he'd check in on us several times during the night, but he did leave the room.

Kestra started to say something to me about her necklace, but I fell asleep without registering what her words had been. Which was too bad. They sounded important.

· NINETEEN ·

KESTRA

Sometime during the night, I sat up straight, struggling to catch my breath and with tears streaming down my face.

"It was only a dream," I whispered in an attempt to comfort myself, but that didn't work because I knew otherwise.

In the dream, I was back in All Spirits Forest, drowning in the river again. A handsome man about twenty years older than me appeared and said help was coming. Then, suddenly, he was injured and pulled away by some unseen force. When I found him again, I promised to save his life. But before I could, he was caught in the explosion of a building.

It was Darrow. I remembered Darrow.

My father.

A sob rose within my chest. In a single memory, I had found my father, loved him, and lost him again.

I clamped a hand over my mouth, hoping to keep myself from crying out loud, but that choked me, and I soon heard Simon's voice pierce the darkness.

"Kes? Are you all right?"

The lone candle in the room had burned out while I was asleep, and I was glad for it now. I steadied my voice the best I could and said, "I'm fine. Go back to sleep."

"You're not. I can hear—"

"I'm fine."

He said nothing more, but his hand reached out and found mine. He gave my fingers a squeeze and then kept his hand there, even after he fell asleep again. I brushed my thumb across his palm, slowly folding my hand in tighter with his.

Meanwhile, I began working to recover every memory of Darrow I could, but for all my efforts, I retrieved nothing but a strong impression that he had loved me, something I realized I'd never felt from Sir Henry. Darrow's current fate was the consequence of his being my father. I understood that too.

Gabe had been correct earlier. Terrible things happened to people who were connected to me. And I had no idea how to make any of it stop.

Simon stirred and I shifted over to sit at the side of his bed. If it was true, that he and I shared some sort of history, then I felt desperate for a single glimpse of it. Not only because of what it meant for us, but also because it would prove that Lord Endrick hadn't saved me in that fall from the castle window.

Maybe Lord Endrick had done to me what he had done to those who wandered All Spirits Forest, giving me enough memories to live in the world, but stealing away those that let me be part of it.

A sound came from outside the room, footsteps near the door, and I quickly retreated to my seat. The last thing I needed was for Gabe to walk in and accuse me of attacking Simon again. Eventually, the footsteps faded and everything returned to quiet.

I fell asleep with thoughts of Simon and Darrow, and questions of what I'd lost without even knowing it. Thankfully, it was a dreamless sleep. My mind couldn't take any more than it already had to work through.

Tillie woke me at dawn. She touched my arm and said, "You must be hungry, child."

I was, beyond my ability to describe it. I looked over at Simon's bed, but he was no longer in it.

"He got up an hour ago, said he was tired of being an invalid. He and Gabe are eating now, but I thought if I didn't give you a chance at the food, there wouldn't be any left."

I smiled and followed her into the small front room with a table full of biscuits, eggs, and bacon. Simon stood when he saw me, and reluctantly, so did Gabe. I understood Gabe's anger. I'd nearly killed his best friend.

Simon wasn't entirely steady on his feet, and his eyes had dark circles beneath them. But he managed a smile and held out a seat for me while Tillie set down a plate of eggs and homemade sausage that I immediately began attacking. I'd had nothing to eat yesterday and very little the day before that.

"You run a fine inn here," I said between bites. "I can't imagine you keep that many guests at any time."

The corners of Tillie's mouth crinkled, pleased to see me enjoying her meal. "True, though there is always room for someone in need."

"I can't pay you for this."

"Give her the necklace in payment," Gabe muttered. "That has to be worth a lot."

It was worth my life, though he didn't know that.

"You can work off the payment instead." Tillie's brows furrowed as she evaluated what type of work I might be fit for. "I need chores done around this place, and Simon needs at least another day to recover."

I noted a rather serious look passing between her and Simon and wondered about that. There was something more she wasn't saying, but I had a guess. Simon knew the Coracks were still searching for us. He had already asked if we could hide here for another day.

"What can we do for you?" Gabe asked.

Tillie started with him. "Winter is coming soon, and I need more meat in my stores. I noticed you have a rather fine disk bow—"

"And when I return this evening, I will have more than you can eat in a year," he said, rising to his feet.

Another meaningful expression passed between him and Simon. Now I was getting irritated. Gabe was actually being sent out to keep watch on the area so he could warn us if he saw any sign of the Coracks. Maybe he'd return tonight with a successful hunt, maybe not. It wasn't the purpose for him leaving. What were they hiding from me?

Now Tillie turned to me. "I don't suppose you've had much experience with housework."

"If not, then I can learn."

Tillie nodded in approval. "Simon can teach you. He used to be a servant boy, you know."

I recalled the dream from the other night with Lord Endrick and the ladybird beetle. Had he been the boy to rescue me?

"Kes, are you all right?"

I blinked and saw Simon staring back at me. I wondered how many times he'd called my name. I merely shook off his silent question and returned to my breakfast. Once I finished, Tillie took my dishes and said she would clean up inside while Simon and I gathered eggs in the yard.

We did, though when Simon teased me for being startled by a hen, I threw an egg his way, barely missing him. After we came back inside, that chore was followed by Tillie's request for us to sweep the day's dust from the floor. I must have been doing it wrong, because Simon wrapped his arms around me to demonstrate the proper sweeping motions. I didn't need the lesson—I would've figured it out, but I didn't mind his arms where they were. At one point, I looked back to ask him a question, which put my face directly in front of his. After a moment in which neither of us moved, he smiled and said, "Share your thoughts and I'll share mine."

"I already know your thoughts," I teased, pushing back from him. Pushing back, because I knew my thoughts as well.

Tillie poked her head in. "If you're finished, I have some bread dough to knead."

Simon followed me into the kitchen, where a large lump of dough was on the table. He folded his hands into the dough, pushing and rolling it together.

"Like this?" I asked, joining him.

"It's hard to do it wrong."

"Are you sure?" I grinned mischievously. "Some of it didn't get mixed in at all."

He looked around. "Where?"

I tapped his nose with some flour. "There!"

He laughed and grabbed a larger pinch of flour and blew it into my face. "No worries, I fixed it!"

Accepting his challenge, I reached for the entire jar of flour, perfectly willing to sweep for the rest of the day just to have the last laugh now. But he grabbed one end of the jar and pulled on it.

I didn't let go, so his tug threw me off balance toward him. I might have stumbled, but his arm went around my waist, steadying me. Holding me. And suddenly, there we were like before, except this time it wasn't a broom between us, but a jar of flour. And this time, there was no question what either of us was thinking.

Hours seemed to pass as we stood there, though it must have only been seconds. He was probably nervous, worried that if he moved too quickly, I'd run. Maybe I would. Maybe I should.

But running would never answer the question of whether these emotions surging through me were real. I had to know. I wanted to know, though it terrified me more than I could ever explain aloud.

If the rush of excited nervousness I felt at being near Simon, the tug to draw even closer, the growing sense of caring for him—if all these feelings were real, then every other facet of my life was a lie.

If so, then I didn't even know who I was.

I couldn't allow this to be real.

I released the jar, forced a smile to my face, then dipped my fingers into the jar and flung the powder at him. He laughed and released me, commenting on what a mess we'd made.

A mess? Yes, that described the swirl of thoughts inside my head with perfect accuracy.

Whatever I felt for Simon, I couldn't seem to hold on to one single, coherent thought, because there was no single thought where he was concerned. He frustrated me, intrigued me, and was constantly on my mind. Did I hate him or like him? . . . Could I have loved him once? It frightened me to get closer to him, but I spent our moments apart wondering what it must be like in his arms. Yet some part of me had already tried to kill him.

He was staring at me again, smiling. I stared back, trying to focus on the question at the forefront of my thoughts. What if I let him kiss me?

Would it prompt a return of memories? And if it did, how would I react?

Would Endrick know? Would he consider it disloyalty?

I just couldn't take the risk.

Tillie walked in at that moment, hands on her hips. "Enough of this, you two! I'll finish the bread. Go fetch me some water. Simon, I hope you can get to the well without creating another disaster."

He winked at me. "For the record, she started it."

"Then I like her even more." Tillie shoved a couple of buckets into his hands and shooed us out the back door.

"Tillie is wonderful," I said as we walked. "How can she be happy, all by herself here, when she is of no value to the Dominion?"

"She's happy *because* she has no value to the Dominion," he said. "And she's not alone. She has a daughter who recently joined the Coracks in the western part of Antora. I come to visit when I can, as do many friends she's made over the years." Simon shifted both buckets to one hand, then offered his other hand to me. "It's a steep slope down to the well. Let me help you."

At first, I thought it was a convenient excuse to hold my hand, but when we started down the hill, it was indeed steep enough that I accepted his offer. He led me to the base, then set the first bucket beneath the pump and began to draw up water.

I said, "Two days ago, I told you that I love Basil."

He stopped pumping and pressed his brows low in earnest. "Do you?"

"No. Before you took me from the Lonetree Camp, I told him that I wouldn't marry him."

"What changed?"

"Nothing. I just didn't want to pretend anymore with him."

He studied me a moment, then said, "Maybe you've had to pretend, to protect yourself. Or perhaps you think that you're protecting me."

A flutter swirled in my belly. "I don't remember you, Simon. All these moments you describe of us, feelings . . . they're in your head, not mine."

"I've only told you the truth."

"I don't have any truth. And without it, I have no trust."

He stepped closer and my breath locked in my throat. "Can you trust me?"

I hesitated, my mouth suddenly dry and with a dull pinch in my heart. I desperately wanted to answer his question the way he wanted to hear it, but I couldn't.

Simon added, "Talk to me, please."

That was impossible—why couldn't he understand that? "You are working against Lord Endrick. I am sworn to obey his orders."

"Since when?"

"For as far back as I can—" I hesitated.

"As far as you can remember? You do not have to obey him." He glanced down to see me fingering the necklace. I hadn't realized I was until he gestured at it. "What is that, really? What is it doing to you?"

I shook my head, releasing the necklace. Whatever it was, I knew one thing for certain. "I *do* have to obey him, Simon. I do."

· TWENTY ·

SIMON

Kestra allowed me to be close to her, until the instant I reached for her necklace. Then she backed off, the expression in her eyes reminding me of a cornered animal.

"Let me see it more closely. I promise to return it." I put my arms around her neck and fingered the clasp, but the second I did, she pushed me away, her breaths becoming shallow and harsh.

"No, Simon."

"You don't want to remove the necklace, or he won't allow it? Which is it?"

"Doesn't matter. I have to keep it on."

"Or else what happens?"

Tears filled her eyes, but she shook her head. I kept my distance and finally she said, "If I ever knew the answer, it's gone now."

"But there are some memories returning to you, correct?"

"Even if there were, I wouldn't trust them." She looked away from me, deliberately. "Some of what's in my head isn't real, and I can't always tell the difference."

"False memories?"

"Maybe."

Taking a step toward her, I suggested, "What if you let everything go but this single moment? What's happening now is real. Can that be enough for now? Ignore everything else and start over."

A shy smile tugged at her mouth. "With you?"

I stepped toward her again and bowed low. "Good afternoon, my lady. My name is Simon Hatch."

Her smile widened, and she gave a polite curtsy. "I'm Kestra."

"No last name?"

She considered that. "No."

She offered me her hand. I brought it to my lips and kissed it, watching her the entire time. Afterward, I didn't release her hand, and she didn't pull away.

Instead, she was watching me intently, as if trying to burrow into my thoughts, and I was more than willing to let her. She asked, "Are you trying to repeat an old memory with me, hoping it will spark something?"

I took another step toward her. "I'm trying to make a new memory with you. And yes, I definitely hope it will spark something."

I watched the smile dance in her eyes while she bit her lip and considered my unspoken suggestion. I pushed a lock of hair behind her ear, then let my hand linger there. But the instant my fingers began to curl around her neck, that smile turned to a sort of worry, a raising of a shield around herself exactly as the old Kestra would have done. At least that much about her was consistent.

She stepped back and brushed at her skirts, an obvious distraction since they weren't dirty. "Tillie will be worried about us. We should bring the water."

Reluctantly, I returned to filling the buckets. Then Kestra insisted on taking one so that I could hold her hand as we climbed the hill. In the end, she climbed ahead of me anyway, so fast that I wondered if she might run once we reached flat ground. I could've kicked myself for making her nervous. I'd ruined a moment I might not get back again.

Tillie had the bread in the oven when we returned, and she followed us outside to gather some vegetables from her garden for supper.

"No sign of Gabe?" I asked her.

"Nothing yet. Let's hope that means his hunt is successful." Tillie smiled as she spoke, but that was only for Kestra's sake. I knew she was as worried about Gabe as I was.

Kestra tilted her head while listening to us, and I wondered if she suspected the real reason Gabe was out there. If she did, she remained quiet, and simply continued gardening.

I worked beside them for nearly an hour before we went in to finish preparing supper. When it was ready, Tillie sat on one side of the table, and Kestra and I were seated beside each other.

"My husband, rest his sweet heart, was always at my side, just as you two now sit." Tillie's smile faded. "He died, many years ago, a soldier in the War of Devastation."

"I'm very sorry," Kestra said. "Whose side—"

"Not the Dallisors," I said.

"Oh . . . of course."

Tillie handed Kestra the bread, still warm from the oven. "There are many of us who remember Antora as it was, before the war. This was never a country that enjoyed a long peace. Either the Dallisors were fighting the Halderians, or the Halderians were fighting the Dallisors. My family is neither, so we managed to stay out of it, until Lord Endrick united with the Dallisors. Then we knew it was time to fight. And we will continue fighting against him until his reign has ended."

Kestra lowered her eyes but said nothing.

It should have been a clue for Tillie, but she continued, "What about you, my dear?"

Her head shot up, a fire in her eyes and a ring of alarm in her voice. "Don't call me that . . . 'my dear.'"

Tillie shrank back. "Oh, I'm sorry, I . . ."

I noticed a trembling of Kestra's hands. "Kes?"

Confusion darkened her expression when she looked at me, as if her mind had wandered elsewhere. She saw my concern and took a slow breath. When she spoke again, her tone had softened. "It's all right. You didn't mean anything by it. I think . . ." Her fingers brushed against her necklace, then she hastily lowered them. "What was your question?"

Tillie cleared her throat and spoke more cautiously. "I wanted to ask if you intend to fight against Lord Endrick. Considering what you did to Simon, you'd be a valuable asset to the rebellion."

If Kestra had been upset before, this was worse. Tillie had meant well, but Kestra's eyes were darting around in every direction. I figured if a gaping hole opened in the floor, she'd gladly dive through it to escape.

I quickly changed the subject. "After supper, maybe Kestra can help you clean up and I'll chop wood for a fire."

"That would be lovely." Tillie smiled at Kestra. "You are such a beautiful girl. I wish I could look into your eyes and see happiness there."

"That's a nice thought, but—"

Now Tillie nodded at me. "You may not realize this, but Simon is a gifted artist. He's made drawings of you before. In those drawings, your eyes are alive and filled with passion and joy. Perhaps he could show them to you someday."

"I've seen them." Kestra quickly glanced at me before turning back to her supper. "But he got the eyes wrong. That's not me, not anymore."

I held her words in my heart for the rest of the meal and noticed she kept her gaze lowered after that. I wasn't sure if she was avoiding me or trying to avoid her own mind. Either way, she was locking up the few thoughts she still trusted and hiding them far from anyone else's reach.

When I came in from chopping the wood, Tillie was in a chair, knitting, and Kestra was seated on the fur rug in the center of the room, pretending to read a book. Obviously pretending, because I built an entire fire and she never turned the page once and her eyes were constantly on me.

When I finished, I sat across from her, giving her room to think, to work through whatever was occupying her mind. Occasionally I put on another log or two, keeping the room comfortably warm.

At one point when I got up, I noticed Tillie's chair was empty. She must have slipped off to bed without saying anything. Now it was only Kes and I. Did Kes know we were alone? She was sitting near the fireplace, staring at the flames, as she had been doing steadily for the past couple of hours.

I sat beside her, our hands almost touching. I wondered if she would slide hers any closer, but she didn't. Maybe she was too lost in her thoughts to know I was here. Several minutes passed before she spoke.

"I've been thinking . . ." She went silent, then tried again. "No, I *know* you're right, that Lord Endrick did something to my memories. There are too many gaps, too many inconsistencies."

I didn't say anything, not yet. She had to work through this on her own.

Several minutes passed before she spoke again. When she finally did, her voice was quieter than before. "I think I'm an Ironheart. Do you know what that means?"

I did know, and it terrified me. "There must be a solution."

"What is it?" When I didn't answer, her eyes narrowed. "You cannot wish a solution into existence."

I hesitated, meaning she knew my answer long before it fell from my mouth. "No." I quickly added, "But I won't give up until I find a way."

"Then you'll never give up, and never succeed." Sadness dimmed the light in her eyes. "Endrick won't surrender control over me. We both know that."

No, he wouldn't.

After a long, heavy minute, she said, "Why did he do this to me, Simon? I'm nobody."

"Nothing could be more false. If only you knew . . ."

Our eyes met and my breath quickened. For nearly the first time since our reunion, there was heat in her expression, a beckoning that burned deep within me. This was the real Kes.

Then she looked down again and the moment passed. "Am I an enemy to him?"

"He would say you are, yes."

"Then why didn't he kill me?"

"Because it's safer to have taken your memories than to have taken your life."

"Safer . . . for him?" She drew in a breath, answering her own question. "If I die, someone takes my place."

"Yes."

It took her time to absorb that, but she was so close to the truth, I had to wait. I had to let her find it for herself. Finally, she said, "Only one person could ever be a true enemy to him, because only one person could ever truly harm him."

My heart drummed against my chest. Kestra knew. She didn't want to say it, but she knew.

She closed her eyes and shook her head. "I've heard the whispers around me, people who speak when they think I'm not listening. Back at the Corack camp, and here between you and Tillie and Gabe, the same word over and over. It can't be a coincidence. They're speaking about me, aren't they?"

"Yes."

She swallowed hard. "I'm the Infidante."

Silence fell between us until she locked eyes with me, demanding an answer. "You are," I whispered.

Her reaction to that was so calm, I wondered if she might not have understood what that role required of her.

Until she said, "I will not do it."

My brows pressed together. That was the last thing I'd expected. "No one else can do it, Kes."

"I almost killed you, Simon, and the pain of it, the guilt, nearly drove me to madness. What if I succeed in killing Endrick? I'll become as evil as he is now."

"If you succeed, you will end his evil for good."

"At what price?" Her voice rose in pitch. "It is not fair to ask such a thing of me."

"No, it's not. But if you refuse this, then Antora is lost!"

"I must have tried it already and failed. That's why he took my memories, why I'm wearing this necklace. If he took a piece of my heart, then he'll use it to make me do something he wants. Maybe he already has and I don't even know it!"

My heart crashed against my chest. "Since leaving Woodcourt, has he given you any orders?"

Tears filled her eyes, and she shrugged, whispering, "I genuinely don't know." Then she sucked in a quick breath and her expression darkened. "I've got to leave. I will not be part of this any longer!"

Before I could reply, she was on her feet and rushing out the door. Still aching from the effects of the poison and a hard day of work, I was slower to follow. By the time I stumbled outside, she was running away.

She was easy to spot in the moonlight, and so although I was walking slower than she was, I knew exactly where she was going. She was headed toward a narrow gap inside a nearby slot.

I understood why she had chosen that path—she thought she could lose me there, but she was wrong. The slot would close up before she went much farther. There was nowhere for her to go.

I could follow her in, and I would, but she couldn't be my prisoner any longer. The only way I'd ever get her back to Rutherhouse was if she chose to come. And as upset as she was, I had no idea if that was possible. This might be my last chance to truly reach her.

· TWENTY-ONE ·

KESTRA

I'd hoped Simon wouldn't see me, but he obviously had. He was still weak, and I had a good lead. If I hurried, I might escape the slot before he caught up to me.

I laughed bitterly to myself. Escape what? I'd never outrun my own mind, my fickle thoughts. I'd never outrun the memories that were seeping back into my life.

Darrow. My father.

My mother dancing with me in the gardens of Woodcourt.

No, she had been my adoptive mother, though I still had no idea who my actual mother was.

The depth of Lord Endrick's evil—I only carried fractions of his crimes in my head now, and they horrified me. Surely he had done far worse than what little I remembered. How could I ever have knelt to such a man?

And with all of that, the question: Were any of these memories real?

A minute later, the slot that was supposed to have offered me an escape ended in straight walls with a few scattered vines crawling up the spine. I'd gone as far as I could here.

Maybe I'd gone as far as I would in every sense. That was obvious by now.

"Come back with me, Kes." I turned with a start. I hadn't realized Simon was already here, only steps behind me. "I meant what I said before, that we will find a way to fix everything."

"You can't fix me!" I lashed out. "No one can. Please just admit that."

His eyes darted away, but slowly he nodded, conceding defeat. I wished he hadn't, even if I had asked him to. Knowing that he believed there was a solution had given me some bit of hope. That was gone now.

A heavy silence followed. Finally, with obvious reluctance, Simon said, "There is one possibility. Tenger and Loelle want to take you to the Blue Caves."

They had said nearly the same thing to me, but I still didn't understand why. "That doesn't make sense, because the Blue Caves only affect—" My breath caught as the truth flooded into me. An awful truth that made my hands tremble and put a hard lump inside my throat. With tears filling my eyes, I shook my head at Simon.

"Tillie told me I wasn't a Dallisor. Loelle said my mind wasn't like other Antorans'."

He nodded solemnly, and white-hot emotions shot through me, burning brighter with each new revelation. Everything became clear now.

Why Tenger believed the Blue Caves could help me. Who my real mother must have been. How I could be the Infidante.

How had I missed this before?

Simon took my hand, but I yanked it away and pushed past him. "Did you know? Did you know that I'm Endrean? That I share *his* blood?"

He followed me without flinching. "Half Endrean, and yes, I do know."

"Does Endrick know too?"

"He believes that he killed every Endrean in his rise to power, so it's possible he doesn't. But maybe he's waiting to see, because if you have magic and he kills you, he can take your powers."

"If I'm half Endrean, maybe I can't get magic."

"Maybe not." He took my hand again and this time I turned back to him. "You might get magic, you might get your memories back, and you might"—with his other hand, he touched the necklace—"you might be able to rid yourself of this. But the price of the answer is high."

"The caves might save my life."

"Or destroy it." Simon shook his head. "Magic sells itself as a solution to problems, but it becomes a parasite, feeding on its host until every trace of good is gone."

"I can resist that, I'm strong—"

"Yes, you are. So imagine how dangerous you will become if it corrupts you."

"What if it's the only way I can return to who I was, this girl in your sketchbook, whom you speak of in nearly every sentence you utter, this girl you wanted to kiss earlier today? If I don't go into the caves, I'll never . . . we'll never . . ." I took a deep breath. "Whatever you and I were before, we'll never get that back."

"And what if you claim your magic? Do you think we'll be free to be together, that it'll be the end of our troubles? Kes, if you have magic, how can there ever be any future for us?"

"There can't." I hated hearing the words empty from my mouth, but they had to be said. "This is where we end. Saving my life with magic will destroy us. If I refuse magic to save us, Endrick will destroy me."

Simon stepped closer and now the sadness in his eyes reflected what surely was in mine. "Let's worry about the future when it comes. We are here tonight. Can this be enough?"

I drew in a sharp breath, trying to hold in my emotions and failing miserably at it. It didn't help when he closed the gap between us, his hands running up my arms, awakening new emotions within me.

"Let's start again," he said. "Tell me something that you remember."

I searched for a memory I trusted, desperate to prove that my mind could overcome Endrick's magic. "I have some memories. Random pieces, here and there. Scattered fragments of a puzzle, and no idea how to put them together."

"Do you remember anything of us?"

A chill went up my spine. "The way you're holding me now. We've been here before."

"Yes." Something in his expression set my heart pounding. Why did he look at me like that, as if I were all that existed, as if we'd known each other forever and were only just meeting?

With his eyes trained directly on mine, he said, "I know you in ways you no longer know yourself. You're my first thought when I wake and you follow me into my dreams each night."

I shook my head, a pathetic attempt to calm the flutters in my stomach. "You're just saying that. It isn't true."

He drew a line up my jaw with his finger. "I know the very place where this bone curves." Now he cupped my cheek in his palm. "The brown in your eyes warms in the sunlight, bringing out tiny flecks of green. And when you're angry, your right brow presses lower than your left."

I knew I should back away, but I didn't. The stroking of his thumb along my cheekbone kept me locked in place, caught in his arms, wondering what would happen if I stayed, if I risked letting myself be with him.

"This is dangerous," I said. "We shouldn't dream of the impossible."

He kissed my cheek, softly, like a whisper against the skin. "Something only becomes possible when you dare to dream of it."

"I poisoned you!"

He leaned back and grinned. "After I kidnapped you. We're even."

I smiled, and let go of my worries, let go of everything but his gentle touch, the beckoning of his eyes. When his hand slid to the small of my back, I leaned into him, letting the flutters in my belly build, so much that I had to remind myself to breathe.

He said, "You see me as a threat, but the truth is, you are far more dangerous to me than I ever could be to you."

"I'm not."

"You are. My heart is in your hands."

Barely able to breathe, I said, "And here I am, in yours."

He smiled and tiny lines formed at the corners of his eyes. He was closer to me now, or maybe I'd moved closer to him.

I wanted him to kiss me. I wanted to feel on my lips what he'd so often expressed with his eyes, to understand in his touch what he wouldn't speak aloud. I suddenly wanted these feelings for him to be real.

Almost automatically, my arm curled around his neck. His fingers returned to my cheek, asking me again to look up.

"If you don't—" he began.

"I do." I kissed him, a cautious, timid kiss. I didn't know what would come next, what should come next. I only knew that I wanted to find out.

I started to pull back, but I caught the expression in his eye, felt the tug of a thousand invisible threads drawing me back to him. He kept his face close, his eyes searching mine for . . . something. When he found whatever he was seeking, he kissed me again, but this was different. Where I had been wary, he was committed. His mouth pressed against mine in a sudden desperation. I felt his kiss throughout my body, echoes of his touch vibrating down to my toes.

Something deep within me must have remembered him—the softness of his lips, the rough tips of his fingers against my cheek, his faint scent of leather—because this stirring within me, this hunger for more of him, felt like an awakening. Like I was alive again.

When we finally pulled apart, I smiled as his fingers traced lines across my cheeks. With a kiss near my ear, he whispered, "I never thought this would be possible, not after the way we began."

I sighed with contentment. "How did we begin?"

He leaned back, chuckling. "You'd probably be glad to have forgotten this. Trina and I forced you to enter Woodcourt, to find the Olden Blade."

Something clicked within me, like a sudden flash inside my head, recalling a memory I did not want. No, not a memory. A command.

At the first pinch on my heart, my eyes immediately filled with tears. "I'm sorry, Simon. I'm so sorry."

He noticed my tears and wiped them away with his thumb. "For the poisoning? It's all right, I understand why you did it. And it ended well."

No, *this* would not end well, being here with him now. He had unwittingly answered a question I didn't even know I had, but now that he did, I couldn't hold back the sharp tone of Lord Endrick's voice inside my head, commanding me, *Find the Corack boy who brought you into Woodcourt and kill him. Fail to do this, and you will die.*

The words exploded through me, more than a passing thought or a casual memory. It was an order that had been placed deep within my heart to ignite at the moment of his confession. This was the reason Lord Endrick had let me live, the reason he had taken that piece of my heart. He wanted revenge on Simon for having breached the walls of Woodcourt, and had given me a week to make it happen.

"How many days?" I asked. "How many days since you took me from Woodcourt?"

Simon mumbled words beneath his breath, counting on his fingers as he did, then said, "Seven. Why?"

I stifled a cry and Simon let me bury my head in his shoulder. I dug my fists into his back, feeling the constriction of my heart. Jolts of pain shot through my chest, down my arms and legs. I drew back, but I couldn't let Simon know how bad it was, or why this was happening. If he knew, he would sacrifice himself to save my life, I knew he would.

"Talk to me," he said. "What's important about seven days?"

"You have to leave now. Something terrible is going to happen."

"What?"

"I don't know." I grabbed his arm and tried to push him away. "I don't know, but you must go, please!"

Endrick must have had a sense of what I was doing, because the punishment he shot through my heart forced me to my knees. He knew I was refusing his order.

And for that, there were consequences.

With that thought, that defiance, Endrick must've squeezed on my heart so fiercely that I nearly fainted. Simon rushed to my side. "What's happening to you?" he asked. "Please tell me!"

I barely heard him as Endrick's order echoed again in my head: *Find the Corack boy who brought you into Woodcourt and kill him. Fail to do this, and you will die.*

"No!" I shouted. Not that it mattered. What I heard was an echo of my past. A memory I wasn't meant to remember until now.

Simon held up his hands, looking utterly helpless. "Tell me how to help you."

"You can't . . ." I struggled for words. "Why did it have to be you who forced me to retrieve the Olden Blade? Why did it have to be you, Simon?"

He reached for me. When I gasped for air, his eyes grew wild with panic. "Is it the necklace?"

"It's you. I won't hurt you again!"

"What are you talking about? Kestra, you're not making sense."

I stumbled to my feet. "I won't let them hurt you."

Then, from outside the gap, a dog began barking. Tillie's dog. My attention flew to Rutherhouse, and without words, without any reason for the fear that suddenly swept through me, I knew what had raised the dog's alarm.

As fast as I could run, I burst out of the gap, blinded by everything but the few lights still burning inside the home and the shadows that passed in front of them, numb to everything but the barking dog and the high-pitched, fluttering call of oropods.

The Dominion had come.

If I could get there first, I had a chance to convince them that I was alone. Whatever happened to me afterward didn't matter. My fate was already sealed.

Except I wasn't there first. Tillie was inside, with them. I was too late.

· TWENTY-TWO ·

SIMON

Kestra had nearly escaped the slot before I realized why she was running.

The dog's barking.

Normally, that wouldn't have alarmed me, but after Kestra's strange behavior just now, I knew something was terribly wrong. And despite still recovering from the poisoning, I found a new strength in me to follow her.

The back side of Rutherhouse came into view and my gut instantly knotted. A prison wagon with green and black markings was parked at the side of the home. I counted eight oropods total. Horror sent a chill through my bones. The Dominion was here.

"No, no!" I breathed.

If this was the Dominion, then why was Kestra running toward them? Would she try to attack?

No, she intended to surrender.

I finally caught up to her when we were within a few paces of Rutherhouse. I put my arms around her waist and pulled her to the ground, then clamped a hand over her mouth as I dragged her behind a tree, almost directly beneath an open window at the back of the house. It became all too easy to hear what was happening inside.

"This is your last chance, woman!" a man shouted. "Where are Kestra Dallisor and your son?"

Kestra locked her widened eyes on mine, asking for a confirmation of what she'd just overheard, and shaking her head in hopes that the soldier was wrong. But I nodded back at her, already feeling the wound splitting my heart. Yes, Tillie was my mother.

Kestra tried to get up, but I kept one arm around her waist and locked her legs down with mine. As I did, I felt my breaths coming in harsh bursts.

What was I supposed to do?

Tillie answered the soldiers, "I'm alone here—" Her voice was cut short by a piercing cry, and I flinched. What had they done?

Kestra struggled again and I tightened my grip on her, though my hands trembled and this moonlit night was blurring in my vision. In my entire life, nothing had ever hurt the way this pain was swelling within me.

"Stop," I hissed in Kestra's ear, not sure whether I meant for her to stop, or if it was a prayer that the soldiers would stop whatever they were doing. I didn't know what to do, I didn't know. All I had with me was a knife, and a body in no condition to fight off eight or more Ironhearts.

Kestra tried again to get away, but I continued to hold her, even as everything within me crumbled apart.

"Lady Kestra was under orders directly from Lord Endrick," an Ironheart said. "She failed, so he is calling her back to face her punishment."

Kestra went still, and suddenly, her odd behavior that ended our kiss made sense. She said she would not hurt me. Those had been her orders, and in anticipation of her disobedience, these soldiers had come for her. But how did they know she was here?

"What sort of evil man uses a sixteen-year-old girl to carry out his orders?" Tillie's question was immediately answered with something that caused her to cry out.

Tears streamed down my face, but if I went in, hoping to save her, they'd kill us both and then find Kestra out here.

If I didn't go, I'd never forgive myself.

I whispered into Kestra's ear, "You get on the nearest horse and you run away as fast and far as you can."

She shook her head, but this time I released her, then stood and withdrew my knife. No sooner had I done so before the soldier said, "We'll find her without your help."

Another cry of pain followed, a final cry punctuated with the slashing sound of one of their swords. I heard my mother's body slump to the ground.

And I fell back to my knees, wanting to scream out every emotion exploding within me, wanting to run into the home and do my worst against every man in there. With only a knife and a weakened body, I knew I was capable of slaughtering them all.

Kestra was kneeling beside me now, maybe crying too, maybe holding me as I silently sobbed, I didn't know. I wouldn't look at her, I couldn't.

I choked on my sorrow until I almost couldn't breathe and funneled that sadness into anger at everything and everyone around me. At Gabe, who was supposed to have been watching for this very danger. At the soldiers who had come here searching for Kestra.

At Kestra.

If she hadn't left, I'd have been at home to defend it. If she hadn't poisoned me, I would not have had to defend it. If she were anyone else, they'd never have come in the first place. This was her fault.

No, it was my fault. I'd chosen the life of the Infidante over the life of my own mother.

I couldn't believe this was happening.

I shook off Kestra's arm. I didn't want her touching me or comforting me. I didn't want her here, reminding me of what I'd just lost, and why.

In the bitter, awful silence that lay around us, I heard the crunch of autumn leaves.

"It's not much, but it'll have to do!" That was Gabe's voice, returning from his hunt, calling into the home. Returning from the end of the house, opposite where the prison wagon was parked and the oropods waited. He wouldn't see them. He wouldn't know what was awaiting him inside.

Kestra stood, intending to warn Gabe, but I grabbed her arm and pulled her back to me, as we'd been before. I felt the tears on her cheeks and wiped at mine. When she continued fighting, I whispered, "They're here to kill you."

"It's supposed to be me," she whispered. "Not you, or Tillie. Not Gabe."

He was next.

A scuffle sounded in the home, and by Gabe's shout of alarm, I knew he'd been caught off guard and that the soldiers had just attacked him too.

"We're looking for Kestra Dallisor," one of the soldiers said. "We know she's with you."

"She was," Gabe said, quick to respond. "But she escaped this morning." That was followed by a hit so hard that I heard it—and Gabe's grunt of pain—from outside. Kestra shuddered within my arms.

"Lies!" an Ironheart said. "Your next one will come with a real punishment."

My gut knotted again, as awful as before. My knife had fallen somewhere on the ground near me, but I felt around in the darkness and couldn't find it.

"Where is Kestra Dallisor?" one of the men asked.

"She isn't—oh!"

I wasn't sure what they'd done, but it sounded as if Gabe had fallen to the floor. Then they kicked him, each strike eliciting a grunt or cry. I knew firsthand that kicks from an Ironheart's boot were merciless.

"Give me a knife," the Ironheart said. "I'll get what I want from him."

Kestra struggled again. "If they kill you," I whispered, "Antora is lost forever."

She shook her head, and I knew my words meant as little to her now as they had meant to me. But even if I hated them, hated what was happening because of *those* words, they were still true.

The soldier asked, "Where is Kestra Dallisor?"

Gabe cried out again, and in my distraction, Kestra elbowed my chest enough to loosen my grip. I reached for her, but she had already bolted to her feet and was running around the side of the house.

I felt around for the knife and found it, but was barely on my feet when I heard the front door bang open. She shouted, "I'm Kestra Dallisor. I'm the one you want."

Heavy footsteps emptied to the front of the home. Toward her.

"Lady Dallisor." The same soldier who'd been speaking before must've shoved her against a wall or door and she gave a cry loud enough for me to hear. "Lord Endrick demands you answer for willful disobedience."

That was followed by another cry and an order to also bind Gabe's hands, though an Ironheart asked why they should bother tying up an unconscious man.

"We're taking them both," the Ironheart replied.

"You only wanted me," Kestra said, and then, obviously referring to Gabe, added, "He's useless to you."

"He's valuable enough that you risked yourself to come in here." The Ironheart chuckled. "I'm sure we'll find plenty of use for him."

By then, the front door opened again, and I ducked around the side of the house, peeking out to see Gabe's still body thrown first into the prison wagon and then Kestra being forced outside, her hands bound in front of her, and her dress torn near the shoulder. I noticed she never looked around, which had to be a deliberate choice. She didn't want to alert the soldiers that I was out here too.

She recoiled at first when they led her to the prison wagon, but the Ironheart pushed her inside and slammed the door behind her. "Oh yes, my lady, you have much to tell us, and you will."

The oropods led the way from Rutherhouse with the prison wagon at the end of the line. I stepped out to see it go and noticed Kestra staring out from the bars at the back. In the darkness, I couldn't see the details of her face and I wondered if she could see mine, but I felt her pain and she surely felt the flood of worry and grief and hopelessness in me.

In less than ten minutes, I had lost my mother, heard my best friend beaten to within a breath of his life, and was now watching the last hope for Antora be carried back to the enemy. I knew what fate awaited her. Thinking of it bored the final hole through my heart.

Ten minutes, in which everything that mattered to me in this life had been taken away.

And I was helpless to make any of it better.

· TWENTY-THREE ·

KESTRA

As we drove away, Simon's face nearly broke my heart—
more than it already was broken. His final expression
had been worse than disgust, worse than hatred. He had
stared at me with utter indifference. In that instant, it seemed, I'd
become nothing to him.

I sank against the floor of the wagon, crying bitterly for him
and his mother, for Gabe who was still lying unconscious beside
me, and even for myself because maybe I really was as selfish as everyone believed the Dallisors to be. Wherever they were taking me, I was
terrified.

Gabe grunted and his hand near me twitched a little, but he
didn't wake up. I had sacrificed myself, hoping to save him. How
foolish that had been, to think they'd ever leave him behind. As cru-
elly as they'd treated him before, I could only imagine what they'd
do now.

And what they'd do to me. I'd heard Endrick's order repeated
in my head and refused it. There would be consequences for that. My
heart was already feeling a squeeze on it, as if the only reason Endrick
was keeping me alive was because something more terrible than death
still awaited me.

When I'd cried out my tears, I crouched beside Gabe and with my hands still tightly bound, I leaned over him. "Gabe? You need to wake up."

He stirred and groaned, but nothing more.

"Gabe!" I gently tapped at one side of his face, the half that wasn't swollen from where an Ironheart foot must have crashed into him. "Please wake up!"

After I'd prodded him enough, finally he moaned, "Stop that, I'm awake." His eyes fluttered open and then widened when he recognized me. "Kestra, you can't be here! How did they find you?"

"I surrendered."

He scowled as his mouth tightened. "How could you be so foolish?"

"I did it to save your life! You'd be dead otherwise."

"If I'm here, I'm a dead man anyway. Where's Simon?"

"Still at Rutherhouse."

Gabe closed his eyes a moment, then spoke more gently. "Does he know what happened there?"

I sat back, sorrow consuming me again. "He knows. He was hiding me out back."

After he'd absorbed that, Gabe mumbled, "You should've stayed with him."

"It wouldn't have mattered."

Gabe looked at me, confused, but when I offered no explanation, he said, "Wherever they're taking us, when we get there, someone important will meet us, someone with authority to make real decisions. They'll try to find out everything you've learned about the Coracks—"

"Which is very little."

"—but that will only be a test to see if you're cooperating. Part of that test will be making you watch whatever they do to me, and it'll be awful."

"No!"

Gabe leaned up on one elbow, then grunted and lay back down again. "Listen, if they think your false memories are still intact, then you have a chance to live. So you'll stand there like a Dallisor and watch it and not flinch in the slightest, because you have to pass their tests or you'll be next."

I lowered my eyes. "I've already failed. I will be next."

His face pinched while he tried to shift positions. "What was the test?"

"That doesn't matter either. But before it happens, I want to try bargaining for you. I can agree to talk to them if they'll let you go."

He scoffed. "The Dallisors don't bargain, they take. Nothing you say will change that. Convince them that you tried to do what they wanted, but we got in your way. The Dominion wants you alive, Kestra. Give them every reason to keep you alive."

"I don't know those reasons!"

"If you say that, they'll send you back to Lord Endrick and he'll take more than your memories. He will take from you everything but a heartbeat, keeping you just alive enough that another Infidante can never take your place, but ridding you of any chance for a life. It will be worse than death."

My hands began to shake but I folded them together, hoping to control my rising panic. "I won't know what to say, and if I do, I won't say it convincingly enough. I can't do this."

Gabe closed his eyes again, for long enough that I thought he'd fallen unconscious. I reached out to prod him awake, but he opened his eyes on his own and said, "There's one other option, and it's very risky. In my vest pocket are the dried leaves of a turilla plant."

I wrinkled my nose. "Never heard of it."

"I've studied a lot about plants—how do you think I knew what to do after you poisoned Simon? And turilla is quite rare. You can't even find it in Antora. I had to go to Brill for this. Chewing on too much can be toxic, but the right dosage will only make it appear to be so."

I tilted my head. "So the leaf almost kills you?"

"That's the idea. It will slow the heartbeat to almost nothing and your body will live off borrowed air until the effects pass, which they do in about fifteen minutes. I experimented for weeks to find the exact amount for my size. I miscalculated a couple of times and Loelle had to bring me back from the brink." He smiled darkly, and when I frowned back, he continued, "The point is that when this wagon stops, we might have a chance if the Ironhearts believe we're dead."

"What if they bury us as soon as we're found?" My head tilted. "Or if we only have fifteen minutes, they may still be near us when we recover."

"Like I said, there are risks."

"If it doesn't work, we're right back where we started. We need a different plan."

Gabe sighed. "Well, I'm sorry that I don't have a long list for you to choose from. There's plan A, in which I'm tortured to death and you end up as a pair of vacant eyes inside a body that Lord Endrick will never allow to die. Or plan B, which gives us a slight chance of escaping plan A."

"Slight?"

"Unless you have a better idea." Gabe nudged his chin toward his vest. "Can you reach into the pocket there? You'll need about half a leaf, I need almost a full one."

"About? If this could kill me, I'd think you'd be more exact."

He glared at me. "Lord Endrick will do worse than that if you don't take this leaf. Is that exact enough for you?"

I found the leaves in his vest and put one in his hands, which he broke to his desired length with his forefinger and thumb. "We'll take them when we see the first signs of a Dominion camp. It's late. I doubt we're traveling far."

I held the leaf in my fingers while we continued to ride, my finger mindlessly stroking the crisp edges. At least an hour passed, and the entire time, I mostly thought of Simon and wondered what he was doing now. I supposed he was tending to his mother's body, perhaps digging a grave for her in the same yard where he had kept me from saving her.

Though I never could've saved her. Therein was the tragedy.

I dreaded what lay ahead for Gabe and me, but I figured it wasn't half of what Simon must be going through right now.

Gabe repeated the plan to me when we first spotted the lights of the Dominion camp. I listened and nodded, and when he put the leaf in his mouth, I pretended to do the same. I waited until he had passed out and then tossed my leaf through the bars of the wagon.

I had told Simon that I could not fulfill my role as Infidante, but that had changed now.

Because I had a plan C. In which my first job was to convince them that Gabe was dead, then to distract them enough to give him time to get away after he woke up. And then to do whatever was necessary to get myself an audience with Lord Endrick. If he had taken my memories, then it was true he could destroy whatever was left of me. But he was also the only one who could return them. I didn't have much to bargain with in order to make him cooperate, but if I was the Infidante, then at some point, I must have had the Olden Blade.

In exchange for my memories, I would offer him the Olden Blade. He would surely agree to that. Then, once he returned them, I would find the Olden Blade again and use it to kill him. I had no memory of using a weapon before, but I'd obviously done so, and I hoped my muscles would remember what my mind could not.

The odds of that were probably remote. Maybe there was no chance at all, but if I truly was the Infidante, I had to at least try my hand against Lord Endrick, and perhaps save my life—and Antora—in the process.

At least, I hoped that would be true as the wagon began to slow. Orders and the announcement that I was with them were shouted out.

The most terrifying game of my life was about to begin.

· TWENTY-FOUR ·

SIMON

In the earth softened by recent rains, it didn't take nearly as long as I'd expected to dig the grave for Tillie. Back when Rutherhouse had been an inn, her guests had all called her Tillie, so I had too. It was hard to think of her now as my mother.

Most of my memories of her were from my youngest years, when she used to sing for me at night, and fill my day with exciting stories as I worked beside her and my younger sister on our small farm. When that wasn't enough, the responsibility of providing for my family fell to me. I went to Woodcourt to work as a servant and still remembered the way she cried when I left. I'd felt mature then, but looking back, I was far too young. After Woodcourt, I was taken in by Gareth, who raised me until his death. I visited Tillie as often as I could, bringing money that I earned working for Gareth. I'd always loved her, but she hadn't felt like a mother to me for years.

I'd just buried my mother.

As I worked, I recited to myself every cliché that might lessen the pain, but none of it helped. It didn't matter that Tillie had offered up her life rather than sacrifice Kestra's. It didn't matter that Kestra had tried to break free in an effort to save her, or that I had refused to let her go. None of it mattered, because none of it outweighed the guilt I felt for having brought Kestra here in the first place.

How did they know?

My fingers clenched into fists. Maybe it was the same way the Halderians knew Kestra was in the Lonetree Camp.

When Trina had passed us on the trail, she had said she knew where I was going. I'd probably mentioned Rutherhouse before, in a time when I had no reason to mistrust her. But although it was easy to believe she might have contacted the Halderians, it was harder to believe she would betray us to the Dominion.

I was kneeling beside the grave when I heard horses approach. It was the middle of the night by now. Was it the Dominion, returning for me?

I swung the shovel over my shoulder, and by now, my sword was in its proper place at my side. If it was the Dominion, I intended to take down every last one of them.

My first peek around the front of the house was little help. I saw several horses, but a few riders held torches, which made it impossible to see their faces. Maybe that made it easier to attack.

I charged around to the front with the shovel ready to swing, but stopped when I heard Tenger shout, "Simon, no!"

I immediately lowered the shovel, and those with the torches lowered them too, illuminating their faces. Tenger was at the front of a dozen Coracks, with Basil at his side. Trina was on the other side of him, and the girl from Brill, Wynnow, whom I still didn't know very well, beside her. Loelle was with them too, and the others were fighters whose faces I recognized, but whose names I didn't know.

Basil leaned forward in his saddle. "Where's Kestra?"

My eyes darted to Trina, hoping to see a reaction from her. "The Dominion took her—and Gabe."

Trina did react, though it wasn't what I'd expected. Her eyes registered what seemed like genuine alarm. Then again, maybe she hadn't intended for Gabe to be caught in their snares too.

Tenger cursed. "We've been monitoring Dominion activity and we saw a prison wagon pass by five miles back."

"They were in it."

"Are you fit to ride?" Trina asked. "You don't look well, Simon."

It took me a minute to answer. I *could* ride, I just didn't want to. I wasn't sure I had it in me to keep pushing for a happy ending that would clearly never happen. But maybe at least I could find an ending I could live with. Which wasn't Kestra and Gabe being tortured in a Dominion camp.

I dropped the shovel. "My satchel is inside. I'll go get it."

I walked back indoors, but froze in the entrance, wondering if this was the last time I'd ever see this place. I should have come here more often. I should have returned here after Woodcourt rather than living with Gareth. While it was true that the money I made sustained my mother and my sister for all those years, what did that matter now? Tenger wanted me to be king of the Halderians. I couldn't even be a son to my mother.

I left a note for my sister, hoping I would find her first to explain in person, then wrapped up what remained of the bread my mother had baked earlier that day, and gathered a few mementos of her, then left my family's home. I had very few memories of my own here.

But at least I had memories.

I imagined how Kestra must be feeling now, being led into a camp where she'd be questioned about what had happened to her over the past several days. They'd figure out that she was not the same girl who Lord Endrick had emptied of her memories. She was in terrible trouble, and I'd been a selfish fool to forget that.

Someone had saddled my horse while I was inside, and I mumbled a general thank-you in the direction of the Coracks, though I didn't care who had done it. I swung into the saddle and felt Tenger's eyes on me.

"You sure you're all right?" he asked.

"Positive."

"What were you doing with a shovel in the middle of the night?"

I closed my eyes and forced myself to breathe. "We're wasting time, Captain."

He clicked his tongue, mumbled something about how we'd discuss this later—I'd make sure we didn't—and rode off. I followed, realizing only after several minutes that Trina and Wynnow were on either side of me.

"That's your mother's house," Trina said.

I glanced over at her. She had confirmed my suspicions that at least she knew about Rutherhouse.

Something sharp must have been in my look, because she drew back, then asked, "What happened there? When the Dominion came . . . the shovel—" She drew in a breath. "Oh, Simon, I'm terribly sorry."

Sorry for sending them there? I wanted to ask, but instead I tightened the grip on my reins.

"I don't wish to be insensitive," Wynnow said, "but surely you can see now why Kestra must go to the Blue Caves. She will need her memories back to have any chance of succeeding against such evil as this."

"Her memories are returning!"

"It's not just the memories," Trina said. "We can't have an Ironheart for an Infidante. And she needs magic to compete with Endrick on his own terms."

I eyed Trina. "What if the chosen Infidante wasn't Endrean and could not acquire magic? What if she were only Halderian, like you? Would you be useless too?"

Trina cocked her head. "Maybe that's why the Blade chose Kestra and not me. Wynnow is correct. Kestra needs to go to the caves."

"No!" I wasn't negotiating this with them.

"That's not your decision to make!" Trina said.

"Nor is it yours. If Kestra possesses magic, it will change who she is."

"If she doesn't go to the caves, she will remain useless as an Infidante. And it doesn't matter anyway: You don't get to decide who she is."

Her words hit me harder than I let on, particularly on this horrible, unending night. As much as I wanted to defend myself, that I was only trying to help Kestra, maybe it was true, that I was forcing her in the direction *I* wanted. Never once had I asked her what she wanted.

I fell behind the group, absorbed in my thoughts, in my grief, my selfishness. I was completely empty of anything else. Trina rode up to Tenger, probably to give him a report on what I'd said. Since they were left to ride beside each other, Basil struck up a conversation with Wynnow. If Kestra had broken off their wedding, maybe he was already seeking a new bride to bring back to Reddengrad.

I became increasingly tired as we traveled, though my exhaustion was immediately forgotten the instant the Dominion camp came into view. This was a temporary camp in a valley east of the Drybelt, beneath scattered homes on the surrounding hillside that had probably been evacuated the moment the first black-and-green flag flew. Its position made it easy to evaluate but hard to attack, especially with our few numbers.

We rode to a home high on the ridge with a decent vantage point and were hardly surprised to find it hastily abandoned. A half-eaten supper was laid out on the table, which a few of our group gulped down while I sulked in a corner.

"The Brillians have some supplies that might be useful here," Wynnow said. "Glues, toxins, explosives—"

"Explosives, that's what I want." Until then, Tenger had been assessing the layout of the camp, debating with Trina and Basil the best way to carry out a rescue. Now Wynnow had his full attention.

She nodded, then joined him at the window, peering through the streaked glass. With the Brillians' exceptional eyesight, she was able to locate the prison wagon.

"It's empty," she said, "but if we assume they drove the wagon close to where they intended to question Gabe and Kestra, then three tents nearby could be reasonable choices."

"Is anyone going or coming from any tents?" Tenger asked. "Any of them with guards standing at the entryways?"

Wynnow looked again. "No to the first question, but I do see one tent that is well guarded."

"They could be in there," Tenger concluded. "Our priority must be in rescuing Kestra, though if we can get Gabe too, then obviously, we should."

"The priority must be Kestra's necklace," Loelle said. "Whatever its purpose, we cannot risk the Dominion getting that back."

"Agreed." Tenger turned to me. "I'm putting you in charge of Kestra's rescue. Of anyone here, I know you'll work the hardest for her. Even after—" His tone softened. "Even after what happened. Trina told me."

"Trina talks to a lot of people," I muttered, then made myself stand. "Let's go."

Tenger would lead Trina and most of our group to the far perimeter of the camp to set off some explosions and draw the Ironhearts to them. A bulky Corack named Hugh would be with us, though his primary goal would be finding Gabe. Hugh only needed a single punch to knock most of his opponents unconscious, so we called him Huge. Wynnow and I were going after Kestra.

"Let me go too," Basil said to Tenger. "That's my betrothed in there."

"Ex-betrothed," I said sharply.

Basil licked his lips, then said, "I want her back safely, as much as you do."

"Fine, but don't get in the way." Tenger looked around the group. "Everyone ready? The faster we get in and out, the better our chances. Go fast, hit hard, and let's rescue our people."

I pulled my knife from its sheath and kept my other hand on my sword, silently counting down from five, then said, "Go!"

· TWENTY-FIVE ·

KESTRA

Even knowing that Gabe had only taken the leaf to appear dead, he appeared so close to it that I worried he'd accidentally given himself too much. He was slumped against the side of the prison wagon with his head tilted forward, his hands at his side, and his eyes closed.

That's how he was when the prison wagon stopped and we were surrounded by Ironhearts.

"What happened to him?" one man growled, frightening me enough that I backed against the far side of the wagon.

"He never recovered from whatever *you* did." Mustering as much courage as possible, I added, "I think he's dead." As soon as the words spilled from my mouth, I felt the pinch again in my chest. Endrick sensed I was lying.

The wagon door opened and lever blades were aimed at me while two soldiers dragged Gabe's body to the ground. The weapons were ridiculous. Did they think I would fight them with my bare hands, that I *could*? Gabe was examined by one of the men for any sign of a pulse. He looked up at his companion and shook his head.

"Toss his body," the second soldier ordered.

I wanted to ask where, and for what purpose. Was it to be tossed into a fire or into a pit for burial? If so, I needed to intervene. But if I did, if I showed any concern for what happened to him now, it would suggest that maybe this was a trick.

Instead, I focused on my plan, to offer enough of a distraction that they would forget about Gabe. I surely could not do this.

"I am Kestra Dallisor," I said, with as much boldness as I could muster. "Sir Henry Dallisor is—"

"Your father is here," a soldier told me, offering his hand to help me from the wagon. "We came for you on his orders."

"With a prison wagon?" I was genuinely insulted by that. If they were going to transport me like a prisoner, I ought to be a prisoner.

"For your protection, my lady, from any further abductions. You seem to be a popular target for that particular crime."

Simon had captured me once, and Trina. And sometime when I was younger, the Halderians had taken me, I vaguely remembered that now. What would the Halderians have wanted with me? What had they wanted two days ago when they attacked the Lonetree Camp?

"Your father has asked to see you." He escorted me to a round tent surrounded by eight guards. *This is not your father,* I reminded myself.

Sir Henry was at a writing desk in the center of the room with a warmed clearstone in the upper corner and a Dominion tablet in front of him. He looked up with a smile that didn't strike me as entirely sincere. Of course it wasn't. That smile was ordered onto his face by Lord Endrick. So were the bland words he spoke.

"You're safe, what a relief." Henry gestured to a chair in front of his desk. "Please be seated."

Where was the talk of punishment, of consequences for my refusal to carry out any orders against Simon? Did Sir Henry know I'd defied those orders?

I obeyed and tried not to appear as nervous as I was. If he knew that my heart was racing, that I was unsteady on my feet, then he'd also know that my memories were returning. Including the truth about who Sir Henry was to me: a stranger and nothing more.

No, not a stranger. Another memory carried through me like a wave. I had told him once that I would never call him father again.

"I never wanted you to call me father in the first place," he had said.

My eyes moistened. Gabe had advised me to address this man as my father, but I couldn't. Darrow was my father. Darrow had loved me, and the man facing me now had been involved in my true father's terrible fate.

Finally, he completed his writing and looked up. "Are you well? Those savages didn't injure you?"

"No . . . sir."

"Basil disappeared the same night as you did. Was he captured too?"

My breathing quickened. I hadn't expected to be discussing Basil; I hadn't thought about him at all. But I needed to lie, or risk exposing Reddengrad to Lord Endrick's revenge.

"He was. They still have him."

"Filling his head with all sorts of lies, no doubt. These people are liars, I hope you know that, Kestra."

What he truly hoped was that I didn't know half of what I already did.

That single thought consumed my mind. I didn't even realize I hadn't spoken until my father continued, "You must tell me everything they said to you. With your recent accident, you might have become confused."

"I'm not confused," I said, staring him in the eye. Staring at a man who only pretended to be my father because he was under orders to do so. "I know who I am, and I know why Lord Endrick attacked my memories. If he ever wants to find the Olden Blade again, then he had better restore my heart to its original condition."

Had I slapped Sir Henry, I could not have gotten a more visceral reaction of rage. He stood, throwing back his chair and shoving his writing table forward. I was startled out of my seat and stumbled back until I was at the door to the tent. I turned to run through it, but a soldier appeared there, wrapping his arms around me and carrying me back inside, dropping me to the floor at Henry's feet.

"How dare you issue demands of your king?" he snarled. "I was ordered here to carry out your execution, Kestra, which I can do simply by removing that necklace you wear."

I clutched the clasp to protect it. "What is this necklace?"

Any warmth remaining in him turned to ice. "It was a gift from your king, and will be a gift *to* your king when I return it to him."

"If you take this, I will die. And by morning, the Coracks will have a new Infidante ready to avenge my death and all of this starts again. But if Endrick returns my memories, then I can be of use to him."

Then I can be a threat to him. That was my real purpose.

"It sounds as if you already have your memories. How is that possible?"

"I will explain that to Lord Endrick, and no one else."

Sir Henry continued, "You demand an audience with the king, after refusing his orders? Do you think Lord Endrick will show you any mercy now?"

I'd never expected him to show me mercy. I doubted that Lord Endrick even knew such a concept existed.

In the face of my silence, Sir Henry said to the soldier behind me, "Take her. Find out everything she knows, and when you are finished, return the necklace to me."

I tried to squirm free, but I barely got two words out before the soldier clamped a hand over my mouth.

"Enough!" My father shouted so loud that the whole camp must know our business. He crouched down until our eyes were level. "Here's the only thing you have any right to know: I am not your true father, which means that I will gladly carry out *my* orders from Lord Endrick." To the soldier, he added, "You know what to do."

With my arms still tied in front of me, I was yanked to my feet and shoved out of the tent. The soldier's grip on my arm was unforgiving and he was walking faster than I could keep up.

"Lord Endrick took my memories," I said. "You'll get nothing from me that he didn't plant there."

"We'll see."

"Let me escape, and I will find Endrick. When the Olden Blade is in my hands again—"

Now he laughed. "In *your* hands? By the time we're finished, your pretty hands won't be holding anything."

"And you'll lose more than your hands if you don't release her to us *now*," a voice said.

The Ironheart stiffened and let go of me. I stepped back and saw Wynnow immediately behind him, with a knife at his back. Basil was with her and heaved a sigh of relief to see me. He took my arm and said, "Let's go."

"Where's Simon?" I asked. No one else could have told the Coracks where I was.

Basil frowned as he hurried me away. "He couldn't . . . Kestra, he just couldn't come."

Behind us, the Ironheart yelled, "She's escaping!"

Wynnow had been running to catch up with us, but twisted around with her disk blade and shot him, and then a few others who had noticed us. Ahead, more soldiers were already gathering. Basil put me behind him and raised his halberd. I hoped he could use it well.

"Come this way!" Wynnow grabbed my hand, but we didn't get far before we were surrounded. "Get down," she yelled. "I've got a plan."

I crouched down, instinctively covering my head with my hands. One of the soldiers around us must have noticed my necklace, because I felt a tug on it. As soon as it snapped loose, my throat began to close up, constricting just as my heart had done, making me labor for each breath.

In nearly the same moment, Wynnow set off a charge that threw every person who had been surrounding us backward into the air. That must have included the person who had grabbed my necklace because suddenly it was gone.

I collapsed on the ground, stricken with pain, desperately feeling around for a necklace I knew wasn't anywhere within reach. A series of explosions came from the far end of camp, drawing Ironhearts and officers that way, some of them right past us in the darkness. None of it mattered. I was choking on my own breath and struggling to keep myself oriented to the chaos around me.

Basil picked me up and began running with me in his arms. "Hold on," he said. "We're getting you out of here."

When we came to a quieter area of camp, I called Simon's name again, but it was almost too soft for my own ears.

"Simon!" Basil repeated, lowering me to the ground.

Within seconds, Simon was hovering over me. I couldn't see him well, but what I did see broke what remained of my heart. Grief was etched into every curve of his face. Heavy bags of exhaustion were under his reddened eyes, and his shoulders bore an unseen weight.

"Where's her necklace?"

"Someone pulled it off. We were surrounded." That sounded like Basil's voice.

I tried telling them about Gabe, and that I needed the necklace back, and that Sir Henry was here. I tried saying anything at all, but I couldn't make myself speak.

Simon cursed. "We need to get her to Loelle. She's dying."

"I'm the fastest rider." That was Wynnow's voice, maybe.

My eyes were closing, and I was trying not to die, but I couldn't see why fighting Endrick mattered anymore. The end was inevitable. He always won.

Basil picked me up again and laid me on a horse that I barely felt beneath me. I was draped over it, utterly helpless, certain each shallow breath I drew would be my last.

"Huge still hasn't returned with Gabe," Simon said. "You keep her alive until she gets to Loelle."

"I promise that I will," Wynnow said.

"No," I mumbled. No, I didn't want Simon to risk himself by going into that camp to find Gabe. But no one heard me.

And maybe none of it mattered. I wouldn't be alive to see what happened next anyway.

· TWENTY-SIX ·

SIMON

Even in her semiconscious state, seeing me had clearly hurt Kestra, and I'd be lying if I didn't admit it hurt me too. I couldn't look at her without hearing the cries of my mother. And maybe the same was true when she looked at me. Had I seen guilt in her eyes, or the reflection of guilt in mine? Any choice I might've made behind Rutherhouse would have been the wrong one.

I watched Wynnow ride off with Kestra's nearly lifeless body and prayed she would make it to Loelle in time. I really didn't know if she would, or if Loelle could save her against such powerful magic.

But once they'd left, Basil handed me the reins to my horse. "We've done all we can here." When I didn't move, he added, "I'm worried about Kestra too, but we have a job to do."

Without replying, I climbed on one horse and he took another. Two horses were left behind for Huge and Gabe, if both returned here. Considering what the Ironhearts had done to Kestra in such a short time, I doubted there was much chance for Gabe.

The explosions had long ago ended when we rode into camp, but that didn't mean the camp was in any better order. Senior officers shouted at junior ones, several of whom found places to hide from their orders and insults, which was convenient for us when we attacked two of them behind a quiet tent. The uniform I stole fit perfectly, but Basil's was a little small. In any other circumstance, I would have laughed at him, but tonight it required all my concentration just to take the next step forward.

Basil had explained he lost his halberd when he carried Kestra from the camp earlier. Now he fixed the Ironheart's sword at his side. "I'm not trained with this weapon," he explained.

"They're simple," I said wryly. "The pointy end goes in first."

We returned to our horses, grateful that with the uniforms and this dark night, we would pass for Ironhearts. I even rode directly past Sir Henry and he never looked my way.

I certainly saw him, though, and heard him. "Heads will roll for this," he yelled. "I've already sent a messenger to notify Lord Endrick. We will have our revenge in Reddengrad!"

Basil eyed me. That was confirmation of where the Dominion was headed next.

Most of those around Sir Henry took a noticeable step back. He saw it too and ordered his officers to round up anyone who had behaved cowardly during this attack. Then he added, "I want to know how many Coracks there were. Fifty? A hundred?"

Twelve. And four of us weren't attacking. This was a temporary Dominion camp, hastily set up, the soldiers unfamiliar with their own area and poorly prepared with defenses. But this would still be seen as an embarrassment to the Dominion. If retribution was coming, then I intended to be there for it. I had a personal score to settle with the Dominion, and now Kestra to avenge along with my mother and possibly Gabe.

When the other soldiers were excused to search for us, we left with them, but turned off at our first opportunity. Basil caught up to me and said, "Gabe could be anywhere. We'll never find him in all this confusion."

"Then let's cause as much damage as we can while we're here," I said.

Basil surveyed the area. "What do we do?"

I tossed him the fire starter kit that Kestra had packed into the saddlebags, then pulled out my own kit.

"Make sure to leave us a way out," I said. "We burn one tent, then ride to another part of the camp, keep them confused."

We started at the tent nearest to us, without any idea of what was inside. Basil lit one corner and I took the other, then we leapt onto our horses again, riding away to shouts of alarm behind us. Three rows down, we did the same, but this time, didn't get far before something inside that tent exploded, startling our horses who bolted away, leaving us on foot in the midst of the damage. It wouldn't be hard for anyone to figure out that we were responsible.

"Stop!" a voice ordered. We turned and saw a young, inexperienced looking boy with a lever blade as long as his arm and shaking in his grip. He could threaten us with it, but I doubted he had the courage to use it.

"Lower that and we'll let you live," I said, a fair warning.

"If I lower it, Lord Endrick will kill me. I'm an Ironheart."

Kestra's nearly lifeless face flashed in my mind. Endrick knew she had disobeyed his orders—an order that had probably involved me—and she was paying for that now. I said to the boy, "Come with us, and help us fight against him."

He licked his lips, considering my offer, which I hadn't expected, then said, "I have to hand you over to my superiors."

"No, you don't." From behind, Huge wrapped a massive arm around the boy's neck, who quickly passed out. "Sleep well," he whispered, then motioned us toward him.

We followed Huge up a hill where Gabe was tucked beneath some bushes, barely conscious. His body bore the marks of having been badly beaten at Rutherhouse, and maybe here as well. We had to get him out.

Huge already had two horses ready. He lifted Gabe onto one, then said, "I'll escape just fine. But Gabe is running out of time."

While Basil rode with Gabe, I pulled out my sword and took the lead, fighting off anyone who got in our path. True to his promise, Huge ran behind us, easily knocking down anyone who was foolish enough to challenge him. Within minutes, we were back at the abandoned home where the two horses we'd left behind still remained. Huge mounted the largest one and then took the reins of the other horse to ride alongside him.

I looked at Basil, almost incredulous that I was putting my trust in him again. "Can you get us to Loelle?"

Basil nodded. "I can. We're going to save your friend's life."

I followed after him with the strangest thought in my mind. That in the most unlikely of ways, Basil had become my friend too.

· TWENTY-SEVEN ·

SIMON

Trina was waiting for us alone when we arrived, at the bottom of a gulch with a shallow cave for shelter. The sun was finally beginning to rise, a welcome end to a night that had cored me from within. I slid off my horse and looked around for the rest of our group. "Where is everyone?"

Trina bit her lip. "I volunteered to stay back until the rest of you came."

"Kestra?" Trina stared back with a blank expression and a wave of panic shot through me. I stepped closer to her and raised my voice. "How is she?"

Her eyes darted to Basil and Huge, then she held out a note. "I didn't write this. Remember that."

I took the note and backed away from the group before opening it. From the very first words, my gut began to twist.

Simon,

If Kestra survives the journey, then by the time you read this, she will be at the Blue Caves. She will leave them with magic in her fingertips and full memories of her role as Infidante.

Therefore, from this moment forward, any connection between you and Kestra is severed.

For your past defiance to me, you will give your life to the Halderians as their king, or I will take your life. I am Captain of the Coracks and I will have my way in the end.

Dominion armies are on their way toward Reddengrad. Trina is in command of your group, and I will join you as soon as possible. When I arrive, I will either greet a king or execute a fool. The choice is yours.

Your captain,

Grey Tenger

I crumpled the note and tossed it into the weeds, watching Trina's shoulders deflate as I did.

"Simon—"

"Now I know why you offered to stay behind. You must have been bouncing on your toes in anticipation of watching me read it."

She pointed at Gabe as Huge lifted him to the ground. "I stayed to treat him. And I need your help."

"Let Basil do it, I won't—"

"Gabe is your best friend, Simon, or he was. Help me!"

Numb to anything else happening around me, I dug through our saddlebags for the supplies Trina listed and passed them to Basil, who carried them over to her. Then I held Gabe while she wrapped the visible wounds.

"I'm sure his worst injuries are internal," Trina said. "We should wait here a few hours and see how he's doing. If he's better, Huge will take him to Loelle."

"I'll take him now." She knew full well why I was offering.

But Trina shook her head. "We have other orders. We're going to the Hiplands."

Of course we were. With a scowl, I asked, "Do you know why he wants me to be king? It's because he can't manipulate Commander Mindall. But he believes he can control me!"

She sighed, obviously tired of arguing. "If you've proven anything over the past couple of weeks, it's that no one can control you. Take the throne or don't, but either way, that's where the Dominion is headed and we both know their plans for the Halderians. We have to help them."

She was right about that much. War was certainly coming to Reddengrad, and the quickest route to their capital was straight through the Hiplands.

I heard the crackle of paper and looked over to see Basil holding the note from Tenger. When he'd read it, he frowned up at me. "Trina's right. The Hiplands have to be our priority now."

I snatched the note from his hands and stuffed it into the pocket of my coat. "You're comfortable, then, abandoning Kestra to go to the Hiplands?"

"Of course not," he replied. "But defending the Halderians must be our priority. Of all people, you should agree with me."

Of all people.

I snorted and marched back to my horse to tend to its needs. Except that wasn't really why I was there. I needed some way to get Kestra out of my mind, maybe forever. For all my efforts to save her from Tenger, he had won in the end. He had ripped her away from me and written that letter to gloat over his victory.

Trina said, "You should all get some sleep while you can. I slept earlier, so I'll keep watch for a few hours."

Huge offered to rest at the far end of camp and to keep one eye open for trouble as he slept. I had no doubt he meant that literally. I laid out my bedroll to guard the opposite end of camp, then groaned when Basil laid his nearby.

I closed my eyes, rolled away from him, and pretended to sleep.

"I do care for her," Basil said. "But there's nothing either of us can do for her now. You know that, right?"

"I'm trying to sleep, Basil."

"The girl who's with her now, the girl from Brill. I don't trust her."

Trina must have been eavesdropping. She said, "Wynnow has done nothing to earn your mistrust."

"It's not just me. Ask your physician—Loelle. She doesn't trust Wynnow either."

"She doesn't *like* Wynnow, which is different. Loelle doesn't like anyone from Brill."

"Nor do we. There are reasons why Reddengrad has no formal relationship with Brill," Basil continued. "They will cheat and lie and destroy others if necessary and without guilt because they consider the rest of us inferior. Worst of all, their long lifespans afford them great patience. Don't you think it's suspicious that they sent you the heir to their throne?"

"Reddengrad also sent us the heir to their throne." I rolled over, making sure Basil felt my eyes on him. "Should we doubt your loyalties too?"

"I risked my kingdom to save Kestra's life!"

"And her gratitude was expressed in promptly ending your engagement." I sat up, though my head swarmed with dizziness. "Let's settle this, shall we?"

Basil studied me a moment. "Still feeling the effects of the other night?"

"No." I straightened up and thought that if I did get sick, I'd aim it all toward him. "Why do you ask?"

He smiled but glanced away. "She never poisoned me, that's all I'm saying."

Near us, Trina chuckled, still listening in. Fortunately, Gabe began coughing, which took her away to tend to him. It left Basil and me free to really talk.

"I don't understand why she broke our engagement," Basil said. "She only told me that she was confused."

"There's no confusion in her feelings. She didn't want your affections before her memory loss and she doesn't want them now."

"Don't you think I know that?" Basil said. "I saw the way she acted whenever you were nearby, and how patiently she endured my company when we were alone. I know where her heart is, where it really is. But," he quickly added, "I truly do care for her."

Trina began walking again through the camp, so I lowered my eyes, and my voice as well. For now, this was only between him and me. "If that's true, then she still needs our help. She'll leave the Blue Caves with magic. You understand what that means?"

Basil took a moment to absorb that, but he finally raked his fingers through his hair and said, "I can't believe I'm saying this, Simon, but I think we may have something to agree on. She needs our help, together."

I reached over and shook his hand, then we lay down to finally get some sleep. Despite my exhaustion, I stayed awake with lines of thoughts streaming in every direction through my head.

If I saw Kestra again, everything would be different. Magic would bring her more enemies, fewer friends, and an indistinguishable line between the two. Tenger was a perfect example of that, the friend who would give her magic, and the enemy who would one day kill her for it.

Stranger still, Basil had just agreed to help me protect her. We were finally on the same side of an idea.

From there, things became more complicated. I would have to go to the Hiplands, and if by some miracle we succeeded in holding back the Dominion, maybe I would have the chance to see Kestra again and determine for myself if things were truly over.

They were. I already knew it.

Tenger was about to destroy her in a way that Lord Endrick never could have dreamed of doing.

At the very least, he intended to separate us, maybe forever.

Which meant he was about to destroy me too.

· TWENTY-EIGHT ·

KESTRA

I had awoken in the night long enough to know that I was in a wagon, that someone was aware of the fierce pain in me, and that they were trying to keep it as far as possible from my heart. It was no use. I was dying.

I tried to speak, and someone who identified herself as Wynnow offered me a drink from a skin. I didn't remember anyone named Wynnow. And I wasn't thirsty. I wasn't anything.

The sun was high in the sky before the wagon stopped, I knew that much, though I didn't know where we were.

A man said something about Blue Caves. I'd heard of them before, somewhere.

"Why are we slowing?" a woman with an older-sounding voice asked. "She's running out of time."

The hourglass had already run out for me. My time was finished, so why did my crushed heart keep beating? Something was sustaining me, something beyond myself.

It was that woman who'd just spoken. Loelle? Somehow, I felt her connection to me. She was using magic to keep me alive, even as Endrick was using magic to kill me.

"We have to be sure there's no Dominion around," the man said. "The last thing we need is a fight here—or worse, to find Lord Endrick."

Lord Endrick. Hearing his name sent a wave of pain through me and I moaned. I didn't want to fight him anymore, I didn't want to fight anything anymore, not even for my own life.

"Hurry!" Loelle said.

"I'll protect us," a girl said, though I faded before she finished speaking.

When I awoke again, I was being lifted from the wagon by a set of arms and then whoever they belonged to was running. Wherever we were going, the air around us was changing. It was bitter and icy cold. I began shivering and vaguely heard a voice say, "Something's wrong."

"No," Loelle said. "She senses the magic."

"Then is she awake?"

Silence passed. I wasn't awake, but I wasn't asleep either. I was just . . . existing.

"Give her to me," Loelle said, and my all-but-lifeless body was passed into her arms. She grunted under my weight, and I perceived through my closed eyes that the light around us was nearly gone.

"Where . . ." I mumbled. That was all I managed to say, and it was a waste of effort. I knew these were the Blue Caves. I knew *where* I was. I wanted to tell her not to take me inside.

But after a few steps, I felt differently. The cold embraced me, enveloping me in its own protective shield. It swirled around me and within me and became part of me. I felt myself breathing easier, breathing deeper, and with each breath, I felt more alive. Light slowly began to fill the darkness, but it wasn't the white light of death or the yellow light of the sun.

It was blue.

Blue like the skies on a summer day. Or like the Ashwater Sea just north of Highwyn. A warmer shade of blue even than sapphires, the same stones that were set into the eyes of the Sentries outside the capital.

I opened my eyes and saw an enormous cave of black rock that appeared almost turquoise in the light. What was causing the strong shades of blue in here? My head felt foggy, making it hard to think.

"Don't be afraid," Loelle whispered. "I'll stay right beside you."

She lowered me gently into a bed of water, where I drew my first comfortable breath in hours. The water was cool, even cold, but I felt warm. More than that, I felt life pouring into me such as I'd never experienced before. It was healing my heart, or returning it to me, freeing it from Endrick's power. I flattened my palm over my chest and felt each beat, stronger than the one before it. I was an Ironheart no longer.

"I should be dead," I whispered, then glanced up at Loelle. "You saved my life."

Her smile was kind. Obviously, this wasn't the first time Loelle had heard those words, but it was the first time I'd ever spoken them with a full realization of how inadequate my gratitude was.

She said, "You will leave these caves a different person than you were before. What will you do with this second chance at life?"

I smiled back at her. "My hopes are what they always were. I want my final words before death to simply be that I lived."

She nodded, pleased with my answer. "Then you had better begin."

I followed her gaze to the far end of the water where the source of the light came from deep below, casting the entire pool in a strong blue glow.

Loelle allowed me to observe that for a few minutes, then I asked, "What is that light?"

"That is the source of Endrean magic. It fills these waters. Kestra, it is filling you."

I knew I was supposed to protest, that the consequences of what was happening to me could be terrible. I remembered how hard Simon had fought to keep me away from here, but as I lay immersed in these waters, my only thought was how wrong he had been. That if he understood how beautiful it was, how beautiful *magic* was, he would know that this was the right place for me.

"I want magic," I said to Loelle.

"You were born to this." Loelle had been dipping her hand into the water and now brushed her wet hand over my hair. "Claim your powers. Claim that which belongs to you."

"I'm only half Endrean. Will that matter?"

"That's what we're here to find out," she said. "But if your body could not tolerate magic, then you would have died in these waters."

"I'm more alive than I've ever been." I smiled over at her. "I want to swim."

She smiled back. "Go, my lady."

I dove into the water, breathing in the cool water as easily as I'd breathe air. Magic became my air instead, my life. The water flowed through my lungs and veins, transforming me, changing me, making me whole. The closer I swam to the blue light, the warmer I felt, the more complete I became. I passed through the blue glow to the light itself, basking in its presence until I knew upon swimming away that the light would come with me, because I was the light and the light was me.

Until I knew I had magic.

I surfaced near where I'd left Loelle, but emerged from the water perfectly dry. Stronger than ever, perfectly whole.

I raised my hands in front of me to examine them, turning them forward, then back. I ran them down my body, checking for signs of anything physically different about me.

Loelle laughed. "You look as you did before, you'll think and act as you did before. But you will not be as you always were. You are greater than that now, or you will be, as soon as you come to understand all that you can do."

"I want to know, I want to understand." I reached my arms into the air, stretching my body as magic continued to spread through me. I felt it building in me, spreading strength as it traveled. Spreading light and power and knowledge. Things I didn't even know that I knew.

Suddenly, I stumbled back, pressing a hand to my temple and gasping. Loelle stood. "My lady?"

It took a moment to catch my breath again, but only because I'd been caught completely off guard. I collapsed to my knees, trying to absorb what was happening to me.

Memories were flashing back into my mind, faster than I could sort them or separate them, like a series of pictures being thrust in front of my eyes, one after another after another.

"It's all right." Loelle brushed her hand across my back, lovingly, like a mother might do. Maybe like my mother had done for me, long ago.

I closed my eyes tight, but that only made it worse. "I can't stop what's happening, Loelle. I can't see everything all at once."

Her hand pressed against my back and my breaths became more even again. "They'll slow down, in time," she said. "And they'll begin to come together."

"Some are wonderful," I said, noting a memory of my adopted mother, Lily, swinging me around by the hands in the gardens of Woodcourt. "Others are not." I wished that closing my eyes was enough to keep out the worst of my history. Awful as those brief glimpses into my past were, no sooner had I retreated from the horror than the best of memories took their place. I tried to latch on to one and explore it further, but then it too turned to another and another again.

"Loelle, please help me!" Dizziness overwhelmed me, and my emotions were becoming stirred up. I collapsed to the ground.

Loelle crouched beside me and placed her hands on either side of my face. It didn't slow the memories, but whatever she was doing calmed my responses to them.

"It takes great courage to relive one's past," Loelle said. "But you are the sum of all your memories. To withhold the bad would be to deprive yourself of all that those difficult times taught you. You can do this, Kestra."

"I have to." I grabbed her arm and she helped me stand again. "I'll tell you what I'm seeing. If you can explain it, I want to know. I want to know who I am."

· TWENTY-NINE ·

SIMON

My eyes were already open when Trina called for us to rise. I'd barely slept ten minutes together and I had a pounding ache in my head, each pulse seeming to repeat Kestra's name, a constant reminder that by now, she had claimed her Endrean heritage.

If that had happened, then I should have been happy that at least she was alive, and I was. But I also understood far too well that her fate was sealed now. I might already be too late to stop the events that were now set in motion against her.

I looked over at Basil as we began saddling our horses. "Before we go to Reddengrad, you need to send word to Tenger about where the Olden Blade is."

Before I'd finished speaking, Basil began shaking his head, as if he'd already known that request was coming. "I'll reveal that after the Halderians agree to fight with my country. Not a moment before."

I stopped working to stare at him openmouthed. "How can you be so stubborn? If Kestra's alive, she needs to retrieve it."

"How can *you* be so stubborn?" Basil countered. "You refuse to do your part to seal our agreement, and then—"

"What you and Tenger decided has never been my agreement!" I shouted. "I owe you nothing!"

"Enough!" Trina pushed between us, then in a calmer voice to Basil added, "We have our orders and not a lot of time. Huge will take Gabe to recover at the Lonetree Camp. The three of us need to be on our way to the Hiplands."

I shook my head, transferring my anger from Basil to her. "I won't obey your orders, Trina. Not when I know your betrayal!"

Her eyes widened. "What are you talking about?"

"You sent a message to the Halderians, telling them where Kestra would be that day. That's why they attacked!"

"I never—"

"I found the etchings in your notepad. I saw what you wrote to them."

Trina shook her head. "I didn't arrange that attack, Simon."

"Then explain how they knew. Explain the note! Explain why your ears perk up every time the Olden Blade is mentioned. If Kestra dies, you will be first to try to claim it!"

"Yes, I would, and I probably would succeed this time. But that's irrelevant, because as far as any of us knows, Kestra is still alive."

"How disappointed you must be."

Trina's voice softened. "I knew Tenger's note would upset you. Especially after your mother—"

"Did you send the Dominion there too?"

I advanced on her, but Basil cut between us. "Simon, stop. Why would she—"

"She wants Kestra dead. The Halderians failed, so she went to the Dominion." I turned to her. "There are very few people who knew that was my mother's home—Gabe didn't know until we went there. But you knew."

Trina's face reddened. "And you think that I would work with the Dominion? That I would help them in any way?"

"Maybe you told yourself that Kestra was an Ironheart and couldn't remember who she truly was. You'd have an easy time justifying what you did."

"Except that I didn't do it. Gabe was with me while we searched for you in the Drybelt. He would know how I felt about finding her safe!"

"If you fight any louder, the Dominion will hear us," Huge said, walking over the hill with his horse already saddled and packed. "But I heard you." He drew a slow breath. "And I will say this. When I was looking for Gabe last night in the Dominion camp, I heard one of the officers near his tent say they never thought they'd have worked with a Corack."

"That could be anyone." The waver in Trina's voice made it clear how nervous she was.

"Not anyone." Huge's wide shoulders hunched and he seemed to be avoiding Trina's eye. "They never mentioned a name, but they did say *she* would finally get the reward she wanted."

That was enough for me. I turned to Trina. "Well?"

She squared her body to mine. "Simon, I have never pretended to like Kestra, and yes, I wish that I were the Infidante and not her. But I am supporting her. I am following the captain's orders to fight so that she can get the Olden Blade back. And if something goes wrong, if she never made it to the Blue Caves, then I might be the next Infidante. You'll have to support me the way you asked me to support Kestra."

"Or the way you're actually supporting her?"

Her hand shifted to her sword, and she made sure I noticed. "We're going to the Halderians *together*. And when we're there, you and I will stand before Commander Mindall and ask him if I've done anything to betray Kestra."

My eyes narrowed. "The day the Halderians attacked Lonetree Camp, did you come out with us to negotiate?"

"You know I didn't. Why?"

"Then how did you know their new commander is named Mindall?" Before she could answer, I grabbed my bedroll and stuffed it into the saddlebags. "I'm ready to ride whenever you are."

If the morning had been cold, it was nothing compared to the icy wind that began gusting around midday. I never complained though. It seemed like a perfect accompaniment to my mood.

Huge and Gabe were on their way to the Lonetree Camp, leaving me with only Trina and Basil for company. I wasn't speaking to Trina, which put me in the awkward position of having to talk to Basil, of all people. He rode at my side as we made our way toward the Halderians, a clan I neither liked nor trusted.

"You haven't said a word for miles," Basil said.

"What do you want me to say?" I replied.

"I want you to explain why you won't claim the throne."

I tossed a glare sideways at him. "That's not your business."

"We need the Halderians' help in defending Reddengrad. Your refusal to claim the throne is very much my business."

"What's your business?" Trina asked, riding up next to Basil. When neither of us answered, she said, "Is this about Simon not wanting to be king? Because I'm the one who figured out who he is. I'm the one who told Tenger."

"Naturally you told someone," I snapped. "That's what you do."

She groaned. "Honestly, Simon, you are impossible! Once you get a thought in your head, you never question it, you just assume you're always right! Well, you are wrong about me, you're wrong in nearly everything you've said about Basil—"

"What has he said about me?" Basil asked.

"—and you're wrong to refuse the Halderian throne. Simon, they need someone with a good heart to lead them."

I cursed under my breath. That wasn't my heart, not anymore.

She continued, "If I'm ever named as the Infidante—"

"Kes is still alive."

She tried again. "*If* I'm ever the Infidante, they will ask me who I choose as king—"

"Don't you dare."

"—and I would name you. Whether you want it or not, whether you deny the truth about the sword and that ring in your saddlebag, I don't care. If it's ever in my power, you will be king of the Halderians."

I glared at her. "If you carry out that threat, then my first order will be your execution for betraying the previous Infidante."

Her laughter quickly faded as she wondered if I was serious. Absolutely, I was.

After a long silence, Basil said, "Well, aren't you Coracks fun? If Reddengrad wins this battle, we'll invite you down for the victory party. I'm sure you two can suck the joy from any celebration." When I didn't reply, he added, "Simon, I wish you would claim the throne, and I haven't heard anything yet that helps me understand why you won't, but you still have a job to do. Get the Halderians to fight for Reddengrad, or I will not say where the Olden Blade is."

I snorted. It was not for him or for anyone to understand my reasons. I would do my best to get the Halderians to fight, and I would go to battle myself if the Dominion came. But nothing more.

Little else was said between any of us as we entered the Hiplands that evening. I'd been here only two weeks ago, with Kestra riding in my arms, smiling back at me as if nothing could ever come between us. The memory was a curse to me now.

As if she could read my thoughts, Trina said, "For what it's worth, Simon, if you see her again, she will probably still be the way you remember her . . . mostly."

It was worth nothing and only made me feel worse. Yet even as she spoke, an advance group of more than twenty Halderians rode toward us with posted colors and visible weapons. The girl who had helped me get Kestra out of Lonetree, Harlyn Mindall, was among them. I hoped we could count on her help here. Little else was in our favor.

Basil leaned toward me. "If you do have any influence with the Halderians, now is the time."

"I don't." But I stopped my horse between Basil and Trina's, hoping that whatever words fell from my mouth would sound more diplomatic than what was actually in my mind.

Commander Mindall was leading the group, and it was obvious from a distance that this wasn't a friendly welcome party. He held up his hand to stop his own procession, leaving us facing each other from a conversational distance.

He began, "We came to your camp three days ago hoping to talk, eager to understand our Infidante better. But you lied to us."

"Who's lying now, Commander Mindall?" I countered. "You weren't there to talk. You had other plans for the Infidante."

His smile thinned. "A necessary act, before she turns on us, and you know that she will, in time. But for now, your captain promised you'd come to help us, and here you are."

I glanced over at Basil, whose furrowed brow suggested I should keep my mouth shut. I started to respond, but Basil tilted his head. "What help do you need?"

Mindall's posture eased as he turned to Basil. "We have a small camp set up nearby. Stay with us tonight, and tomorrow we will escort you into Nessel."

He turned his horse with the obvious implication that we were to follow him. When we did, Trina rode up closer to him and said, "Commander, I hoped you might clear up a misunderstanding among my friends."

"If I can."

She tossed me a sideways glance. "How did you know where Kestra was three days ago?"

His laugh was cold. "You cannot possibly think I will reveal that source."

"This one is important. Did you receive a communication from a Corack telling you where she was?"

Mindall gave her what appeared to be a sincere nod of respect. "I will say this. On the night the Infidante was chosen, few of us cheered when we saw the blade in the hand of a Dallisor. We admired the way you fought for the Olden Blade, Trina, and we remember your mother. *If* you had contacted us, we would have heeded your call."

Trina's eyes widened at what Mindall had just implied. I only sent her an icy glare. "Was that the denial you were hoping for?"

"Simon, listen—"

"I will fight with you to protect the Hiplands, but do not mistake that for believing that you and I are on the same side of anything. I want nothing more to do with you."

She started to answer, then clamped her mouth shut. Whatever else she denied, we both knew that a part of her hoped Kestra had never made it to the Blue Caves. Trina would never give up her wish to be the Infidante of Antora.

And I would never trust her again.

· THIRTY ·

KESTRA

Loelle had explained to me every memory that she could, though she only knew a fraction of the thousands of images flashing through my head, some of them tiny details, and others, significant, life-changing events.

I remembered running through the corridors of Woodcourt and being scolded by Sir Henry. How I'd resented him, even then.

The opposite was true of my adoptive mother Lily, whom I'd loved more than life. I had a memory of leaning against a wall of her bedroom as her handmaiden dressed her in stiff formals for a supper in Lord Endrick's palace. She'd smiled at me but there was a clear pool of dread in her eyes.

There often was. My mother must have felt like a sort of prisoner at Woodcourt.

So had I, at times. I used to climb trees in the gardens, keeping a silent perch overhead when Sir Henry passed by with his officers, making plans in support of Lord Endrick. I'd learned early to avoid the king, though I now hoped the day would come when he'd wish he had avoided me.

Other memories filled my mind too, though I couldn't always place the year they had happened, or the setting, or who else had been with me. And when the memory conflicted with an idea that Lord Endrick had inserted into my mind, I couldn't always separate one from the other.

With one exception: I understood perfectly that the Dominion was my enemy, and that any memory that suggested otherwise was false. Everything else was like a dammed-up river, a route my mind desperately wanted to travel upon, but which only leaked out the smallest of details.

"Give yourself time," Loelle assured me. "You will sort this out."

If only time was on my side.

And although I had thought Loelle and I were only in the Blue Caves for an hour or two, when we finally emerged, the sun was already peeking over the horizon. I stared at it, grateful for the promise of a new day rather than more cyclings from my past. "Is it morning already?"

Loelle smiled. "My lady, it's been a full day and night since we entered the caves."

I turned to her, confused. How was that possible, when I'd not felt tired or hungry once?

Tenger and Wynnow were waiting in a cove of trees near the cave entrance, seated around a small morning campfire. I recalled asking Simon for a fire only four nights ago, but he had refused, claiming it would be unsafe. I'd been cold then, when I should have been warm in his company. And I was warm now, standing before people who emanated a cold desire to use me for their own ends.

They stood when they saw me, and from the corner of my eye, I saw Loelle signal to them to sit back down, and I was grateful for it. I didn't want any questions, nor could I offer any explanations for what had happened to me, what was still happening. I felt the magic stretching through my veins, even if it wasn't as strong as it had been in the caves. But I couldn't properly explain the feeling, nor was I certain if this was my own developing magic or whether I was simply reflecting the glow of the caves. And when I asked Loelle, she replied that we would have to wait and see.

Wait and see. How I hated that concept. I always had.

That made me smile. Whatever else magic had done for me, it was still not powerful enough to overcome my innate lack of patience.

Wynnow invited me to sit at the campfire and offered some boiled eggs. I knew I should've been half-starved, but I wasn't. I wasn't anything other than aware of the magic. It pulsed with every beat of my heart. *My* heart, free of Lord Endrick's grip. Every easy breath I drew was a reminder of my freedom from him.

"I will know when she's hungry," Loelle said sharply, motioning to Wynnow to withdraw the offer of eggs. "Kestra is in *my* care."

Wynnow straightened up, her face pinched with irritation, yet the only logical place to sit at the campfire was on the fallen log beside her. When I sat there, Loelle pressed her lips together, something Wynnow obviously took as a victory.

"Your appetite will return soon," Loelle explained, pretending not to be as irritated as I knew she was. "Quite voraciously at first, but that too, will pass."

She sent a look to Tenger as she finished speaking, and he nodded back at her. "If it involves me, you should say it aloud," I reminded them.

Wynnow smiled. "The captain and I were discussing what is the proper next step for you."

"That's obvious. I need to retrieve the Olden Blade, and . . ." Panic shot through me. "I don't know where it is! What if that memory doesn't return?"

"You don't have that particular memory," Tenger said, more calmly than I'd have expected, considering the stakes. "From what I can piece together, you made an attempt on Lord Endrick's life, which ended with you jumping through a window to escape. Basil was waiting for you. You gave him the Olden Blade and asked him to hide it from everyone, including you."

"And where did he hide it?"

Tenger clapped his hands together. "Well, that's the problem. Basil won't tell us yet, not until the Halderians agree to join in Reddengrad's defense."

I kicked at a pebble near my boot, wishing I had a better distraction for the frustration that was beginning to burn in my chest. "I don't trust the Halderians."

Tenger smiled. "You'll trust them less once your memory from about three years ago starts to rebuild itself."

I cocked my head, but he gave no further explanation. I asked, "Are we joining the battle too?"

Loelle leaned forward. "You're feeling strong, which is a good thing, but obtaining magic has placed you in a precarious state. You must take some time to understand yourself, as you now are."

"I'll figure it out, on the way to the battle."

Wynnow's stormy glare leveled in Loelle's direction became a much friendlier smile in mine. "If you are willing, my lady, I will take you over the border to Brill, where you will have refuge among my people until you are recovered."

I tilted my head. "How long will that take? I feel fine."

"It's not necessary for you to go all the way to Brill," Loelle said. "Your mind is clear of Lord Endrick's magic now, so you should begin to sort out the real from the unreal. And within a few days, we should know more about the magic within you. Then we can determine exactly what powers you have, if any."

I stared down at my hands, feeling the pulse of magic course through me, wondering what lay ahead for me now. I was at once nervous, excited, wary, and eager to begin experimenting with possibilities.

Loelle reached over and gave my hands a comforting squeeze, as if she sensed how I was feeling. I smiled back at her, grateful to be understood.

"Experimenting with her magic is better done in Brill," Wynnow said. "She has many enemies here in Antora, and none in my country."

Wynnow was right about that. I liked the idea of learning about magic somewhere my life wasn't constantly at risk. "We can go to Brill," I said, immediately hoping I wouldn't regret the decision. Loelle obviously disagreed. Her lips were pinched into such a fine line, I barely saw them anymore.

While the others broke camp, I wandered up the hillside to survey the land. We were in the lower elevations of the mountains, so I couldn't see to the horizon, but the view was extraordinary. The mountains here were snowcapped almost year-round, with striking peaks, rocky hills, and a dramatic waterfall that was already beginning to freeze for the winter months. Before the War of Desolation, before Lord Endrick destroyed his own people, this had been Endrean territory. A part of me belonged to this land, and despite whatever people might say about me one day, Antora was my home. I was determined to save it from Endrick's clutches.

Even if I needed magic to do so.

Even if it meant risking my life, and losing everything I valued—Simon.

I drew in a sharp breath, horrified at the direction of my thoughts. What if victory against Lord Endrick cost me a future with Simon? I didn't want that, I'd never choose that.

But I probably had already lost him. I'd be a fool to think otherwise.

I'd lost him. Nothing else would have stopped him from rescuing me in the Dominion camp. Instead, he sent Basil. Simon would be here now too, if he had wanted that. He was letting me go.

And the worst part was that I didn't blame him. Not after my role in the loss of his mother. Whether I deserved such blame didn't matter; I remembered with perfect clarity his last expression as he looked at me. How broken he'd looked, how empty.

"Kestra?" Wynnow was climbing the hillside and stopped by my side. "We're ready to leave."

I started toward the camp, but Wynnow touched my arm and lowered her voice. "You should tell Loelle not to join us."

"Why?"

"Tenger and I spoke last night of his plans for you. He wants Loelle to come to be sure they are carried out."

"What plans?"

She huffed, as if she was reluctant to say anything more, and yet knew it had to be done. "They want you to complete your quest as the Infidante. But when it's complete, they will . . . well, they do not want another Endrean with magic."

"Loelle is another Endrean with magic."

"They do not want *you* to have magic, my lady."

My fists curled. I marched down the hillside to find Tenger saddling my horse, and Loelle already on hers, ready to leave. But I held my temper enough to say, "Wynnow and I will go to Brill alone."

Unaware of how furious I was, Tenger casually shook his head. "Loelle needs to go. If the last few days have proved nothing else, it should be that a lot of people mean to harm you. You may need her help."

My laugh sounded bitter, and I'd intended it be so. "What kind of help do you mean? After I kill Endrick, will I need Loelle's help to die?"

Tenger suddenly looked as if he'd just swallowed his tongue, which was all the answer I needed. I yanked my horse's reins away from him and started to follow Wynnow out of camp, but he called out, "Yes, Kestra, what you are saying is true."

I stopped and turned with my mouth half-opened, incredulous that he would be so forthcoming.

He wasn't finished. "The truth is that because you're only half Endrean, we don't know how magic will affect you, but we do know what it's done to full-blooded Endreans. If I see signs of corruption in you, then it will force me to act." Tenger spoke so dispassionately, I wondered if he remembered we were discussing my life, and not some tactical battle plan. "I know how harsh that sounds, but if you had seen the destruction waged by the Endreans on this land during the war, you'd agree with me."

I shifted my weight, unable to counter his argument with anything more compelling than my desire to live. All I could think to say was, "I will not let that happen to me."

He smiled. "It is my sincerest hope not. But until then, should anything go wrong, Loelle can save your life. She is also the only one who understands magic, unless you plan to ask Endrick for advice. Complete your quest and then we can discuss your future."

Wynnow had descended the hill to stand at my side. With her eyes narrowed on Loelle, she said, "The Brillians will protect you. If necessary, from the Coracks."

"The Coracks aren't the problem," I mumbled. "It's the reason I might need protection from them that matters."

I stared at Loelle, then reluctantly nodded my permission for her to come. She fell in behind Wynnow and me as we rode away, though we'd only rounded the first bend before she caught up with me. "I can explain."

"Don't." Whatever she said would either be a lie or yet another conversation about the ever-growing number of people in line for my life. Neither was worth the effort of listening.

But Loelle talked anyway. "Kestra, your mother—your real mother, Anaya, had a powerful magic, that of cloaking her presence from others. But her true strength was simply in her determination, her forceful will. We see that same strength in you, and we'd be fools to overlook its potential for danger."

"I'd think you'd be glad to see an Infidante with such willpower."

"As Infidante, yes. You will need those traits to succeed. But what happens after you do, after you are an Endrean holding the Olden Blade, able to wield it just as he did?"

I looked back at her. "What do you mean? That the powers of the Olden Blade will pass to me?"

"We don't know. Nor are we sure how the magic will affect you."

"My mother was never corrupted."

Loelle's voice was firm. "Pardon me, my lady, but there were signs."

I wheeled my horse around to face her directly. "What are you talking about?"

"After you became the Infidante, Captain Tenger began learning more about Anaya. Many people believe the reason she had to pass the Blade to her servant, Risha, is because her powers were gone."

Yes, that was the story everyone knew.

But Loelle continued, "Except that wasn't true. Anaya had some magic in the closing days of her life; that's how she was able to write in the rock of the dungeon walls. So why did Risha really have the Blade? It wasn't because Anaya lost her magic."

I was quickly losing patience. "Why was it?"

"Risha had to take the Olden Blade from Anaya, because she had begun to talk about what she would do once she possessed the Scarlet Throne, the revenge she would seek on all Loyalists, and anyone who failed to bow to her."

"That doesn't mean she was corrupted."

"What else could it be?" Loelle pressed her lips together. "My lady, this magic now inside you is a weapon and it can be used for good or for evil. The line between the two is thinner than you may realize. Walk too close to the edge and you will fall."

"You never have," I said. "Why have you never been corrupted?"

"There is a reason," she said. "The truth is that—"

"We should keep going," Wynnow called back to us. I hadn't realized we'd fallen so far behind. "The sooner we get to Brill, the better."

Loelle glanced at me, a silent promise that she would explain when she could. I hoped the explanation would assure me that I was right to bring her along. Because my gut told me that I was headed into something far more dangerous than I was prepared to face.

Maybe I should've trusted Wynnow's warnings after all.

· THIRTY-ONE ·

SIMON

Last evening, I'd successfully ignored nearly everyone in the Halderian camp, and I hoped for the same luck today. As angry as I was, as broken as I was, and as sharp as my sword remained, it was better for everyone if I kept to myself.

For most of the day, I rode with Trina and Basil at the end of a long line of Halderians. Trina had already tried several times to open a conversation with me, but I'd had nothing to say to her before. She should have no reason to believe that would change now.

Finally, she asked, "Can you at least put aside your suspicions enough to focus on why we're here?"

I continued to ignore her, but Basil, who was riding between us, said, "She's right, Simon. We must work together to persuade the Halderians to fight with us in Reddengrad."

"Bring Reddengrad's soldiers here," I said. "If we defend the Hiplands, then the Dominion will never reach Reddengrad."

Basil shook his head. "If our soldiers cross the border, the Dominion will interpret that as an act of war."

"The Dominion is coming to make war on you!" I said. "They won't care which side of the border you're on."

"If we are wrong, and I hope we are wrong, then we cannot give the Dominion an excuse to attack us."

I sighed. "And if I am right, and you know that I am, then you have doomed the Halderians."

Basil said, "Claim the throne, Simon. Then you can order them into Reddengrad, to fight with us. Behind our borders, at least they will have some chance of survival."

"They don't need me. If Commander Mindall cares about his people, then he will do what's best for them."

Trina said, "If we explain that helping Reddengrad is the only way to get the Olden Blade back—"

"No!" I couldn't believe I had to explain this. "If they hear that Kestra doesn't have the Blade, they will feel even more license to go after her."

After a moment's contemplation, Trina turned to Basil. "You need to tell us where it is."

"I will, when I've got the Halderians' support in Reddengrad." Basil gestured at me. "You can make that happen now, Simon."

Trina started to argue with me too, but through a clenched jaw I said, "Both of you listen carefully, because I will never explain this again. King Gareth adopted me as his son, but we never spoke of me inheriting his throne. Never. The day the Dominion came to arrest him, he gave me his sword and his ring and told me to hide and protect them with my life, which I did, and which I have done ever since. Gareth never came back. I still have his sword and ring, but only because I hid like a coward while he gave his life for his people. I was never anointed, I never asked to be his heir, and I certainly won't stand before his people and claim otherwise."

Silence followed, then Basil said, "Gareth adopted you. That means he chose you as his heir."

"Well, I don't want it. Not that way."

"How can you be this selfish?" Trina's face twisted in anger. "When did this rebellion become about what *you* want?"

"It's never been about what I want!" Now my own temper flared, and it was all I could do to keep my voice down. "I fought when I was ordered to and killed when I had to, every single time hoping *this* would be the moment that made a difference! And finally, through battles and chaos and every kind of treason, I found someone that I *want* to make part of my life, but she's gone now. Accuse me of being foolish, or shortsighted, or cowardly, but don't you ever say that I am here because this is what I want!"

"Hush!" Trina said, her eyes locked forward.

Commander Mindall had fallen to the side of his soldiers, waiting for us to catch up. I worried that he'd overheard me, but instead he fell in beside Basil as Trina and I rode directly behind them.

In one hand he carried a halberd, which he handed to Basil. "Your weapon of choice, I believe?" Basil thanked him, but Mindall immediately moved on to strategy. "Captain Tenger informed me of the Dominion's plans. I've ordered a full defense of Nessel, and of all the Hiplands. It's time for the Halderians to stand our ground."

"That ground is not worth their lives," Trina said. "Sooner or later, the Dominion will break through whatever defenses you have in place, and they won't distinguish between a Halderian with a weapon and a civilian."

"Send them to Reddengrad instead," Basil offered. "We'll offer protection to your civilians in exchange for your soldiers fighting with us against the Dominion."

Mindall laughed. "You mean, in exchange for our men dying for you? It is not our fault that the Dominion is headed our way. That blame rests with Kestra Dallisor."

"How is it her fault?" He must've sensed my irritation for he reacted with a sharp turn of his head.

But Mindall quickly recovered to say, "The Infidante was supposed to marry this prince of Reddengrad beside me. If she had, the Dominion would have had their alliance. But thanks to her defiance, my people are facing extinction." Addressing Basil again, he said, "We've worked hard for what little land we have. I won't lose it."

"What if you had a king who ordered otherwise?" Trina asked. I cast her a glare, but she ignored me.

Mindall turned back to her. "The Halderians have not had a king since Gareth was executed by the Dallisors three years ago."

"He might've named an heir."

Now Mindall turned his horse to face her directly. "Gareth died after living alone in hiding for some time. He could not have named an heir, and if he had, surely that person would have come forward by now."

"Sir," one of Mindall's men said, a note of warning in his voice.

But Mindall continued, "The Halderians have no king, and the Infidante is missing. I am in command." His eyes shifted to me. "We welcome your help in fighting alongside our people. With a little luck, a few of us might survive."

After that he signaled to his men to pick up their pace. We followed, but I felt as if a stone had lodged in my gut. When had the Halderians ever benefitted from a little luck?

It surely wasn't now. Because one of Mindall's men, highest on the hill of the road ahead, suddenly called back, "The Dominion! They are coming!"

I withdrew my sword and turned my horse to get a look for myself, but the worst of my imagination could not have prepared me for what I saw in the distance. Hundreds of Dominion soldiers were on the march toward us. Most were on foot, but with a garrison this size, I knew Endrick would also send his oropods and giant condors and every other foul creation of his magic. We were now only skimming the surface of the battle that was coming for us.

Trina was beside me but leaned forward in her saddle and squinted ahead at a horde of four-legged hairy beasts trampling over everything in their path. "I think those are carnoxen."

I hadn't heard of them and apparently, neither had Basil, but between us, Trina cursed and added, "The carnox has the body of an ox but the ferocity and speed of a wolf. Their flesh is thick and leathery, so you'll have to stab direct and hard. Above all, don't let them gore you with their tusks. That's how they tear their prey apart."

Basil had a sword but reached for his new halberd instead, rotating it with one hand as if he'd fought with one many times before. I doubted it would be enough for the creatures who were quickly approaching. However, before either of us could act, Mindall rode up near us.

"How fast can the three of you ride?"

"Fast." Trina didn't blink as she spoke.

"I've already sent my daughter to Nessel, and she has no idea any of this is coming." Mindall gathered his reins in his hands. "I need you to ride ahead and warn my people to arm themselves."

"You see now what we're facing," I said. "Send your people to Reddengrad."

I noticed that Mindall had been examining my sword as I spoke, but if he recognized it, he said nothing. Instead, he stifled a deep cough before saying, "Anyone who can hold a weapon will stand at the gates of Nessel and defend it. We'll try to delay them here, but we might only give you until dawn to be ready."

I scowled, but immediately started down the hill toward the Hiplands, flanked by Basil and Trina.

"If we obey Mindall's orders, the Halderians will die," Trina said.

"Then we ignore them," I said.

They were the last words we spoke as we raced through the night toward the Hiplands, arriving on the outskirts of Nessel long after midnight. An advance party of three fully armed women met us there with clearstone torches, with Harlyn in the center of the trio. Wisps of her short hair fluttered against her cheeks, but her focus was such that she seemed not to notice.

Instead, her eyes quickly settled on me, boring through me with the intensity of her stare. Then her brows pressed together, and she said, "Something happened to you, Simon. What is it?"

I looked away, intensely uncomfortable. It was a relief when Trina said, "Your father sent us to warn you. The Dominion has sent a much larger army than we'd expected. They're headed this way."

Harlyn's attention shifted. "Is my father still alive?"

Basil said, "He intends to hold off the Dominion army for as long as he can, but the enemy has probably already broken through his lines on their way here. Your people are invited to take shelter in Reddengrad, if all those who can wield a weapon will stand with us and fight."

"Stay in Nessel and your deaths are certain," I said. "But if you go to Reddengrad and join the strength of their army, your people have some chance of survival."

Harlyn's eyes narrowed. "How long do we have?"

"Till dawn, if we're lucky. Tell the people to take nothing with them but their families and to leave now."

Harlyn gestured to the women on either side of her. "Begin the evacuation at once. I'll help out here."

While she was speaking with them, Basil looked over at me. "This is the right thing to do, Simon."

"Is it?" A weight roughly the size of a boulder had settled on my shoulders, and I returned Basil's stare. "Tell me that Reddengrad can protect these people."

His silence told me more than I wished it did: There was little chance for any of us to survive a Dominion attack, no matter where we were.

Harlyn rode up to us but addressed me directly. "I saw the look you just gave Basil, but all is not lost. We have some surprises waiting in Nessel."

Trina patted a large satchel on the side of her horse and even laughed a little. "I have a surprise here too, thanks to the Brillians. This battle is not lost yet!"

· THIRTY-TWO ·

KESTRA

With Wynnow's expert guidance, we made excellent time through the Watchman Mountains, reaching Snowbourne shortly after dark. This small village was the last stop before the Brillian border, and populated almost entirely by Loyalists, so I kept up the hood of my cloak and went straight into the room of the inn that Wynnow arranged for us.

When she left to order our supper, Loelle asked, "Any changes to your memories?"

"I can't remember anything more of Simon," I mumbled. "Maybe I'm afraid to remember him because I know Lord Endrick wants those memories too."

She smiled. "The king has no more access to your memories, nor your mind. What do you remember?"

"Darrow. But it isn't the old memories. I think—" Tears welled in my eyes. "After Simon took me from Woodcourt a few days ago, I nearly drowned in a river at the edge of All Spirits Forest. Darrow saved me; I know it was Darrow who pushed me from the water. He must be there, in that forest. I think Lord Endrick banished him there as punishment."

Loelle reacted without surprise and took hold of the conversation as if she had been waiting for this very moment. "Hundreds of people eternally wander those woods. Just alive enough to be aware of the world. Too dead to ever join it. They are cursed."

As was I. I remembered that too. Endrick had told me I would reach a point when there were no more paths to victory.

Loelle said my name and started to say something more, but when Wynnow entered with a servant of the inn carrying bowls of stew, she closed her mouth and said almost nothing the rest of the night.

At dawn, we were back on the road toward Brill, crossing the border by late afternoon. To my surprise, a box carriage was waiting there for us, though it was a far greater surprise when the door opened and I recognized the woman who stepped out to greet us.

"Imri Stout?" This was the handmaiden who had been assigned to my service after I attacked Lord Endrick. I was beyond confused and my expression surely showed it.

Imri nodded. "Wynnow sent me to Woodcourt for your protection until the Coracks could rescue you. A Brillian would never be a captured servant."

By then, Wynnow had already dismounted and said, "Imri is here now for a very different purpose. She will teach you to use your magic."

"That isn't necessary." Loelle's voice betrayed her irritation. "I can teach Kestra all she needs to know."

Imri looked at Loelle with pure disdain. "Lady Dallisor is in Brill now. She will train with us." Imri motioned us toward the carriage. "Let's ride together in there. Our drivers can handle your horses."

Wynnow strode forward first, and I noticed the men who opened the doors for her gave her the appropriate bows. Somehow,

I'd never thought of her as royalty, but now that she was in her home country, she certainly played her role well.

At Imri's gesture, I started to follow Wynnow into the carriage, then stopped, as if my feet had suddenly turned to lead. Wynnow leaned out. "What's wrong?"

"I don't like small . . ." My voice trailed off as I gritted my teeth and balled my hands into fists. I knew I'd have to get in the carriage, and showing weakness in front of the Brillians over such a minor thing was the last thing I wanted. Closing my eyes, I entered before I could think better of it, followed by Loelle. The door shut behind us and I gripped the seat, only releasing it when Imri noticed. If she had disapproved of me when the biggest problem on my mind was a potential marriage, she would have far more reason to doubt me now.

We rode for about an hour in silence before I noticed Loelle had fallen asleep. As if she had been waiting for such an opportunity, Wynnow immediately gestured at her companion.

"Aside from being a brave and loyal spy for the Brillians, Imri is also the foremost expert on magic in our land. She knows some tests to help us narrow down what cluster of magic you may have."

I arched a brow. "Cluster?"

Imri leaned forward. "There are ten, although the powers within each cluster may vary according to strength and ability. To draw upon your powers, no matter how powerful or weak, you must have full concentration. I know when we last met, your mind was altered due to Lord Endrick's magic. I hope you can be more serious now." Before I could answer, she began counting off her fingers. "First is the ability to influence another's mind."

"How Endrick took my memories," I said.

"Or how he communicates orders to his Ironhearts," Wynnow added.

Imri said, "Second is the ability to influence another's actions."

I thought of when Endrick ordered me to kneel. Despite every effort on my part not to obey him, I had fallen to my knees. One day, I would find a way to resist him. I was determined never again to kneel before him.

Imri said, "Third is an influence on objects and fourth is the influence on nature."

I wondered if that was the way my mother, Anaya, had carved into the rock of the dungeons, leaving clues for how to find the Olden Blade the first time. If only there were any clues for how to find it again, without having to rely on Basil's help.

Imri nodded at Loelle. "She has the fifth cluster, to influence health. The same ability allows Endrick to create Ironhearts. Sixth is the ability to become undetectable, or to mask one's thoughts from others."

I straightened up. "That was my mother's gift. Endrick never took it from her. He doesn't have this ability."

"Unless he obtained it elsewhere," Wynnow said. "Surely other Endreans possessed this gift."

"Seventh is the ability to expand one's own strength or talents," Imri continued. "Eighth is the ability to create."

"Endrick's creatures, his technologies and weapons," Wynnow clarified. The explanation wasn't necessary. I had already understood that.

"Ninth is what we simply call recalling," Imri said. "In the moment of need, a person with this magic will recall the information they require, even if it vanishes from their mind once it's no longer necessary."

Maybe Loelle had that too. She seemed to always have a solution for any problem a person had.

"And tenth is the power to take magic from others—by killing them," Imri finished. "As far as we know, Endrick is the only Endrean ever to have this power."

"Is there any way to guess at what cluster is mine?" I asked.

Imri steepled her fingers, as if preparing herself to work. "We must test you, one cluster at a time. Since we're in this carriage, I think we should start at the beginning, the influence of another mind."

Wynnow leaned in toward me. "Do you know what I'm thinking?"

I grinned back at her. "With my confused mind, I can't even tell you what *I'm* thinking at any given moment."

"Be serious, Kestra. Do you know what I'm thinking about?"

I looked deeply into her eyes, hoping for a window into her thoughts to open, or for any sort of clue to decipher an answer. But I wasn't supposed to figure it out. If that was my power, then shouldn't I just *know*?

And I didn't.

I leaned back and rolled my eyes. "Next."

Wynnow pointed at Loelle. "Give her a silent command, from your mind to hers, to wake up and ask what we're having for supper tonight."

"What *are* we having?" I asked.

"Kestra!"

"All right." I focused on Loelle, my immediate goal simply being to cause her to stir. But again, nothing happened.

"We can eliminate the first cluster," I said. "And the second, for that matter. I can't make Loelle yawn, much less influence her to wake up."

A vein popped out in Imri's neck, I swore it did. "Let's try the third cluster, then, to influence objects." She widened her palm, revealing a single pearl earring on it. "Can you move this to your hand, without touching it?"

I tried it. And no, I couldn't. Nor could I move it on her hand, crush it, or cause it to do anything.

I slumped back in my seat. "Enough. I'm done being tested for now."

"My lady—" Wynnow began, but Imri touched her arm, and whispered something to her. I distinctly heard the word *defect*. Meaning those who are capable of magic but fail to develop it.

When she caught me looking, Imri tried to cover it up by saying, "Don't worry. You're probably tired, or the magic is still too fresh."

"Of course." I tried to sound hopeful, though I didn't believe either of those reasons was to blame. The problem was that a part of me hoped I was a defect. Yes, I needed magic to have a chance against Lord Endrick.

But if I never developed magic, then I might still have a chance with Simon.

I doubted there was any future where I could have both.

· THIRTY-THREE ·

SIMON

Harlyn had certainly sparked our curiosity about how Nessel might be prepared for a Dominion attack, but then, I was equally curious about what might be inside the satchel dangling from Trina's saddle. The two girls stared at each other a moment, silently negotiating who might announce their news first.

It would be Trina. Arching her neck, she dismounted and withdrew from her satchel a wood box, then carefully laid it on the ground while we gathered around it. She slid open the lid to reveal a roll of burlap packed in straw, then glanced up at us with excitement dancing in her eyes. "You remember the Dominion fire pellets?"

Of course we did. They were shot from shoulder cannons and exploded almost instantly upon hitting metal. We could avoid the worst of their impact if only a few came our way, but in numbers, they were lethal.

Trina added, "Packed in here is a single fire pellet, one large enough to explode a hillside. You only have to squeeze on it, then throw."

Or have it thrown at us, should we lose control of such a device. I shook my head. "It's a dangerous thing for the Brillians to want

Lord Endrick's technologies, his mutations. And it's more dangerous for us to fight him with his own tools of war."

"I disagree." Harlyn crouched beside Trina, hoping to examine the contents of the box more closely, but Trina shut the lid again and added, "This is Brillian technology, not Endrick's magic."

I exchanged a cautious look with Basil. "What good will that do us here?" he asked.

Trina shrugged. "Maybe none, unless it's our last chance to stop the Dominion."

"We're not there yet," Harlyn said, rising again. "Come with me and see what we've been doing."

We returned to our horses, dividing into pairs to fit on the narrow road toward Nessel. Harlyn rode near me, lowering her voice to keep our conversation from the others. "If something is wrong, you can talk to me."

I looked over at her, ready to explain that we barely knew each other, ready to lie and say that I was fine. I couldn't say the truth, not to anyone, maybe not even to myself. It'd only worsen the damage to my heart, or what was left of it. Harlyn only nodded at me as if she knew that and understood.

I was relieved when the city came into better view, anything for a distraction from my thoughts. Since my last visit here only weeks ago, walls of tall wood slats had been built up around Nessel with what appeared to be a single gated entrance. With the advent of a new Infidante, obviously the Halderians had known war would eventually come to the Hiplands.

"You said you have ways of defending this city?" Trina asked Harlyn.

"Yes, though we've never had to test them." Harlyn motioned for us to follow her through the gates. The evacuation must be ahead of us, since I saw no other people, though it was still dark enough I might have missed them in the shadows of the side roads.

Other than the high walls, Nessel was exactly how I remembered it, with cobblestone walkways and smooth dirt roads for the horses and wagons. When we'd come before, it had felt as abandoned as it was now, except then, it was because the people had gathered at the edge of town for a meeting. That was where Kestra had been named the Infidante.

It was also where Tenger had tried to kill her. And she was with Tenger now. Every time my thoughts drifted there, I became nearly paralyzed with worry. But for now, I had to put it aside. I *had to*, or else I'd be no use here.

"Stay on the stone paths," Harlyn warned.

"Why?" Basil asked, scurrying back off the road.

She smiled back at him. "We don't normally advertise this to outsiders, but our city is founded on an underground river. Believing that the Dominion would come for us one day, we built in quick escape routes everywhere we could. Holes have been dug into the roads, then covered with fabric and wood and disguised to look like dirt roads. If we are attacked, the plan is to pull out the wood and lower ourselves by rope into boats to go downriver. There are hundreds of holes throughout the city."

"That was why your father wanted everyone to stay and defend this place," I said.

She groaned. "No, my father wanted us to stay because his only instinct is to fight. An evacuation is better." She dismounted, motioning for us to do the same, then crouched beside an unremarkable spot in the road, aiming the clearstone torch downward. Only then did I see the outlines of a light brown fabric with dirt scattered over the top of it. She lifted up one corner and we peeked in to see a long drop-off into darkness below. "Before everyone left, we had them remove the wood, but this fabric disguise remains. When the Dominion rides over the holes, they'll fall into the underground river. My idea, by the way."

"It's brilliant," I said. She blushed, but it had been a sincere compliment. I was genuinely impressed.

"And is that for the condors?" Trina asked, pointing to a tower in the center of the city, clearly visible in the moonlight.

I squinted, seeing what appeared to be a cannon there, but I hoped that wasn't the plan. These birds were large enough to carry a grown man and had talons capable of killing him. They'd easily outfly a heavy cannonball.

"Nets." Harlyn kept her eyes on me as she answered Trina's question. "Big nets."

"I'll go into the tower," Basil offered. "I'll watch for the enemy's approach."

While he ran off in one direction, Trina's attention turned to the path along which we'd come. "I'll go shut the gates, slow them down when they do come." When Harlyn didn't respond, still keeping her eyes on me instead, Trina added, "Then I'll single-handedly defeat the entire horde with my sword, a toothpick, and a sewing needle, shall I?"

I rolled my eyes at Trina's sarcasm, still aware of Harlyn's focus on me. And more than a little bothered to realize that I had been staring back.

To Trina, I said, "If you're at the entrance, I'll go to the far end of town for any soldiers who get past the traps."

"I'm coming with you," Harlyn offered. "You'll want my help."

"Help?" Trina echoed with a smile. "That's what you two are calling it?"

If Harlyn heard, she pretended not to and only led me along the cobblestones on a winding maze through the city. "Nessel is a fine city and worth protecting," she explained. "I didn't think you would come here, not after the confrontation at the Corack camp."

"How did you know to come to the Corack camp?" I asked. "Who told you that Kestra would be there? Was it Trina?"

Harlyn laughed. "Trina? No, they'd have told me if it was Risha Halderian's daughter. My father only said it was someone the Coracks trust with their lives." Which wasn't helpful at all. We trusted every Corack with our lives.

We rounded a corner, then Harlyn continued, "The Halderians don't hate the Infidante. But half of us believe she cannot succeed. The other half worry that her success will make her the next tyrant to assume the Scarlet Throne."

"She will succeed, Harlyn. And she is no tyrant. She fights with us."

"Where is she now?" I turned forward again, and after a loud and lengthy silence, she added, "At least you are here, and your two friends."

Friends. One whom I'd accused of every sort of betrayal, and one who'd behaved far better toward me than I ever had to him.

At the far end of Nessel, Harlyn warmed a clearstone, then led me into a shop with shelves loaded with bags marked as saltpeter. "Is that really what's in there?" I asked, brushing my knuckles along the bags as I walked down the row. My mind was already racing with possibilities.

"Trina may have a single fire pellet the size of a small boulder, but we can make the saltpeter into hundreds of explosives. And since I know you're about to ask, yes, we have an excellent wagon for hauling it all to Reddengrad." She touched my shoulder and I turned back to her, though she was standing so close, I had to step away. "You should rest now, Simon. I can see that you're exhausted."

"I'm fine." Which was a lie and she knew it.

"Your eyes are bloodshot, your shoulders look as if you're carrying a mountain on your back, your movements are wooden. It's as if something inside you died." She drew in a sharp breath, and when our eyes connected again, I knew she was seeing deeper into my heart than I dared to admit. In the gentlest of tones, she asked, "Who was it?"

My heart raced, hurting again, breaking again. Since the night my mother . . . since that night, I'd tried my best not to feel anything, not pain or despair or grief . . . or love, which hurt most of all. My emotions were so knotted that if I pulled a single thread to explain myself, I feared I would unravel entirely. But Harlyn wasn't about to let this go.

She said, "A year ago, my family set out northward, hoping to trade with some Antorans along the coast. On our way, we saw Dominion soldiers approaching us on the road. My mother had some silver bars in the back and she went to hide them. As expected, the Dominion stopped our wagon to collect for the king. When they realized we were the Banished, as they call us, they set the wagon on fire and we ran for our lives." Harlyn's right foot had been jittering while she spoke, but now it went perfectly still as she added, "My mother didn't make it."

A tear rolled down my cheek, pairing the image of her mother with the cries of my mother. I knew exactly how awful that must have been, because I knew how awful it was for me too.

She sniffed, getting my attention. "I don't know who you lost, but whoever it was—"

"My mother too," I said, barely above a whisper.

Without another word, Harlyn drew me into her arms. After an awkward few seconds, I folded my arms around her too, accepting the healing she was attempting to offer. She let me grieve there, let me feel selfish and weak and foolish while silently communicating an understanding that if I was any of those things, what happened to my mother still wasn't my fault.

I wasn't sure how long we remained that way, only that at some point, it wasn't a hug of comfort or compassion. Her fingers combed through the back of my hair, stirring me up inside, her touch filling holes that had been punched through me over the last couple of days. I tightened my arms and pressed my hands into her back, aware of how very close she was, her dark hair against my cheek, her breath on my neck. And I still hadn't let her go.

She pulled away first, but only enough to stand face-to-face with me. With her thumb, she brushed a stray tear from my cheek and left her hand there.

I'd needed someone to understand my loss. But at some point, the hug that I'd needed had become an embrace that a part of me wanted. And not just an embrace.

What if Harlyn and I—

"You need to rest, Simon." Harlyn led me to a chair in the corner, sitting close beside me with her arms around my shoulders for comfort. No sooner had I settled in than I was asleep, awakening what felt like minutes later to the sound of a screech overhead. It was lighter outside, so a few hours must have passed, but Harlyn was at the window now and I leapt to my feet to join her. There we saw a giant condor flying overhead, a black shadow against the early morning sky. Its rider would seek out any signs of life, and if found, would use a shoulder cannon to rain the Dominion's fire pellets over the city. Though small, if they dropped enough of them, the shop where Harlyn and I were hiding would be flattened within seconds.

With a swooshing sound, a net flew out from the clock tower in the town square. It wasn't a direct hit, but a corner caught hold of the condor's wing, which began tilting, as if attempting to shake off the net. It tilted hard enough at one point that it dropped its rider, then flew away.

Harlyn winked at me. "We have nothing like Brillian technology or Endrick's magic, but never say the Halderians can't make the best glue in the region."

More condors were coming. From his position in the tower, Basil hit the second one directly, a riderless bird which sharply nose-dived. He hit the third as well, though by now, the others seemed to know he was in there. They began circling over the tower, higher than Basil could reach with his nets, if he even knew they were there.

"Get out," I mumbled beneath my breath. Did Basil understand he was being targeted?

Whether he did or not, the largest condor suddenly angled toward the tower. At the last moment, it dropped downward and the rider launched fire pellets into the open tower windows. Seconds later, the entire tower exploded, crumpling like it was made of twigs. My breath caught in my throat. If Basil was anywhere inside that tower, he could not have survived.

That's when I heard the first call of the oropods, their screeches and cries as they fell into the underground river. It was followed by the shouts of other riders to stay off the dirt. I also recognized angry growls that must have come from carnoxen falling into the holes and becoming trapped midway.

But it was only minutes later when those that had survived flooded the street directly ahead of us. Harlyn emptied her disk bow as they approached, though it took multiple disks to bring down any single carnox. When more kept coming, I withdrew my sword, then said to Harlyn. "I'm going out there."

"Me too." Harlyn withdrew a thinner blade from a sheath at her side. "I'm with you, Simon."

My smile at her was grim, but there was no time for anything more before beasts began entering the square.

Once outside, I first engaged an oropod that had been charging directly at me, stabbing it from the front, then pulling it down by the reins. The rider leapt to his feet, but Harlyn caught him from behind. When he fell, she smiled at me, though her grin immediately dropped as a new sound entered the square.

"Carnoxen!" Harlyn cried.

At least twenty of the beasts streamed toward us, most of them stampeding for the city's rear gates, but a few had noticed us. Trina had described them well, though she had failed to mention their thick dark fur from their shoulders to the tail. That would make it harder to know where to aim.

"Stay near me," I called to Harlyn. I raised my sword at the beast, but the blade merely grazed it across the shoulder. Its flesh was more than leathery; it was like stone. The carnox turned on me, baring its teeth, but Harlyn caught it from the side, stabbing it from above, at the back of its neck. It howled with a gravelly cry, then fell dead.

"There're too many!" Harlyn cried as she was nearly overrun by another incoming horde of animals.

I grabbed her hand and pulled her back into the shop, hoping we hadn't been seen by any riders. I didn't think so, but Harlyn and I still stood with our backs against the door to hold it closed, in the event anyone tried to get in.

Gradually, the noise outside faded away, the danger passing by. Harlyn rolled toward me, keeping one shoulder against the door. With only the single clearstone for light, I felt her gaze more than I saw it, and it seemed to heat the air around me. Finally, she said, "That probably wasn't the way you hoped to wake up."

I peered out the window and indeed, the streets had gone silent. Seconds later, Harlyn was at my side, her hand on my shoulder. She whispered, "You're a good fighter. Your mother would be proud of you."

Instinctively, I stepped back. "Harlyn, last night—"

That was as far as I got before Harlyn leaned forward and kissed my cheek. "My mother would be proud of me too, Simon. Don't ruin this moment with logic."

"Simon! Harlyn!" Basil's voice startled us apart. I flung open the door and was relieved to see both Basil and Trina on horseback. Basil was filthy, as if he'd rolled in sweat and dirt, but both of them were uninjured, better news than I had dared to hope for.

Basil trained his eyes on the city's rear gates. The army that had emptied out through there was no longer visible, but he continued staring as if watching them flee. "It's time to follow the battle into Reddengrad, my friends. I daresay it will be far more difficult there."

"We've honored our half of the agreement," I said, facing him. "Now honor yours."

Basil smiled. "I already have, days ago. Before we left the Lonetree Camp, I asked one of the Coracks to give Tenger a message. It will tell him everything he needs to know of where I hid the Olden Blade. He's probably on his way to retrieve it right now."

"Where is it?" Trina asked, sounding far too eager.

But Basil shook his head. "It's better if no one else knows. If you're captured in the coming battle, I don't want that information tortured out of you."

I'd been wrong about Basil. He was neither the fool nor the villain I had made him out to be. More likely, I'd been wrong about nearly everything thus far.

I showed Basil and Trina the storehouse of saltpeter and together we loaded it into a wagon while Harlyn fetched other supplies I'd asked for, namely salt, sugar, and any food that was easily available.

Once we were ready, Harlyn invited me to ride along in the wagon with her but I made excuses to go on horseback, claiming it was safer. That was true enough. My emotions were brittle and fragile, and Harlyn was eager to heal them. I knew what would happen if I spent too much time alone with her, what had almost happened back in that shop. So I accompanied Trina and Basil out on horseback, following the wide path of destruction torn by the oropods and carnoxen.

We'd stopped a good number of them, but not enough. Far too many had gotten past us, and surely the Dominion had another wave still coming, which meant by morning, the planned devastation of Reddengrad would already be under way.

· THIRTY-FOUR ·

KESTRA

It was dark when we arrived at Brill's capital city of Osterran. I wasn't sure what the buildings here were made of, but the walls were as white as Brillian hair and glistened in the starlight. Rather than the cobblestone or hardened dirt roads of Antora, the Brillian streets were like glass, slightly translucent, appearing almost as if water flowed beneath them. The homes were equally smooth, with no clear seams in the corners. Instead, one home connected fluidly to the next.

The only exception was the palace, which sat alone in the center of a large and rolling field of grass, still green despite the late season. The palace was made of the same smooth material as the houses, but the gold Brillian flag with the black circle in the center flew from every spire. It was entirely unlike what Endrick had made of his palace back in Highwyn, which felt as foreboding and cloistered as Endrick himself was.

Thinking of him, of my responsibilities against him, I shuddered in my seat. "I shouldn't have come," I murmured.

At first, I didn't think anyone had heard me, but then I noticed Wynnow's eyes had narrowed sharply. "What are you talking about?"

"The Dominion will seek revenge for my rescue," I said. "They'll bring war to the Halderians, or to Reddengrad or the Coracks. I've got to go back to Antora, do my part."

Wynnow shook her head, suddenly in the role of a stern governess. "Your part is to learn magic! Don't you see how vulnerable you are right now? Your memories are incomplete, your magic is nonexistent, and you do not have the Olden Blade. Where is it?"

"I don't know! But I can still help in that battle."

I'd spoken more sharply than I should have, and Wynnow's tone now reflected mine. "Your purpose is bigger than that battle! Learn magic. Nothing else matters, because without the Olden Blade, magic is your only chance to stand against Lord Endrick. Until you can use it, his terrible reign will continue." She leaned forward. "If you can't learn to stop him, then every death, every burning village, every prisoner filling your father's dungeons will be your fault."

Her words hung in the air like a dense fog. I nearly choked on them, unable to offer any defense for myself.

"That's unfair, Wynnow." Loelle put a hand on my arm and gave it a comforting squeeze. "Kestra is not responsible for Lord Endrick's crimes."

Imri leaned forward, her eyes on me. "No, not for the crimes, but if she does not learn magic, the crimes will continue, and she must accept blame for that."

"She will learn it," Loelle said. "With my help."

"Or ours." Wynnow spoke as if that were the end of the matter, timing her words exactly as the carriage door opened for us.

Four men in long gold robes awaited us on the steps to the palace entrance. They bowed low to Wynnow as she passed, and after they straightened, one man stepped forward.

With a voice of confident authority, Wynnow asked, "Where is my mother? I have good news for the queen."

The spokesman simply said, "The queen sent us." As if that was enough of an explanation.

Wynnow sighed before saying, "Counselors, this is Kestra Dall—Kestra, the Infidante of Antora. With her is a physician in service of the Coracks." Who apparently would go unnamed, and I knew from Loelle's clenched jaw that she felt the insult. Wynnow had no need of introducing Imri, who took her place at their side, facing me with an expression of disapproval far worse than anything I'd seen when she served me at Woodcourt.

I decided to mirror them. It seemed appropriate. Or at least, equally rude.

"What can you do?" the spokesman asked.

Already irritated, my brows furrowed. *"Do?"*

"You are tasked with killing Lord Endrick, correct? What skills do you have to accomplish this? Can you use a sword?"

I would have loved to demonstrate my skills right then, preferably on him. "Yes, reasonably well."

A grunt followed that. "Do you have any special access to Endrick's court?"

Lately? "I highly doubt it."

A longer grunt, to be sure I heard it. Then, "Is it true, that you lost the Olden Blade?"

I'd had enough. Rolling my eyes as visibly as possible, I said, "It is true that I am the Infidante, and I will do my best to succeed in my quest."

Loelle stepped forward, addressing Wynnow. "The Infidante is tired. Perhaps you would show her to her quarters?"

"Of course." Wynnow dismissed the men who descended the stairs while we continued up.

In a voice not nearly as quiet as it ought to have been, Loelle said to me, "Don't worry about what anyone here thinks, you're doing fine. Among other flaws, Brillians are not patient. They don't understand that you need time to figure out your magic."

"I'm not patient either," I snapped, then took a breath. *If* she was a friend to me, then Loelle was one of the few I had. I couldn't afford to lose her help. In a calmer voice, I added, "Wynnow isn't the only one who's wondering if I can complete this task, or how my magic might manifest. I doubt myself more than anyone."

Loelle put an arm around my shoulders. "Maybe they couldn't figure it out inside the carriage because your magic won't fit in such a small place. Tomorrow, we'll try something on a bigger scale."

I knew she intended that to comfort me, but it had the very opposite effect. I kept hearing Simon's words in my head, that the more powerful I became, the more dangerous I would be if I turned bad.

When I turned bad.

Loelle said nothing more while Wynnow finished escorting me to the south wing of the palace. She opened the door for me, revealing a room far more elegant than anyplace I'd ever been, even when

I was recognized as Sir Henry's daughter. The ceiling was tall and painted to resemble the clouds in the daytime and to produce starlight at night, as it did now. The curtains were shear and radiated various pastel colors at different angles. The carpets were soft and thick, but nothing to compare with the bed that beckoned me to enter and disappear within its blankets. How I longed just to sleep.

Wynnow said, "I'm sorry for what happened in the carriage, and for the ill manners of the men who greeted us. That was about me, not you. My mother is disappointed that my joining the Coracks has not produced quicker results, and I've passed that burden on to you."

So Brillians even spurned their own. I said, "The burden was already mine. I'm the one who must complete the quest. All that the rest of you can do is hold our battle lines until I do my part."

"Agreed." Wynnow stepped in closer. Her eyes gave the appearance of sympathy, but something deeper in them was calculating the exact words she wanted. "And we will do our part until you can use magic. But you must remain here to learn it, no matter what is happening to our friends in Antora. If you leave before you're ready, you could become the reason the rebellion fails."

As she'd intended, her words struck me like a hot iron. They triggered another memory in me, similar words that had come from Lord Endrick.

I'd be his wolf among the Coracks.

Unaware that my heart was nearly pounding out of my chest, Wynnow wished me a goodnight and I stumbled into my bedroom, shutting the door, then sliding to the floor beside it.

I was the reason the rebellion would fail.

My hand flew to my throat, to where Endrick's necklace had been. My eyes closed, and I tried to collect the memory. It was the necklace. What was the necklace?

With the question came the answer, twisting deeply in my gut. Endrick's words returned to my mind, almost perfectly. *This gift will register everything you see and hear while you are with the Coracks. Once I get it back, I will have the means to find the Olden Blade. Then I will destroy them all.*

"My lady?" Loelle's voice on the other side of the door accompanied her knock.

I flew to my feet and flung the door open, words tumbling from my mouth. "Before I was rescued from the Dominion camp, my necklace was pulled off. Someone would have found it and it will make its way back to Lord Endrick. I know what the necklace was for."

Loelle's eyes darted to either end of the corridor, then she pushed past me inside the room and shut the door behind us. "You must be more cautious, my lady."

I shook my head. "Loelle, that necklace was collecting information about the rebellion. Everything I've seen, everything I know. It will destroy them." I started to open the door again. "I have to warn them!"

Loelle grabbed my hand and held it tight, then took a deep breath. "I wasn't going to show you this, but I think I must." With her free hand, she reached into a pocket of her overcoat and withdrew the necklace.

At first, I froze, incredulous at not only seeing it again, but seeing it with her, of all people. "You had it? How?"

"Wynnow had it. She pulled it from your neck that night, knowing it would force you to enter the Blue Caves to survive. When we stopped in Snowbourne, I stole it from her satchel, to protect it. It's safe from the Dominion now."

I exhaled an enormous breath of relief. Whatever else I'd done, at least the necklace was in Corack hands.

Loelle added, "Wynnow doesn't know I have the necklace, and she'll expel me from Brill if she learns the truth. I ask you to keep this a secret between the two of us . . . and"—she lowered her voice—"one other secret as well."

Curious, I nodded, and Loelle led me to a chair on one side of a grand fireplace, then she took the other.

After nearly a full minute of gathering her thoughts, Loelle began, "I know this is a difficult time for you. You're full of questions and doubts, and as the last hour has proved, being here certainly won't help with that."

"Maybe what I feel isn't magic. Or maybe my power might be so small, we won't even know that we've discovered it."

"Used correctly, even a small power can be dangerous. But bear in mind, that you may also be developing a power that we will have to curtail, lest it becomes too dangerous after Endrick is defeated."

I sighed. "That's what most Antorans believe will happen to me, no? That this magic—powerful or not—will corrupt me. But it might not, since it has never corrupted you." I leaned forward. "Why not, Loelle? When it has corrupted all other Endreans?"

She smiled back at me. "This is the reason I came, to answer that question. The answer is simpler than you probably suspect. I cannot be corrupted like an Endrean because I'm not Endrean. I come from a different race, filled with magic, but from far across the sea."

That took me a minute to absorb, though I didn't doubt her words. Uncharted lands extended in every direction from the seas around Antora. Of course, Endreans would not be the only ones to have magic.

Loelle continued, "Many years ago, war came to our land. My family was destroyed—most families were. I was rushed onto a boat with a few survivors, but our ship crashed on the rocky shores off southern Antora. It didn't take long to understand what was happening to the Endreans. We decided to blend in with the other countrymen and say nothing of our magical abilities. I ended up with the Coracks, and over time, they have come to believe I'm Endrean. I've never corrected them."

"How many of you are left?" I asked.

Her smile fell. "I'm nearly the last one who is . . . fully alive. The majority of our people settled in All Spirits Forest."

I bit my lip, thinking of Darrow again. "Where they were cursed by Lord Endrick during the war."

"He calls it the eternal punishment." It took a long time for Loelle to finish her thought. "Every day since losing them, I've tried to find a way to bring them back. So far, it's all been in vain. I can heal a person on the edge of death. But once they've gone over that edge, if only by a whisper, they are beyond my reach. My people will likely be extinct within a few years."

"I'm sorry," I told her. But I was also sorry for myself, because if she wasn't Endrean, then maybe Simon had been right, and there wasn't much hope for me now.

Loelle acknowledged that with a brief nod, then asked, "How sure are you that Darrow is in All Spirits Forest?"

My vision blurred through my tears. "I'm sure. Shortly before Endrick took my memories, he told me that Darrow received an eternal punishment." I shook my head. "Gabe once told me that bad things happen to people who are around me. I think it's true."

"Nonsense." She gave my hand a brief squeeze. "Find your magic and stop Lord Endrick from cursing any others to the same fate. Time is of the essence. Open battles have begun in the south, involving people we both care for very much. You may be their sole hope."

Her implication was clear, that if I failed here, the Coracks would fail there. Whatever weight was already lain on my shoulders, she had just doubled it.

Loelle stood to leave, and I asked, "Why don't you trust Wynnow?"

"I don't trust any Brillians, and nor should you. But—" Loelle added with a smile. "They don't trust you or me either. Because for all we lack, we have the one thing they most desire. We have magic."

· THIRTY-FIVE ·

SIMON

Near the border of Reddengrad, we finally admitted that we needed to stop and rest for the night. Harlyn shared the food she had brought, though I ate only because I knew I had to. For most of that time, I had my eye on Trina, thinking of Harlyn's statement that it had not been her who told the Halderians that Kestra was in Lonetree Camp.

I supposed it could have been anyone—we had hundreds of Coracks in that camp, many who were also from the Halderian clan. I'd been too hasty in accusing Trina, which meant I owed her an enormous apology. After all I'd said and the petty way I'd behaved, I'd rather have cuddled up to a snake, but this had to be done.

So when Trina got up to do a sweep of the area to ensure we were safe for the night, I offered to go with her. She looked at me, clearly surprised, but when our eyes met, she nodded her permission for me to come.

Once we were alone, she said, "I thought you weren't speaking to me."

"I wasn't, which proves what a great fool I can be. I'm sorry, Trina. Harlyn told me that it wasn't you who contacted the Halderians."

I'd already prepared myself for any cruel response. If she boasted that she'd told me so, demanded that I apologize on my knees, or refused outright to accept my apology, I deserved all of it.

But she only bumped against my side as we walked and said, "You've fallen so hard for Kestra that she's turned you senseless. You know that, I hope?"

I chuckled lightly. "Yes, I know that."

"These past couple of days, I really wondered if you were. The night we found you at Rutherhouse, had you just buried—"

"Yes." I didn't want her to finish the sentence, didn't want to hear my mother's name.

The silence between us only grew heavier when Trina asked, "Was Kestra involved?"

I shrugged, finding it impossible to explain the clash of emotions inside me whenever I thought about Kestra. What happened that night wasn't her fault . . . yet it was, maybe almost as much as it was mine. I felt awful for being angry with her, and angry with myself for not having been part of Kestra's rescue from that Dominion camp afterward. If I'd gone, maybe her necklace wouldn't have been lost, maybe I could have kept her from the Blue Caves. Maybe I could have held us together, with some chance for a future.

Trina took my arm and gave it a comforting squeeze. "If it helps, I don't entirely hate Kestra anymore. I think she really believes in our cause, that she isn't doing this just because she used to care for you."

Used to. I clenched my jaw and tried to focus only on putting one foot in front of the other. Trina probably didn't realize how those two words pierced me.

Or how much worse it was when she added, "You'll be angry when I say this, but you've got to hear it, so remember that I just forgave you for being horrible to me."

I stopped walking, barely daring to ask. "What is it?"

"When you become king, they'll expect you to choose a Halderian as a wife, someone who connects you to their clan. Perhaps someone with a prominent father."

"Harlyn?" An uncomfortable few seconds passed while Trina waited for me to say something more. Finally, I asked, "Do you think there's any chance Kestra and I could still—"

"I doubt you'll ever accept her with magic. And she'll never accept you as king of the clan that's caused her such extensive harm."

I waved that away. "That much won't be a problem. I haven't changed my mind."

Something about that gave her a half-smile, but in the face of my solemn expression, she merely said, "I've never known anyone who works harder at fighting the inevitable. You cannot hold back the tide forever."

Deep inside, I knew she was right, and not only about whether I might eventually have to claim the throne, but about whether I had to let Kestra go. That also seemed inevitable now. I held out an arm for Trina. "Let's go, or Harlyn may become jealous."

She laughed again, though once we returned to camp, we became far more serious. Basil had drawn a rough map of Reddengrad into the dirt, and he and Harlyn were discussing strategy.

We were currently camped on the north side of the wide Mistriver, which marked the boundary between Reddengrad and

Antora. Immediately after crossing, we'd have a half day's ride through a pass between steep mountain ranges. If we turned east, the pass would lead us to a forest encompassing King's Lake, which Basil represented on his map with a large leaf. The capital, Lynsk, was in the west, marked with a small rock.

We gathered around the map. A little moonlight helped us to see in the gathering dark, though we still needed to press in close as Basil explained the plans.

"The Dominion army is probably two or three hours ahead of us. That will put them in position to attack Lynsk early in the morning. But my father will have the bulk of his forces waiting for them. If we come in from behind, they'll be trapped."

"All *four* of us?" I snorted. "That's not a plan; it's a death wish."

Basil considered that a moment, then asked, "What do you propose?"

I used another stick to draw a line eastward. "Draw the enemy away from your capital." I pointed to the area around King's Lake. "What's out there?"

"The Nesting Woods. In most ways, they would be perfect, but—" Basil's eyes widened. "No, we should not fight from there."

"Why not?"

"Do you remember I told you about the Rawkyren?" Seeing blank expressions on our faces, Basil added, "I assumed everyone knew. The Rawkyren is a particularly fierce breed of dragon—"

"Dragons don't exist," Harlyn said flatly.

Basil blinked twice at her before continuing. "We had thought so too, until seventy years ago when one was discovered deep within the

Nesting Woods, a female. Rawkyren start out small but they eventually grow to a wingspan three times the size of Endrick's condors. Their scales are reflective so they blend in with their environment, and they are deadly."

Harlyn shivered. "You're right. We're not going to the Nesting Woods."

"My grandfather killed the Rawkyren he found and another one has never been seen," Basil said. "A canopy track was built overhead for travel through the woods so that people wouldn't accidentally disturb a sleeping dragon, but no one goes there anyway."

"If a dragon hasn't been seen in seventy years, then the Rawkyren are probably extinct." Trina spoke with conviction, though I wondered if the only reason one had not been found was because the woods had been abandoned. She added, "Can we mount a defense there?"

Basil nodded. "The canopy is too thick for their condors to pass through and the undergrowth may trip up their oropods." His eyes suddenly lit with excitement. "Maybe we should go there! My grandfather stocked the tracks with pole weapons, so that if another Rawkyren was ever discovered, we'd be ready for it." He drew in a sharp, excited gasp. "I need to leave." With that, he stood and hurried toward his horse.

"Where?" Trina asked. "Now?"

"I know a secret way in to Lynsk. I must speak with my father, tonight."

"Someone should go with you." Trina gave me a sympathetic smile, knowing this meant we'd have to pair off, and there was only one logical way to divide. "How about I do?"

"Thank you." Basil shifted an eye from Harlyn to me, and warned, "If we can't stop the Dominion at our border, then we'll meet you at the woods tomorrow."

"Stay safe," I said, and nodded when Trina wished us the same.

After we bid farewell to Trina and Basil, Harlyn sat back down on the log where she'd been before, so reluctantly, I did too. After the embrace Harlyn and I had shared in Nessel, I knew something lingered between us, something that was making my heart race now. If she felt it too, this would be an uncomfortable night.

After drawing in the dirt for a moment with a stick, Harlyn said, "May I ask you a question?"

I tilted my head, already suspicious, then decided I wouldn't be able to avoid conversation with her for the entire evening. "Go ahead."

"Do you know why my father took command of the Halderians?"

I shrugged, but I was genuinely curious. Almost since the end of the war, the Halderians had been led by a man I knew only as Thorne, who had spent most of those years trying to prove to his people, and to Kestra herself, that she was meant to become the Infidante. He had finally succeeded, but it had apparently cost him his life.

"The night the Infidante was chosen, we had tremendous hope for her. But by morning, Kestra Dallisor was gone. She gave us no explanation of her plans. She made no effort to get us on her side."

"To be fair," I said, "the Halderians have never been Kestra's friends in the past."

"Which was why she needed to stay and help us understand her! After she left, the Halderians broke out in fighting amongst ourselves, some of us wanting to give her a chance, others who claimed that she had taken the sword back as a gift to Endrick, her king."

"That was never true, Harlyn."

"I know. Haven't I already proved to be on her side? But the truth didn't matter, only what people believed. Finally, my father challenged Thorne for leadership over our people, not because he wanted the power, but because Thorne couldn't control the fighting."

"Your father was part of the fighting!"

"My father agreed to follow the voice of the people. The head of every house was invited to a meeting to give their opinion. The decision was overwhelming: Kestra Dallisor cannot be our Infidante. The Halderians want her replaced."

I glared back at her. "Then the Halderians voted for her death."

"Yes." But she quickly added, "There is a reason I'm telling you this. It's because I know who you are . . . Your Grace."

My glare darkened. "How?"

She blushed, as if we were flirting rather than on the verge of a shouting match. "I admit that on the night the Infidante was chosen, you caught my eye. And after Gerald escaped from Woodcourt, he came back to Nessel. I knew you'd been there with him, so I asked about you. It took some persuasion, but he finally told me."

"Uh-huh. And who else knows?"

She shrugged. "Nobody, as far as I can tell. I figured since you haven't claimed the throne that maybe you have reasons not to, but I think you should reconsider, for her sake. You can't force the people to accept Kestra Dallisor, but as king, you might be able to protect her from us."

I stared at her, then reached for my bedroll. "Good night, Harlyn."

She grabbed my arm first and scooted toward me until our knees were touching. "What aren't you telling me?"

I'd told her almost nothing of my feelings for Kestra—whatever they were now—or of my plans for the future. I certainly wouldn't admit that having her so close shrouded my mind in a constant fog.

After I failed to answer, she leaned forward, keeping her eyes on me the entire time, and pausing briefly when her face was directly in front of mine. Then she smiled, grabbed my bedroll, and thrust it into my hands. "I'll keep first watch," she said, fully aware that for a moment, I had stopped breathing.

I stood and lay on the bedroll, but even as I rolled away from her, I felt the weight of her eyes on me. Maybe she didn't know what first watch meant.

However, that wasn't why I felt unable to sleep. It was becoming increasingly clear that in the end, I might be forced into claiming the title of king. Not for the Halderians, and certainly not for myself, but because Kestra would need me there.

She would obtain her magic, thinking it would save me, but it would corrupt her. I would claim the throne, hoping to save her, and no doubt it would corrupt me too.

And Harlyn was probably still watching me, having made it perfectly clear that when my heart was open to other possibilities, she would be there waiting.

If any relationship remained between Kestra and me, Harlyn threatened to corrupt that too.

· THIRTY-SIX ·

SIMON

Harlyn was already awake when my eyes opened the next morning. I'd taken the second watch, but she insisted on a third, claiming that she rarely slept much anyway. She was tending to our small fire now, and whatever she was cooking smelled delicious. When she noticed me, she said, "There's some hot tea and biscuits, if you're interested."

I definitely was, and by the time I got there, she had poured a mug for me and had three firecake biscuits ready. I thanked her, though when she smiled back, I quickly looked away. I'd spent half the night thinking about my conversation with Trina, and the other half thinking of everything Harlyn had said. If I'd slept at all, then Kestra was in those dreams. I'd watched as she faded away from me, like mist in the sunlight.

By the time I finished eating, Harlyn had packed up most of our camp, including tethering my horse to the other animals already pulling her wagon. "We should leave soon. Who knows how much time we'll have?"

"Probably not much." I did a quick check of my satchel to be sure everything was still in there. My eyes rested on my sketchbook as a wave of sadness washed over me. I doubted I'd ever draw in it again. Hoping to distract myself, I asked Harlyn, "Have you been to the Nesting Woods before? Do you know anything about them?"

"Nothing beyond what Basil told us last night." She drew a deep breath and looked at me. "My father won't be happy that you changed his orders. He doesn't see the point of defending Reddengrad."

"He should. Because if the Dominion—"

She laughed, putting a hand on my shoulder. "Simon, *I* understand it. I agree with you, and when he joins us, I will tell him so. But I thought I should warn you that he'll be angry." Now she patted my arm before walking away, sending echoes into my heart, awakening what I thought had died in me. "It would be easier if you'd claim the throne now."

I said nothing to that and instead simply climbed onto the bench of the wagon. She joined me but rode us away at a fast clip that, thankfully, made conversation difficult. I rather wished it had been impossible.

We traveled that way for most of the day, taking breaks only when necessary. When we had to talk, I spoke only about the coming battle. How many Halderians did she expect would fight? What were their skills? Halderians were far more experienced on horseback than on foot—could they compensate if the thick forest was too dense for horses?

Harlyn answered every question precisely and confidently, making it clear why her father relied on her as much as he did. I'd have to rely on her too when the battle came.

By late afternoon, we saw a thick forested area cresting on the horizon. The Nesting Woods.

Harlyn stopped the wagon so we could get a better look from a distance. "At a good pace, I think we could arrive in another hour or two."

"Then let's go."

"First we have to talk."

I took a deep breath and clenched my jaw. "We'll lose our light soon. Can this wait?"

"I'm afraid not."

I knew what conversation was coming. The unspoken words between us had been the invisible third member of our party through-out the journey, and if it were up to me, they would remain that way. Reluctantly, I turned to face her and despite my bristling irritation, I couldn't help but smile. Her cheeks and nose were windburned, and her hair was tousled, but she finger-combed the curls back with one hand and gave a shy grin. Harlyn was anything but shy.

She said, "This is about us."

I bumped a fist against my thigh. "There is no us."

"But there could be. I'm not a subtle person, Simon, that should be obvious by now. I like you. And while I relish the idea of a long courtship in which I convince you to like me too, the fact is that we might not even survive the rest of this day."

"And?"

"And my father is sick, though he hides it well. He will not be around to command the Halderians much longer. His replacement will be a disgusting, scaly man who escaped torture years ago at the hands of Kestra's father." She took a deep breath, then added, "This man offered to marry me in exchange for my father naming him as the next commander of the Halderians. He has a specific grudge against Kestra, because of her father. He cannot be allowed anywhere near the throne."

My eyes darted away, looking at anything but her. "Do you want me to take the throne for Kestra's sake or for yours?"

"I want you to take the throne. When you do, if I'm at your side, everyone wins. The Infidante will be protected. The Halderians get a just king, and a wonderful queen, trust me on that. Instead of a scaly old man, I get you. And instead of an empty seat at your side . . ." She took my hand. "There's me." Her eyes bored into mine and a rush of heat flooded through my chest. "We could be a good match, and I think you know it. That's why you've been so nervous around me."

I didn't answer. Nor did I release her hand. Instead, I froze as a debate raged within me. My heart wanted Kestra at my side, only her, and it begged me to ignore the logic and reason of Harlyn's plan. Begged me to believe in a dream.

A memory. A possibility that no longer existed.

Harlyn squeezed my fingers, drawing my attention back to her again. "Give me a chance, Simon."

I stared back at her, feeling pulled to her in ways I couldn't understand. My emotions had been blown apart over the past few days. Maybe all that I was feeling was gratitude at having someone nearby to help me pick up the pieces. Or was there something between us? Was this heat she was generating in me real? It would be so easy to lean forward, to open that door with Harlyn and accept the future that I was being funneled into anyway. One kiss, that's all it would take.

One kiss.

With her free hand, Harlyn reached up and touched my cheek. I jerked away, shaking reality back into my mind.

"I'm sorry," she said. "I just noticed a bruise forming there. I wondered if it hurts."

"We should get back on the road." I faced forward again, trying to slow my breathing. Failing miserably at it.

"Some bruises are visible," Harlyn said, picking up the reins. "But the deepest wounds are rarely seen. Some are in you, Simon. No one should have to hurt alone."

I said nothing, but once our wagon started up again, she placed a hand over mine as it rested on the bench. And this time, I let it stay.

Nearly an hour later, we reached the outer borders of the Nesting Woods. The undergrowth was impossibly thick to bring a wagon through. We tied off the horses in a safe place, then left to explore the woods on foot.

It quickly became obvious that the undergrowth was denser than what it had first seemed, with vines that grew unseen beneath thick brush and fallen autumn leaves. Every footstep had to be deliberate and slow, and even then Harlyn tripped at one point. I reached out and grabbed her, pulling her back to her feet, but when I did, she came closer than I'd expected. Much closer.

She blushed, but didn't immediately step back. "This isn't a hint . . . unless you want it to be."

Something in her tone made me smile, which relieved some of the tension between us. We hadn't gone much farther before we heard the sounds of an approaching army from the same direction we had just come. I pulled out my sword and Harlyn did the same, then we crept back to the edge of the forest, keeping ourselves masked by the undergrowth. Whoever it was, they were on horseback, and the rumbling sounds suggested we were about to receive dozens of riders, or more.

Harlyn was the first to recognize them. She let out a cry and ran from the woods, waving them down. That was when I first saw the brown flag with the blue Halderian stripe.

I wasn't sure whether to be relieved or upset, but either way, I sheathed my sword, and walked from the woods in time to see Commander Mindall dismounting. He put an arm around Harlyn and gave her an affectionate squeeze, then they both approached me.

"You changed my orders." Mindall's stern expression matched his tone.

"I did." If this was where our argument began, I was more than ready for it.

Except that Mindall reached out to shake my hand. "I know what happened in Nessel. I believe we'd have lost a lot of people had we stayed there."

"We have a chance here." Harlyn gestured to the woods behind us. "Basil told us there are rope ladders into the trees and access up there to a canopy from which we can fight."

"Fight from the tree canopy?" Mindall shook his head. "We'd do better to meet them here in open battle. That's a more honorable way to fight."

"And an honorable way to die," I said. "I've fought the Dominion in the open, and we always lose."

"You think we'll win up there, poking at the enemy from above like we're spearing a fish? You're still a boy, and I admire your courage and ambition, but you obviously don't know what a terrible plan that would be."

"If that were my plan, I'd agree with you." I pointed to Harlyn's wagon. "Inside there, we have enough raw ingredients to give us a chance in this battle. But we have to hurry."

Mindall arched a brow and looked over at his daughter, who said, "Simon's right. Give his plan a chance."

Mindall pushed past us and peeked inside the wagon, then without speaking, he walked into the forest. He returned several minutes later and pushed past me once again to announce to his men, "Anyone who has experience working with saltpeter stays here with my daughter, who will show you what to do. Simon will take the rest of you into the forest and give you instructions there. Everyone, move!"

I nodded and started back into the forest, but Mindall grabbed my arm. "You'd better know what you're doing," he warned.

I stared back at him. "I never said this will guarantee our victory, and we will lose men. But I firmly believe that we have a better chance in the canopy."

"'*We* will lose men'?" Mindall held out his arms as he turned around. "Tell me, where are *your* people, the Coracks? Since your captain begged us to come here, even forced us here, I would expect him to be here too."

"He'll come," I said firmly, hoping I was right. But it bothered me that we had not seen any other Coracks by now. Even if Tenger was trying to retrieve Kestra's blade, surely he had ordered everyone who could be spared down to this battle. Something must have gone wrong.

I kept that thought to myself, but as the day passed, it was a growing concern on my mind, constantly interrupting my thoughts while we stationed weapons and explosives in key positions among the trees.

At a halberd's reach overhead, an entire system of wooden pathways had been built into the canopy of the trees. Basil had called them tracks. The width varied to accommodate one to three people. There were no railings for support, but the construction seemed sturdy and allowed easy passage over great distances. Several of the trees had rope ladders to provide access to the tracks, though I couldn't detect any system for which tree had a ladder and which did not.

We worked hard but were less than halfway through our search that late afternoon when the Halderians standing guard at the border of the forest called out that more soldiers were coming. Hoping to see Coracks, I hurried out, only to be greeted by Basil and Trina, and a sizable number of Reddengrad soldiers behind them, though not as many as I'd have wanted.

Trina was clearly disheartened and Basil looked exhausted. When I studied his army more carefully, I saw their bloodstained uniforms, dirty and bruised faces, and expressions of defeat.

"It was a slaughter," Basil said quietly. "And they aren't far behind. I hope you've got a bigger army in hiding than what I can see now."

My attention shifted to Trina, who must have been wondering the same thing I did. But it was Mindall who asked the same question as before: "When can we expect to fight with the Coracks?"

"We'll fight with what we have," I replied, then to Basil, I added, "Let's get everyone onto the tracks. I doubt we have much time."

We had less time than I had expected. For even as I spoke, I heard the first screech of a giant condor.

The battle was about to begin. We weren't likely to win, but I hoped what we were facing was a mere defeat, not the near decimation Basil and Trina had just endured.

Either way, I raced up the nearest ladder, grabbed one of the many halberds that Reddengrad had stationed in the trees, and readied myself to find out.

· THIRTY-SEVEN ·

KESTRA

I began my morning in a rotten mood, fueled by exhaustion and starvation from the sweet cream and air that passed as Brillian food, and perfectly aware it would be a long day of disappointing everyone around me.

So I was already irritated when I was led to an open field near the castle where Wynnow and Imri Stout stood with a stern reminder that they had been waiting for nearly fifteen minutes. Thinking of the stolen necklace, I approached them with caution. "Where's Loelle?"

"We have no need of a physician," Wynnow said, eyeing Imri. When she saw my concern, she added, "I told you before, Kestra, that I don't trust her. I think she wants to use your magic for her own purposes. Not as Infidante, but something she wants from you."

I'd gotten the same feeling from Loelle last night. But then, I had the same feeling from Wynnow too, that there was something more behind her offer to train me than simply wanting Lord Endrick's defeat. I'd been naïve far too often, but no longer.

"Let's be clear about something," I said. "The decision whether to trust Loelle is entirely mine. You are the princess of these lands, but I am the Infidante of Antora and I will not yield that decision to you."

Surprisingly, Wynnow nodded her head in respect. "Agreed. Shall we begin?"

Imri stepped forward. "It's a beautiful morning. I thought perhaps we might start by testing your influence on nature."

I shook my head. "I already tried—"

"We rushed you yesterday in the carriage. That wasn't fair, especially given your . . . fears in there, which would prevent the proper focus and relaxation." Her false smile turned sour. "I suspect that with your memories returning, you are rarely relaxed and that your focus on any given topic shifts like leaves in the wind."

There was more truth to her words than I wanted to admit. I tried to remember a time in my life when I'd been perfectly relaxed and came up with nothing. I wished I could recall—or trust—who I'd once been. As I was now, was this always me?

"Kestra?" Wynnow touched my arm.

My eyes flew open. "We should wait to do this. I'm still not entirely myself."

"Will Endrick wait until your memories are intact? Until you've had proper time to understand your powers?"

I nodded and tried to push the nagging worries from my mind. "You're right. Let's begin."

Imri shook her head, doubting me only slightly less than I already doubted myself. "I fear you lack—"

"What's the first test?"

Imri smiled and gestured to the skies. "Something simple, perhaps. Can you give us a slight breeze?"

A slight breeze wouldn't trouble Lord Endrick. Instead, I focused on creating a storm. Gathering clouds, generating lightning.

If I could control the weather, in combination with the Olden Blade, I could do more than defeat Lord Endrick. I could singlehandedly defeat the Dominion.

But for all my concentration, my determination, and a full hour of sincere effort, I couldn't generate a storm, nor a slight breeze, nor the rustle of a single blade of grass. The effort exhausted me, but I wouldn't admit that to Imri or Winnow. They'd only rattle on about how Brillians never became tired from mental work.

"Pity," Imri said. "I rather hoped that would be your power."

She shifted to testing me for what had once been my mother's ability, to become undetectable. "Without this power, Anaya never could have stolen the Olden Blade. It would be natural for you to have inherited it." She angled away from me. "When I turn around again, I should not notice you, even if you are directly in front of me."

It was a nice thought, but when she did turn back to me, her lips pressed together in utter disappointment. There I was, my arms widened in a hopeless gesture.

Wynnow stepped in and took my hand. "What are you thinking about right now?"

I twisted my expression. "Do you want the full list?"

"It's cruel that the Brillians weren't given the gift of magic," Imri said. "We'd never struggle so much to find our own powers."

"Imri!" Wynnow scolded.

The older woman dipped her head. "My apologies, princess."

No apologies were offered to me, whom she'd actually insulted. I had been trying to remain focused and to do as Imri had instructed. Maybe Imri was right, that I couldn't be taught.

Imri frowned at me. Again. "Perhaps you are meant to create."

"If I am, I refuse to test it." We'd all seen what Lord Endrick did when he combined one cruel animal with another. I wanted no part of it.

"What if this is your power?" Wynnow asked.

"It's not!" I was losing patience with her, and Imri, and mostly with myself. "Maybe I have no powers."

"You need to start trying."

My temper warmed, and I opened my mouth for what was about to be a sharp retort when we noticed Loelle crossing the field.

"What Kestra needs is to rest," Loelle said. "Her magic is young and it will take more energy from her at first." Her eyes fell upon Wynnow and their expression was cool. "Forgive me for coming late. I believe the servant you sent to tell me of this meeting must have gone astray, for she never made it to my room."

Wynnow folded her arms and faced Loelle. "The servant made it to Kestra's room last night while you were there. What do you want from her, if she gains her powers?"

Loelle's eyes flashed with guilt. But rather than answer, she asked, "Have you tested her yet for the influence of health?"

"As you must know, in battle that would be a less desirable power," Imri said. "The Coracks already have you for a physician, and such abilities would have limited use for an Infidante. I was saving that one for nearer to the end."

"Well, I'd like to test it now," Loelle said, "because since walking onto this field I've developed a piercing headache. Kestra, can you heal it?"

I stared back at her. "I don't know how."

"Put your hand on my head, here." Loelle lifted my hand and placed my fingers on her forehead. I immediately yanked them away and leapt back as a sudden fear rushed through me. Endrick had placed his hands on me thus, when he stole my memories.

"What's wrong?" Wynnow asked.

I shook my head, unwilling to explain the emotions that were overwhelming my heart and mind. The fear that I'd experienced in that room was awful, but it was nothing compared to the helplessness of having one memory after another pulled from my head, knowing I was losing pieces of myself. It was almost as terrible now to have to relive it again.

"We'll try again tomorrow," Loelle said.

"No." I closed my eyes and tried to calm myself. Perhaps the panic now was only because I had panicked then. After a few deep breaths, I lifted my hand again and placed it on Loelle's forehead. "Tell me what to do."

"Let all thoughts empty from your mind, except what you feel with your fingers. Can you find the pain in me?"

I tried, sincerely and wholeheartedly, until I was worn out from the attempt. Finally, I pulled my hand away. "I can't."

"You should be able to. I felt the magic working within you, through your hand. It knows I'm hurting."

"No, *I know* you're hurting because you told me that. I can't feel anything special and even if I did, I wouldn't know what to do about it."

"You need time," Imri said, "and more patience."

"I have no time." My attention shifted to Wynnow, who was inspecting her nails as if she'd given up on me. "Hasn't that been your point all along?"

Wynnow glanced over to Loelle. "Will you fetch the Infidante some tea? I believe it will refresh her."

Loelle grunted with the insult of being treated as a servant, but she nodded to me and returned to the castle.

Meanwhile, Imri said, "There are other clusters. Recalling, taking power from others. And endless possibilities for powers within the clusters we've already tested. We could easily have missed something."

My eyes narrowed. "But Brillians never miss anything, do they." I shook my head, then began walking from the field. "I'm done with these tests!"

"You're not concentrating!" Imri scolded. "It's obvious your mind is elsewhere."

"And it should be obvious why!" I could scarcely hold two thoughts together with all my worries for what was happening in Reddengrad. "Has there been any word about the Dominion attack in the south? Has the battle begun?"

Wynnow nodded at Imri. "Leave us alone. You need a rest."

I scoffed. *Imri* needed the rest? Why? Was it tiring for her to scold me, demean me? Was it hard for her to be as cruel as she had been?

When we were alone, Wynnow said, "We have a Dominion tablet, and have been carefully following any news of the battles."

My eyes widened. "You have a tablet?" When she nodded, I added, "They can't be trusted. Everything written on them comes from Endrick himself."

"Yes, but I believe what I've seen on the tablet is real." Wynnow paced, biting her lip. "The battle is not going well. The Dominion entered Reddengrad. They fight there with giant condors, oropods, carnoxen, and a full slate of weapons. This battle's ending has already been written."

I took her hand in mine, hoping to make her understand how desperate I was to help them. "Speak to your mother. Convince her to send Brillian armies into Reddengrad to help them fight."

"Brillians do not act in the interest of other countries. Only for our own."

"Defeating the Dominion is in Brill's interest, wherever it happens! If Reddengrad falls, you must know Endrick's eye will turn to Brill."

That didn't seem to bother her. "Brill is safe from the Dominion."

"No, it's not. In the end, arrogance will not save you, imitating Endrick's technologies will not save you. And if all else has been destroyed on his path to Brill, then no ally will come to save you either." I released her hands and marched away.

"Nor, it seems, will you save us."

Her words hit me like a knife. My muscles tightened, and I began walking again, anything to get as far from her as possible, shouting back, "That is not fair!"

"When were you ever promised that your duties would be fair? What is your magic, Kestra? How many lives must be destroyed before you care enough to find it?"

I swung around to face her. "I'm trying my best!"

"*This* is your best?"

Just then, the gardener's door near us opened and Loelle came through it with a cup of tea in her hands. "I heard arguing—"

Wynnow frowned at me. "If this is truly your best, then Loelle dies." Before I realized what was happening, she pulled out her dagger and threw it at Loelle. With the perfect aim of the Brillians, it pierced Loelle in the stomach.

"What have you done?" I cried, racing toward Loelle and catching her as she fell to the ground.

Wynnow followed me. "Maybe you haven't found your magic because everything is too safe. Heal her."

"We've tried that! I can't heal people!"

"Loelle said she felt your magic working. Maybe you can do something more than heal. She is dying, my lady. You'd better hurry."

I knelt beside Loelle, whose eyes were fluttering open and then closed. "Tell me what to do."

"Pull out the knife."

I gritted my teeth together, grabbed the handle, and said, "This will hurt, I'm so sorry." I pulled and Loelle's body stiffened, but she didn't cry out.

"Now what?" I asked.

Loelle's eyes fluttered again, then closed.

"Loelle!" I cried, but she didn't answer. I pressed my fingers against her neck, checking for a pulse. It was there, but wouldn't be for long.

"I can't do anything for her!" I turned back to Wynnow. "Please call for help."

"I did. I called for you." Then Wynnow casually folded her arms and leaned against the door, apparently indifferent to whatever happened next. I cursed, putting my hands over Loelle's wound to slow the bleeding. I had to think. What would be the next thing to do?

I didn't know. The bleeding had to be stopped, but simply pressing my hands here wouldn't help nearly enough. She needed healing from within.

And with that singular thought, I shuddered as something emptied from me. I wasn't sure what it was: Strength? A parcel of my own life? I only knew that I felt weaker than before, and in the same moment, Loelle began breathing easier.

"Something is happening." With hopefulness in her voice, Wynnow stepped forward. "Kestra, keep going!"

I did, not for her, but for Loelle. I concentrated on her injury and offered my strength to close the wounds, to seal every tear. I knew it was working, because the pain of it transferred to me. I felt the knife, the broken tissue, the fierce sting, as if the wound was mine. Everything I gave took something from me. As she became stronger, I weakened.

"Enough," Loelle whispered, placing her hands over mine. "Enough, Kestra."

"You're not whole yet." I tried to keep working but she pushed my hands away from her. "I can do more."

"No, you cannot. You must not." Loelle sat up, though with significant effort. "My lady, I felt your strength pouring into me. If you give too much of yourself, you will die. No more than half, ever."

"How do I know what is half?"

"This is half. Never give more than this." She put her hand on my cheek and smiled. "So there is an eleventh cluster of magic, one that is yours alone. You are not a healer as I am; you are a giver of life. This is a powerful gift, Kestra. Use it well."

I stared at my hands, trying to calm their shaking, cursing my weakness. Loelle was wrong. In my hands, this was not a powerful gift. Not with such a high price for using it. I'd never be capable of helping on a large scale.

Wynnow walked forward, triumphantly standing over us. "This is wonderful news, and a significant power." As if this were her achievement.

I turned to her. "How did you know that would bring out my magic?"

She only shrugged. "I didn't."

Anger washed through me, giving me enough strength to stand and begin walking off the field, this time determined to get away from her. "I am finished here. Finished with Brillian superiority, your dismissal of all races but your own, your disregard for anything that does not benefit you. I will not fight for you or use magic for you. I'll be gone by morning."

She started to speak, but I pushed open the door and stormed away. Yet as angry as I felt, that wasn't the problem, not really. I didn't even make it to my room before I began openly sobbing. I wrapped my arms around myself, consumed with pain, then crouched in a quiet corner of the palace and let the tears fall.

I had acquired a magic of only marginal significance, and for what? This supposed gift would have little impact in the fight against the Dominion, and to discover it I'd just traded away the thing I valued most.

In the moment of saving Loelle's life, I had sealed the end of my relationship with Simon. It was over.

· THIRTY-EIGHT ·

SIMON

The battle began much as I'd expected. The condors flew over the forest canopy, but the leaves were far too dense for the riders to set targets with their shoulder cannons.

Many of the early Ironhearts who entered attempted to do so on their oropods, but they quickly realized their mistake. The forest floor was covered in such heavy brush and thicket, their oropods became tangled and fell, making them easy targets for us from the canopy tracks above.

We killed or wounded almost half of that first wave of Ironhearts, but those who survived quickly responded, firing disks upward. It was easier for us to hide than it was for them, and in a few cases, the disks fell back to their archers, piercing them. Where the canopy tracks were lower to the ground, if we lay on our stomachs, we could aim the halberd downward and stab a soldier before he knew we were there.

But our easy victories could not last. After an hour of their side taking heavy losses, the carnoxen were sent in. Their bodies were too low for us to reach with our pole weapons, and from this distance, our disk blades couldn't pierce their hides. They also trampled the undergrowth, creating easy trails for the next wave of Ironhearts.

"Now?" Basil asked, looking over at me.

I nodded, and with a silent gesture to men waiting in key positions around the canopy, a handful of rope ladders quietly descended.

The Ironhearts returned, angrier than before and apparently with orders to flush us out of the canopy, just as I'd hoped. One of their officers called out that the rebels had made a mistake and he'd found a ladder. I grinned. A mistake had certainly been made, but not by us.

I gave a whistle that was immediately echoed by our fighters in the distance. The Ironhearts climbed the ladders, certain they would trap us, while we led them deeper into the forest, quietly descending in prearranged locations and waiting to counteract their next order. Basil and I descended together but took up hiding places as far apart as possible while staying in visual range.

Within minutes, the Dominion officers shouted that they had taken control of the canopy. This was true, though we had taken the pole weapons with us and their swords wouldn't reach low enough to threaten any of us.

That hardly made us safe. Plenty of carnoxen and oropods were down here along with the majority of Ironhearts. I heard fighting already breaking out in some areas ahead.

It was time for the battle to shift again. Basil had assigned one hundred men as fire starters, their first job to burn any rope ladders that came down from above, keeping the Ironhearts overhead trapped. Their second job was to light smoke bombs as needed, ones Harlyn had shown the Halderians how to make from the saltpeter and sugar.

With the first fires lit, the forest immediately began filling with thick white smoke, rising fast and becoming trapped in the canopy. As the Ironhearts ran for breathable air, they often ran directly off the track, with men following so close behind them that several fell before anyone changed course.

We weren't finished. We had also converted some of the salt-peter into gunpowder that exploded at the base of trees, bringing down the entire track and everyone on it.

"Retreat!" someone called from above.

"How?" another voice answered. "We're trapped up here!"

"Find a way!"

While I fought below, I ordered our fire starters to stay ahead of the Ironheart retreat, keeping as many as possible in the canopy. The rest of us moved deeper into the forest. The Dominion hadn't come this far yet, granting us a little time to rest.

I leaned against a tree, uneasy with unused energy that still pulsed with the urge to fight. Meanwhile, Commander Mindall and Harlyn were checking on their soldiers, and Trina was nursing a long cut on her arm. After a quick review of his men, Basil headed toward me, looking cautiously hopeful. I wished he didn't. There was still little hope for us.

"Gather the wounded," one of Basil's officers ordered. "And bury the dead."

"Our dead." All eyes fell on me and I added, "Not theirs."

Basil shifted his weight. "Simon, out of respect . . ."

"If we bury everyone, the Dominion returns to an even battle-ground, any memory of today's losses a thing of the past. No, I want them to see how many men they lost and wonder if they got any of ours."

Basil nodded, then called to his men, "Find a quiet place for our dead. Somewhere they won't be disturbed."

The first wave of battle had gone well, with far more Dominion losses than ours. Still, we had too many fallen fighters, which meant when I saw Commander Mindall walk toward me, my stomach filled with dread. I was scolding myself plenty. I didn't need his criticism too.

But he stood beside me, looking back on the white smoke still filtering through the forest and said, "It's a terrible thing to lead a battle. No matter how it ends, you'll inevitably spend the rest of your days obsessing over every choice you made, berating yourself for any mistakes you made. Learn from them, then let them go. If you can, then today's mistakes become tomorrow's victories. Refusing to move on is simply another mistake." When I only frowned at him, he clapped a hand on my shoulder and added, "It was a good day for our people."

He gave me a respectful nod, then left, yet my mind lingered on his words, that it had been a good day for *our people*. Not *his* Halderians. It didn't bother me that he'd said it that way; it bothered me that I cared.

The Dominion set up their overnight camp outside the forest, where they could build fires for warmth in the wintry air and cook some hearty food, its mouthwatering scent easily carrying on the wind toward us.

Forced to make camp among the trees, we did our best to relax within the lingering smoke and haze and within easy sight of the unburied dead. Without enough food to go around, Mindall ordered some of his men to hunt for anything remotely edible, and a few others offered to fish from King's Lake in a clearing deeper in the woods.

"A bridge runs over the east end, before it empties into a river," Basil suggested. "That'll be your best place to fish."

The idea of eating appealed to me, but sleep sounded even better. Trina had built a small fire and I sat beside her and stared at the flames, wondering if the Dominion would wait until morning before attacking again. Hoping so. Every part of my body ached, and I'd begun to notice small injuries that had escaped my attention before. I was beyond exhausted and might've fallen asleep until one of our watchmen called, "We have prisoners!"

Mindall and I stood in time to see Halderian fighters leading two people forward. I recognized Huge first, his arms propping up Gabe as they walked. I gave a shout of happiness and ran toward them.

"These aren't prisoners!" I wrapped an arm across Huge's shoulder, then nodded at Gabe, who was half-bent over, clearly still mending from his injuries. To the fighters, I added, "Release my friends!"

Trina had joined us by then and helped me lead Gabe toward a bedroll Harlyn laid out. Carefully, we lowered him onto it.

"Thanks," Gabe mumbled as Harlyn spread a blanket over his bruised body.

Huge settled onto a log near the fire and someone passed him a flask of water, which he gratefully accepted, taking a long draw before offering it to Gabe, who also seemed eager for a drink.

Mindall's eye passed from Huge to Gabe to me, his expression souring with every turn of his head. "At last the great Corack army has arrived," he said wryly. "All two of you."

"Where is everyone else?" I asked Huge. "And why did you bring Gabe here? He should recover at Lonetree Camp."

Huge's eyes darted from me to Trina, then in a low voice he said, "There is no Lonetree Camp. It's been destroyed."

My heart stopped. "Dominion?"

When Huge nodded, Trina leaned forward. "What happened to the Coracks who were stationed there?"

Huge gave her a knowing look but said nothing. Too many other listeners were around.

"Was Tenger there?" I asked.

Huge's eye briefly shifted to Mindall, then he slowly nodded.

Near me, Gabe mumbled something. I leaned in and asked him to repeat himself, but he only said, "Tell him, Huge."

I looked up to Huge for an explanation, but his gaze shifted across the group. I stood and said to Trina, "Keep an eye on Gabe. Huge, come with me."

"If he has something important to say, he should say it to all of us," Mindall said. "I am in command here, after all."

"But this is Corack business," Harlyn said, which earned her a harsh glare from her father. He started to scold her, but I wasn't around for that. Huge and I had already walked away.

A small tent had been set up near King's Lake, which was a long walk, but it was the one place where I knew we'd be alone, especially as the other fighters were waking up to begin morning preparations. Once inside the tent, I folded my arms and squared my body to Huge. "Tell me everything."

He took a deep breath. "The Dominion has never known where Lonetree was—that's what made it such a strong camp. Their soldiers plowed straight through it, emptying it within minutes. Our hope is that most of our people escaped, but we know the Dominion captured quite a few of them."

I shifted my weight while I let that sink in. "How could the Dominion have found it?"

"Gabe knows Dominion technology better than any other Corack, and he has a theory about the necklace that Kestra wore. He believes it might have been some sort of tracker, registering everything Kestra was seeing in that camp. It must have been something like that, because the Dominion breached every security system we had. They knew about the tunnels and how to navigate them. They knew our escape routes, our hiding places. They had to have inside knowledge about what to expect."

"Then that necklace was taken from her in the Dominion camp." I ran my fingers through my hair. "We should've gotten to her before they could take it." No, *I* should have gotten to her. I should have come.

"We did get to her by then," Huge said. "I saw them drag Kestra out from her father's tent, with the necklace. But it was gone by the time Wynnow rescued her."

My eyes narrowed. "Are you saying that Wynnow took the necklace?" Huge shrugged, but I continued, speaking aloud my thoughts as they came to me. "Wynnow wanted Kestra to go to the Blue Caves. If she removed the necklace, she'd force Kestra to go there, to save her life."

"But she couldn't have known that removing the necklace would kill Kestra," Huge said. "None of us could have sensed its magic."

I couldn't answer that, but I was beginning to piece together the clues. She and Trina had worked closely together back at Lonetree Camp. If Wynnow had wanted to send a message to the Halderians, she might have written that note on Trina's notepad, especially if she wanted to divert suspicion to Trina. Trina also could have told Wynnow where my mother lived, information she might have passed on to the Dominion. The night Kestra poisoned me, Trina and Gabe were searching for us together. Wynnow was missing for that entire night. She easily could have made contact with the Dominion during that time.

And when he was attacked, hadn't Gabe overheard the Ironhearts saying the Corack traitor was female?

"Where is Kestra now?" The tension in my body came through in the urgency of my voice.

Huge shrugged. "Tenger would've sent her somewhere safe to recover—"

"With Wynnow."

"We're getting ahead of ourselves," Huge said. "This is all speculation. There's no proof."

"No, but there're plenty of reasons to make sure Kestra isn't alone with Wynnow. Who knows what might happen?"

"Simon—" Trina ducked her head through the tent door.

"I've got to find her and pray it's not too late."

"Simon!" Trina said, more firmly. "Listen!"

I did and heard the first shouts from the Reddengrad guards at watch. The Dominion had returned, and we were out of tricks. We could not expect any Corack reinforcements, and our one hope for success—Kestra arriving with the Olden Blade in hand—probably wouldn't happen. Not if Wynnow had betrayed us.

If she had, our battle here was already lost.

· THIRTY-NINE ·

KESTRA

I awoke sometime around midnight, barely able to breathe and with sweat on my palms and throat. I flung my bedcovers aside and stood, trying to orient myself in the darkness. Where were my day clothes?

It didn't matter. I collapsed on the floor, wrapping my arms around my legs, hoping simply to breathe again. What I'd just experienced was no ordinary dream. It was a memory, so real that I felt as if I were there again.

Thanks to the starry ceiling overhead, my eyes gradually adjusted, but I had yet to calm my racing pulse or to collect an even breath.

I remembered being in the room with Lord Endrick on the day he took my memories. I remembered all of it. The acidic smell of the walls and furniture. The smooth binding cords that had tied me to the chair. Lord Endrick with his scarred gray face close to mine, eagerly anticipating the theft of my memories.

I remembered everything, and recalling what had been missing before was worse than I had imagined.

He had ordered me to kill Simon, an order I had later refused. He had instructed me to wear his necklace to spy upon the Coracks;

at least it was safe now with Loelle. But he had also assured Sir Henry that even if I failed, he had another spy in place among the Coracks.

Whoever that was, I needed to warn Captain Tenger. If I didn't, the spy would find the Olden Blade. He would betray all information about the rebellion to Endrick.

The spy would kill Simon.

I had to leave immediately.

With that decision made, I stood and dressed myself in riding breeches and a fresh tunic, then slung a satchel over my shoulder for what few possessions I had here. Wynnow already knew I was leaving so it should be little surprise to find me gone when morning came. She would be angry at my decision, but no angrier than I still was for what she had done to Loelle. Wynnow would call me a fool for entering a battle with such insignificant magic, powers that could never change the battle's outcome. I was going to Reddengrad anyway.

I tiptoed from my room, avoiding any servants I could and ignoring those I couldn't. Once in the stables, the horse I chose was a Brillian breed of far greater strength and power than what we had in Antora. It wouldn't beat an oropod in a race, but it would get me to the battle sometime tomorrow.

Once the horse was saddled, I led him by the reins, intending to mount him after passing through the stable doors. But I didn't get five steps forward before Wynnow entered the stables to stand directly in front of me, deliberately blocking the doors with her body. A disk bow was in her hand and a thin-blade sword hung at her side.

"You will not leave." Every muscle in her face was tightened in anger, but no more than mine.

"I'm no prisoner, nor servant. I do not follow your orders."

"You are staying here, Kestra."

As proof of her intentions, she reached into the satchel at her side and pulled out a black disk, inserting it into the pocket of the disk bow. My pulse quickened. "Only the Dominion have black disks."

Something in her smile turned my stomach. "Then I must have gotten this from the Dominion."

"Stolen?"

"No."

As coldly as she had behaved since we arrived here, that single word of hers sent an icy shiver through me. I began backing away. "You're a Corack. We're on the same side."

"I'm Brillian, doing what is right for my people."

"I'm no threat to your people," I said.

"But you are part of a bargain I made *for* my people . . . now." She had backed me into a corner of the stables, her bow trained on me. "This wasn't what I wanted, Kestra. I sent Imri Stout to serve you in Woodcourt, and she would have gotten you safely out, had Simon not interfered. Meanwhile, I joined the Coracks, fully intending to be your friend, and the one you trusted as your memories returned. But Simon interfered with that as well."

"Lord Endrick said he had a spy among the Coracks. That was you?"

She sighed. "I must do what is best for my people, and whatever is necessary to protect my mother and her throne, and I have. Lord Endrick and I have just completed an agreement that assures the Dominion will never attack Brill."

I shook my head as the pit in my gut swelled. "He's *here*?"

"He's on his way to these stables now, to collect the second of his two demands. They were steep sacrifices, but they were necessary."

"What demands?"

"The first was that Lord Endrick wanted the necklace back. It shouldn't have mattered—I already told him everything he wanted to know about the Coracks, but perhaps he's sentimental. Imagine how dismayed I was to discover that Loelle had stolen it. She barely escaped Brill earlier tonight, but I retrieved it from her."

Hoping against what I already knew, I said, "You fought with the Coracks. How could you betray them like this?"

"Without you, the Coracks will be extinguished anyway."

"Without me." Now my heart sank. I bit my lip and nodded in understanding. "Because I'm the second demand."

"You, with your newfound powers. He can take them from you now."

"And once he does, he will become even more powerful." I was terrified and fighting the instinct to run, but mostly I was angry at the feelings of betrayal, the coldness of her having pushed magic on me and then traded it away with my life. I said, "Whatever he's promised, he will come for Brill eventually."

"But not today," she said, refocusing the bow at me. "I really do wish we could have been friends. This isn't personal."

My heart thundered against my chest as I spoke. "I disagree. What is about to happen is very personal." Even at the expense of my life, Lord Endrick could not have my magic. Holding my breath for what was coming, I leapt at Wynnow, arms out.

Immediately, she fired the disk, which sliced into my shoulder. Pain seared through me, and I looked down to see the black disk embedded deep in my flesh. I had seconds to live.

"Why did you make me do that?" she screamed. "He'll be angry!"

"Good." I fell to the ground.

"He's come all this way. If you die now, he'll destroy us."

"Starting with you, I'm sure." I was in immense pain and felt my body shutting down. But I'd use my last breath to get at her.

Wynnow knelt beside me. "Maybe if I take the disk out, you'll live until he gets here. I can save you until he arrives." She ripped the disk from my shoulder, which hurt almost worse than it did going in. I cried out and the lights began fading around me.

I grabbed her arm, holding her near me so that when Endrick walked in, he would know this was her fault, that she had broken her own promise. I wished she could feel my pain.

In that very moment, Wynnow gasped and started to pull back. I'd have thought little of it, but just as she weakened, I felt a surge of life.

Her life. I was pulling her life back to myself.

"What are you doing?" Her voice sounded weaker—it *was* weaker.

And I was beginning to understand why. My shoulder was healing, even as Wynnow was crumpling to the floor. I wouldn't kill her, I never wanted to be that person. But I held my hand where it was until I was restored enough to sit up, then I staggered to my feet, leaving her on the ground in a semiconscious stupor. I didn't know how long that would last, but since Brillians were superior at nearly everything, she was bound to recover soon. I had to leave *now*.

No, I should have already been gone. Behind me, in the palace, footsteps marched down the corridor, heavy enough that their echoes carried all the way out here. Endrick's footsteps.

I looked around the open stables. There was nowhere to hide, and I had no weapons of my own. I grabbed Wynnow's bow and her satchel that had held the black disk, hoping to find another one, but when I checked, it only held the stone tablet she'd shown me earlier. So I grabbed the sword at her side and sheathed it. And finally, I picked up the black disk she'd used on me and returned it to its pocket. Then I stood back, doing my best to aim the weapon at where I thought Lord Endrick would appear when he came through the doors. It wouldn't kill him, but perhaps I could slow him down long enough to escape.

The door opened, and as soon as I saw his scarred face, I fired. The disk went higher than I'd hoped but still flew toward his shoulder. He reached up and grabbed the sharp disk out of the air with his hand. On it was the grip glove, and his hand was uncut. He crushed the disk with his fingers, dropping shards of black dust to the ground.

"I gather that crude attempt on my life means your memories are restored," he said.

In my anger, I forgot to be afraid. "My memories are returned, along with my strength and my determination to complete my quest. You are no king, no Lord of anything. The Scarlet Throne does not belong to you, and I will not rest until the rightful king has the throne, and you are in the grave."

He smiled, amused by what he surely considered my idle talk. "Then you will never rest, my dear. Certainly, you will not do so today. Go to your knees."

My legs began to weaken, folding to his order, but I refused to kneel. I faced him with all the fire and determination inside me. I would not kneel.

"I gave you an order." With the grip glove, he grabbed my arm like a vise and I immediately collapsed to my knees. He kept the pressure there, intending to punish me.

But I was furious. I would not kneel to him any longer, I'd decided that already. Not by choice or by force or by weakness, I would *not* kneel.

Or if I had to, then so would he. I put one hand over his as it gripped my arm and sent the full force of my magic into pulling at his life force, just as I had done with Wynnow. He cried out in anger and sent a bolt of pain through me. It weakened me, but I filled my strength again by taking it from him.

Again, he filled me with daggers of pain that I survived only by sapping his own strength. He believed he was hurting me, and he was, but if he continued this way, he might kill himself.

Endrick tried to pry my hand off his, but this cycle of taking and giving life seemed to have bound us together. As long as his grip glove was on me, I could no longer release my hold on him. Slowly, I stood again. His hand was still on my arm, flooding my body with pain, but I sent every bit of it back to him, pulling from his strength to make myself stronger.

Not only stronger physically, but my mind was stronger, my will, my very spirit. I was feeling power such as I never had before. His power. I was borrowing a little of what he'd gained from the hundreds of Endreans he'd killed.

Under my hold, the grip glove became brittle, and then crumbled beneath my fingers. Endrick cried out with fury, "Curse you, girl!" and this time, he grabbed me with both hands, sending something like fire through my body.

I fell backward onto the ground, struggling for air, my thoughts flying apart; I was close to blacking out.

"Do you know what it feels like when I take someone's magic?" he asked, striding toward me. My vision was fading to nothing. I only saw the hem of his cloak, coming ever closer.

Balancing on my forearms, I scrambled away from him, but he hovered over me, eager to strike, to punish me to the point of death. My heart was nearly pounding its way free of my chest, but I was determined to keep fighting. This was not over yet.

"It will feel like you're separating from within, as I take one layer of your magic at a time. Once I start, no one will be able to stop me. You will beg for mercy, but the time for mercy has passed. I will hear your pleas as laughter, and when I have wrung you out and you are nothing but a hollow shell that used to be a person, then I will do the laughing for us both."

"Is that what it felt like for you just now?" I asked. "When my hand was on yours, did you feel me taking life from you, one layer at a time?"

"What little bit you borrowed from me is inconsequential," he said.

My smile back at him was full of fury. "I took more than your life. I borrowed your magic too." And I shoved my hands forward through the air. It threw him backward through the doors where he had entered, so forcefully that they shattered apart and crumbled the walls around him. I wouldn't be able to do that again, it was all I'd been able to take in those few moments, but it did buy me some time.

I flew to my feet and scrambled toward the horse I'd saddled. The second I was on its back, I kicked him away and raced down the hill. Violent fires sprang up beside me—Endrick's attempt to slow me down—but this was a Brillian horse and it nimbly dodged the hazards. A roar sounded up the hill ending in the collapse of the entire Brillian palace, and the earth shuddered around me. I didn't dare stop or even look back, but I felt as if all the air had been sucked from my body. How many people would have been inside that palace? Dozens? Hundreds?

Wynnow.

Wynnow, who had thought it was merciful to kill me. And when mercy didn't work, she turned to total betrayal.

And received the worst of all possible fates in return.

Not only her. The entire government of Brill had probably just perished. No doubt that would come to haunt me, but for now, I had to get to Reddengrad.

· FORTY ·

SIMON

The fighting resumed with greater ferocity than before. The Dominion had regrouped and may have oriented their soldiers to expect more tricks from us. Except that this time, we were out of surprises. Moreover, it was a dark night beneath this forest canopy, and we often didn't know whether the person approaching us was friend or enemy until it was too late to avoid a clash.

I found myself fighting from positions deeper and deeper within the forest, at times pursued when the numbers were greater than me, and then the pursuer when those groups inevitably became separated by the tangle of the undergrowth and narrow paths. More often, I didn't know which of them I was, or why I was even fighting.

Eventually, the morning sun broke through the canopy, offering a small bit of hope that at least some fighters on my side yet remained. I was cutting my way toward a clearing when I heard the shouts of men ahead followed by a screeching sound that turned my stomach. Hadn't there been enough death, enough pain? It sounded like the soldiers were torturing a creature weaker and smaller than they. I wouldn't tolerate this. Readying my sword, I crept in their direction, unsure of what to expect.

I reached the crest of a small hill and looked down to see four soldiers in Dominion colors firing disk blades at something ahead of them I could not see. Most of their disks made a clanging sound when they hit their target, but then whatever they were firing at would screech again and they'd cheer.

"Simon!"

I nearly jumped from my flesh at hearing the hiss of my name, but Trina put a hand on my shoulder, then crouched beside me. "You followed the sounds here too?"

"I think it's a Rawkyren," I whispered. "That dragon Basil told us about, and probably a young one. I'm going to rescue it."

I began to stand but Trina grabbed my arm and pulled me down again. "If they're as dangerous as Basil said, maybe what they're doing is for the best."

No, it wasn't. I shook my head. "I don't expect you to understand this, Trina, but I can't sit here and listen to what they're doing. After hearing my mother . . . I just can't."

Trina pressed her lips together and nodded in sympathy, then reached for the disk bow at her side. She checked her pouch and pulled out five disks, one for each of the men below and an extra. "I'll give you cover, but we both know this is a terrible idea."

"When has a terrible idea ever stopped us?" I winked at her, then redoubled my grip on the sword and started down the hill as quietly as I could. The men were so engrossed in the cruelty of their actions that they failed to notice me until I was more than halfway down.

With a shout of alarm, they turned, and one moved to fire his disk bow at me, but Trina caught him first, knocking him backward into the pond. I locked swords with the first man to reach me, then heard a whoosh directly in front of me where Trina must have fired another disk, hitting a man who was still targeting the Rawkyren.

When he fell, I got my first look at the creature, very briefly as it balanced on a rock in the center of a pond. It was no larger than a bird of prey, so it must have been a very young dragon, its silvery wings outstretched and flapping vigorously, but unable to fly due to a disk stuck into its front leg.

With increased anger, I attacked both of the two remaining men simultaneously, stabbing the first in the shoulder, then kicking at the man coming up behind me until I could face him directly.

"Do you know what those are, what they become?" that man said as I wheeled around with my sword ready again.

"I might ask the same question of you," I answered. "Can't you see what *you* have become?"

He scowled and charged at me. I dodged it, but he continued running past me into the pond for another attack on the young dragon. It screeched again, though this time it sounded like fear more than pain. Its cry stung my ears and burned holes through my heart. How could this man be so unfeeling?

I attacked him from behind, but he grabbed me and threw me sideways into the pond, then stabbed downward, slicing my arm. I felt the sting of the injury, but something worse came with it, like vinegar was seeping into the wound.

"Simon!" Trina darted from the trees and shot the man who had stabbed me, but my attention was on the Rawkyren perched within easy reach of me now. It had enormous eyes, filled with as much pain as I felt. It widened its mouth, revealing developing rows of teeth, and let out a cry that could have easily come from me too.

I reached up with my injured arm to remove the disk stuck in its leg. The instant I pulled it out, the Rawkyren recoiled, then opened its mouth again and shot fire onto my arm.

I screamed as it seared my flesh, but the instant it was over, Trina grabbed my other hand, pulling me from the mud pit. With her arm around my shoulders to brace me, I took another glance back at the dragon, hoping for a better look at it, but it had somehow disappeared. The voices of more soldiers weren't far off. We needed to go.

Trina nodded at my arm as she helped me hurry away. "We need to get some water on it. Different water . . . than what was in that pond."

We had passed a stream a short distance back, and I followed Trina there now. I knelt beside it and dipped my right arm in the water. The dragon breath had burned much of the sleeve of my longcoat, exposing the flesh, which was bright red from the burn except for the line created by the stab wound. It wasn't bleeding anymore, but instead was a solid black line. Whether intended or not, the dragon's breath had cauterized the wound. My arm stung beyond anything I could describe, not only the skin, but inside my arm, as if sealing the wound had kept something inside me that shouldn't be there.

Trina gasped when I pulled my burned arm from the water. "Does it hurt?"

I tilted my head at her, unwilling to explain the obvious. When she nodded in understanding, I shrugged and said the only thing I could: "Let's rejoin the others."

By the time we returned to the main part of the forest, the morning sun was higher in the sky, and I recoiled in horror. The forest was littered with the dead and wounded from both sides. And still the

Dominion kept coming. Their condors had broken holes through the forest canopy and rained fire pellets down whenever they spotted a valuable enough target. Carnoxen and oropods ran wild without riders, attacking fighters from both sides who happened to be in their way, and I saw no discernable leadership in place, meaning the fighting had become exactly what Mindall had predicted: chaotic and brutal.

This was entirely different from my past experience as a Corack. We hit hard and fast, with sharply focused targets and clear goals. I wasn't at all prepared for open warfare such as this.

Trina led us toward the clearing around King's Lake, where the fighting worsened considerably. Here, the casualties carpeted the ground, making it impossible to travel five steps in any direction without nearly tripping over a fallen body. Black smoke rose from a patch of burned trees, the air reeked of blood, and the only noises were the clashes of steel blades and grunts of soldiers fighting for their lives.

I recognized Harlyn in the battle and was relieved to see her safe. She had just rescued a Reddengrad soldier whose halberd was broken in half. She offered a hand to help him up and briefly smiled at me.

Commander Mindall was with his fighters to my left, attempting to hold back a line of Ironhearts to stop them from entering the clearing. While Trina ran in one direction, I joined the Commander, but when I reached for my sword, I lacked the strength to even pull it from its scabbard. I backed into the thicket until I was alone and examined my injury again. The burn had turned darker but wasn't blistering as a severe wound should. Which would have given me hope, except my arm also felt weaker than it had when I'd first been burned. Something was definitely wrong.

Out in the clearing, Mindall called for all available Halderians to come for reinforcement. I made a fist and grimaced at how weak it was, then heeded his call.

When I emerged, I almost careened into a large Ironheart riding a carnox. The animal reared up, and while I fumbled for my knife, it pushed me to the ground with its front paws. I landed on a small stump of a fallen tree, which dug into my back and stole my breath.

"Simon!" Harlyn cried.

The Ironheart leaned over the animal and gave a booming laugh. "You're Simon Hatch? We assumed this would be harder!"

"That what would be harder?" Better we talked than he ordered his carnox to take a bite from me.

"Finding you in all this chaos. We expected they'd have protected you better. Don't you know that every soldier here has orders to find you?"

By then, I had squirmed free enough to reach my knife with my left hand. I pierced the hide of the carnox but that made it angrier and it stomped a paw down on my leg. Hoping to ease the pain, I rolled sideways, but it didn't help and put me in a worse position defensively.

The Ironheart started to give his animal an order, but then he grunted loudly. By the time I looked back, he was already falling from the animal, with Harlyn standing directly behind him, her sword now in the carnox's side. It stumbled back, freeing my leg, and fell dead.

She rushed over to me. "Are you hurt?"

"Hurting, but not hurt," I said, though it took her help to stand again.

However, before she released my hand, she rotated it to see the burn on my arm and the cauterized wound. "What happened?"

I pulled my hand away. "I'm sure someone in the Reddengrad army knows what to do. Or our physician, Loelle." I wished I knew where she was.

"It looks painful."

I started to shake my head but Harlyn put a hand on my shoulder. "Why do the soldiers here have orders to find you?"

"Long story."

"Well, for now, stay with me and maybe you'll live long enough to tell me the story."

I balled my hand into a fist but felt even less strength in it than before. If I fought, it would have to be with my left hand, which was far less useable. I'd do better at Harlyn's side.

Harlyn ran with me toward the far end of King's Lake, where a bridge had been built to allow crossing over the wide river. On our side of the lake, Basil was with Trina and at least fifty men, all of them laying fallen trees in a tall horizontal stack. It would give us a firm position to gather when the battle made it this far.

I pulled Basil aside. "You need to get under cover. If there's a target on me, surely there is on you too."

"I'm a prince," Basil said. "And you should be a king. We're always targeted." He took a deep breath. "I was sorry to hear about the loss of the Lonetree Camp. How will that affect the rebellion?"

"It will crush us," Trina said. "That one assault on the camp probably scattered or killed eighty percent of our people." She glanced over at me. "How is your arm?"

Harlyn grabbed my hand and lifted it for Basil to see the injury. He stared up at me with widened eyes. "You found a Rawkyren." It wasn't a question, nor did he look at all happy to have spoken those words.

"What can we do for him?" Harlyn asked.

"I know what this means." Basil's frown became pronounced. "When we have time, I'll explain. But this may change everything."

His words were drowned out by another screeching sound overhead, different from the Rawkyren's. "Everyone get behind the barricades!" Basil ordered.

His own men were calling for him to come, but he waited for Trina and me to run ahead of him. A shadow passed over him and he paused to look up. Trina screamed out a warning, but it was too late. A giant condor swooped down, grabbing Basil with its talons and carrying him into the air.

"Bring down that bird!" I shouted, running out from behind the barricades. His men threw their pikes and the few who had disk bows aimed them upward, but the condor was already out of range. Both Basil and the bird disappeared into the morning sun, almost certainly headed to the dungeons of Highwyn. Almost certainly headed to his doom.

· FORTY-ONE ·

SIMON

Watching Basil be carried away had hit me like cannon fire, and I was still reeling, staying on my feet only with sheer willpower. Through all the commotion around me, I stared at the sky until his body disappeared, fully aware of the torture and terror that awaited him, and how little any of us could do to stop it.

Almost immediately after I last saw him, the Dominion army crashed into the clearing, breaking through Commander Mindall's lines. We had nowhere to retreat.

A gray-haired Reddengrad soldier took up command, ordering half the men to raise their pikes while the rest of the men continued to build new barricades behind us. My sword was in my left hand, almost entirely useless. Harlyn looked over at me with widened eyes, and asked, "Is this the end?"

A horn sang out in the distance and suddenly everything went silent. No more thundering of running animals, no whooshing sound of blades from the thicket. No orders being shouted. Basil's men froze in their work too, looking to their new captain for answers. It became eerily quiet, with only the rushing river echoing in my ears.

From up on the hillside, a sound slowly grew from a soft, rhythmic beat to dozens of footsteps in a precise march. I turned toward the top of the hill on the south side of the river. My heart sank the instant I saw them.

These were some of the Coracks from the Lonetree Camp, fifty or more. I recognized many of them, though even from this distance, I knew something was wrong. Their expressions were flat, and their eyes were fixed toward the Dominion armies, as though they were waiting for orders. There could only be one reason for it.

"Ironhearts," I mumbled, the single word washing a chill over me. Endrick was clearly directing their every move from afar.

One of the men from the back of the two lines moved forward, taking a position in the center. My gut twisted. That was Captain Tenger. Endrick must have known who he was and wanted us to see him so that we'd understand this wasn't only the end of the battle; this was the end of the rebellion.

Above us, more condors swooped in from overhead, firing pellets that demolished our barricades and forced us back out into the open fields. I charged out with the men, though with one injured arm now holding only a knife, I knew I had the disadvantage. No, it was worse than that. I had little hope for myself or anyone else here.

Near the edge of the forest, a soldier at least a head taller than me raised his sword in my direction. I sighed and lowered my knife like I'd accepted defeat. And maybe I had, though not to this oversized fool. When he was nearly to me, I ducked away from his sword and instead plunged the knife directly into his chest. It cost me a deep slice on my shoulder, but he fell at my feet.

Nauseous and overwhelmed with pain, I stumbled into the forest to collect myself, finally settling in the brush against a tree. My shoulder was bleeding and I covered it with my hand, then closed my eyes to rest, to figure out what to do next.

Though as far as I could tell, we were entirely out of options.

We had lost, and every one of us would pay for it with our lives.

· FORTY-TWO ·

KESTRA

I crossed the Mistriver Bridge without being noticed, but on the outskirts of the Nesting Woods, I met my first Ironheart, a man who must have been captive to Lord Endrick for so long that his eyes were utterly deadened. He charged at me with his sword out, forcing me to react. I felled him with the Brillian sword I had taken from Wynnow's palace, amazed at how light the metal was, and how sharp. It truly was a superior weapon.

On his heels, four more soldiers rushed toward me, all with swords positioned for attack. I swung at the first two and left my mark, but the third one cut my arm as he rode by, so deep I nearly fell from my horse. With my free hand, I grabbed the outstretched arm of the nearest soldier and drew enough strength from him to heal my wound, and then took more until he toppled to the ground without a single visible injury.

This group must have been assigned to protect the perimeter of the forest, for I saw the smoke rising from the canopy and the condors flying overhead. That's where the real battle would be. That's where Simon would be.

Because of the thick undergrowth, it was necessary to leave my horse outside the forest, and so I tied it off, then headed as quietly as possible toward the fighting. I kept the hood of my cloak raised and the sword beneath its folds. There was no sense in announcing myself any sooner than necessary.

I saw signs of a few skirmishes that must have happened here, but the deeper I went, the louder the sounds of battle became, the thicker the scent of blood and smoke. I couldn't imagine what yet awaited me.

Then up ahead, I saw a body resting against a tree and drew in a sharp breath. That was Simon! Was he—

I crept up to him, crouching at his side and watching for the rise and fall of his chest beneath his coat. I saw it and finally released the tense breath locked in my throat. His face was dirty, and speckles of blood flecked one cheek. His shoulder bore a deep cut and was still bleeding. I put my hand over his wound and with a little concentration, felt the injury come to me. Not all of it—Loelle had said no more than half. But I gave enough to stop the bleeding.

He'd be angry when he figured out I'd used magic to heal the wound, but what did that matter now? I wouldn't apologize for having magic, nor should I have to. Still, I wished we had spoken about it before he got a demonstration.

Simon stirred and then his eyes flickered open, immediately settling on me. They creased at the corners as he took me in, blinking a few times in disbelief. I knew I should say something, but in the moment, I didn't know how to begin the conversation. Or how to continue it past "hello." Or how to speak to him at all.

"Kes?" he mumbled, looking genuinely confused.

Then from out of nowhere, I heard a shout and saw a Dominion soldier headed toward me, his sword out. I stood in time to clash swords with him, but when he swung at me again, I snatched his hand and immediately pulled as much strength as I could from him, enough to instantly drop him to his knees. He stumbled through a few words of bewilderment, then fell unconscious.

I immediately turned to Simon, whose eyes had become wary, maybe even fearful of me. Without speaking, he looked down at his healed shoulder and then over at the fallen soldier, taking time to absorb what he'd seen. "What have you done?"

"He would've killed you!"

Simon closed his eyes, though the tension in his face remained and his disappointment was as evident as his despair. "But the way you stopped him . . . with magic."

Kneeling beside him, I said, "The things I can do now . . . I can change this battle. I can defeat Lord Endrick."

I'd never expected him to cheer for the news that I'd acquired magic, but couldn't he at least try to see the good it might accomplish? Instead, he sat up straighter and rubbed his shoulder, taking far longer than he should have. When he looked up again, his eyes were even colder than before.

"Be careful, Kes. It's dangerous to play with the power of life and death."

I pointed to the sword at his side. "And what is that you carry? Does it not also let you play with life and death?"

"That is not the same! I never *want* to use this sword!"

"And I never asked for this power! But if you must sometimes take life, why is it wrong for me to give life?"

"Because it comes at a price. You give to someone who is dying, and a piece of you disappears. You take life and absorb a piece of them. In time, how do you know that won't fracture you?"

I stood, full of fire and frustration, but trying not to shout. "Simon, I'm still me!"

"What does that mean?" Something burst inside him too. "Because at any given moment, I don't know who *you* are anymore. Are you a Dallisor? Corack? Endrean?"

His words cut me deeper than he might have known. Barely able to look at him, I said, "I remember you telling me that no matter who I was, you'd always care for me."

"Care for you?" He grunted. "All you remember of us is that I care for you?"

His words hung in the air like a fog growing between us. I continued staring at him, but I no longer saw him, not really. A tear escaped my eye. "I'm alive, Simon. I thought you'd at least be happy about that."

A heavy silence followed before he finally stood, though he wasn't making the effort to get any closer to me. "After all that we've been through, how can you believe that I only *care* for you?"

"Simon?" A rather pretty Halderian girl was running toward him, her sword out. "I saw—oh."

She had noticed me and immediately lowered her sword. She tossed a look from Simon to the fallen Dominion soldier, and finally back to me, then said, "I'm Harlyn Mindall. And you're the Infidante."

"This is Kestra Dallisor," Simon said, blandly motioning toward me.

An awkward silence fell between the three of us. My head was spinning from the words Simon and I had just exchanged. If I'd been unsure before of his feelings for me, I was more confused now. I didn't even know if we were still friends—let alone whatever we used to be. And it was obvious that he and Harlyn were. Maybe even more than friends.

She finally said to him, "I didn't mean to intrude. It's just that the battle—"

"That's why I came," I said, eager for any reason to escape. "For the battle. Only the battle." And I left.

Simon called my name, but I ran until I emerged into the clearing, instantly assaulted by the sights and sounds of a terrible battle. I became surrounded by a tangle of soldiers and fighters wearing Reddengrad uniforms and Halderian colors, and scattered animals, some running about in a leaderless frenzy, others injured, others still attacking whoever was within reach of their claws or teeth, without regard to uniform.

I continued running, dodging every possible fight while Simon's words streamed through my head, asking if the powers I had would eventually fracture me. It was only a question, only an idea concocted from his belief that all magic was inherently bad.

But it had also unnerved me, and I was no longer sure if I should use these powers again. That is, until my gaze turned onto a hill on the far side of the lake, to the strangest thing I'd ever seen: Coracks I recognized from the Lonetree Camp, simply standing there watching, with Tenger at the forefront. They were statues that breathed and blinked but did nothing, even as the battle raged on. They were Ironhearts now.

Thanks to Wynnow's betrayal, and the necklace I'd worn in camp, Endrick had captured them and done this. I knew what they were experiencing, how it felt to be controlled by orders that took over thought or reason, to instinctively know that disobedience equaled death. I also understood that if Endrick killed Tenger, the rebellion would receive a fatal blow.

Whether Simon was right or wrong about the magic within me, I had to help the Coracks now. I charged up the hillside, fighting only when necessary. Tenger was too visible for me to dare rescuing him, but I put a hand on the heart of the nearest Corack at the back of their two lines, the boy who had shown admiration for Simon when he first brought me into the camp.

I gave him from my strength, hoping to heal the piece of his heart that Endrick had taken as his own. It put a pinch in my chest, but I was strong enough to manage that, and seconds later, the boy came to, as if awoken from a daze.

He recognized me and seemed to know exactly what was going on. "We can see the fighting, my lady," he said. "We just can't do anything about it."

"Now you can. Go!" I did the same to a dozen other Coracks along the back line. I wanted to do more, and I knew I had to get to Tenger. But by then, I was too weak to help anyone else. I needed to take some strength too.

But not yet.

Instead, I hid within the tall grasses of the hill and watched the unfolding battle. For as fiercely as the Halderian soldiers and Reddengrad armies were fighting, we had no chance of winning. Not unless I could get stronger and return to the battle.

Then, from out of the forest, eight men on horseback entered the clearing, all in Dominion colors. I immediately recognized the man in front, Sir Henry, and my fingers grew numb. Despite knowing exactly the kind of monster he was, including what I'd suffered at his hand, it disturbed me to know I might have to use magic on him as well, whether today or in the coming weeks. He was my enemy, he served the king who had tortured me, and he detested me above most others in his world. But in some small way, he'd also been my father once, and maybe deep inside me, I had a measure of love for him. Henry surveyed the scene and by his gestures to his officers, he seemed to be pleased with their progress in battle.

A horn was sounded, loud enough that most fighters stopped in their places and turned toward Sir Henry, who called out, "I am told that my beloved daughter is here. You may know her as the Infidante. I will guarantee the life of anyone who turns her in to me. However, if she is not turned over in the next fifteen minutes, all of you must die."

My shoulders fell. Apparently, to him, I was only an enemy. Nothing more.

· FORTY-THREE ·

KESTRA

They must not have known where I was, or Sir Henry simply would have ordered the remaining Corack Ironhearts near me to attack, knowing I'd never harm them. That bought me a little time . . . but time to do what?

I wasn't as strong yet as I wished to be, but even if I were, I couldn't turn this battle. At best, I'd take down a few of their soldiers, and in response, the Dominion would finish the battle with total destruction laid at my feet.

There was only one solution. My hands trembled at the thought of it, and I didn't know how I'd get the courage to walk down the hill, but I had to do it.

I had to surrender.

I rose to my feet, but paused to see a girl riding across the clearing toward Sir Henry. I squinted, trying to get a better look. It was that Halderian girl I'd met earlier—Harlyn Mindall. I snorted and shook my head. Of course she would be the one to turn me in. I wondered if Simon knew what she was doing.

Did he?

Simon's reaction to seeing me again had been even colder than I'd expected, proof of the pain he must still be feeling. I couldn't fully understand it, but I did know that when I'd seen fear—of me—in his eyes, it had shattered my last hope for us, if there ever was much hope.

Harlyn finished her conversation with Sir Henry, ending with a handshake, and her wiping tears from her eyes. Then she gestured some sort of signal toward my side of the lake, where the bulk of the Halderians had gathered.

Harlyn would not shed tears for me, so they must've had a different conversation. Which meant there was no point in delaying my surrender. Feeling stronger now, I began to walk downhill, but a hand grabbed me from behind, covering my mouth. I thrust an elbow backward and heard a grunt, then a hand clutched my sword arm. Trina said, "Kestra, stop, it's me!"

I turned enough to see Trina behind me, though I was being held by an enormous Corack she introduced only as Huge. As soon as I relaxed, he released me. I said, "This isn't necessary. I was already going down there."

"What?" Trina's face twisted. "No, Kestra, that's not the plan. Follow us."

I glanced down to the clearing. The fighting had ceased as everyone silently counted down their fifteen minutes to a fate that now depended entirely on me.

With a heavy sigh, I lowered my sword then followed Huge and Trina behind a ridge of the hill, as heavily wooded as the rest of the surrounding forest, which meant I didn't see Simon until I was almost beside him. But he certainly was looking at me, his gaze as intense as it ever was.

If only it had not come so late. My time was running out.

"Will everyone leave us?" Simon asked, keeping his eyes on me. His request was honored. Trina and Huge and a few of the Coracks I'd rescued immediately vacated the area.

"You left before our conversation was over," he said.

I shifted my weight, too uncomfortable to remain in one position. "Your feelings were clear. You're afraid of me, maybe even revolted by me now, with magic."

I turned to leave, but Simon moved so as to block my path and to keep himself in front of me. "I'm afraid of your magic, yes, of what it means for your future, but what I feel for you"—he stopped, as if overcome by his own words—"is so much more than simply caring." Now he took my hand in his, adding, "I wanted to share your life, share in every moment I could. I start each day hoping you will be there. I haven't ended a day since we parted without torturing myself by wondering where you are."

There was no more fear in his eyes, no more suspicion or silent accusations against me. All I saw was tenderness and affection. I gave his fingers a squeeze and he smiled, but it was hollow and forced. Something was still terribly wrong, I just didn't know what it was.

From wherever she was stationed, Trina called out, "It's almost time."

I nodded, accepting my fate. It was good they had kept track of the time, because I'd almost forgotten about it.

Simon grabbed my arm, pulling me back. "You're not going out there. Henry saw you storm into the clearing a few minutes ago, how upset you were. Harlyn convinced him that you left the battle."

That was why she'd ridden out there? I was missing something. "Henry set new terms?"

He nodded. "They favor us. He's agreed to release the Coracks, and all our fighters here can leave in peace. We couldn't have hoped for more."

My eyes narrowed. "What did we promise him in exchange?" It must have been something big, and if it wasn't me . . .

Simon kicked at the leaves beneath his feet and my heart sank. "No, Simon. You are not taking my place!"

"I'm not as valuable a prize to the Dominion as you'd be, but I'm enough for them to claim some sort of victory."

Anger rose in me. "I have no value as Infidante. I still don't know where the Olden Blade is. I have few friends and even fewer people I can trust. Nowhere is safe for me, especially now that I have magic."

He shook his head. "I've made the agreement with Sir Henry. Let it be."

"I will not! He won't save the Coracks, he probably won't even end the fighting. Your agreement is madness."

Simon gestured toward the valley below us. "This battle is madness! The fact that we continue fighting despite everything Lord Endrick has done to us is madness!"

"It's nothing to what he'll still do if he is not stopped."

"Yes, he must be stopped. That's why you have to live."

"No, you listen to me!" I felt how quickly each second was passing before I'd lose him all over again. "I can't fight him alone. I came here for you. I came to save you."

"Kestra—"

"How could you make such a foolish bargain?"

"I did it for you!" He drew in a sharp breath. "If I go out there, you will live."

Silence followed his words and every thought in my head emptied, except for one: This was for me.

He stepped closer and wiped the tears from my cheek. "You will defeat Endrick one day." How tender his voice was, how gentle. "I wish I could be there to see it."

"Don't do this," I said.

He shrugged. "It's done."

"Not for me. Your mother's life was a sacrifice so that I would live. Do you know how that tortures me? I will not play these games of whose life is most valuable."

Now Trina crossed the ridge and coughed to get our attention. "We have to go, Simon."

He nodded and started to climb up to her, but turned back long enough to say, "*Your* life is most valuable. If necessary, we will all die for you."

Words that would haunt me forever. Unless . . .

I waited until he crossed the ridge, then started off in a different direction, immediately bumping into Huge, who must have been sent to keep me here.

I folded my arms and in my sternest voice said, "How will they do it?"

Huge frowned, though it still took him a moment to say, "Simon will go halfway across the bridge. Our archer will fire the shot and he will fall into the river."

"The disk?" I asked.

As if he hardly dared to speak the words, he whispered, "White. They're not taking any chances."

My breath caught in my throat. A white disk. A fate worse than death, forever suspending Simon in a half-life of wandering and misery.

"I'm leaving," I said. "And you will not stop me."

Huge blocked my way. "I have to stop you. Those were Simon's orders."

"Simon is not your captain."

"Nor are you, Infidante."

"Huge, if you saw me on the battlefield, you know that I can get past you if I want to. Don't make me hurt you."

He widened his stance. "My lady, it's not only Simon who will die for you. If you want to get past me, you'll have to take my life, for I will give it if necessary to keep you here."

I sighed, then reached out a hand. "As you wish." Before he could react, he dropped to the ground. Seconds after that, he was flat upon it.

· FORTY-FOUR ·

SIMON

I hated the way I'd left. I hated that a fight would be our last moment together. Maybe that was for the best. It might be worse for her to have a final memory of us that was happy . . . that was hopeful.

Except that I knew Kestra wasn't out there dwelling on hope. She'd be searching for a solution, for some way to save me. And knowing Kestra, she'd convince herself that whatever plan she came up with actually had a chance.

It didn't. I knew what the Dominion had planned for me. It was terrifying, but it had to be me. Justice demanded it. I was the one who'd infiltrated Woodcourt, embarrassed the Dominion, and forced Kestra to find the Olden Blade. Trina had been there too, of course, but Sir Henry didn't know about her, and I intended to keep it that way.

Trina had silently accompanied me down the hillside, but before we left the thicket, she touched my arm. Her face was deeply lined with worry and she was blinking too fast, as if fighting back tears. That was all right. So was I.

"Are you ready?" she asked, her voice quivering.

I took a deep breath before turning to her. Nothing could possibly make me *ready* for what was about to happen.

"Let's keep walking," I said. We had to keep walking because if I stopped too long, I knew I'd turn and run.

"I need to tell you . . ." Trina's eyes darted, then she exhaled and looked at me again. "Someone needs to thank you for doing this. It might as well be me."

"He's not really going through with this!" Harlyn ran into the thicket and must have been close enough to overhear us. She looked at me and her eyes widened with fear. "There has to be a distraction, Simon, a trick. Let me help."

When neither of us answered her, she stepped toward me, and now her breaths came out in harsh gasps. "I only made the bargain with Sir Henry because you said it was part of a larger plan!"

"It is." I forced myself to look at her, knowing how she'd respond. "But not to save me."

Harlyn shook her head, becoming angrier as she did. "Kestra Dallisor's life is not worth losing yours! We can find another Infidante."

"But not another Kestra." I frowned at her, deeply sorry to be causing her so much pain, then kissed her cheek and walked from the grove with Trina at my side. Harlyn called after me, "What kind of person is Kestra anyway, that she would let you die to save herself?"

I started to turn, but Trina linked her arm with mine, keeping us moving forward. "You won't change her mind, Simon, and besides, we're already late."

Also, we'd been spotted. A lookout on the bridge called that I was on my way. As the bridge came better into view, I saw Dominion armies lined up in formation on the far side of the lake while the fighters from Reddengrad and the Hiplands were on this side.

Without looking directly at me, Trina said, "I know we haven't always agreed with each other, but my heart is breaking right now. I—"

I cut her off, saying only, "You'll have to protect Kestra from now on. Including from Harlyn, I think."

"I will, I promise." Trina paused a moment, then added, "Your sacrifice on that bridge won't be in vain. Promise me that you'll look Sir Henry in the eye in your final moments. For your own sake."

I stopped to look at her. "Why?"

She only teared up again, then pulled me into a hug, wrapping one arm around my neck and keeping the other at my waist. Into my ear, she whispered, "You don't deserve the fate of a white disk."

I stepped back from her and wiped a stray tear from her cheek. "Don't join me on the bridge. It's too much of a risk."

"You and Kestra are not the only ones willing to take risks," Trina said. "I am going up there. I need a final assurance of his word to free the Coracks."

As if Sir Henry's word meant anything. "All right, but keep your head down and let me do the talking."

Trina snorted, but I hoped she'd do as I asked. This was hardly the moment to be proud of taking risks.

With those thoughts, the remaining walk to the bridge seemed to last for hours, the worst of it being when the Reddengrad and Halderian fighters parted to allow Trina and me to pass through. They looked at me with respect, as if I were doing this for them, or for Antora. As if I'd thought of anyone but Kestra when I suggested this plan.

Sir Henry stood halfway across the bridge with what I guessed were most of his officers from the battle, along with an entire squad of men surrounding them, well-armed and with expressions of victory on their faces. Any one of them seemed capable of crushing me between his fists without breaking a sweat.

Meanwhile, I had Trina.

I faced Sir Henry, arms folded and as defiant as I could make myself appear. Inside, I felt made of pudding, as if I'd collapse at the slightest touch, but I'd faint in this position before letting him know it.

Sir Henry *tsked*. "I must admit, I didn't think you would come. I had suspected you sent that pretty Halderian girl out as a distraction while you escaped with my daughter . . . again."

"Kestra is not your daughter," I countered.

He smiled, his only acknowledgment of my comment. "I almost wish you hadn't come. It forces me to end a battle in which we were performing quite well. We would have won, although as soon as you fall, I'll order my men to follow Kestra and return her to Lord Endrick's control."

"She's probably already past the Mistriver by now." Trina's lie was surprisingly bold and hardly what I'd had in mind by suggesting she keep her head down. "But if Simon keeps his word, will you keep yours? Lord Endrick will release the Coracks on that hill?"

Sir Henry's smile reeked of insincerity. "Of course."

Trina nodded at him, then looked in my eyes to say a sorrowful, "Good-bye, Simon."

My heart pounded, but I no longer trusted myself with words. I merely squeezed her hand and nodded back at her. Notably, she turned me to face Sir Henry before she released my hand. Whatever her purpose in doing so, that was obviously her real reason for coming onto the bridge.

Trina started to leave when Henry said, "Wait. Turn around, girl."

Trina huffed, but obeyed, looking down as she turned to face him. *Now* her eyes were down.

"You were at Woodcourt too," Henry said. "My daughter's handmaiden. Correct?"

Before Trina could protest, he cocked his head and three of his thugs stepped forward, grabbing Trina by the hands and feet. She tried pulling away but failed and screamed as they lifted her into the air.

I touched Trina's arm but was pushed back before I could help her. The terror in her expression turned to a calm realization that her fate was now as sealed as mine. She locked eyes with me and mouthed, "I'm sorry!"

"Let the Coracks die!" Henry screamed to our side of the lake. "With my authority as Lord Endrick's representative, I order your hearts to be crushed!"

"No!" Trina cried. But even as she did, every single Corack that had been on the hillside instantly fell to the ground, unmoving. Dead. Including Tenger. There was nothing I could do for them, but I could still save Trina.

I tried again to reach her, but another of Henry's men grabbed me from behind. "She was only following my orders!" I shouted, still struggling.

"Then she'll receive your punishment." With another nod, Trina was thrown backward off the bridge, screaming as she fell into the icy water, her voice immediately drowned out as she sank.

Halderians watching us gave audible gasps, but I heard none of their shouts above the man holding me, who said, "What is this?"

Henry's face reddened as he reached into the left pocket of my longcoat and withdrew the Brillian fire pellet, about the size of my fist.

I cursed under my breath and looked down while I put everything together. This was why Trina had apologized. In our brief embrace back on land, she must have slipped this into my coat, telling me she would save me from the white disk. And she had wanted me to face Sir Henry so that when she left the bridge, the pocket with the fire pellet would be closest to her. It would explode when squeezed, but I suspected her alternate plan was to shoot me with something to ignite the pellet, killing me before I was hit with the white disk and bringing down everyone on this bridge.

Sir Henry must have realized this too. His eyes became thin slits as he said, "How dare you?" He speared a fist into my gut and I doubled over with pain. I hadn't fully regained my breath when I straightened up, hoping to get a hand on the pellet, but Sir Henry lifted it out of my reach.

And I was too late. Directly in front of me, a Dominion archer already had me in his sights with a white disk in the pocket. Tenger had once told me there was peace in a person's final breath of life. In that moment, I knew he was wrong.

The instant the blade hit me, I fell backward over the thin railing, just as Trina had done. It felt like hours until my body splashed in, fueling the pain in my chest where the disk had hit. Somewhere above me came a loud thundering noise but I couldn't imagine what it was, nor did it matter. The current was rapidly carrying me downstream, but I felt myself separating from my body as if part of me was already somewhere else, somewhere dark and bleak.

I clutched at the blade in my chest, hoping to pull it out, then gave up. It wouldn't matter. The water blurred my vision, or maybe this was the beginning of my end, to lose focus on the real world. At least I wasn't in pain anymore. I wasn't anything.

From the corner of my eye, some movement caught my attention. I wished I were stronger, or that I could make myself care. But this wasn't my world anymore. This wasn't my life.

An arm wrapped tightly around me, but I didn't feel it. I only knew it was there.

The arm was holding a body that might've been mine, once, whoever I was, whatever I was. I felt no connection to flesh anymore. I felt no connection to life.

· FORTY-FIVE ·

KESTRA

Downstream from the bridge, I was stationed in some thick brush beside the river. I doubted anyone would see me here, though I had a good view of both the bridge and the Coracks on the hillside. My heart was racing with anticipation, but so far, everything was going according to plan.

Huge must have only been unconscious for a few minutes. Only moments ago, he'd raced past me on horseback headed farther downstream, nodding distinctly at me as he did. I hoped he'd already guessed my plans and intended to help.

My plans . . . such as they were. I hadn't had time to consider any details beyond where I now sat. After leaving Huge, my first stop had been the Ironheart Coracks, and it was a good thing I did because Sir Henry wasted no time in breaking his promise regarding them.

Up on the bridge, I saw the Dominion soldiers grab Trina and then Henry shouted, "With my authority as Lord Endrick's representative, I order your hearts to be crushed!"

A gasp rang out through the assembled armies on our side of the river as one by one, the Coracks collapsed to the ground. A flawless performance. I'd gotten to them just in time.

Before coming here, I'd restored Tenger and the other Coracks, borrowing the health of the few Dominion fighters who'd lain injured on the hillside nearby. The Coracks who'd fallen were very much alive, but for now, we wanted the Dominion to believe the rebellion had been crushed here.

Yet, as smoothly as everything had happened up till this point, it all fell apart on the bridge. Immediately after the Coracks collapsed, Trina was tossed over the bridge, making the long drop into the water. I crouched forward, ready to pull her out if I could, but when her body drifted past me seconds later, she was out of reach and looked unconscious. It twisted my heart to sacrifice her while I waited to help Simon, but I hoped Huge would see her. Why had she come to the bridge anyway?

On the bridge now, a Dominion officer pulled something from the left pocket of Simon's longcoat. I squinted to see it, but only saw something that appeared to be a rock or some sort of dark-colored ball. Whatever it was, it clearly enraged Henry, who slammed his fist so hard into Simon's stomach, he might've fallen without the officer still holding him from behind.

Simon was bent over, so he didn't see Henry's gesture for the archer to take aim. But I saw it, and the white disk that was loaded into his bow. As soon as Simon straightened up, he was hit somewhere in the chest and fell backward into the water. I probably had thirty seconds before he'd drift down to where I was.

A cheer went up on the Dominion side of the bridge when Simon fell, but my attention had shifted to movement on Reddengrad's side. Harlyn Mindall stepped forward from the crowd with her own disk bow raised. She took aim at the bridge and fired.

It hit directly on the ball that Henry had pulled from Simon's coat, and in that instant, the entire bridge exploded. I leapt to my feet, stunned at what was happening. The center collapsed and fell into the river. No one on the bridge could have survived the initial explosion. Including Sir Henry.

He couldn't have survived that.

Simon's body rounded the bend in the river. I was still shaking when I dove in, catching the current barely in time to see him go completely underwater. The water was icy, stealing my breath, but it was nothing compared to what must be happening to Simon now, so I forced myself to keep swimming.

By the time I grabbed hold of him, he was completely unresponsive, possibly already . . . whatever he would be once that disk took effect. I yanked the disk from his chest and blood spilled into the water, but I pressed my hand over the wound to slow the bleeding.

I needed to get us out of the water, but I wasn't sure how far we had to go before it was safe, and I wondered how I'd have the strength to do it. Simon was pulling life from me faster than I could keep us together.

Once I was sure we'd be out of sight, we surfaced, but Simon wasn't breathing and that sent waves of horror through me. Had he already passed the point where I could help him?

Then, from nowhere, hands reached into the water, plucking both me and Simon out of the water. I looked up and saw Huge standing over us. "Two fish with one hook," he said proudly, pulling us to shore. This was where he'd been in such a hurry to go. He must've guessed at my intentions.

"I . . ." I couldn't muster the words to explain myself and instead only managed, "I'm sorry . . . for before." To which he nodded in reply.

Trina was on the shoreline shivering, but on her feet with wide eyes and the same expression of panic as I felt. She cried, "Is he——"

Huge lowered Simon to the ground first then I knelt beside him, rolling Simon's lifeless face toward me. He was visibly shaking and his skin was draining of color. It terrified me to my core, and from that same place I yelled, "You are *not* leaving this way, do you hear me?"

If he heard, he didn't respond.

I put my hand back on his chest, near where the disk blade had entered. The wound was slowly healing, but it didn't matter because that wasn't the true threat against him. Louder, I cried, "Simon, don't you walk away without a fight!"

His lashes fluttered, which I supposed was the best fight he could manage. I knew he'd disapprove of what was coming next, but I hardly cared. If he objected, he could wake up and tell me so.

The white blade was stealing away his soul. The only cure would be to give him half of mine, half of everything I was to pull him back to himself. It wasn't enough to give him from my strength. I had to give him a piece of me.

With my other hand over my chest, I willed any power in me to transfer to him. Instantly, I felt a gathering of energy toward my hand, a swelling of something deeper than the beat of my heart or the blood in my veins. It was whatever force kept me alive, and I sent it to him through my hand.

Emptying out so much of myself immediately took its toll. A wave of dizziness washed over me, but I kept my hand in place, holding on to him with only tendrils of hope to connect us.

A piece of my own soul must have transferred too, because suddenly I was part of him. Whatever of Simon remained.

How very empty he was, little more than a shell of who he had been. Hoping for anything I could latch on to, I dug deeper and through our connection, found remnants of his soul, scattered like leaves in the wind. His worries still remained, stronger now with no reason or thought to control them. No wonder he had been shaking. I felt those same emotions too, and they filled me with ice. I understood now why he didn't want to take the throne, how he feared he'd be less than he should. Then I saw myself through his eyes. Not as I was now, but as he feared I might become with magic. Corrupted, vengeful, rotted from within. With gray scarred lines on my face, one for each death I had caused.

Just like Endrick.

I recoiled from that with so much force, so much terror, that I returned to myself beside the river. Nothing had changed. I leaned in closer, hoping he could sense that I was here with him, very much alive, and that I needed him to stay alive too.

"Simon, you come back to me!" I shouted. "I can't fight alone!"

"His finger twitched!" Trina cried. "Kestra, keep going!"

I wanted to, but there wasn't much of me left either. Simon was borrowing more than half of my soul; he was feeding on my emotions, my physical strength. He was emptying me out just to keep a thread of himself connected to reality.

But with that thread, he must have been aware of my presence inside him, for I felt his soul wrap around mine as if it were an object of curiosity. He needed to do this, but every piece of him that was being pulled away took more of me too.

That piece of me entered the world of Endrick's eternal punishment and it was worse than anything I could have imagined. Nothing was here but a dark empty field, where hundreds of others who had been given similar fates wandered, forever restless. They were in a dense maze of trees, burned to nothing but blackened sticks in sterilized soil. Seeking to cure a hunger that could not be filled, searching for relief from pain that could not be healed. These were the souls who wandered All Spirits Forest. It was more than a prison for those who had tried to take shelter there during the War of Devastation, many of them Loelle's people. It was also the worst sort of prison Lord Endrick could have created. Simon would go here too.

"Kestra?" In this vision, I saw a man staring at me, familiar but part of a distant memory. He was clothed as I last remembered him, but entirely without color and with gray wisps fluttering from his body, each loss a slow deterioration of what it was to be him.

"Darrow?" I blinked hard. "Father?"

"This is no place for you," he said. "Get out while you can!" And he interlocked his fingers, shoving a rush of energy toward me that thrust me back into my own reality, even as I clutched for one last glimpse of him and watched him vanish before my eyes.

I was here again by the side of the river, kneeling over Simon and now fully aware of his destination if I could not pull him back.

I shook Simon's body, then put both hands on his chest again, willing to sacrifice my whole life if it saved him from that place, from that doomed forest. "Come back," I ordered him. "Now!"

And with a final burst of magic, something rushed into him with so much force that it knocked my hands from his chest and rolled me backward. When I opened my eyes, Simon was staring at me, confused, but slowly becoming aware of his surroundings. It was him.

I sat up again and touched his face. He whispered my name, but I wasn't finished. I couldn't be finished because the wound in his chest was open again. I hadn't pulled him back together only to lose him to physical injury now.

My hand was shaking when I placed it near the wound. I tried to pull the injury to myself, but it wouldn't come. I put one hand over the other, ignoring his whispers for me to stop, ignoring the warnings in my own head that I'd gone too far.

"Enough!" From behind, Trina pulled me away from him. "Kestra, you've done enough."

I shook my head and tried to get back to his side, but I had no strength for it. When I looked at her, I realized we were no longer alone. It wasn't only Huge and Trina here. A man on horseback in a brown uniform with a blue sash was here along with another dozen Halderians.

I spoke to the man on horseback, assuming he was in charge. "You can bind his wound now—you can save him."

Trina addressed the same man. "Commander Mindall, he needs your help."

"I respect his courage, but fixing this injury would require too many of our supplies. We'll use them on our own men."

Somehow, I found it in me to look up at the commander and say, "He is the most important of all your men."

"Kes, no," Simon mumbled, though he was weaker than I was and could not stop me.

Simon's satchel was still around his shoulder. Trina dug through it to find his ring, then held it up as I said, "King Gareth chose this boy as his successor. Simon has the king's ring and if you look closely, you will recognize the sword he wears. He is your king, and you will do everything in your power to save his life now."

All eyes turned to Mindall, who took a few deliberate breaths before saying, "Give this boy everything he needs to stay alive."

Simon's eyes fluttered as he was carried away. I didn't care if he was angry with me. He was alive.

And only once he was gone did I collapse too.

· FORTY-SIX ·

KESTRA

oon after Simon was taken away, Huge leaned over me as I
lay on the sand, struggling to remain conscious. "Take some
strength from me, my lady. I've got plenty."

I shook my head, mumbling, "I already did that. I won't do it
again."

Trina knelt at my side. "Then use me." She nudged my hand
onto her arm. "Just don't get greedy."

I didn't want to, but the truth was that I had given too much to
Simon and I was having trouble keeping my eyes open. The way I felt,
if I closed them for too long, they might remain that way.

"I'm sorry for this." I tried to control the pull of Trina's strength
toward me, but even then, she gasped when she felt the tug of my
magic.

I took from her the least I needed to keep myself alive, and it lasted
only a few seconds, but when I pulled my hand free, she was leaning
heavily on one arm to prevent herself from falling to the ground.

"Still a Dallisor, taking as much as you can," she muttered,
though I thought I saw a hint of a smile.

"Let's get you both to safety." Huge lifted me first, lowering
me into a wagon I hadn't noticed before. Trina was laid beside me,

and we were both fully covered in sheets as would be done for the dead. That seemed appropriate. Even if they were intended to prevent any Dominion soldiers from spotting us, I felt more dead than alive. Before the wagon's first bump, I was asleep.

After waking up, the first words I heard were a scolding.

"You were never to use your skills beyond half of your own strength! That nearly killed you!"

Loelle.

I smiled weakly. "How will I know what half is if I don't go beyond it?" With that, I opened my eyes. I didn't recognize the tent where they were keeping me, but it was small and simple, and I was warm. Better still, I was alive.

"Where are we?" I asked.

"We're in the Hiplands, just outside Nessel. I got here in time to save you from your own foolishness."

"Where's Simon?"

Loelle licked her lips and her eyes darted away from me. "Someone else should answer that question." She stood and parted the tent flap. "She's awake."

A moment later, Captain Tenger and Gabe walked in, surely noticing how my expression deflated. I'd hoped to see Simon.

Gabe leaned against the door, his attempt at guard duty while Tenger took Loelle's seat beside me. "Well, young lady, you have exceeded my expectations."

"How low were your expectations?" I smiled, but it hadn't been a joke.

"Whatever they were, we must ask greater things of you now."

"I'm ready. Just give me the Olden Blade." When he didn't move, my stomach twisted. "You don't have it?"

"Lonetree Camp was destroyed before I got Basil's note. I was hoping he might've told you where it is or offered any clues."

"He didn't. Can't we just ask him now?" I sat up on my elbows, feeling short of breath and desperately worried. "Where's Basil? Is he—"

"Captured by the Dominion. We'll do our best to get him back, Kestra, but if the Dominion realizes he holds the secret of the Olden Blade—"

"Then we're finished." I lay back and closed my eyes, suddenly exhausted.

Tenger patted my arm. "He should have a little extra time, thanks to Trina's bravery."

With my eyes closed, it was far too easy to picture the sudden fire on the bridge, all the bodies that fell. "Trina was responsible for the bridge collapse?"

"And Harlyn Mindall, one of the Halderians. We believe it led to the deaths of at least four senior officers in the Dominion army . . . as well as Sir Henry Dallisor, Lord Endrick's second in command."

I appreciated that Tenger didn't reference him as my father. He was only a name to me now.

Yet, he was more than a name too, though I had no wish to dwell on that.

When I opened my eyes again, Loelle was standing behind the captain, looking as if a terrible weight had settled on her shoulders. Tenger wasn't smiling either. He said, "There is something else of great concern to us. An explosion that makes the bridge collapse look like child's play." He looked up at Loelle to continue.

She said, "After Wynnow caught me with the necklace, she ordered my arrest, but I escaped. For your sake, I remained hidden near the Brillian palace." Loelle paused, possibly recalling the sounds and smells of that night, just as I had so often done. "I saw the explosion, Kestra. It must have destroyed half the capital city, including the entire palace. Seconds later, I saw you race down the hillside as fast as that horse could carry you."

"I didn't cause that!" I said, realizing only after I spoke where this conversation was headed.

"Of course not," Tenger said. "Nothing could explain such extensive damage . . . outside of magic."

Loelle added, "We believe that Lord Endrick was there and that he now has the necklace. Is that true?"

I lowered my eyes, letting my silence answer them. Confirming it aloud would invite more questions, none of which I wanted to revisit.

Tenger gave a long sigh, then said, "I'll require your full explanation . . . when you're stronger. Then we'll figure out how to explain it to the Brillians when they come to you for answers."

I could only imagine how that conversation would go. But for now, I had other worries. "May I see Simon?"

"Not now, I'm afraid."

Alarmed, I started to sit up. "Is he still—"

"Alive? Yes, but he is a king now . . . thanks to you. And he has his duties, as you have yours."

"Five minutes, Tenger. Haven't I earned that much?"

His smile became almost sympathetic. "You have, but that's not my decision. Even I have no access to him. Trust me, I've tried."

Biting on one lip, I asked, "Does he know I'm here?"

"I don't know." Tenger said Gabe's name, then, "You heard the Infidante. Will you try to answer her question? You too, Loelle."

Gabe nodded. "Yes, sir." Then he parted the tent flap for Loelle and followed her out, leaving me alone with Tenger. That was no accident.

Tenger turned back to me, and the time for sympathy had passed. "There's no future for you and Simon, no hope. Do you understand that?"

"Why not? Because you don't believe it's possible?"

"Because you have bigger concerns. Lord Endrick knows by now that you have magic."

I half smiled, though I took no joy in it. "You have no idea how well he knows it."

Tenger clicked his tongue, then leaned forward, one arm on each knee. "If it's true that Endrick has the necklace, then he knows about Simon. If you stay in Nessel, you will bring Endrick here."

Just as I started to reply, Gabe burst in with a scroll in one hand. "A message has come from the Halderians. On behalf of the new king of the Halderian clan, Commander Mindall would like to invite all distinguished Coracks to a supper tonight."

I sat up in bed. "I've got to see him, Tenger."

"The necklace—"

"It's just to say good-bye. Allow me that."

Tenger frowned, but gave me a slight nod. "Just to say good-bye."

· FORTY-SEVEN ·

SIMON

The day after I awoke looked to be unbearably long and utterly without mercy.

I was in a bed of carved wood, tucked between silken sheets that never could belong to someone of my station. But when I tried to get up, the bandages tightly wrapped around my chest, shoulder, and right arm were a reminder that the nightmare I vaguely remembered actually had happened.

Kestra had saved me from the worst of the white disk's consequences. Yet in an entirely different way, I still felt split in half. Based on my surroundings, it seemed that I was now recognized as a king, a title that no more described me than had I been declared ruler of the imaginary Bingebrushies. The other half was simply a boy who'd seen far too much for his years yet was still too young to have any idea what to do now. I was part of the rebellion, a protector at times, and a fool more often than I wished. But I was no king.

Gerald was my first visitor of the day, meeting me in my chambers since the Halderian doctors had apparently asked me not to move about more than was necessary. I had no intention of ignoring them. Moving felt roughly akin to running a saw through my shoulder. I was far from healed.

He sat in a chair next to my bed and smiled over at me. "King Simon. It feels right to call you that."

"I never wanted . . . I don't want . . ." I abandoned that argument. There was no point in debating this with Gerald. "How is Kestra?"

"She's recovering elsewhere. She'll be all right."

But something was wrong. The tension in his voice revealed that much. "Gerald—"

"She is not your concern any longer. The Halderians are your people now."

"She's my main concern, and *my people* should feel the same way. We need her!"

"No, they need *you*." Gerald lowered his voice, trying a more reasonable approach. "Since the war's end, the Halderians have been scattered, hunted . . . broken. And surviving only because they hold to the belief that the Scarlet Throne should be theirs and will be again one day. You must give it back to them."

"How? I am a king with no history, no gold, no claim to the throne other than I happened to be plucked half-dead off a roadside by the right man. We both know I shouldn't be here."

"Yet the people will bow to you." Gerald leaned forward. "Give them a reason for it. Love them, serve them, and give them hope for the future."

I closed my eyes again, sensing the direction of this conversation. "Kestra is our only hope, not me. The people must know that."

Enough silence passed that I finally looked at him again, and when I did, I observed a sincere sadness in his eyes. "My king, she cannot be allowed to remain here. Surely you understand why."

I did understand, in ways I wished I didn't. And in ways I didn't dare explain to anyone else.

Except that Gerald already seemed to know. In a near whisper, he said, "While you've been recovering, you've repeatedly murmured a distinct word in your sleep: *corrupt*."

My eyes darted away from him. "Who else heard?"

They closed entirely when he murmured Harlyn's name, adding, "She's barely left your side. My king, why that word?"

I paused, trying to swallow a lump that had formed in my throat, then finally gave up and said, "I don't know exactly what Kestra did after she pulled me from that river, but for a while, we shared a piece of each other's souls. I don't remember most of it, but I remember sensing that it was already . . ." I hesitated again. I didn't want to think of what I'd felt from her.

"Already corrupting?" Gerald nodded, answering his own question.

In those few seconds between us, I had felt bound to her, wrapped in warmth and love and her unparalleled strength to hold on to me. I'd reached back for her, but instead found a piece of soul that was ice cold, a piece that was dead and spreading. It had frightened me then, and chilled me now.

Gerald continued, "Every time she draws strength in from others, she pulls a portion of themselves to her. Imagine if she ever attempted to do that with someone truly evil, such as Lord Endrick himself."

"It would shatter her." After a pause in which I had to force myself to breathe, I added, "We must find a way to heal it. We'll start by keeping her here, around good people."

"The people saw what she did, and they are grateful. But if they were wary of a Dallisor girl, imagine how they would feel to see her now: an Endrean with exceptionally powerful magic, abilities that will make her the sole target of Lord Endrick. If she remains here, the Dominion will return and destroy whatever we have left."

"We will have nothing left if she fails!"

Gerald nodded, though he clearly didn't agree. "It's possible to make the wrong decision, even for the right reasons. Be wise instead and trust her to leave. If she is strong enough to challenge Lord Endrick, then she can defend herself out there."

"Yes, but the greatest danger—"

"The greatest danger may be the people here who have repeatedly sought her life. Imagine how quickly the Halderians will try again if they believe she is corrupting and if she has any influence over their king."

"Then I won't be king!"

"Who will replace you? Commander Mindall, whose first order will be the same as his last, to find and destroy the Infidante? Execute Mindall and another one just like him will take his place."

I sighed. "I won't lose her, Gerald."

The corners of his eyes creased as he asked, "My king, did you ever have her?" He let me absorb that as he continued, "Send her away for your sake. For the people's sake. Send her away, and let her complete her quest, as she must do. Then you are free to take the Scarlet Throne and restore these people to their proper place in Antora."

"And what happens to her afterward?"

Gerald shrugged. "If she is lucky, she will be allowed to leave Antora. If she is unlucky, or if the corruption worsens before this is over . . ." He glanced up at me without ending his thought.

I shook my head, the only movement I could manage due to the crushing weight resting on my chest. My mind raced to find any scenario in which Kestra and I remained together. And came up with nothing.

"The people surely know how I feel about her. I'll never convince them otherwise."

He sighed. "I've considered that. We must give you a cover. I suggest Harlyn Mindall. She likes you. And maybe in time, you will learn to like her too."

I grunted with irritation. "Am I supposed to like her . . . or marry her?"

"Both. Although the sequence is up to you." Gerald leaned forward. "The people respect her. If she is at your side, they will learn to respect you too. You need her."

I cursed and banged my fist against the bedpost, but even as I did, I received my second visitor, Harlyn herself. Who was admitted in under the pretense of examining my wound, though I doubted this seventeen-year-old girl was the pinnacle of the Halderian medical team.

With a quick wink at me, she did a brief check of my bandages, but when she examined my right arm, her brows pressed together and her expression at Gerald was filled with deep concern.

"What?" I asked.

"I think we can remove the bandage on your chest by tonight, which is good news. But there's a bump beneath the wound in your arm, and the flesh is hotter than it should be, even with a burn. I think you should keep it bandaged until we figure out what to do." She frowned. "The Infidante was not as thorough as she might have been in healing you."

"The Infidante saved my life," I snapped.

"We cannot delay the crowning ceremony," Gerald said. "The people need to see a leader in place as soon as possible."

"I'm well enough," I said, sensing an opportunity. "Out of respect for the Coracks who fought with us, please invite any who wish to intend."

Kestra. I hoped she'd come.

And I waited the entire day to find out.

With all the patience I could muster, I endured the tailors who fitted me for an outfit suitable for a crowning, a black tunic with a brown sash and three blue stripes on my shoulder, and a longcoat over the top.

With less patience, I endured the visits of those who hoped to gain my favor and be named to a position of power. If only they knew what I really thought of them.

And with no attempt at being patient, I endured the slow passage of time. I genuinely had no idea if Kestra would come—our last several encounters had been disasters. But I hoped she would.

Finally, it was time for the ceremony, which would be followed by a supper in the town square. The ceremony itself would be held in the same outdoor theater where Kestra had become Infidante, built on a hillside with the stage at the lowest point. Every Halderian was invited, regardless of wealth, status, or rank. From my position on a seat in front, I watched the people enter, some with excitement to have a king again, some with dread at the same. A few rows back, I overheard mothers pointing me out to their children, and young women offering their opinions on which of them would be most suitable as my queen.

None of them. Especially when I heard them giggle. I wondered if a king could outlaw giggling.

"Ignore them." Harlyn casually sat beside me. A seat, which I hadn't realized, must have been reserved for her. Of course it was. She was dressed in formal attire with her hair slicked back, and in a long blue dress with brown trimmings. She looked beautiful.

Harlyn asked, "How are you feeling?"

"Not great. The Coracks have a physician. When this is over, I'll ask her to come."

"Our doctors are already speaking with Loelle about your arm. I'm sure they'll figure out a solution soon. Until then, this will be a historic night. Can you feel the anticipation around us?"

Around *us*?

I turned to her, needing to be firm, but also hoping to be as gentle as possible. "Harlyn, you asked me to give you a chance, but I have to explain—"

"No, I have to explain." Harlyn took my hand in both of hers and leaned forward to speak directly into my ear. "I'm ready to be your queen, but only when you are ready too. Until then, I will let the people think that because their commander has entrusted his daughter with you, that they should trust you too. I will stay by your side and do all I can to help you retake the Scarlet Throne. But marry me because you love me, and for no other reason."

She smiled, then left a soft kiss on my cheek. I heard giggling behind us again and quickly faced forward. We would continue this conversation later, when my stomach wasn't churning with nerves, and we were in a less public place.

Only a minute later, Gerald took the stage with Commander Mindall. Gerald quieted the audience, then said, "I knew Simon Hatch before he claimed his royalty. I can testify that he is a person of immense courage, skill, and wholehearted determination to end the reign of Lord Endrick. He is the adopted son of King Gareth as he lived in exile and has the king's ring and sword to prove it." Gerald had the ring and held it up. Harlyn squeezed my hand with anticipation. I'd been so nervous, I'd forgotten she was holding it.

Commander Mindall had also raised my sword, but when he lowered it, he continued the narrative. "My people, I have served as a military leader on your behalf almost since our banishment, and as your political leader for this past month."

He failed to mention that he'd become the political leader after challenging Thorne for power, angry that Thorne had helped Kestra to become the Infidante. Maybe that didn't matter to these people, but it did to me.

Mindall continued, "His courage in Reddengrad caused the deaths of four senior officers in the Dominion army as well as the death of Sir Henry Dallisor, second in command to Lord Endrick. I have offered him the hand of my daughter, Harlyn, and he has accepted."

I pulled my hand free of Harlyn's. She leaned over and whispered in my ear, "They're only words."

Words that put us one step closer to the wedding arch.

Next, Mindall invited me to the stage. Harlyn took my arm to walk with me and gave it a squeeze, without realizing she had pressed in directly on my wound, igniting the sting again. Yet that was the least on my mind. The next fifteen steps in front of the crowd were the hardest of my life.

Once we were up front, Harlyn formally curtsied to me, then rose and kissed my cheek again, whispering as we parted, "My king."

"Kneel, Simon Hatch." Mindall's tone showed respect, but I couldn't tell if there was any sincerity to it. I nodded at him, unsure of how much respect I felt for him either.

I gave the same nod to Gerald, then gazed out across the audience, but from my position, I couldn't see Kestra anywhere. Maybe that was for the best. I doubted she'd take well to the announcement about me and Harlyn. I wasn't even sure how well *I* was taking it.

I knelt on a blue velvet pillow and lowered my head. Mindall raised the sword above me and used it to touch my right shoulder and then my left, saying, "With my authority as General of the Halderian Armies, I pronounce you King of the Halderians, heir to the Scarlet Throne of Antora and the leader of our victory against the Dominion. Rise, King Simon!"

A cheer burst from the audience and as shouts rose in honor of my health and happiness, Gerald took my hand and placed Gareth's ring upon the center finger.

"You have become the person your adopted father wished for you to be," he said. "And truly a king I will honor with my loyalty, respect, and service." Then he went to his knees, followed by Mindall.

Next to kneel was Harlyn, directly in front of me, and looking up with an expression that sent a rush of heat through me. She offered me her hand, and when I took it, she held my gaze as I lifted her to her feet. In turn, the rest of the audience knelt for me, yet from the corner of my eye, one particular movement caught my eye, the flash of a cloak in the wind as someone hurriedly left.

Kestra. I knew it had been Kestra.

· FORTY-EIGHT ·

KESTRA

Simon would be a good king. A great king. I was certain of that, and I hoped his new subjects would agree. The Halderians needed someone like him. He would help them rebuild, but more importantly, he would organize them to eventually return to Highwyn, and there he would claim the Scarlet Throne, ruling not over one people, but over one nation. Then it would be his responsibility to restore an entire country.

If I were less selfish, that would've been enough. I should have been happy for him, and excited about his future, and humbled to have had a small role in putting him on the throne.

But none of that mattered to me. My heart was hurting far more now than from anything Endrick had ever done to it, and it was about to get worse. I had to say good-bye.

Following the ceremony, a banquet was held in the town square for anyone who wished to attend. I only caught fleeting glimpses of Simon, who was surrounded by a parade of well-wishers hoping to gain his favor.

Those who weren't buttering themselves up to the new king stood in lines alongside the rows of tables crowded with breads, cheeses, and a variety of meats. Notably, fewer people were here than on the night I'd been named as Infidante. The Halderians had lost many of their fighters. Reddengrad had lost many more.

Including their prince, now a captive of the Dominion. Tenger was planning his rescue, and I intended to be part of it. Basil deserved that much after all he'd risked to get me out of Woodcourt.

Trina joined me on the edge of the square where I sat on another low rock wall, trying to pretend I wasn't watching every move Simon made. Trying to ignore the pretty Harlyn Mindall who had become a fixture at his side.

Trina offered me some bread from her plate, but I had no appetite for it. She followed my gaze over to Simon. "You've changed."

I turned to her. "How?"

"The girl I once knew would never sit over here when what she really wants is over there."

"Maybe because that girl has decided to accept reality. You heard the announcement, Trina. He's agreed to marry that Halderian girl."

"If he did agree, then it's only because he had to. Talk to him."

My eyes misted. That's why I'd come and what I had planned to do, but now that I was looking at him, I'd lost my courage. I stood and brushed at my eyes before she noticed. "I'd better go. It was a mistake to come here." Then I hurried from the square, vaguely aware that people darted from my path in fear, as if simply being near me was dangerous.

"Kestra, wait!" I glanced back and saw Simon hurrying toward me.

"Go back to your subjects. Go back to *her*."

"Kes . . . stop, please."

I did, but folded my arms, unwilling to look at him. He stood silently beside me until someone in the crowd behind us called,

"Where is the king?" Simon sighed, then put a hand on my back to lead me forward. "Let's talk in private."

My heart pounded, and a shiver ran up my spine, but for entirely different reasons than it once had. When Tenger had spoken to me, it had been an easy thing to understand that if Endrick had the necklace, then he knew there were feelings between me and Simon. Maybe Tenger was right; I should put as much distance between us as possible.

But now that I was near him, it was even easier to tell myself that the damage was already done. Whether I stayed or left made no difference to what Endrick would do with the information in the necklace.

When I finally dared to steal a glance at Simon, he immediately met my eyes and I caught my breath in my throat. I'd never seen him like this before, the ferocity of his intent chilling and warming me with every look he sent my way.

We walked in silence for some distance, into a walled-off vege-table garden, one which might have provided much of the evening's feast. The sun had already been low on the horizon, stars beginning to shine in the deep blue sky. The glow of sunset tinted the air around us, casting golden tones on Simon's profile.

I froze in the entry, but he grabbed my hand instead and pulled me deeper into the darkening corner.

I didn't want another fight, but that seemed to be his intention. I yanked my hand away and stepped back, squaring my body to his. Time stopped between us. His breaths were deep and deliberate. I'd barely breathed since the moment I faced him. Finally, I mumbled, "Simon—"

In a single stride, he closed the space between us, cupped my cheek with one hand, and kissed me. The kiss was fierce and hungry and instantly melted every defense I had. He followed it with another, one which created a fire in me that burned for his next kiss, the next beat of his heart against mine. His left hand curled around my waist, pressing us closer, and then slid up the small of my back, leaving me to tremble in his arms, wanting more. Wanting only him.

I longed to live in this imaginary world where only he and I existed. Where our existence together wasn't questioned or challenged or . . . torn apart. But that's all we could ever have now, an imagined life within a temporary dream.

I tilted my face away from him, then slowly backed deeper into the corner, each step away like splitting myself in half. When I found the courage for it, my eyes rose to his and I saw the hurt in his expression. But neither of us spoke. He didn't seem to know what to say any more than I did.

He finally began, "Since we left Woodcourt, I can't count the number of times you've tried to leave me."

I shrugged. "You should have let me go." But even though I said the words, even though I believed them, I still couldn't make myself walk away.

He rubbed one hand over his mouth and jaw, but dropped it before saying, "Please stay." As if a simple request could fix everything. Or was it a command? He was a king now, after all.

"You ask me to stay and watch you marry that girl?"

His eyes darted away before returning to me. "Those were only words for the people's sake."

"Yes, but after Harlyn bowed to you, the way you looked at her was more than words." He started to shake his head, but I said, "It makes sense to choose her, Simon, more than it'll ever make sense to choose me. She will secure your rule. I threaten it. She agrees with everything you say, and I think we only fight. She has no magic—"

He stepped forward. "Your magic, Kes. Is there anything I should know?"

I lowered my eyes. "What do you mean?"

A pause, then, "These powers you have . . . are they affecting you?"

When I looked up again, his expression had changed. No longer with the soft gaze of his eyes or the intensity of his feelings, but with suspicion, just as it had after I'd healed him in the forest. Like that, we were there again, with his doubt, his mistrust. How were we ever to build a relationship on that foundation?

The answer took me back to where it always did: We couldn't.

Blinking back the sting in my eyes, I said, "The truth is that we've gone as far as we'll ever go together."

"Because you have magic? We can figure out—"

"There is nothing to figure out. This is who I am, what I am. Whether you like it or not, we have to face reality."

"I agree. It is reality that my heart stops every time I see you. The knot in my gut when you turn away is real, because *this* is real, Kes. This moment. You and I here, right now, *this* is all that's real."

A pressure rose in my chest. "What is *this*, then? You and I sneaking off for a moment alone, hoping not to be caught because then you'll be pulled in one direction and I in the other? This is our future?"

"It's a start." He crossed to me again, and his hands slid up my arms, coming to rest as they tangled in my hair and wrapped around my shoulders. "I know you've got battles ahead, on the ground, and in your heart. Let me fight them with you."

I tried to absorb his words the way he wanted me to. Tried to pretend that wanting the words to be true would make them true. But that wasn't enough.

He asked, "Do you *want* to go? Or do you feel you have to go?"

My answer froze in my throat. I was only aware that his hands were circling around my back and he was drawing me to him again.

"Because if you want to stay here, we'll find a way."

"Tenger said—"

His eyes rolled. "And Gerald says, and Loelle says, and everyone has something to say about whether we can be together. But we don't have to listen to them. I'm telling you, Kes, they're wrong."

"How do you know?"

His answer came with another brush of his lips against mine, sending my heart racing. Before he pulled away, I stole a second kiss, a deeper kiss, and one that invited him to stay for a third. He backed me against the garden wall, and I molded my body to his, shivering beneath the lines of his fingers, warming when his hand flattened across my back, bringing me even closer.

His lips drifted to my jaw, then close to my ear where he whispered, "I know they're wrong, because I know that what I feel for you is real. I'm in love with you, Kes."

I pulled back, my heart pounding in my ears. Had I truly heard those words? Happiness flooded through me, carrying a peace such as I'd never felt before.

But nothing so good could ever last.

From the entrance of the garden, someone coughed loudly, then called, "Your Grace?"

Simon leaned back and rolled his eyes. "Yes?"

"You are wanted, my king."

Simon's expression was full of irritation when he looked back at me, but I said, "Go to your people."

"Please don't leave. We'll speak tomorrow. We'll figure this out." When I nodded, he smiled and gave me a final kiss. "I will see you again soon. I promise."

I returned his smile as he left, though I didn't miss the tender way he brushed a hand over his right arm. Something there was bothering him. I could help, when I was stronger. Tomorrow. Until then, I ran a finger over my lips, sealing the memory of what had just passed between us.

He loved me. That was real.

And for now, it was enough.

· FORTY-NINE ·

KESTRA

Because of the rapidly cooling weather, Simon offered us rooms in the manor that was serving as his castle-in-exile. It was smaller than Woodcourt and far less grand, but it seemed to be the finest home here in Nessel and had escaped any damage from when the Dominion had come through. I was assigned a room with Trina and Loelle while the men were in another room down the corridor.

Sometime in the middle of the night, someone jostled my shoulder. I bolted upright in bed, instinctively reaching for the Brillian sword until Loelle's hand came over my mine and she whispered my name.

"What's wrong?" I asked, deeply alarmed by the terse set of Loelle's expression and the late hour.

"Get dressed." Loelle handed me an overdress for my shift. "Trina will help you."

Like Loelle, Trina was already awake and dressed. While I laced and buttoned the overdress, she fetched my boots, then handed me the satchel I'd taken from Wynnow when I escaped Brill. "You'll want this," she whispered.

"What's happening?" I asked. "Are we leaving?"

Before anyone answered, a knock came at the door. Loelle opened it and I heard her brief mumblings with Gerald, then she turned and said, "Trina, will you keep watch in the corridor?"

Trina handed me the Brillian sword to strap to my side, gave me a grim smile, and obeyed.

"Keep watch for what?" I asked, worry beginning to claw at my heart.

Gerald entered and shut the door, then he and Loelle faced me, looking deadly serious.

"Will you sit down, my lady?" Gerald asked, offering me a chair.

"I will not."

"That's for the best anyway," Loelle said. "We must leave at once."

My eyes narrowed. "Why now?"

Her frown deepened, and she glanced at Gerald before continuing, "You are in danger, from Captain Tenger."

By now, my pulse was racing and I shook my head, incredulous. "He means to harm me? Because I didn't end the relationship with Simon?"

"No, my lady. It's because—" Gerald sighed. "When you healed the king before, was there a moment when your souls connected?"

I hesitated, but if my life was in danger, I had to be honest. "Yes. It was the only way to keep Simon . . . with us."

"Of course." Gerald cleared his throat before continuing. "During that connection, the king observed something in you that is very concerning."

I stared over at him with no idea of what he could possibly mean. Finally, he added a single word: "Corruption."

My face felt hot. "That's impossible. I've not had magic for even a week."

"Yes." Gerald nodded. "So you can understand the problem."

I crossed my hands over my stomach, as if the corruption were there, as if it were a tangible mass that could be cut out surgically. Simon had tried to talk to me about this in the garden. And apparently Tenger already knew about the corruption too. He wasn't going to wait for me to kill Endrick. He'd replace me with a new Infidante instead.

Trina.

I shook my head. "I won't run away—I can defend myself against Tenger and against anyone else."

"Defending yourself is not the problem," Loelle said. "And you're not running away."

"You must be sent away." Gerald took a step toward me before adding, "When the Halderians came to Lonetree, Captain Tenger offered us a compromise. If we backed down and allowed him to restore your memories, in exchange, you would stay out of the Hiplands."

I looked to Loelle for confirmation and she nodded, twisting my heart even deeper. So Tenger had always intended to separate me and Simon. The necklace was only an excuse.

As gently as possible, Gerald continued, "You must leave the Hiplands tonight and promise to never return. You bring danger to our king, and to all our people."

"I saved your king, and I'm trying to save your people!"

"We are grateful for what you did in the battle, please believe that. But many Halderians are frightened of you."

What had started as a tremor of worry was quickly swelling, filling my entire chest with heartache. "Simon asked me to stay, and I agreed. When he wakes up and finds I'm gone, he'll come after me. He always does."

Gerald's eyes saddened. "My lady, if you do not leave, then the king will never wake up."

My attention shifted to Loelle. "What is he talking about? Is Simon sick?"

"There's an infection in Simon's arm, and it's spreading."

"Infection?" This must have been in the arm he'd been favoring earlier. Why had he hidden that from me? "Is it serious?"

Loelle's eyes betrayed her answer. "Very serious."

Without another word, I pushed past them both and marched into the corridor. Trina stood upright, though from her position, she had obviously been listening through the door.

She quickly said, "I swear to you, Kestra, I'm not part of any plot to replace you as Infidante."

I ignored her and went to the east wing of the home, where Simon's room was supposed to be. I wouldn't have known which one was his except that two guards stood at either side of a door.

They saw me coming and raised their sabers. I stopped with one hand on the Brillian sword and my other hand directed at them. "Let me pass and you will survive."

"You'll have to get through us," one guard said, a challenge I was more than happy to meet.

But Gerald and Loelle must have followed. Gerald said to the guards, "Let her pass."

They lowered their weapons, and without another word, I entered Simon's mostly darkened room. It was larger than I'd expected, divided into areas for living space, grooming, resting, and study.

Yet Simon was all that mattered. He was in the bed, but restless, throwing off his bedcovers then shivering and clutching at them again. I started forward, but Harlyn Mindall, the girl who had been attached to his side before he was crowned, was apparently also attached to him here. She entered the room from a side door, seemingly unaware of my presence.

She carried a bowl of water and a rag, then sat on a stool beside his bed. She dipped the rag in the water and began gently washing his face. Her fingers traced over his cheeks as she did, and he briefly stirred beneath her touch, then went still again. She slowly leaned forward as if to kiss him.

Anger boiled inside me, erupting in a voice loud enough to ensure she heard my every word. "His arm is injured. You will not cure him that way."

Harlyn jumped, nearly dropping the bowl of water. But she stood and placed it on the stool behind her. Barely looking at me, she said, "I only meant to comfort him." Then she lifted her gaze until our eyes locked. "Why are you here?"

"I want to see the infection." And heal it, if I could.

After a brief hesitation, Harlyn pulled at the bandage on Simon's right arm. The flesh was burned and bright red, except for a cauterized wound running up his vein. On either side of that line, the flesh was raised and lighter in color. That must be the infection. I didn't know what it would cost me to heal it, but I had to try.

I moved to lay my hand on his arm, when Loelle said, "Not this, my lady. We don't know what that infection is. It's different than anything I've seen before."

And Loelle had surely seen everything. She pulled me back, then Harlyn returned to the chair beside Simon, protectively placing an arm on his shoulder.

"There must be something you can do for him," I said to Loelle.

"I've offered them medications." Loelle frowned at me. "But he is the Halderian king. They insist on administering the treatment."

I grabbed Gerald's arm. "Then do it!" But he only stared back at me, which was infuriating.

"Let me talk to her alone." Harlyn stood and nodded for Loelle and Gerald to leave.

My temper warmed while I waited for them to go. Then she stepped closer to me, and this time I noticed tears were in her eyes.

"I care for Simon," she began. "Sincerely care for him, and I beg you not to let him die."

"Then tell your people to give him those medicines."

The expression in her eyes shifted to something between sadness and suspicion, enough that when she spoke, I'd already known what was coming. "You kissed Simon earlier tonight, in that little garden."

"He kissed me."

Her eyes flashed. "Word of it spread to the heads of houses. They don't like the idea of an Endrean being so . . . close to the king. They set conditions that must be met before he can receive Loelle's treatments."

"How dare they? He's their king!"

She sniffed. "By morning, he might not be."

I looked from Simon back to Harlyn. The depth of her emotion carried through the air, piercing me and answering my unspoken question. "I'm the condition."

"Loelle claims to have a place where you can go and be safe . . . far from here."

I closed my eyes, trying to keep my composure. "And when Simon is healed, you two will marry."

"As soon as it can be arranged. Whatever feelings he has for you will fade in time."

And grow for her. I knew how this game worked.

Simon rolled in his bed again. I started forward but Harlyn blocked my path, saying, "If you have feelings for him too, then please let us save him. Please go."

Tears welled in my eyes, but I nodded, barely trusting myself with words. With one final look at Simon, I turned and left the room, walking directly past Gerald, Loelle, and Trina, who all silently followed in my wake. Shortly before reaching my own room, I turned to them, addressing Gerald specifically.

I said, "If you don't save him then know this: I will return with my magic and my blade and an unquenchable fury. I will destroy every Halderian who is responsible for his death, and it will start with you."

Gerald's eyes became solemn. "This, my lady, is why the Halderians fear you."

The first tear spilled onto my cheek. "I ask only one favor before I go."

Gerald dipped his head at me. "If I can."

"Will you tell him, please, that I wanted to go, that I chose this? Tell him the corruption is worse than he suspects, and that I am irredeemable." My face felt hot, but I closed my eyes, trying to steady my emotions. When I had, I added, "Tell Simon anything you must to keep his heart from breaking too."

He nodded at me again, then Loelle took my arm. "A carriage is waiting for us outside. Trina, gather anything from our room that we may have left behind, and hurry. You will ride with us."

Loelle led me farther down the empty corridor to a rear exit of the manor where two Halderian guards were waiting to admit us into the carriage. I slumped against the side wall, determined to ignore Loelle's attempts at conversation.

"For what it's worth," she said, "I am sorry it has to be this way."

It was worth nothing. She was simply the last in a long line of people who'd trampled over me, bent me to their will, then apologized with the excuse that they had no other choice.

My eyes were closed and I was facing away from her when Trina joined us in the carriage, ready to leave. Loelle called up to the driver and we rode away.

"You should sleep," Loelle said. "We have a long journey ahead."

I had no intention of sleeping. I just needed enough quiet so that I could plan. This wasn't over yet.

· FIFTY ·

SIMON

From the moment I awoke, I knew Kestra was gone. I saw it in Gerald's terse expression as he hastily sent the other attendants in the room away. I heard it in Harlyn's voice as she described the efforts of the doctors who had stopped the infection in my arm from spreading into my shoulder. And I felt her absence, deep within my heart.

I knew Kestra was gone. I just didn't know why, or how long it had been.

"Which of you is responsible?" I asked.

After a silent exchange of looks with Gerald, Harlyn began with the easiest part of the conversation.

"You've been unconscious for three days. Your arm is still—"

"Did Kestra leave by choice, or was she forced away?"

Harlyn's eyes darted, and her fingers twitched with discomfort. She barely looked at me to say, "A little of both, I suppose. Once she understood the danger of staying, she willingly left."

My glare at Harlyn darkened. "The danger of staying? Who threatened her?"

Now Gerald answered, "No one threatened her. But surely you have considered who she is—"

"The Infidante."

"Who she is . . . now that both her adopted parents are dead."

I groaned and leaned against the headboard of my bed. "Kestra is the heir to Woodcourt."

"And if Lord Endrick is removed?" Gerald prompted.

"The Scarlet Throne would be hers."

"Yes, *if* the Dallisors are in power. As King of the Halderians, obviously you cannot allow that."

"Obviously." I closed my eyes and tried to keep hold of my temper. "Where is she?"

"I don't know," Harlyn whispered.

I spoke louder. "Where is she?"

"Harlyn does not know, nor do I," Gerald said. "Loelle promised to take her somewhere she would not be found. Not by Lord Endrick or the Dominion. Not by us and—"

"Not by me." I pressed my lips together and let my fist beat on the mattress beneath me. If anyone but Loelle had arranged this, I might've had a chance. But Loelle would hide Kestra with the benefit of magic. For all I knew, she could be right under my nose and I wouldn't know it.

Gerald cleared his throat again. "I might add, my king, that you have responsibilities now. The Halderians lost a good many fighters in Reddengrad, but the Dominion sustained heavy losses as well. We must prepare strategies for taking the Scarlet Throne once Endrick is gone." He hesitated, then added, "If Kestra attempts to take the throne, you must order her removal. Anything else, and the Halderians will consider you—"

"A traitor." I was finished with this conversation and snarled, "Get out, both of you."

Gerald said, "Do not be angry with Harlyn, nor with me. I warned you not to give your heart to Kestra. Your feelings for her may be sincere and deep, but now they may also be a form of treason." He put a hand on Harlyn's shoulder, who looked like she wished she could vanish as completely as Kestra had done. "This girl will be your queen one day, the sooner the better. Open your heart to her now. That's all I ask."

"Ask?" I nearly spat out the word. "I was never *asked* about any of this!"

"No, you weren't. But you were warned." Gerald sighed with regret, as if this was my fault. "All the heads of households are meeting downstairs in an hour, expecting to welcome their king. We hope you will be a good one, Simon. And you will be . . . if you can let her go."

With a sharpness in her expression I had not expected, Harlyn stood and started to follow him out the door, but turned back and said, "If I had known about her, I wouldn't have let things get this far. I'm not eager to play the role of future queen when it's obvious that your heart is already spoken for. But I'll do it because it's in the best interest of my people. *I* am in your best interest, Simon, even if you're too blind right now to see that." With that, she stormed out the door.

Blindness wasn't the problem. If anything, I saw far too clearly what had happened while I was unconscious.

Except for what was required of me in my new role as fool king of the Halderians, I remained in my room all day, staring out at the dark clouds as they rolled in, wondering if their rain would become snow by morning and if Kestra was warm and safe, wherever she was. Wondering if she was thinking of me, if she missed me. I couldn't seem to put two thoughts together without her being in at least one of them.

Very late that night, a knock came to my balcony door. At first, I mistook it for the pouring rain, but it came again, more urgently this time. My first instinct was to call for the guards, but I quickly reminded myself that an intruder would simply burst in, not knock. And second, that until a few days ago, I had been involved with the rebellion, and a rather competent fighter in its ranks. I shouldn't need to call for help.

Still, after pulling a robe around myself, I carried my sword to the door, inched open the curtains, and saw Trina, soaking wet.

I immediately opened the door and invited Trina in. To calm her shivering, I pulled the top blanket from my bed and wrapped it around her, then sat her in front of the fire in my room.

Out of basic courtesy, I should have waited until she was warmer before speaking, but I had no patience for it. I asked, "What are you doing here? Is there trouble?"

"Well, Kestra is involved, if that's enough of an answer." Trina frowned over at me. "Is Tenger still here?"

I shook my head. "I'm told he's on his way to Highwyn to rescue Basil and to retrieve the Olden Blade for Kestra. Why?"

She mumbled to herself, "He wasn't going to harm Kestra. Loelle lied about that."

I wasn't following her reasoning. "Why would Loelle have lied?"

Another shiver went through Trina, one that probably had nothing to do with the cold. Forgetting the blanket around her,

Trina leaned forward and said, "Let's go back earlier, to the note you accused me of writing to the Halderians about the location of Lonetree Camp."

I nodded. "Harlyn told me it came from someone the Coracks trust with their lives."

Tilting her head, Trina said, "I think that's true in the most literal sense."

"Loelle?" My expression twisted. "Impossible. She'd never endanger so many people."

"Wouldn't she? I was there when she asked to be the one to take Kestra into hiding. Why her? Loelle is no fighter, no protector."

"No, but she understands magic better than anyone on our side."

"Which also makes her the best person to understand the purpose of Kestra's necklace. Remember that she told everyone the priority in rescuing Kestra from the Dominion camp was the necklace, even above Kestra herself. That's why Wynnow grabbed it during the rescue."

My heart pounded harder. "Do you think Loelle knew what removing the necklace would do to Kestra?"

"I think Loelle could sense the magic in it, something none of the rest of us could. She knew Kestra was an Ironheart, so she must have at least suspected what would happen if it was removed."

I understood that, but this didn't sound like the Loelle I'd ever known. Unless I'd never fully known her.

Trina leaned into me. "There's more, Simon, and it's worse. Kestra told me that on the way to Brill, Loelle stole the necklace back from Wynnow. Why would Loelle have wanted it?"

I shook my head. "We know it lured Lord Endrick to Brill. But Loelle wouldn't have planned it that way. After going to so much effort to give magic to Kes, she wouldn't risk it all by forcing a confrontation with Lord Endrick."

Trina had an answer for that too. "I don't think Loelle intended for Kestra to face Lord Endrick, but I do believe she wanted him to go to Brill. Loelle didn't like the Brillians and never trusted Wynnow. The Brillians were close to being able to replicate everything Endrick can do, only without magic. I believe that Loelle thought Endrick would see it and destroy Brill for it."

"So Wynnow never betrayed Kes?"

"No, she absolutely did, but I think her betrayal happened after Lord Endrick came to Brill. He probably threatened to destroy Brill, just as Loelle wanted, and so Wynnow needed to offer him something even better. Wynnow must have offered up Kestra as a trade for a guaranteed peace."

"Only Kestra didn't cooperate. She fought back, maybe even achieved some level of victory over Endrick."

Trina added, "And in his anger, he destroyed most of Brill's capital city, including the royal palace. Including Wynnow." She touched my arm. "Whether she intended it or not, Loelle is the one who corrupted Kes. And now Kes is with her."

A hard lump formed in my throat. "Where are they?"

"I don't know. All I can tell you is that when we stopped for a change of drivers, Loelle insisted on driving the carriage herself, claiming only she and Kestra could go the rest of the way. I was dismissed."

"We've got to find them. If Loelle went that far to get Kestra under her control, then she's got a much bigger plan in mind."

"Agreed." Now she smiled. "But it's not all bad news. I also have a special message for you. Kestra wants you to know that she remembers everything now. More importantly—" Trina stopped mid-sentence as she noticed my exposed arm. Her eyes widened with alarm. "The burn!"

Instinctively, I pulled it toward myself. Except when the physicians had applied creams to the flesh, I'd kept my arm tightly bandaged since the crowning ceremony. I'd forgotten it was unwrapped now. "It's not as bad as it looks."

"I think it's just the other way around." Trina leaned forward enough to get a closer look at my arm. Most of the skin from my wrist to my elbow remained as red as when it had first been burned, but the heat generated from my flesh made my entire body feel like I was constantly standing too close to a fire. The cauterized line had turned to a dark shade of red and the lump beneath the skin was hardening. Trina tenderly pressed on the lump and I yanked my arm away.

"Did that hurt?"

I looked at my arm. "No, it just . . . I felt something happen when you pressed on it." It was like a thousand vibrations coursed through me, all of them gathering in my arm.

Frowning at me, Trina said, "When you fell into that pond, with the cut on your arm, the Rawkyren was in the water too, a cut on its leg. What if its blood got into your blood? Simon, what if that dragon is somehow connected to you now?"

Almost in answer to her question, a fluttering sound came at the balcony door, ending with a thump on the balcony floor. Trina stood, withdrawing her sword, and I crept to the door, parting the curtains again. I barely breathed at what I saw: the Rawkyren from the forest, slightly larger than a falcon now, and obviously here for a reason.

It must have cauterized the wound on its own leg, which had a black line similar to the one on my arm. Its silvery scales were like mirrors, reflecting the stormy night, so I might not have seen it except it was looking through the window directly at me, with large piercing eyes. I reached for the door handle.

"Don't go out there!" Trina said.

I opened the door and the Rawkyren flew in, landing on my injured arm, which I'd instinctively raised to hold it. I felt the talons dig into my flesh but with the thick mass beneath the skin, I wasn't hurt. It was almost as if . . . as if that were the purpose for the lump.

Trina stood back as the young dragon stretched its wings and looked around the room, like it had come home.

"I think you're right about me being connected to this dragon," I said, almost to myself. Then to Trina, I added, "If only I still had any connection with Kestra."

Trina smiled. "I think you do; I have a message Kestra asked me to deliver." She looked me directly in the eye, then added, "Simon, she wants me to tell you that she loves you too."

· ACKNOWLEDGMENTS ·

It would be impossible to properly acknowledge everyone who deserves my recognition and gratitude for their amazing work. Certainly, I owe my family infinite thanks for their support, encouragement, and faith in me. I am also blessed by the thoughtfulness and expertise of my agent, Ammi-Joan Paquette, and by the skill and intelligence of my editor, Lisa Sandell, and I am amazed at what it means to be a member of the Scholastic family. To those at every stage of the process, I see only a fraction of the total work you do, and it is first class.

Finally, I wish to thank my readers, fans, and cheerleaders. Nothing I do would matter without you. Every time you pick up one of my books, recommend, review, or pass it on to a friend, you are paying me the finest of compliments, and for that, I will always think more fondly of you than you ever could of me.

· ABOUT THE AUTHOR ·

JENNIFER A. NIELSEN is the critically acclaimed author of the *New York Times* bestselling first book of the Traitor's Game series, *The Traitor's Game*, as well as the *New York Times* and *USA Today* bestselling Ascendance Trilogy: *The False Prince*, *The Runaway King*, and *The Shadow Throne*. She also wrote the *New York Times* bestselling Mark of the Thief trilogy: *Mark of the Thief*, *Rise of the Wolf*, and *Wrath of the Storm*; the standalone fantasy *The Scourge*; the historical novels *Resistance* and *A Night Divided*; Book Two in the Horizon series, *Deadzone*; and Book Six of the Infinity Ring series, *Behind Enemy Lines*.

Jennifer collects old books, loves good theater, and thinks that a quiet afternoon in the mountains makes for a nearly perfect moment. She lives in northern Utah with her husband, their three children, and a perpetually muddy dog. You can visit her at jennielsen.com.